Diane Moore

About the Author

CATHERINE O'CONNELL lives in Aspen and is active with the Aspen Writers' Foundation. She has worked as a sales executive for the importers of Taittinger Champagne and Louis Jadot wines. She is a graduate of the University of Colorado School of Journalism.

WELL BRED AND DEAD

WELL BRED AND DEAD

A HIGH SOCIETY MYSTERY

Catherine O'Connell

HARPER

NEW YORK • LONDON • TORONTO • SYDNEY

HARPER

HarperCollins books may be purchased for educational, business, or sales promotional use. For information please write: Special Markets Department, HarperCollins Publishers, 10 East 53rd Street, New York, NY 10022.

FIRST EDITION

Designed by Justin Dodd

Library of Congress Cataloging-in-Publication Data is available upon request.

ISBN: 978-0-06-112215-6
ISBN-10: 0-06-112215-7

07   08   09   10   11   ❖/RRD   10   9   8   7   6   5   4   3   2   1

For Fred
With gratitude and love

It is not with whom thou are bred, but with whom thou are fed.

—MIGUEL DE CERVANTES, *Don Quixote*

WELL BRED AND DEAD

Prologue

The clock ticked the morning away slowly, each second an eternity as I battled the alternating demons of boredom and fear. I was hungry and thirsty and, worst of all, I had to use the bathroom, as my captors had not given me the opportunity to do so before taking their leave. My body ached from the pull of the ropes, but any attempt to shift my position made it feel like my joints were dislocating. My hair stuck to my face in greasy copper clumps with the exception of one obnoxious strand that tickled my nose in an excruciating manner. Since the duct tape over my mouth prevented me from simply blowing the hair away, I turned my head into the pillow and painfully managed to rub it aside. Throughout the ordeal Fleur remained faithfully at my side, flicking her tail as she studied my predicament with feline curiosity.

Wondering just how much longer I could hold out before soiling both myself and my Frette sheets, not daring to contemplate how long I might last without food and water, I stared at the ceiling and reflected upon my life. I thought about what I would have done differently given the opportunity to live it over again. I would have been a kinder, more caring person. I would have spent less on couture clothes and high-end cosmetics and more on others. I would have gotten involved in philanthropic activities that actually touched the needy, like food banks and homeless shelters, instead of the high-profile events that put one on the A-list, like the Tiffany Ball. I would have been more sympathetic to my mother's plight and her struggle for dignity, instead of blaming her for Grandmother's disinheritance.

I might have even had children.

Of the many things I would have done differently, two stood out far and above the others. I never would have invested my money in derivatives, and I *never, never, never* would have befriended Ethan Campbell.

1
Cold Lunch

The thing that really irks me is that I paid for Ethan's funeral. At the time it seemed like the right thing to do, seeing as he had made me his heir. Had I known then what I know now, I wouldn't have put out a single sou, much less the small fortune I spent to see to it that he had a proper send-off. But Ethan knew me all too well and knew I would tidy things for him, that I wouldn't be able to live with the thought of his remains ending up in some unmarked grave or as an anonymous pile of ash in the county morgue.

Looking back, much of his deception shouldn't have come as a surprise. There were inconsistencies about him all along, starting with his awkward table manners and ending with the seedy area in which he lived. These are not customarily the ways of one *to the manner born*. But Ethan was a writer, and since writers are known for their eccentricities, I simply chose to attribute Ethan's to his literary bent. Thus, not only did Ethan's charade take me completely unaware but the depth of it was as unanticipated as an earthquake in the Midwest.

Now I'm getting ahead of myself. Though Ethan's story really begins the moment he was conceived, it became my undoing the day I went to his apartment and found the body. Prior to that, the thought of Ethan as anything other than my best friend would never have crossed my mind. What followed afterward just shows how little we know those we think we know best.

It was the rare spring day in Chicago, a city whose climate can best be summed up in two words: winter and August. The sky was a cloudless silky blue, the air wrung dry by a westerly wind that whisked the city's notorious humidity out over the lake. The swollen buds on the trees looked ready to burst their seams, and the sweet scent of cherry blossoms perfumed the breeze. Venus rising from the foam, spring coaxed, and her public was happily seduced.

My mood was exceptional as I stepped from my co-op building onto the short costly street known as East Lake Shore Drive. Across the busy lanes of the outer drive, Lake Michigan stretched endlessly before me, her slate blue waves folding gently onto the shore. The public beach bristled with humanity as the prisoners of Midwestern winter took advantage of the unexpected parole. Joggers and bicyclists crowded the paved trail while sunbathers sprawled across the sand, guilelessly soaking up the sun's disfiguring rays. Apart from the crowd, two lovers were entwined on a hastily thrown blanket, groping each other with abandon. Indifferent to the presence of other beachgoers or the vantage point of the high-rise buildings that loomed above them, they acted as though they were the only souls on earth. I watched their antics with a pang of envy, realizing that far more than a few lanes of asphalt separated our worlds.

I turned and walked away at a leisurely pace, past the tulip-filled gardens and Beaux Arts facades of the city's priciest real estate. When I reached the Drake at the end of the block, the doorman nodded at me in polite recognition. "Good afternoon, Mrs. Cook," he said, tipping his hat. He swept the door open with a gloved hand. "Beautiful day, isn't it?"

"It is indeed, Raymond." I acknowledged him with a polite smile. Ethan and I had a standing twelve-thirty reservation in the Cape Cod Room every Wednesday afternoon, so our faces were well known at the hotel. Our ritual had been established after our very first meeting more than five years before, and was never broken unless one of us was out of town—or if something of greater urgency came up.

I stopped inside the arcade to check my watch and noted with satisfaction that the time was one o'clock, making me precisely thirty minutes late for my lunch date. I seldom arrive anyplace on time. I feel it makes one look desperate. Farther down the corridor, a couple of attractive men in business suits were locked in what appeared to be serious conversation. Upon seeing me they fell silent, their heads pivoting as their eyes followed me to the restaurant entrance. When one is a five-foot-ten redhead with extremely long legs, one becomes accustomed to such responses. Although I'm certain it didn't hurt that I was wearing my new magenta suit from Feraud's spring collection, an acquisition that cost far more than I had any right to spend at the time. But it fit me as though it were designed with me in mind, and besides, I'm a winter. Bright colors flatter me. As a woman ages, she must learn to become less dependent on her looks and more dependent on her style. With my half-century mark looming ominously before me in the coming year, mere days before the world would pass into the new millennium, I had already learned to appreciate how one's clothes can carry the day as the other attributes fade.

Not that I conceded to fading quite yet. One thing I had to thank my mother for was good genes. From her side of the gene pool came my long legs; auburn hair; a compact, slightly upturned nose; luminous skin; and an ample bosom. I say ample, not large, thankfully. Nothing like those dreadful drooping appendages Sunny Livermore was cursed with or the overinflated balloons Whitney Armstrong had surgically installed. Finding couture to hang properly over bustlines like those must be challenging at best.

The only thing I inherited from my father was my eyes. Ironically, many say they are my best feature. Deep-set and emerald green, they tilt slightly upward at the corners like a cat's. When we first met, Henry used to tease me about their color, saying he thought my eyes couldn't possibly get any greener until he saw them reflect money.

Michel, the longtime maître d' of the Cape Cod Room, greeted me warmly from his post just inside the restaurant door. My eyes darted immediately to Ethan and my regular table expecting to see his small figure patiently awaiting me as always. But his chair sat empty, which was a puzzlement. Ethan was seldom late. If anything, he was usually insufferably early. Scanning the dimly lit room to see if he could be visiting elsewhere, I spotted Marjorie Wilcock lunching in a corner booth with Franklin James. Their affair was one of the worst-kept secrets in town—no surprise since they chose places like the Cape Cod Room for their illicit rendezvous. Half the Gold Coast dines there weekly.

Marjorie looked up and our eyes locked. Not the least bit abashed, she raised a hand and waved me over. I fixed my most gracious smile and navigated the busy room to their table. Franklin appeared to have aged since I last saw him at the Zoo benefit with his wife. His face was puffy and swollen, his eyes saggy and red-rimmed. Marjorie's bony face was as put-together and perfectly made-up as always, but she was so thin that she looked a bit . . . tired. Both had voluminous stemmed glasses parked in front of them. We made small talk as if there were nothing untoward about the two of them huddling together in a dark corner, closer than a pair of Siamese twins.

"Pauline, that suit is divine," Marjorie said, salaciously eyeing my latest purchase over the rim of her glass. "Wherever did you get it?"

WELL BRED AND DEAD

"This? It's just a little something I picked up for spring at Nei-man's," I replied with masterful understatement. "You haven't seen Ethan, have you? We're supposed to meet for lunch."

"No, I haven't," Marjorie gushed in a manner telling me the mar-tini she held in her hand hadn't been her first. "Haven't seen him in ages, actually. How's his book on Daisy Fellowes coming along, by the way?"

"Remarkably well," I lied, loyally stretching the truth on Ethan's behalf. Though he had conducted countless interviews and compiled reams of material about the Singer sewing machine heiress, he con-fided in me that he hadn't actually written much yet. His agent and I were the only people alive who knew this. Had his publisher known, he would have gone into an apoplexy. Ethan had received his advance well over a year ago.

"Well, if it's as juicy as the Gloria Guinness book was, I can hardly wait to read it. He certainly leaves no stone unturned." She winked in a conspiratorial way I wasn't quite sure how to interpret. Everyone knew about Daisy Fellowes's legendary sexual prowess, her countless lovers—among them several ebony ones—and her discarding of them when they no longer suited her purpose. However, Marjorie was capable of giving Daisy a run for her money. Franklin wasn't the first man to share martini lunches with her in the bowels of a convenient hotel.

We made some more small talk before I excused myself to go tele-phone Ethan. At the time, I believe I was one of the few people in the Western hemisphere who hadn't yet succumbed to the cell phone, considering them the rudest assault on good manners in recent his-tory. I was appalled by the way strangers suddenly felt free to share the intricacies of their personal lives with anyone within hearing dis-tance, from last-minute grocery items to be picked up to their latest stock market acquisitions to their nocturnal successes. Being of the mind that anyone with the slightest bit of decorum conducted one's business in private, I chose to remain a hold-out from their ranks.

In the ladies lounge the attendant changed a dollar for me. I put fifty cents in the pay phone and listened as Ethan's phone rang repeatedly with no answer. Assuming him to be in transit, I hung up and took a seat at the vanity, fussing with my makeup in order to give him ample time to arrive.

I always looked forward to lunch with Ethan. It was often the high point of my week. Ethan was my oasis of civility in the cut-throat competitiveness of everyday living, the one person to whom I could bare my soul. He knew just about everything about me, from my past lovers to my sorry financial situation. Aside from that, he was witty and engaging and a virtual font of information who counted the better part of Chicago's socially elite women among his acquaintances. Ethan had the inside scoop on nearly everything, from who joined AA after planting her face in her sole meuniere while dining with her in-laws at oh-so-proper Onwentsia to who was sleeping with their soon-to-be-ex's divorce attorney. But despite Ethan's vast collection of female friends, he and I shared a special relationship that rose above the others. Ours was a friendship rooted in far more than societal dictates and idle chatter.

I tipped the attendant my remaining fifty cents and returned to the restaurant where Ethan's seat remained glaringly empty. This time I had Michel seat me, nonetheless, and ordered my usual seafood salad and a glass of Premier Cru Chablis. I sipped at my wine in silent irritation and avoided glancing in the direction of Franklin and Marjorie. Not that it made any difference at that point. By then the two of them were more oblivious to others than the couple on the beach. According to Ethan, Franklin's wife had recently caught on to his hijinks and filled Marjorie's husband in on the gory details. He told me they had recently been served with divorce papers and were in shock over it, though probably more over what it was going to cost them than the lost affection of their respective spouses. Maybe that explained why Franklin looked so tired.

My salad arrived and I picked at a crab lump in solitary displeasure, wondering what could possibly be delaying Ethan. And then it struck me like a misplayed chord of Rachmaninoff. Ethan's answering machine hadn't picked up! He was positively religious about leaving that machine on at all times, lest he miss a returned call from an interviewee for his book or, even worse, a social invitation. Last night on the phone he had complained that his new blood pressure medication caused his ankles to swell. Since Ethan was a confirmed hypochondriac, I hadn't paid attention to his complaint at the time. Now it reverberated in my brain.

I placed my fork upon my plate and signaled Michel for the check.

Traffic was light on Lake Shore Drive as I sped north toward Rogers Park and the fringe neighborhood Ethan called home. Whenever I dropped him off there, on those rainy or snowy nights when I couldn't bear the thought of him shivering away at a bus stop, I was all too happy to see it retreating in my rearview mirror. I turned onto Ethan's street and nearly collided with three unsavory characters standing smack dab in the middle of it smoking cigarettes. With their spiked hair and with chains dangling from not only their belts but their ears and noses as well, I imagine they would be called punk rockers. When I honked at them, they glared at me with defiant glassy eyes, as if I were the problem, before moving sluggishly aside like sheep on an Irish country road.

Ethan's dreary gray mid-rise stood mid-block. My spirits were buoyed to see an open parking space directly in front of it. I angled in between two wrecks and turned off the car, noticing in my mirror that the punk rockers had shuffled back into the street behind me. Though genuinely concerned about Ethan, I found myself suddenly apprehensive about the security of my car. Not only was mine the only luxury vehicle in sight, it was most certainly the only 1972 limited edition Jaguar XKE in opalescent metallic bronze.

Feeling I had no other choice, I got out and hurriedly locked the car. As I walked around to the other side, I discovered why the parking space had been open. There was a fire hydrant situated squarely in front of the passenger-side door. Having yet to see a police car anywhere in the area, I calculated the risk of getting a parking ticket as low, certainly lower than that of having my hubcaps stolen. Glad my insurance premiums were paid up, I left my late husband's prize possession and prayed it would remain in the same condition until my return.

The entry of Ethan's building was even seedier than one might imagine. The drab floor tiles were chipped away in several places, revealing a lighter shade tile suggestive of the floor's color in an earlier, cleaner era. Junk mail and flyers from local eateries were strewn about, and a freestanding ashtray, the type that usually holds sand, held no sand at all, though the metal bowl overflowed with cigarette butts just the same.

A second glass door that led to the interior lobby was locked. I located a directory listing of the tenants and pressed the button next to CAMPBELL, E. After several tries and no response, I turned back to the directory and located a button simply marked MANAGER. After pushing it repeatedly and getting no answer, I held it down with my index finger. Finally, a coarse metallic voice crackled at me through a small vented intercom.

"Yah?"

"Hello, I'd like to speak to someone about getting into an apartment."

"About getting an apartment?"

"No. About getting *into* an apartment."

"What?"

"I said I would like to get into one of your apartments. I have a friend who resides here, and I'm fearful something has happened to him. I would greatly appreciate it if you would come to the door and speak with me in person so I can explain. It is quite difficult talking into this box."

The box clicked which I took to mean the manager was on his way. After several minutes the lobby elevator opened and discharged an enormous man with oily brown hair plastered to his head. He wore a torn T-shirt stretched tight by a rotund belly one might describe as hanging over his belt, had he seen fit to wear one. He scrutinized me from his side of the door as if I posed him some threat, the clogged pores on his nose visible through the glass.

"I would be ever so grateful if you would let me in," I said.

His eyes rolled up toward his forehead as he visibly deliberated. After some consideration he must have deemed me harmless, and he opened the door, deigning me entry to the inner lobby. With its worn red industrial carpeting, token sofa, and another freestanding ashtray, it was no cleaner than the outside lobby. It also had the additional drawback of smelling like the Paris Metro at the height of summer. Or perhaps it was the slovenly giant who smelled. Regardless, I had come for a reason and precious time was ticking away. I quickly introduced myself and learned he was Mr. Desmond Keifer, the building's manager and superintendent. I explained the reason for my visit to this outpost of civilization, how Ethan stood me up for our regular luncheon engagement and how he had complained about his ankles swelling the night before. I pointed out that it was critical I be let into Ethan's apartment immediately in the event that he had taken ill and was unable to come to the door himself. I noted with satisfaction that Mr. Desmond Keifer nodded his head in agreement the entire time I spoke.

"So may I go up then and have a look?" I asked, growing almost as eager to distance myself from the odoriferous lobby and him as I was to check Ethan's status.

He stopped nodding. "No," he said simply.

"I beg your pardon?"

"I can't do it, lady. I just can't go around opening apartment doors whenever some renter don't answer his phone. How do I know you're not a thief or a jilted lover who wants revenge or something?"

"I can assure you I am none of the aforementioned. It is imperative that I get into Mr. Campbell's apartment at once."

"You'll have to get the police to do it."

Though perturbed, I had no intention of being put off. I had not come this far, risking life, limb, and loss of property to hear "no." I crossed my arms and stood my ground, contemplating what tack might be best with this unreasonable man while stealing an occasional glance outside to assure myself my car still had four tires. Mr. Keifer must have noticed this, because there was a sudden change in his demeanor. "Is that your car?" he solicited.

"Yes, it is, and I'd like to get to the bottom of this while it's still there. Now would you please let me into Mr. Campbell's apartment?"

He looked from the car to me. "Car like that costs a lot of money, don't it?"

"It certainly does," I replied, not quite catching his insinuation. After all, this was uncharted territory to me. When he looked down at my Chanel bag in a none-too-subtle manner, I entered a state of enlightenment. "Oh, I see," I said. I took out my billfold and opened it. It contained two dozen credit cards and seven dollars. I removed the five-dollar bill and held it out to him.

"Five bucks? You've got to be kidding," he said.

"That's five good dollars, take it or leave it. You certainly don't think I'm going to give you my last two dollars as well. If you don't want the money, then I suppose I will have go to the police as you suggested, and you will have passed up five perfectly good dollars."

His eyes lolled back into the sagging creases of his fat eyelids and he snapped the five-dollar bill from my hand. "Drives a Jaguar and only has seven dollars in her wallet. Now I've seen everything."

*   *   *

The elevator was insufferably slow, especially when considering I was sharing the small unventilated space with a large man whose hygienic practices were reminiscent of the Middle Ages. We finally creaked to a halt at the seventh floor. Mr. Keifer lumbered out and led the way down the dimly lit hallway like a giant fish struggling to swim upstream. I followed at a distance, the worn carpet beneath my feet even more dreary than that in the lobby.

He came to a stop in front of 7F and pounded ferociously on the door with a hairy balled-up fist. "Anyone in there?" he shouted. When a minute passed with no response to his barrage, he reached deeply into the pocket of his baggy pants and unearthed a huge keyring with dozens of keys. Considering the number of keys he had to sort through, he found the appropriate one in an amazingly short time. A second later, the door opened and Mr. Keifer was standing aside for me to enter.

I walked into the apartment and found myself in the small living room. My first thought was that it had been ransacked. There was paper everywhere, blanketing the floor as well as the couch and coffee table. The walls were barren, causing me to think that whoever had made this mess had also taken Ethan's art, since he professed to be an aficionado. But after taking a moment to focus in closer, I realized that the papers were stacked in piles. The chaos I was viewing was actually a room being used as a gigantic filing cabinet. Though Ethan professed to being somewhat disorganized, I never suspected he was this bad. I bent over and picked up a note card from the top of the stack nearest me. There, in Ethan's trademark loops and curlicues, was written: *Daisy, early years.*

I put the card back and moved into the adjacent kitchen, a narrow galley with metal cabinets painted yellow and a gray tile floor. In stark contrast to the living room, it was remarkably orderly, with a solitary coffee mug turned upside down on a towel next to the sink. A hall off the kitchen led to two doors, one open and one closed. The clear view of a sink through the open door told me it was the bathroom. The closed one had to be Ethan's bedroom. My heart pounded with apprehension as I gave it a light tap, a ridiculous gesture in light of the brutal pounding Mr. Keifer had administered to the front door minutes before. My resolve began to waver. I have never been good with sick people and matters of health. Perhaps Mr. Keifer had been right when he said we should call the authorities. Being a very private person myself, the prospect of violating another's inner sanctum went against my grain. Somewhere in the back of my mind was the notion I might be intruding. Or was it more the sense that there was something in that room I didn't want to see?

"Ethan, are you in there? It's Pauline. I was worried about you." I cracked the door open the tiniest bit. Through the crack I could see a small desk with a typewriter. Above it a piece of yellow legal paper was taped to the wall. It read: FINISH CHAPTER ONE. While my eyes locked on the note, an iron-like scent drifted to my nostrils.

"No!" I cried aloud, throwing the door open without giving it further thought.

The sight that greeted me will remain forever etched in my memory like the prehistoric images are in the cave at Lascaux. Ethan was slumped over on a narrow twin bed, clad only in a pair of boxer shorts, his concave chest sporting an embarrassing half-dozen wiry gray hairs. His head was situated so that he stared at me with empty black eyes. His right hand rested alongside him on the covers; the left dangled in space. It dawned on me he was dead at the same time it dawned on me that the mural on the wall behind him was pieces of his head.

I must have screamed because the next thing I knew, Mr. Keifer was squeezing his bulk past me into the room. When he saw the body on the bed, his jaw fell open. "Oh, shit," he uttered, and then with growing emphasis each time, "shit, shIT, SHIT."

"I imagine we should call the police," said my pragmatic side while my emotional one was trying to sort out the scene before me.

"Yeah," he agreed, the two of us on the same side for the time being. We backed out of the room and Mr. Keifer closed the door behind us. He muttered something about this being the last thing he needed as he headed into the kitchen, repeating his pet phrase the entire way. "Oh, shit."

I leaned into the doorframe. My hands were trembling and my insides felt as if they had just been vacuumed out. It was an emptiness I had not experienced since my husband's death twelve years before. But with Henry's death there had been one big difference. His illness had given me plenty of time to prepare for his loss. Nothing had prepared me for this.

I felt confused and immensely sad, my head spinning as though I were being sucked down into a vortex. Then the questions began to form, the most pressing one being what had happened on the other side of that door and why.

One thing was crystal clear. Ethan had not died from swollen ankles.

2

It's Not Who You Know

I refused to think the unthinkable—suicide. Having lost several friends and acquaintances over the years to this most unnatural cause of death, it inevitably leads one to ask oneself, *How could I have missed the signs?* Certainly Ethan had given me no signs. Or had he? I recalled cutting him short on the phone last night, and did not want to think I had missed a cry for help. But Armand Peckles's car had been waiting out front, and there was no time for dallying if we were going to make the opening curtain of *Tosca* at the Lyric. If there is one occasion that demands punctuality it is the opera. A scant minute of tardiness can mean watching the entire first act on video monitors in the lobby.

Coming from the kitchen, Mr. Keifer's gravelly voice gave out Ethan's address over the phone. In no time at all, the small apartment would be overrun with police and coroners and what have you. Once they arrived, they would take over and things would be beyond my control. I wanted some answers now, but in order to get them, I would have to go back into that room with Ethan. I had to know if the violence that occurred therein was of his own doing or if something of a more sinister nature had taken place.

I put my hand to the knob and it froze there as if it were paralyzed. The picture of the gore just the other side of the wooden barrier was still fresh in my mind. I'd never witnessed such vulgarity before, and my psyche balked at facing it again. But if I wanted my answer I had to go back in.

Once, when Henry and I were trekking in the Himalayas, we had gotten lost and ended up in front of a deep chasm. It was not too terribly wide, two feet at the most, but it was bottomless. An electrical storm was moving in quickly, jagged bolts of lightning crackling from the sky to the earth, and we had no choice but to jump across the gap in order to get back to safety before it struck in all its fury. But, in spite of the greater danger the storm posed, my gut terror stopped me like a steer at a cattle guard. Henry tried everything to get me to jump to no avail. It wasn't until he quoted Goethe that he was finally able to get me across. *Be bold and mighty forces will come to your aid.*

I boldly threw the door open and stepped back into the room. The calm was eerie, Ethan's face staring at me in mute slumber with glassy blank eyes. The iron smell of blood was sharper now, and layered over more offensive odors, the foulness of human waste. Barely able to draw breath, my eyes glossed over the pointy-nosed face to the wall behind it where vestiges of gray matter stuck in ragged bits and pieces. My stomach lurched momentarily, and the thought occurred to me it was a good thing I hadn't finished lunch.

Turning my head away from the body, I rummaged the bedclothes searching for a gun. To my great relief I didn't find one. The absence of a weapon would prove that someone else had performed this horrific act and not Ethan himself. I preferred it be that way, so that I could absolve myself from any blame. But my relief was to prove shorter lived than a fourth marriage as I looked downward and caught the cold glimmer of a metal cylinder peeking out from under the bed, just beyond the reach of Ethan's dangling left hand. I had known that Ethan was left-handed. I had not known he owned a gun.

"Oh, Ethan, what possessed you?" I cried aloud, angry and devastated at the same time. Nothing made sense. For all appearances, Ethan had been enjoying his life to the fullest and seemed far too self-centered to take it. Not to mention squeamish. It simply wasn't logical. But then what is logical about suicide? I forced myself to look back at the pale pathetic body and found myself burning with shame for him—not only for what he had done but that he had done it in such an undignified manner.

There had to be some kind of explanation. Certainly a writer would have left a note. I went to his desk where a sheet of paper stuck from the carriage of his typewriter. I rolled it forward and read the two lines of type centered on the page.

DAISY FELLOWES—A WOMAN REINVENTED
by Ethan Campbell

Evidently he had written even less than I thought.

Still hoping to find a note, I decided to search his desk. I opened the top drawer and saw his appointment book laying atop a jumble of papers. His self-declared "lifeline," he never went anywhere without it. I picked up the slender leather book and thumbed through it. The ink-filled pages testified to a full social agenda: lunch dates and dinner parties, library board meetings, a fundraiser at the Historical Society, a speaking engagement at the Women's Athletic Club. No wonder he never got anything written; he was never at home. I suspected he would have been better served putting more time into writing at his typewriter and less in his appointment book.

I flipped to the current date: Wednesday, March 30. Our lunch engagement was carefully inked-in at twelve-thirty, *Pauline, Lunch, Drake.* On Tuesday, I noticed he'd had lunch with Sunny Livermore at the Four Seasons. Funny, he hadn't mentioned it to me. That made Sunny the last of his friends to see him alive, I thought jealously. Though the emotion was probably misplaced, it stung just the same to think that someone other than I spent his last afternoon with him.

I was startled by the sound of someone coming into the room and turned to see a tall Latino man standing in the doorway, an inexpensive navy suit hanging loosely on his lanky frame. His features were those one might see on the cover of a grocery store romance novel: deep black eyes, a cropped mustache, a helmet of thick dark hair, a tremendously macho scar that traced a line from his right cheek to his jawbone. His gaze flicked from me to the corpse, and then back to me again. Assuming him to be some sort of authority figure, I also assumed he was not terribly pleased to see me rifling through Ethan's personal effects. I was correct on both counts.

"What are you doing?" he demanded.

"And who is asking?" I countered.

Though his eyes telegraphed impatience, he accommodated me by reaching into his breast pocket and pulling out a worn-looking wallet. He flipped it open with one hand to reveal a silver star. "Detective Velez from the Chicago Police Department. Homicide. And you are . . . ?"

"My name is Pauline Cook," I said, scrutinizing the badge as if I had the foggiest notion what I should look for. It could have been a child's plaything for all I knew. After finishing my examination, I pointed at the body on the bed. "We were friends," I said softly.

"I'm sorry, Ms. Cook—"

"Missus," I corrected him.

"*Mrs.* Cook, but I'm going to ask you to step into the other room. And leave that." He was staring at the appointment book in my hand. I laid it obediently on the desk.

"Now, Mrs. Cook. If you'd please . . ." He indicated the door with a gesture that could only be taken one way.

*   *   *

Mr. Keifer and I were led from the apartment and asked to wait in the hall until someone could interview us. Not long afterward, a second detective arrived on the scene, Detective Jerry Malloy. Younger than his counterpart, he was dressed entirely in black: black leather blazer, black T-shirt, black polyester pants. With a broad freckled face, sandy hair in serious need of a cut, and eyes an insignificant murky shade of green, Detective Malloy had the sort of bland looks that made him easily forgettable. However, there was one thing about the young detective that was quite indelible: his unique butchery of the English language. An assault upon the ears akin to fingernails on a chalkboard, it would have driven Henry Higgins to take up serious drinking. Not only was his grammar atrocious, but it was punctuated by the occasional replacement of the *you* pronoun with *youse* and the consonants *th* with the letter *d*.

Take, for example, his first question. "Mrs. Cook, Mr. Keifer, I got a couple of t'ings to ask youse here." His pen poised in the air over a small note pad. "For one, could youse please explain for me what prompted the two of youse to gain entry to the deceased's apartment?"

Aside from the fact that I found him somewhat insolent, I didn't take kindly to the implication that somehow Mr. Keifer and I were associated. For a moment, I considered being difficult and telling him to contact my attorney for his answers. But being uncooperative wouldn't have served the best interest of Ethan's memory, and besides, my attorney was ridiculously expensive.

"We went in to see if he was all right," I said, reigning in my indignation. "Which clearly he wasn't." I explained my relationship to *the deceased* and his failure to appear at lunch. "And after getting no answer on the telephone, I recalled Ethan complaining about his ankles swelling just last night. Naturally, I got worried and drove up here right away. I insisted Mr. Keifer let me in."

"I told her she should call the police," Mr. Keifer piped up in his own defense.

"Uh-huh. And what did youse do after entering to the apartment?"

"I went into Ethan's bedroom and found him in the same condition that your people are now studying, I imagine."

"I didn't go nowhere near there until I heard her scream." Mr. Keifer was obviously trying to distance himself from any involvement with me. I suppressed the urge to ask him for my five dollars back.

"Uh-huh. D'jouse touch anything while you was in there?"

I contemplated my every move inside Ethan's apartment. "Well, let's see, the doorknob, his desk, some papers. And I happened to take a glance at his appointment book."

Detective Malloy looked appalled. "So in other words, while you was in the room with da deceased, you was going tru' his personal things?"

"Just his appointment book. Is there something wrong with that?"

"Of course there is. You don't touch dead people's stuff. You could have contaminated the scene. Don't youse ever watch police shows on television?"

I assured him I did not. After rolling his eyes in a manner suggesting I was one of the more vacuous people he had ever met, he went on to ask, "Do you know what Mr. Campbell did for a living?"

"He was a writer."

"Like for newspapers?"

"No, *like*, for books. He wrote biographies about socialites. He had two in print and was working on his third."

His eyebrows arched over his dull green eyes. "Anybody I ever heard of?"

"Are you familiar with Berthe Palmer or Gloria Guinness?" His perplexed look told me this was uncharted terrain. I went on to explain.

"Berthe was the wife of Potter Palmer who built the Palmer House Hotel. She was a grand patron of the arts, one of the earliest devotees of the French Impressionists. Berthe is responsible for that tremendous collection of Monets we have in the Art Institute. As for Gloria, she was the quintessential social climber. Her parents were Mexican peasants—her mother was a seamstress. But that didn't stop her from marrying her way up. Her last husband was the international banker, Loel Guinness."

"Do you think what he wrote about dem could have pissed 'em off?"

"Lord, no. They're long dead. To include Daisy Fellowes, the subject of his latest book. Singer sewing machine heiress," I added before he could ask. I neglected to mention Daisy's sexual proclivities, though I suspect he would have found them of great interest.

"Why d'ya suppose he wrote about dem?"

"Ethan was intrigued by rich and famous women."

The detective contemplated. "So was he light in da loafers?"

"You mean, homosexual? I believe so." Though Ethan and I never actually discussed it, it went without saying that if he had any sexual inclinations, they were toward men.

"Did he have any lovers?"

"Not that I knew of."

He jotted on the pad. "How about enemies? Anybody who had a beef with him?"

I thought carefully. Ethan's tongue could be acerbic and had irritated more than a few people on occasion. But true enemies? The closest I could come was Connie Chan who wrote the society page for *The Tribune*. She had panned the Gloria Guinness book in her popular column, calling it simple, shallow, and rife with name dropping and inaccuracies. Since then Ethan always referred to her as "that slanty-eyed bitch," blaming her for lost book sales. Just last week at a reception for Philip Roth, he had referred to her writing as sophomoric within earshot of the author himself. Connie had been livid. Still,

I couldn't fathom petite Connie Chan driving across town to blow Ethan's brains out. Connie wasn't exactly the sort to win popularity contests. If this was her response to insults, the streets would have been littered with her victims. I ruled her out.

"No enemies to speak of," I replied.

"What about family?"

I had heard Ethan's family story so many times I could recite it aloud. It read like a Greek tragedy: He was born to wealth, his mother somehow related to the Eastman fortune. An only child, he was sickly and had to be schooled at home, so he had few childhood friends. By the time he was ten, his father had squandered most of the family finances and committed suicide. When he was eighteen, his beloved mother died in a car crash honeymooning with her third husband in San Sebastian. His new stepfather had survived the crash and inherited what remained of the estate, leaving Ethan penniless. As he told it, it wasn't the loss of the genteel life that hurt the most, but more so the overwhelming loneliness of not being tied to anyone. I could relate to him on both counts, the father's squandered inheritance and being an orphaned only child—though Mother's death of breast cancer didn't occur until after I was a grown woman. But still, Ethan and I shared the unenviable status of having no one obligated to invite us for holidays.

"No immediate family," I replied.

"None at all? No brothers, sisters, cousins?"

"Not that I am aware of."

"Was he depressed about being all alone like dat?"

"Ethan was not depressed. And he was not alone. He had many, many friends."

Detective Malloy directed his next string of questions at Desmond Keifer and learned that Ethan had lived in the building for ten years, usually paid his monthly rent of four hundred fifty-five dollars on time, and was often a "major pain in the ass."

"What d'ya mean by pain in da ass?" the detective asked.

"He was always complaining. About security. About sanitation—which I can't understand seeing how I run a clean building here. About noise. He drove me nuts complaining about noise."

And then, as if providence was intervening on Ethan's behalf, a reverberating jackhammer-like sound rattled the walls. It was coming from the apartment at the far end of the hall. Detective Malloy dispatched a policewoman to instruct the occupants to "turn down that racket." Then he asked us to "stay put," and went back into Ethan's apartment.

Mr. Keifer and I remained obediently stationed in the dim hall while a steady parade of civil servants streamed past us. A photographer and a medical examiner were followed by more police and two young paramedics pushing an empty gurney. One by one they disappeared into the apartment leaving us standing there. Finally, someone thought to bring a couple of chairs from Ethan's kitchenette, so at least we had something to sit on during our detention. The minutes ticked past at an excruciating pace as one hour turned to two. I was growing increasingly perturbed. Not a very patient person to begin with, the little patience I do have was sorely tried by the occasional burst of flatulence coming from Mr. Keifer's direction—the aftermath of which was competition for the mythological harpies. It was so painful I nearly forgot why I was sitting there. But then the reason presented itself coldly when the two paramedics reappeared in the doorway. This time a sheet-covered body rested on top of their gurney.

I stood up and gasped aloud. And then, in a manner quite unlike my usual self, I grabbed hold of Ethan's lifeless arm and held onto it tightly. It felt like cold putty in my hand. "Ma'am, ma'am, you can't do that" a voice was saying while someone else's fingers were trying to pry mine off my dead friend. I finally let go and watched in surrender as Ethan made his last trip down the dingy hallway.

"Goodbye, Ethan," I whispered under my breath as they loaded him into the elevator. "Goodbye, mon cher ami."

Detective Velez made his second appearance a minute later, this time to dismiss us.

"I'm sorry to have kept you so long. You two can go now," he said matter-of-factly, offering no explanation about the long wait.

"About time," grumbled the corpulent building manager. There was a loud squeak as he lumbered to his feet and the chair cried out in blessed relief. He pointed a thumb over his shoulder to the apartment behind him. "Hey, who cleans up this mess anyway?"

"No one goes in there until the crime scene tape comes down," the detective warned. "After that, I'm afraid it's yours."

"Don't the city send someone in?"

"I'm afraid not."

Mr. Keifer's fat pout rolled from his sagging cheeks to his protruding lower lip. He clearly wasn't up to the unpleasant task. "What about all his junk?"

"I'll oversee the disposition of his things. This is where I can be reached," I heard myself volunteer, eager to be rid of Mr. Keifer for more reasons than the obvious one. I needed to speak to the detective by myself. Reaching into my wallet, I handed him one of my calling cards. He studied it for a minute, made an impressed clucking sound at my address, and deposited it into the pocket with all the keys. Then he turned wordlessly and headed down the hall with surprising speed, no doubt anxious to get back to his television, a frozen pizza, and a can of beer.

Detective Velez noticed I had made no move to leave. "You're free to go too, Mrs. Cook. We'll call you if we have any more questions."

"Actually, I have some questions for you, Detective."

The jagged scar on his cheek darkened, and he looked at me like he would a pesky fly. However, I was not about to be intimidated by a public servant who earned his living off my tax dollars. Lord knows, I paid enough of them, and I had every intention of getting my money's worth. Besides, the painful hours spent sitting in the hall had not been a total waste. They had given me plenty of time to come to my own conclusion regarding Ethan's death, and it had to do with one of the first thoughts to cross my mind after finding him.

"What can I do for you, Mrs. Cook?" he acquiesced.

"I want to know if you are treating this death as a suicide or a homicide."

"Any suspicious death is treated as a potential homicide until the coroner makes a ruling," he said, sounding like he was quoting directly from the police manual. Then his voice softened and turned sympathetic as he added, "But murderers generally don't leave the weapon behind."

"Did you find a suicide note?" I asked.

"No, but contrary to popular belief, suicides rarely leave them."

This was news to me. I would have guessed that people miserable enough to time their release from this world would have no qualms about sharing the reason for it with those left behind. But Ethan wasn't miserable and he didn't take his own life.

"Detective, Ethan did not kill himself. I'm certain of it. He was extremely vain, so vain that I can guarantee one thing unequivocally." I paused for emphasis before delivering my coup. "There is no way in creation that he would have ever permitted himself to be found wearing only his undershorts."

At that moment, Detective Malloy chose to interrupt us. He crooked his head at his superior in a manner that indicated something significant had happened.

"George," he said. "Got something here you might find interesting."

"We'll take all your comments into consideration, Mrs. Cook. Now thank you for your cooperation," said Detective Velez, dismissing me with a finality that even a taxpayer such as myself could not challenge.

By the time I stepped out of Ethan's building, the sun was low in the sky, like an enormous gold coin being deposited into the high-rise buildings to the west. To my great relief, my car was still intact. However, a bright orange parking ticket was stuck to the middle of the windshield. I plucked it off and read in disbelief that the fine for parking in front of a fire hydrant was one hundred dollars. A police car with two officers inside was double parked in front of the building. I marched over and thrust the ticket through the open window on the passenger's side.

"Excuse me, but would you happen to know anything about this?" I demanded of a ruddy-faced man chewing gum with aerobic intensity. His jaws stopped momentarily as he glanced down at the financial outrage and back at me.

"Yeah, lady. That's called a parking ticket. We put them on cars that are parked where they aren't supposed to be."

"Yes, well, I wonder if you might cancel it for me."

His expression suggested I had just asked him to shoot someone on my behalf.

"Lady, in case you didn't know, it's illegal to park your car in front of fire hydrants. Even if it's a Jaguar."

"You don't understand. It was an emergency. My friend was found dead in this building. This was the only available space." He stared at me blandly. Then a glimmer of compassion came into his eyes as he realized my connection to the lifeless body that had just been wheeled out. But I was to learn who one knows doesn't carry much weight when it comes to the Department of Motor Vehicles.

"I'm sorry about your friend, lady, but we can't cancel parking tickets once they are written. All you can do is go to court and tell your story. Mark here to protest," he said and he pointed to a box on the orange ticket. "But if you want my opinion, I'd just pay the fine. You're driving an expensive car. You can afford it. It ain't worth wasting the day in court."

I was incensed that simply because I owned a luxury car he thought a hundred dollars did not mean a great deal to me. It meant far more than he could know. But I was too physically and emotionally drained to take on another challenge. I walked away without a fight and got into my car, throwing the ticket onto the passenger's seat in righteous anger. Then a bout of sorrow swept me. I thought of Ethan's scrawny white body and wondered where it was now. Most likely laying on a cold slab of concrete in some morgue. And then another, equally troubling, thought occurred to me. When the coroner finished with Ethan's body, who would take responsibility for its final disposition?

I remembered what it cost to bury Henry and felt the noose of financial strangulation tighten itself ever firmer around my neck.

3

Finding Solace

The black cloud that had formed between the sky and myself followed me into the paneled lobby of my building. Jeffrey was on duty, looking incongruous in his staid hunter green uniform. His young muscular body was far better suited for a pair of shorts on the beach, playing volleyball with the wind teasing his wavy blond hair onto his face.

"Good evening, Mrs. Cook," he greeted me in his perpetually cheery voice. "That's a beautiful suit you're wearing."

It seemed so long ago since I put the suit on that it didn't even feel new anymore. I was too disheartened to even acknowledge the compliment. My entire being was overwhelmed with the sense of something going missing. "Jeffrey, my car is out front. Could someone take it to the garage?"

I know it's difficult to believe that anyone could live in a multimillion dollar apartment and not have parking, but such was the case with many of the vintage buildings on the Gold Coast, and mine was no exception. My building was erected during the twenties when the wealthy expected to have drivers. As a result my car was housed around the corner which was often an inconvenience. But I so adored my penthouse, with its three-hundred-sixty-degree views and spacious elegant rooms, that I wouldn't have considered living anywhere else. The inconvenience was acceptable.

"I'll see to it immediately, Mrs. Cook." It was then that he must have noticed the misery in my face, because he added, "Is everything all right, Mrs. Cook?"

"I'm afraid it's not, Jeffrey. Mr. Campbell has died."

He looked shocked. Ethan was a regular visitor to my home, so all the doormen knew him. "I'm sorry to hear that, Mrs. Cook. What happened?"

"That is the question, Jeffrey."

He accompanied me through the lobby to the single elevator that serviced the building. The gilded door stood open, and he reached inside and pushed twenty for the penthouse. I managed a weak smile while the door closed upon his comely face. The door reopened onto my private foyer, the hardwood floor gleaming from a fresh coat of wax, the crystals of my Venetian chandelier glimmering overhead. Wondering how much longer before I would have to discontinue the service that kept my home so polished, I unlocked the antique knob to the interior foyer and entered the apartment.

I went directly to my bedroom and changed into a pair of slacks and a sweater, hanging my new suit, thankfully no worse for the wear after my ordeal. Then I took the back hall to my library to check my answering machine. The few messages were unimportant and none related to Ethan. Then again, Ethan's death was still so fresh no one would know about it yet. I contemplated calling Sunny and some of the others who considered themselves his closest friends, those who would be insulted if they weren't among the first to hear the news, but just couldn't summon up the energy. The day had been long and draining and I didn't feel like talking. The personal touch would have to wait until the morrow.

I shut off the volume to the machine, turned to my bar, and poured myself a stiff Scotch over ice. As a general rule wine is my drink, much better for the skin, but the occasion called for more drastic measures. The first sip went down with an amber glow. I drank more and waited for the alcohol to take its numbing effect. But instead of anesthetizing my sadness, it seemed to be magnifying it. With each swallow, my grief grew stronger until it merged with anger and betrayal as well. Regardless of what caused Ethan's death, his own hand or someone else's, I railed against him for leaving me with no warning.

The phone rang and I let the machine take it as I carried my drink into the living room and sat down on one of the empire sofas in front of the window. The antique-filled room usually generated a sense of warmth and calm in me, but at the moment it felt cold and alien. My gaze drifted to the lake. In the setting sun, the buildings of Lake Shore Drive cast long shadows onto the water like fingers reaching for the unobtainable.

Suddenly, the tears I had so stoically stanched all day began to flow. They came with a fury, and I sobbed my heart out, exhausting two embroidered handkerchiefs before turning to a far more practical box of tissues. My best friend in the entire world was gone, the very person I called when I felt as miserable as this. Ethan was always available to meet me for a drink or a cup of coffee and listen patiently to my sorrows. Now I was left to suffer them on my own. It felt like trying to play the piano with one hand.

The tears finally tapered off. I remained on the sofa and listened as my grandfather clock sounded eight desolate chimes. An oppressive loneliness came over me, and my thoughts drifted to Sean. He worked a short shift on Wednesdays. I picked up the phone and hung up without dialing. Ethan strongly disapproved of my young lover, saying not only was he far beneath my standards but that he was using me. I thought Ethan was really jealous. Whatever the case, I decided it would be disrespectful of Ethan's memory to call Sean now. Instead, I went back into the library and poured myself another Scotch.

Fresh drink in hand, I resumed my position at the window. Fleur emerged from somewhere in the apartment and jumped onto my lap. I found some comfort in stroking my Siamese's silky coat, some solace in the rhythm of her purr. Outside, the lake was a vast ebony expanse broken only by the pearls of the breakwater lights and the soft glow of the offshore pumping station. A solitary boat came into view and disappeared into the lonely black. Spring could bring quick changes on Lake Michigan and the water was dangerously cold. Boats overturned and people died of hypothermia. Whoever was out there was either foolhardy or a devoted boater.

I was reminded how Ethan had always wanted a boat. It was one of his greatest desires. He claimed the passion was born during his summers in Newport as a youth and nurtured during his adult years in Puerto Rico. In a way, my friendship with Ethan was owed to his fondness for boats. Years ago, when Ethan had spent a winter in Palm Beach doing research for the Gloria book, he happened to meet my good friend and former Radcliffe roommate, Sandy St. Clair, disembarking her ninety-foot Hatteras, *The Sandy Saint*. They struck up a conversation, and when she learned he wrote biographies about famous women, she took him under her wing. That entire social season she squired him around town and introduced him to everyone. When the lease on the apartment he was renting ran out, she installed him as a resident guest on the Hatteras.

Ethan always spoke fondly of Sandy. But when he spoke of *The Sandy Saint* his dark eyes enlarged in their sockets and a glow came over him as if he were in a trance. In fact, he was enamored of most things involving the trappings of wealth, from fine dining and wine to expensive clothes, exotic locales and grand estates. Though he had little money himself—his two books made far less than one might expect—he was obsessed with the rich and the glamour associated with them. At times he reminded me of a shoeless waif with his face pressed to a candy store window, seeing his heart's desire right there in front of him but beyond his reach just the same. He had confided in me once that he felt entitled to more and hoped to attain it through his writing. Though that hardly seemed likely considering his lack of discipline and disdain for deadlines.

When Ethan left Palm Beach to come back up north, Sandy St. Clair insisted he look me up "the very moment you set foot in Chicago." And so he called me the very day he returned. I shall never forget the sound of his voice the first time I heard it. It had a captivating quality as if some grand secret lingered beneath the deep resonant tones. He invited me to lunch, and naturally I accepted, adding that "any friend of Sandy's is a friend of mine."

The day we were to meet for the first time, I primped as if I were going to be featured on the cover of *Town and Country*. I worried more about what to wear that day than I did when Princess Diana visited Chicago. The potential of a new male acquaintance, especially one with Palm Beach connections, could not be looked upon lightly. As any single woman over the age of forty can attest, the dearth of quality men available in the mature age bracket is deplorable. Those who aren't married or aren't with women half their age either have one foot in the grave or some crippling emotional disorder—the ones with decent portfolios that is. I wouldn't have a clue about the others, though I suspect it's the same. Ethan had to be taken seriously as a possible suitor or, at the very least, a suitable escort for a fundraiser or two.

Eager to set eyes upon the face that accompanied the enticing voice, I arrived at the Cape Cod Room a mere fifteen minutes late, wearing a moss-colored Chanel suit that really accentuated my eyes. Michel escorted me to the table, and my lofty hopes for romance deflated as I laid eyes on my new friend for the first time. The voice that had so enchanted me on the telephone was in direct contrast to the man who rose to greet me. Slight and frail looking with pockmarked skin, his narrow face tapered off into a pointed chin. Though he appeared to be around sixty, the long strands of hair combed over his pate were an unnaturally deep brown. He was meticulously dressed, however, his tweed jacket of good quality, his white shirt starched, and his red tie such a good Hermès knock-off it very nearly fooled me.

"Hello, dear lady." He greeted me with a yellow-toothed smile and an ebullience that suggested we were the oldest of acquaintances reuniting after a long interval. He kissed me on both cheeks in the European style as if no well-bred person ever met without doing so. Then he extended his hand and I took it. It was cool and slightly damp with short manicured fingers. My smile was pasted on lest it drop and my disappointment show on my face. I wondered why I hadn't had the presence of mind to call Sandy and get the low-down on Ethan before meeting him. But then his magical voice poured forth, causing me to nearly overlook his less than comely appearance. "Sandy told me you were a beautiful woman, but I had no idea you were this stunning."

"How kind of you to say so," I replied, always receptive to a compliment. Hardly as honest or as frequent as when I was younger, it made them all the more pleasurable. His words rang with such heartfelt sincerity, it's possible I may have even blushed. It was then I realized that Michel was still holding my chair out, so I took my seat and Ethan took his.

"How are things with Sandy?" I asked him. "I want to hear all about her."

"Well, she was very busy when I last saw her. With the end of the season nearing, she was preparing to close the house and cruise *The Sandy Saint* up to Newport."

"Lovely boat, isn't it?"

"First-rate," he said, his eyes glazing over briefly.

"Was Mark with her in Palm Beach?" I pried.

"Not while I was there. I understand his business kept him in New York for most of the winter this year."

"Of course. Mark St. Clair is a *very* busy man," I said, knowing fully well what kind of business had prevented Mark St. Clair from migrating south for the winter—monkey business. He had been having an affair with a department store clerk from the cosmetic counter at Bloomingdale's for the last year, putting her up in a tony flat in the east nineties. Everyone in New York knew about it, including Sandy, though she would never admit to it. Denial was the safest avenue. To acknowledge her husband's philandering would mean taking some kind of action, and that might jeopardize her status as Mrs. Mark St. Clair, not to mention risk installing her rival in her own position. Sandy was more than happy simply to turn her head to her husband's illicit liaison and spend her winter unencumbered by him in Palm Beach.

Ethan knew of this dalliance as well, and we found ourselves exchanging none too subtle knowing looks. We connected in that moment and our friendship was sealed. The afternoon flew past in a heartbeat. Ethan updated me on the most select gossip coming out of Palm Beach, about Pilar Zenda leaving her husband's dead body on ice for three months so that she wouldn't have to miss out on any of the social season, about Pug Witherspoon's looming fraud indictment for overselling memberships in his golf developments, of the personal secretary who was having an affair with both her employer and his wife. Ethan seemed to know everything about everybody.

And that included me—information gleaned from Sandy, no doubt. He knew all about Henry's death twelve years prior, and he made several references to my matriarchal grandmother. He was polite enough not to mention my father's side of the family or my mother's disinheritance. But for some reason I didn't find any of his knowledge about me threatening. He already felt like a dearest friend, and it only seemed fitting that such a friend should know all about me.

"You know, I'm just finishing up a book about Gloria Guinness," he said with pride evident in his voice. "Sandy told me that your mother knew Gloria. Did you ever meet her?"

"Once—in New York at Grandmother's Park Avenue apartment," I told him, the memory coming back to me vividly. "It was a summer day and Gloria would have been, well, about my age now. As I recall she was dressed entirely in white. She literally floated across the room smoking a cigarette from a long cigarette holder. I was barely a teenager at the time, but I was struck how everything about her personified beauty and elegance. She projected a style one rarely finds these days. My own mother appeared almost dowdy next to her."

"Did your mother ever tell you any interesting stories about her?" he probed, always eager for another anecdote to add to the biography.

"Not really, aside from the fact that she had a mouth like a sailor. Mother wasn't terribly fond of Gloria, and she was disturbed because I was awestruck by her. I suspect my mother was jealous because even though Gloria had come from humble beginnings, she had managed to catapult herself to the top, while Mother, coming from all the advantages, always struggled to make ends meet. She said that Gloria claimed her father was a Mexican diplomat when in reality he was little more than a peasant, and her mother a seamstress. Mother also told me Gloria was a spy for the wrong side during World War II. Is that true?"

"According to my research there's some truth in it. She was married to von Furstenberg at the time."

"Anyhow, Mother said Gloria was a pro at rewriting history and a pro at reinventing herself."

Ethan's black eyes gleamed as he leaned back in his chair digesting my words. "I like what your mother said—about Gloria reinventing herself. That she did indeed. Imagine essentially being born in the gutter and rising to move in the smartest circles in the world. Then end up marrying one of the world's wealthiest men? Most people never even had a clue as to her actual history; she veiled it so well.

"I have a great appreciation for those who are able to scale the walls of their pasts. Though when they get to the other side they forget their yesterdays, I find them some of the most interesting people of all."

"Well then, Ethan, I suppose you will find me rather dull, because I've never reinvented myself and wouldn't even think of it. I am who I am and the devil to anyone who doesn't care for me this way."

"Then you are a rarity, Pauline," he said, his tone of whimsy turning into one of utmost sincerity. "Have you any faults?"

"Just two. The first is insatiable curiosity. The second shall remain nameless."

We ruminated over the latest issues: Ivana Trump peddling clothes on television, Miglin's murder and the subsequent murder of Versace by the same sociopath, and the recent death of a well-known socialite from a botched liposuction. Before I knew it the afternoon had slipped away and I had to rush off to get ready for the theater. But before parting, we arranged to meet the following Wednesday, and the tradition was established.

Over time our friendship continued to blossom. Before long, we were talking on the phone every day at least once, sometimes several times. Ethan was great company, attentive and fawning, and had a way of making one feel elevated when in his presence. He had such a good eye for fashion that I seldom made a major purchase without his approval. He was a wonderful escort who carried himself in a manner that transcended both his unseemly looks and his sometimes tired sartorial appearance, a presence I attributed to his aristocratic pedigree. We attended the symphony and opera together, the latest art gallery openings, the fashion shows, the Lincoln Park Zoo Ball, parties at the Casino Club, and countless other events. All at my expense, of course. But having Ethan was like having a really best girlfriend that one never had to compete with in any way.

Ethan had already lived in Chicago for years before I met him, working on the Berthe Palmer book, but hadn't established himself in the best circles. After the Gloria book was published, and made several bestseller lists, his status changed overnight. Suddenly he was embraced by the social elite, was invited to speak in their clubs and attend their parties. Rarely was there a night or a lunch that he didn't have some kind of an engagement. As his popularity grew, so did his entourage of women friends, and many afternoons he could be found holding court at high tea at the Drake.

Personally, I avoided those sessions like the plague, having only so much tolerance for my own gender. Though I must confess to appreciating the morsels of the gossip Ethan gleaned from his tea parties and shared with me later.

The phone rang and once again I let the answering machine do its job. In my misery, the last thing I wanted to do was talk. My thoughts reverted back to Sean and the mindless pleasure of his strong arms around me. After all, I was only human, and humans seek comfort in their misery. My resolve against calling him wilted with the last ice cubes in my Scotch. I looked skyward to ask for Ethan's understanding. I got up and called Sean at work.

"Bertucci's." A nasal female voice fought to be heard over background noise that sounded like the Las Vegas prizefight Henry took me to the year after we were married. He had some business interest there at the time. The roar of the crowd had been deafening as two shiny, sweaty black men pummeled each other in a most savage manner while blood and sweat rained upon us in the first row like Paris drizzle. My new suit was ruined. It was my first and last fight.

I asked for Sean and heard the woman scream over the din. "Romero, it's for you." I held the receiver away from my ear until his unmistakably masculine voice came on the line. It never failed to appeal to my carnal side.

"This is Sean speaking."

"Sean, dear, it's Pauline."

His mouth moved closer to the phone, and his tone turned attentive. "Pauline, I've missed you."

"Sean, I'm feeling a bit blue. I wondered if you might stop over after work." There was no reason to tell him about Ethan yet. It could wait.

"I sure can. I'll be finished about ten-thirty. Is that all right?"

"That's lovely. I'll tell Jeffrey to expect you."

I hung up and went into the bathroom. The image that stared back at me from the mirror was frightening. Red, swollen eyes and a face blown up like a balloon. Thank God Sean wasn't expected for a couple of hours. I hoped that would be enough time to pull myself together. Then I laughed aloud at my own audacity. Time wasn't the answer. Time was the enemy. There wasn't enough of it left in eternity for a forty-nine-year-old woman to hide nature's ravages from a thirty-year-old man. To feel secure, older women should be with older men, preferably ones with plenty of money and diminishing eyesight.

Insecure or not, the relationship with Sean filled a void in my life—the one involving my second fault. My biological clock may have been winding down, but it hadn't given any indication of being in its final hour yet. In fact, it was just the opposite. It's my understanding that as estrogen levels drop in pre-menopausal women, there is a surge of testosterone that fuels sexual desire. If this is the case, I was no exception to the rule. My carnal desires were stronger than ever. Maybe playing doctor with this man-child was ludicrous, but it worked well for me. And tonight my needs flared stronger than ever. I needed the cushion of human flesh to soften the sharp pain of loss.

I put a cold towel to my face to reduce the swelling.

When the elevator door opened, I awaited in the foyer, wearing a silk dressing gown over a bustier and garter belt. Without even saying "hello," he picked me up in those Herculean, supple-skinned, muscular arms and carried me directly into my bedroom. He practically tore my undergarments off and buried himself inside me. All was forgotten save the exquisite realm of mortal pleasure.

Only later, as we lay in exhaustion on sweat-soaked sheets, beneath the canopy of my four-poster bed, did I tell him about Ethan.

4
No Good News

The sun dawned brightly again the next morning, but I was not party to it. Fortuitously, my bedroom faces west so the morning sun never intrudes. The combination of the Scotch and the stamina of a young lover left me in need of extra sleep. Besides, I have no great affinity for the morning. It's a pleasant time for coffee and a piece of dry toast, but serves no purpose that I can see other than that. I far prefer the other side of the clock. After Henry died, I found it difficult to sleep, so I started reading and answering correspondence into the wee hours. The habit stuck. Now I seldom even think of going to sleep before midnight.

It was after ten when I awakened. Sean was gone. He had an early morning shoot and knew better than to disturb me. Looking over to the crumpled sheets on his side of the bed, I took a selfish moment to luxuriate in the memory of the night before. A note was propped up on his nightstand next to the Trojan wrapper, an indispensable prerequisite to intimacy in these days of disease. Sean was, after all, an aspiring model. I turned on my bedside lamp and read what he had written. *You were sleeping so soundly I didn't want to wake you up. I'll call you later. I'm sorry about Ethan.* So very Sean. Simple and to the point.

The reminder of Ethan brought a feeling to my stomach like that of an undigested meal in a third-world country. Past experience told me it would get worse before it got better. When one is first confronted with death, the numbing shock basically gets one through the initial days. But it's the ensuing weeks and months and even years after the death that prove far more difficult, when the totality of the passing settles in. Death is in the times the phone doesn't ring, the day one doesn't have to seek out a birthday gift or send a postcard from abroad, the emptiness of unlocking the door to a lifeless home. The wasted thought, Henry/Mother/Grandmother, would love this place/dress/vase. That was where death affected me the most, in the staggering weight of the small details rather than the grand.

That day I wouldn't wonder where Ethan was because my mind told me he was gone. I knew that I wouldn't be picking up the phone to talk to him. I knew I wouldn't clip out a juicy bit from the newspaper to share with him. His death would hit hardest when something nice occurred in the future and I realized he wasn't there to hear about it. There was to be no more idle gossip between us. I would never hear the rare magic of his musical voice again. Ethan left a gaping hole that a thousand Seans could never fill. Like a schoolgirl mourning the loss of her first love, I turned onto my stomach and cried into my empty pillow.

After showering and dressing, I fed Fleur her breakfast of Albacore tuna and took my coffee in the library. The answering machine's red light flashed with urgency. A look at the digital display told me I had eleven messages. I pressed the play button and waited for the tape to rewind. It took quite a while.

The first message was from Detective Velez. His call must have been the one I ignored shortly after arriving home yesterday evening. He wanted me to call him as soon as possible.

My next caller was Sunny Livermore. In public we kissed cheeks like the best of friends, but in truth we shared an unhealthy rivalry. She was pure parvenu, and insanely jealous of people such as I who came from the East, attended all the right schools, and had families of social standing. Her husband Nat traded at the Mercantile and was obscenely wealthy. They had catapulted into the social scene years ago by attending fund-raisers and putting one more zero on their checks than everyone else. Sunny reeked of nouveau, from her ridiculously expensive clothes, to her opulent house, to her vulgar parties. At Nat's birthday celebration at the Saddle and Cycle last fall, Comtes de Champagne ran in the fountain, Beluga was served up in tubs, and guests were handed Lalique figurines as party favors. Some might think I was jealous of her, but as I told Ethan, I simply hated to see money squandered. He replied by telling me that Sunny planned to rent out the Field Museum for Nat's next birthday. I shuddered to think what they would do when their daughter married.

Sunny's name reflected neither her coloring nor her disposition. It was bestowed upon her by her Italian father when his sixth child turned out to be his sixth daughter, and his wife shut down the baby facility. So instead of a son he settled for a Sunny. She was extremely insecure and covered it with a tough veneer. Nat Livermore was a short, squat, bald man with swollen fingers and and a face to match, who more often than not had a large cigar clenched between his teeth. Though he had married a short brunette, he had a penchant for both tall women and redheads, so do the math: Sunny was a basketcase whenever he and I were in the same place. Though she really needn't have wasted the negative energy. Nat held no more appeal to me than a weekend in the Poconos. Even though his bank account *was* quite impressive, it was not impressive enough for me to ever consider soiling the sheets with him.

Sunny's nasal voice showed no evidence of the elocution classes Ethan told me she was taking to temper her Midwestern twang. "Pauline, the police just left. I can't believe it. Our Ethan. What do you think happened? Please call me first chance you get."

Our Ethan, indeed. Sunny hadn't seen fit to give him the time of day until the Gloria book came out. After that she was on him like a call girl on a commodities broker. He was her leg up into the literary world without having to actually read a book. I wondered why the police had seen fit to pay her a visit. Did they really think that she could tell them more about Ethan than I, his best friend? Then I remembered their lunch date in his appointment book. They must have wanted to know his frame of mind Tuesday afternoon. Then a delicious thought occurred to me. Perhaps they suspected she killed him.

The next message was from Marjorie Wilcock, who had watched me wait for an already dead Ethan in the Cape Cod Room, that is when she hadn't been riveted to Franklin or her martini glass. She expressed her surprise in a contained and proper voice. "Darling, I just saw it on the news. No wonder he stood you up. The newscaster made it sound most mysterious. Call me when you know the arrangements."

The news? Ethan had made the news? Then I thought about what she said about the arrangements. Things were as I had feared. People would look to me for the funeral plans.

A string of messages expressing condolences followed, the callers' voices ranging from shocked to saddened: Susanne Free, the sweet young concierge from the Drake; Raoul Simone and Bharrie Williams, Ethan's decorator friends who hung on his coattails and managed to garner more than a few good commissions along the way; Elsa Tower, who wrote the society column for the Gold Coast's bible, *Pipeline*; Sarah Page from the Goodman Theater; Carkey Bunting from Barney's. All lamented his death and losing him as a part of their lives.

Message nine took me by surprise. *Tribune* columnist Connie Chan, the one who gave Ethan bad press, made a wry attempt to sound saddened about Ethan's passing, saying he would have appreciated the spot on the ten o'clock news. Then she asked me to call her with details. I hoped she wasn't waiting near the phone. She wouldn't be receiving any fodder for her column from me.

Message ten had been left earlier this morning while I was still sleeping. Detective once again Velez entreated me to call adding it was urgent.

The final message was from Whitney Armstrong. Though Ethan always treated her civilly to her face, behind her back he called her all kinds of names, the gentlest of them being riffraff. One would have thought he would have been fonder of her since she fell into his beloved category of those who reinvent themselves. The former coat check girl from Gibson's met her husband Jack Armstrong, president and CEO of Verry Lingerie, while moonlighting as a lingerie model in a gentlemen's lunch club. The story goes he took one look at what Whitney did for his thong and his wife didn't stand a chance.

Whitney's figure was drop-dead gorgeous, despite her oversized implants, honed to perfection through the combined efforts of body building and technology. Never shy about showing it off, she nearly always wore something tight, low-cut, slit, short, or a combination of all the aforementioned. Needless to say she was a great devotee of Jean Paul Gaultier. Her face was a scientific marvel, as well, with a suspicious resemblance to a young Bo Derek, her hair golden blond, her cheeks as implanted as her breasts. She spoke in a breathy delicate voice reminiscent of Marilyn Monroe, causing me to wonder if it was manufactured, too. But oddly enough, despite her plebeian origins and Ethan's disdain for her, I found myself genuinely drawn to Whitney for reasons even I didn't understand.

"Pauline, is it true about Ethan, that he killed himself? I simply can't believe it. How terrible it must have been for you to find the body. I . . . I . . . well, I can't really say what I want to. Please call me."

My machine clicked off with a loud beep. Whitney had sounded truly devastated, more so than anyone at the news of Ethan's death. But I didn't understand why she said he had killed himself. That had yet to be proven. I still didn't believe Ethan took his own life. Which reminded me of Detective Velez and his two messages. I decided I best get back to him.

"Mrs. Cook, where have you been?" he demanded in a voice colored with impatience. In my mind's eye, I could picture him drumming his fingers restlessly on top of a desk. Evidently, he had forgotten the way he had left me cooling my heels for the better part of the previous afternoon in an airless hallway with an uncivilized cretin. Quid pro quo.

"I've been incognito, Detective. I decided to recuse myself from civilization for a bit."

"Well, something important has come up regarding your friend. There's something we'd like you to take a look at. Can you come down here as soon as possible?"

"Where might 'here' be?"

"Area Three Headquarters, Belmont and Clybourne."

The location he was referring to, this Area Three, was a tedious drive over dozens of congested city blocks. There were still so many calls to return. "Perhaps this afternoon . . ." I started to say.

"Look, if transportation is a problem, we can send a car for you. I'd come over by you, except I'm in it up to my neck at the moment."

I toyed with asking him what exactly he was into "up to his neck" but let it go. The thought of a police car picking me up did have its appeal. My building is renowned for being particularly highbrow. Any potential buyer must go through a rigorous background check and the slightest hint of impropriety in either their life or their portfolio is grounds for rejection. My being seen getting into a police car might raise a few blood pressures. I did have my impish side. "You won't hold me hostage like you did yesterday, will you?"

"You'll be my first priority."

"All right then, Detective. I think I can be ready within the half hour. You may send a car for me then."

The big question now was what to wear. I wondered if peach Escada would be a bit much for a trip to the police station.

5

A Letter from the Grave

Edgar rang from downstairs to tell me that I had a visitor. At nearly eighty years old, Edgar had a longer tenure at 213 East Lake Shore Drive than any of its residents. He had been employed at the building for more than fifty years. The board had tried to get him to retire on his golden anniversary, but he was a widower without any children and probably would have died of loneliness if he stopped working. Though he still maintained a professional appearance, his uniform always neatly pressed and his cap worn squarely upon his silver head, he was slipping mentally. The board was alarmed at the increasing frequency with which he dialed up the wrong apartment when announcing guests.

"Good morning, Mrs. Cook," he greeted me, waiting dutifully as I stepped out of the elevator. "Your gentleman caller is out front."

"Thank you, Edgar," I replied, wondering if perhaps he really was losing it. "But that is no gentleman caller. That is a cop."

"I see, Mrs. Cook," he said unfazed.

I followed his stooped figure out the entrance and saw that Edgar had made an honest mistake. To my great disappointment, the carriage awaiting me was a nondescript white sedan in dire need of washing. I had expected a standard police car with the stack of blue lights on top and bold letters spelling out CHICAGO POLICE on the side. My disposition was further tested upon seeing who had been sent to collect me. It was Detective Malloy, the butcher of the English tongue. He leaned against the car smoking a cigarette, flicking its ashes into the wind. When he saw me he straightened up and crushed his cigarette out on the drive.

"Sorry to inconvenience you like dis," he said. "A couple a things come up, and Velez thought it'd be better if he spoke to you in person."

"That's quite all right. I am happy to do anything that might help solve Ethan's death," I said generously. Edgar opened the car's rear door and reached in to brush off the seat for me. Detective Malloy stared at him strangely.

"Is there something wrong, detective?" I asked.

"Well, most a' my passengers ride in the back seat, but then again, most a' dem are wearing bracelets and, well, they're kind a nervous if you know what I mean. You never know what's been on the seat back der. I mean with what you're wearing and all, you might be more comfortable riding shotgun. "

Not wanting to expose peach silk to Lord only knew what, I took the front seat. Edgar had barely closed the door before we were on our way, Detective Malloy reminding me to put on my seat belt. He drove erratically, taking a route I always avoid, down Division Street through the housing project of Cabrini Green. The exterior staircases and halls of the blighted high-rises were wrapped in mesh barriers—presumably to prevent the tossing of something or someone from their heights. It was general knowledge that the buildings were coming down soon, though as I stared at the population of dark faces on the street, I wondered where all these people were going to go.

"Pretty fancy digs you live in over der," he said, cutting in and out of traffic with the confident authority of being the law. "What'cho got up der, a two-bedroom?"

"Actually, I have three."

"Tree. Must be nice. Which way you facin'? The lake?"

"My salon and dining rooms face the lake, two of the bedrooms face west, and the third faces south—as does my library."

He was silent as he drew himself a floor plan. "Wait a minute. Lemme get this straight. You got north, west, and south views? What do'ya got? Half the floor?"

"Well, actually I have the entire floor. My kitchen faces east."

He whistled. "Whooowee. Bet that set you back a pretty penny."

"I wouldn't know," I fibbed. "My husband bought it before we were married."

"Wow, he must be loaded. What's he do?"

"He doesn't do anything now, I'm afraid. He's dead."

One would think that would have stopped Jerry Malloy's prying, but it didn't. I suppose one who sees the more unseemly sides of life isn't much bothered by conventional social graces such as tact. He continued, saying what most people think, but don't have the nerve to ask.

"Bet'ya he left you a bundle."

Unwilling to inform him he would be betting wrong, I changed the subject. "So what is this all about, detective?"

"Velez has got a couple of issues he want to talk to you about concerning your friend. Now in all likelihood, your friend's death was most likely a suicide. But there's something kind of strange the M.E. come up with. With most gunshot suicides, the shooter holds da weapon right up against his head like dis." He panto-mimed a gun with his forefinger and thumb and pressed it to his temple, flicking his thumb as if it were a trigger. "Or the shooter eats it."

He started to put his hand into his mouth. "That's not necessary, Detective Malloy. I get the picture."

"Yeah, well, in the case of Mr. Campbell, the M.E. is saying it looks like he shot himself from about six to eight inches away. Dat's what we call an intermediate range wound. Dat's kind a unusual. True suicides don't want to miss. Den again, maybe he wasn't really sure he wanted to kill himself, was changing his mind at da last minute."

"I've already made it clear, I don't believe Ethan killed himself. What's the other issue Detective Velez wants to talk about?"

He was uncharacteristically quiet before saying, "I better let him tell you himself."

Area Three Headquarters at Belmont and Clybourne was quite unlike anything I had ever seen in my life. Not the building itself, which was a drab, low-slung brick structure resembling an institution, but rather the chaos surrounding it. The parking lot overflowed with people milling about and cars were parked all along the sidewalk in front of the building despite signs that read NO PARKING. When we pulled into the fenced-off section marked DETECTIVES ONLY all the spaces were filled drawing Detective Malloy's ire.

"Motherfuckers! Dey come here for court and dey park wherever the hell dey please. Those ain't police cars. Show's how much respect dey have for da system."

He pondered for a moment before parallel parking behind two cars, blocking them in. "Don' worry. Dey'll find me if dey wanna leave," he said. I didn't bother telling him I wasn't worried about his parking. I was more worried about what might lay inside this center of justice if no one obeyed the laws outside.

The interior of the building turned out to be an introduction to a side of life I had heard but had never seen. Just inside the glass doors, we were met by a series of metal detectors like those in an airport. Several lines of slouchy, untidily dressed people were waiting to pass through, the majority of them young black males. Nearly all wore baseball caps turned backward and pants so enormous that the crotch hung down near their knees. This called to mind the story of Eleanor McFardle's Jamaican fling several years ago, causing me to wonder if they wore the baggy trousers because they needed the space.

Detective Malloy nodded to a female police officer with a very large derriere, and we moved to the front of her line. I passed uneventfully through the metal detector, but this was not enough to satisfy the somber-faced woman. Clearly a stickler for details, she wanted to search my purse. The detective let out a stream of angry air and rolled his eyes at her.

"For Chrissake, she's a witness," he said.

"I don't care if she's the Virgin Mary coming to testify against Judas. All purses get searched. If she's got a gun in there and decides to become Missus Vigilante, I'm the one who's gotta answer."

He looked at me apologetically. "Ya mind?"

Though I wasn't terribly keen on the idea of someone's greasy hand rummaging through my Ferragamo bag, I played the good sport and did not make a fuss. The woman sifted through my personal belongings, commenting on my gold compact, before declaring me "clean."

Detective Malloy and I proceeded into a large open lobby teeming with people, the sort who might set me to running were I to encounter any of them on a quiet street at night. They were people with tattoos and facial scars and hard-looking eyes. Studying the faces of this assembled humanity, I saw desperation and hopelessness, as well as anger. I found myself both fearing and pitying them at the same time, reminding myself I was in a police station, so that meant I was safe. Still, I kept close on the heels of the detective, afraid of bumping into one of the aimless bodies, unsure of what might rub off on me if I did. There was an underlying sense of danger, of something dark, in the air.

"What exactly happens here?" I inquired.

"This is where preliminary hearings are held," my escort replied. "Most a dese scumbags are waitin' to get der murder cases continued or der armed robberies trone out. Sometimes I don't even know why we bother to arrest 'em."

He led me past a bank of elevators and up a flight of dismal concrete stairs. "The elevators ain't worth waitin' for," he explained. On the second floor, we passed through a pair of swinging doors into a large room filled with gray metal desks, all facing forward so that it looked like a classroom for adults. Fluorescent lighting exacerbated the putrid green shade of paint. Most of the desks were empty, but those that were occupied were occupied by men. The majority of them were on the phone except for a few speaking with people whom I took to be victims, their voices flaring occasionally, their faces twisted in anger or woe.

"Velez is over there," said Malloy, pointing at a dark bowed head on the far side of the room. "I gotta go. I better move my car before somebody gets a hair up his ass over me blocking 'em in." He gave me a naive smile as if we were now the best of friends. "Hey, if you ever think of selling your joint, gimme a call."

"You'll be at the top of my list," I replied.

I felt oddly conspicuous as I walked to Detective Velez's desk. Heads were turning, but it wasn't quite the same as in the Drake. I suppose peach Escada isn't often seen at Area Three. I decided too late I had overdressed.

Detective Velez was engaged in a phone conversation, but acknowledged me by pointing his index finger at the plastic chair beside his desk. He then held up the same finger to indicate the number one. I wasn't sure if this meant it would be one second, one minute, or one hour, but he had promised to get to me swiftly, so I sat down. On his desk, three raven-haired children smiled from one side of a silver frame and a raven-haired wife smiled from the other. While waiting, I couldn't help but overhear the detective's conversation.

"I don't care," he shouted into the phone. "Tell them to go back and search the basement again. There's got to be more. You don't just take the hands and leave the head. Get the picture?"

Silence. While the party on the other end responded, I drew a picture of my own. A rather unpleasant one I might add. "Yeah, you're right, could have been scared off halfway through. Well, hopefully we'll be able to I.D. from dental charts. Maybe the feds should start taking dental impressions instead of fingerprints, for Chrissakes."

Another long pause, and then the detective laughed out loud. "You've got to be shittin' me. The wallet, huh? Look, I've got someone here. Don't move him. I'll be there as soon as I'm finished." He replaced the receiver and looked at me. His slightly flushed face caused the jagged scar on his cheek to turn purple.

"My apologies, Mrs. Cook," he said, indicating the phone. "I hope that wasn't too gruesome for you."

"Au contraire, detective. I found the conversation rather . . . enlightening. I've been known to read a mystery novel from time to time; they serve a purpose for an insomniac such as myself. If you don't mind my asking, why would the culprit take someone's hands?"

"Oh, so we can't identify the body by the fingerprints. But here's the irony of the whole deal: the goofs who killed him left the guy's wallet in his back pocket. Like we always say around here, " 'Thank God they're stupid. If they had brains we'd be in trouble.' "

He covered his mouth with his hand and collected his thoughts. When he took his hand away his visage had changed. Any trace of a smile was gone, and I knew he had mentally filed the case of the handless corpse away for the time being. He had pulled out a fresh one, the Ethan Campbell file.

"Now as to your friend. We've got a match between his prints and the prints on the gun, and there's residue on his hand that indicates he was the shooter. That pretty much says suicide. But . . ." The hesitation lasted a few seconds as he collected his thoughts. "We've also seen evidence that the bullet was fired from an intermediate range. That's not real common in suicides."

"I told you Ethan wouldn't have killed himself," I interrupted. "Maybe someone put the gun in his hand and forced him to shoot it."

He didn't respond. Instead, he picked up three yellowed papers that lay before him on the desk. They appeared to be documents of some kind. He shuffled through them once and then looked back at me with ponderous brown eyes.

"How well did you say you knew Mr. Campbell?"

"Quite well. We've been good friends for more than five years."

"And you've always known him as Ethan Campbell?"

"Of course."

"Does the name Daniel Kehoe mean anything to you?"

"No," I replied, wondering what sort of game the detective was playing. "Why are you asking all these ridiculous questions?"

He pushed the yellowed pages across the desk to me. Even a lay person such as myself could see they were birth certificates. They appeared to be ancient, falling apart at the seams where they had been folded and unfolded numerous times over the years.

I looked at the first one. It was issued to a baby boy. Daniel Kehoe, born to Moira McMahon Kehoe and Patrick Kehoe on June 1, 1940, in Boston, Massachusetts. I wondered who these people were and what connection they had to Ethan. The second document was foreign issued with a very official looking stamp from Her Majesty's Government. It gave testimony to the birth of Moira McMahon in Limerick, Ireland, on February 14, 1922. Obviously Daniel Kehoe's mother. It still didn't mean anything to me.

It was the third birth certificate that gave me pause. It too bore the stamp of the English crown and documented the birth of an Ethan Campbell in Bury St. Edmunds, England. Parents: Sara and Lawrence Campbell. Date of birth: December 24, 1942.

Mystified, I looked back at the detective. "Who is *this* Ethan Campbell? What does all this mean?"

"I was hoping you might know. We found them in his apartment. In the same drawer as his appointment book."

To say I was confused would be a vast understatement. My friend Ethan had never owned up to his age, so I couldn't know for certain the year he was born. But I did know his birthday was on Valentine's Day—not Christmas Eve. One of Ethan's extravagances every year was the celebratory birthday lunch he threw for himself at the Drake, inviting all his lady friends and insisting everyone wear red. I pictured him at the party just last month, seated at the head of a long table wearing a pink shirt and red tie, drinking Taittinger Rose Champagne and eating strawberry mousse, beaming as we sang "Happy Birthday" to him.

"Whoever this Englishman is, he isn't the same Ethan Campbell I knew," I told the detective. "For one, my friend Ethan's birthday was February 14. Secondly, he was not born in England. He was born in New York City."

"You're certain of that."

"Yes, I am." I would run out of fingers and toes if I tried to count how many times Ethan had spoken of his christening at St. Patrick's Cathedral and the sumptuous party thrown afterward. He could recite the list of attendees, the creme of New York society at the time— names found in the Social Register including his godfather—one of the Eastmans. The Kodak Eastmans.

And then the first spark of doubt. A glimmer that perhaps Ethan hadn't been completely honest about his past. Aside from the way he watched me before picking up his silverware at fund-raisers, not to mention his occasional use of my bread plate instead of his, there was something else. Like the embers of a dying fire being fed a fresh piece of wood, a repressed memory flared to life. When Ethan's publisher sent him to New York years ago to promote the Gloria book, Sandy St. Clair, my former college room-mate, happened to be up from Palm Beach. To celebrate his new publication, she arranged a little reception in his honor at Sardi's, a place he had waxed long and eloquently about being a fixture at during his New York days. She called me afterward to tell me she had found his behavior a bit disturbing. From the minute she picked him up at the Pierre, he had been completely disoriented, unsure of where he was going, making a wrong turn more often than not. And when they reached the theater district, he hadn't even known where Sardi's was located or that it was on two levels. She said it was as if he had never set foot in the restaurant in his life, much less the city. On top of that, Sandy added, though she had invited a good cross section of New York society to the recep-tion, Ethan had not known one person there.

I hadn't paid her call much heed at the time, and forgotten about it shortly afterward. Now the papers sitting on the desk in front of me loosened it from the recesses of my mind.

Detective Velez must have been speaking because his lips were moving. I hadn't heard a word. I brought myself back to the cold, ster-ile precinct with a shake of my head.

"I'm sorry, what was that?" I asked.

"I said is there anyone you can think of who might be able to tell us more about him? Someone who has known him longer than you?"

"Well, there's Juan Cardoza in Puerto Rico." Ethan lived there for twenty-five years before moving to Chicago. He wrote the society col-umn for Juan's newspaper. "He worked for Juan for a long time."

"Would you know how to reach him?"

"No, but I would guess you could find him through directory assis-tance. He's the publisher of *Puerto Rico Hoy*," I said, fairly certain Detec-tive Velez would have no problem negotiating his way through the Puerto Rican telephone system.

He wrote Juan's name down on a pad of paper. Then he put the pen down and stared at me. "If we can't be certain of who your friend was, I'm afraid we're going to have to run a fingerprint check with the FBI."

"And that will tell us who he was?"

"If he had a criminal record it will."

"I hardly think Ethan had a criminal record. May I ask what happens to his body in the meantime?"

"Well, because of the nature of his wound, we're still waiting for the M.E. to make a ruling on cause of death. After that, it will belong to the Public Administrators Office until we identify it. The F.B.I. check could take up to three weeks. Then we'll release him to next of kin or anyone else who wants to take responsibility for him. If no one comes forward the state disposes of him."

It all seemed so cold. My mind was overloaded as I tried to assimilate the past twenty-four hours. My best friend, who never gave any indication of unhappiness, died a violent death that may or may not have been at his own hand. Now there was some convoluted mystery regarding his very identity. I didn't know if I was more stunned, shocked, surprised or dismayed. One thing was for certain, I planned to find out who he really was. I tapped a finger on the mysterious birth certificates. "Would it be possible to get copies of these?"

Detective Velez shrugged indifferently. "I don't see any reason why not." He picked up the tattered documents and disappeared, returning minutes later with sheets of crisp white copy paper. He remained standing as he handed them to me. A sure sign our time together had come to an end.

"I'll get someone to take you home," he offered. Then he smiled as if he was just greeting me. "That's a beautiful suit you're wearing by the way. I'd love to buy my wife something like that. Where did you get it?"

Though I doubted his budget had room for a two-thousand-dollar suit, I gave him the store name anyway. I hoped he would never go there. I wouldn't want him to leave disappointed. He led me through the sea of desks to the front of the room where he barked some orders to a uniformed policeman in the front. With a quick nod he was off, presumably to learn more about the handless corpse. I followed the uniformed police officer back through Dante's Inferno and out to the parking lot. This time I had the good fortune to ride in an actual squad car. The experience turned out to be especially delightful because Edna Atchison was walking her poodles on the parkway when we pulled up in front of the building.

I gave Edna a playful wave and went inside.

Edgar handed me my mail with a quivering hand and I tucked it into my purse. The entire ride up in the elevator, my mind was completely preoccupied with the photocopied birth certificates Detective Velez had given me. Daniel Kehoe of Boston. Moira McMahon Kehoe of Limerick, Ireland. Ethan Campbell of Bury St. Edmunds, England. Who were these people? What was their role in my friend's life?

I let myself into the apartment and went into the library to sort through the mail. A postcard from Emily Whitehead vacationing in Patagonia praised the beef. A creamy white envelope contained an invitation to Anne and Vincent Williamson's daughter's wedding, which meant the purchase of an expensive gift. Two bills from credit card companies got tossed into my desk drawer. They contained my stratospheric credit card statements—debt that had been riding for months now at 18 percent interest. A piece of junk from a different credit card company went into the trash.

The final piece of mail nearly caused my knees to buckle. It was addressed in Ethan's all too familiar hand, elaborate loops and curlicues that danced their way across the front of the plain white envelope. There was no return address.

My entire body trembled. The letter was postmarked Wednesday. But that was impossible. Ethan died Tuesday night. For a ridiculous moment I thought maybe there had been a mixup and he wasn't dead after all. Then I flashed back to the grotesque scene in his bedroom. One couldn't get much deader.

I waited for my adrenaline to slow enough that my hands weren't shaking. Then I opened the envelope from the great beyond. There were two sheets of typing paper inside. I unfolded them slowly, my heart pounding as if it would like to come through my chest. With tear-filled eyes, I read the first page.

Tuesday

Dearest friend, Paulina:

By the time you read this I will be dead.

First I must say how sorry I am to have to do this to you this way. You were my best friend on earth and it wasn't fair for me to bow out without giving you any warning. But I was unhappy, far more unhappy than you will ever know. My soul was so tormented that I felt I could no longer go on. There are things about me that you never knew—terrible things—and they ate at me night and day. I hope you need never suffer as I did.

Please don't ever think you weren't a good friend to not pick up on my unhappiness. I had become a master at hiding it. No one could have ever known, not even you, my dear. I hope your life is long and wonderful, you deserve it, you deserve happiness. For me, this was not possible in this form.

I'm afraid I'm not leaving much behind, but whatever I have, I want it to be yours. I am leaving you all my worldly goods, all my bank accounts, all my possessions. I want you and only you to have any future income I may derive from royalties or in any other way. You are the only person I want to inherit from me, and I write this as a person of sound body and mind. An odd thing for a person about to commit suicide to say, I realize this, but I can't stress how much I want everything I have to go to you and only you. You deserve it for being such a dear, dear friend to me when I was alive.

Goodbye and Godspeed,

Ethan Campbell

I reread the letter several times before I turned to the second sheet, his will. It was also written in longhand, a simple two sentences.

I, Ethan Campbell, being of sound body and mind, do leave all my worldly goods to Pauline Cook. This will replaces any other will that may have come before it.

It was dated March 29. Two people whose names I did not recognize served as witnesses, and there was a notary stamp from a local currency exchange.

I felt immensely sad. I tried to imagine Ethan's frame of mind, writing a will and then running out to notarize it before taking his own life. He referred to being in deep pain. He never seemed in any pain to me. In fact, he seemed to be having the time of his life. Although he wrote I couldn't have known about his unhappiness, we were so close I just couldn't believe I completely missed it. He had been tormented enough to take his own life and I saw no signs? His ear had always been ready for my fears and problems. Had my ear been closed to his?

I suspected that the birth certificates found in his apartment had something to do with his torment, but nothing in his note explained them. However, the note did clear up one thing. There was no longer any doubt that Ethan's death was a suicide.

I looked at the Wednesday postmark. His letter must have been dropped into the mailbox after Tuesday's last pickup—before he went home and shot himself. I wondered why he had chosen to mail it instead of simply leaving it in his room. Maybe he feared it would be overlooked in his paper jungle. Then a frightening thought occurred to me. Maybe his rationale was that once he mailed the letter, he would have no choice but to go through with the act it described.

After sitting quietly for some time, I called Detective Velez and told him what the day's mail had yielded. Though he tried to sound sympathetic, it was clear he was relieved to have one less case to worry about. He asked if he could send Detective Malloy around to pick up the correspondence, assuring me that it would be returned to me as soon as they finished with it. While I wasn't overly thrilled at the prospect of yet another visit with Detective Malloy, I told him it would be fine.

After hanging up, I read and reread Ethan's last words. There was something bittersweet about him making me his heir. Though to my knowledge there wasn't much to inherit. He'd been living off the advance on the Daisy book for so long there probably wasn't anything left of it. Nonetheless, I found the gesture to be truly thoughtful on his part.

If only I had known how truly thoughtful it was.

6

The April Fool

Black. It had to be black. Though fully one third of my closet is dedicated to the mourning color, I was hard-pressed to find the appropriate ensemble. The Valentino suit was too elegant, the Thierry Mugler too over-the-top. Then I spotted it buried in the back behind some formal gowns: an ancient St. John knit. It would serve perfectly.

On the first Friday of every month, we ladies lunch at Scarlet's, and it just so happened that this first day of April was the designated day. I initially toyed with skipping the monthly gathering in deference to Ethan, but then decided it would be better to attend. For several reasons. First, my peers would be expecting to hear every detail of Ethan's death directly from my lips, and it would be inconsiderate on my part to deprive them of the maudlin pleasure. Secondly, it would be far more expeditious to get the story told in one fell swoop instead of having to repeat it ad nauseam over the next weeks.

And then there was the third reason which, to my thinking, was the most important of all. I felt duty-bound to defend Ethan's honor.

This call to arms had been prompted by my phone conversation with Sunny the night before. I had finally returned her call after putting if off as long as humanly possible. We consoled each other over the loss of our friend, and Sunny actually shed some tears, though real or for effect I couldn't say. Then I told her about Ethan's suicide letter to me, leaving out both the will and his reference to having committed some terrible deed. Sunny loved to gossip, and I didn't want his memory sullied over some incident that was most likely overblown in his depressed mind. She sniffled loudly and lamented that she hadn't noticed anything wrong with him at lunch on Tuesday.

Then to my complete surprise, she brought up the matter of the birth certificates. At first I was stunned that she knew of their existence, but then it dawned on me that of course Detective Velez would have asked her if she knew anything about them, too. After all, she was the last one of us to see him.

"What do you think they mean?" she asked. "Do you think Ethan was some kind of a fake?"

"Fake?" I leapt to his defense. "Fake what? He wrote books. How can writing books make anyone a fake? One certainly can't fake a book."

"I don't know. I just find it disturbing. Maybe he had something to hide. Maybe he wasn't who he claimed to be."

"Sunny, I would suggest we not jump to rash conclusions here. There's probably some completely reasonable explanation for those documents. Maybe they belong to some of his relatives."

"Ethan made a point of saying he didn't have any relatives."

"Living relatives. Maybe these belonged to some cousins or some other relation." I didn't want to admit to her how disturbed I was, too—that not only had Ethan killed himself but that he might have deceived me on top of it. "Listen, would you mind if we kept the birth certificates as our little secret for now—until we learn more? There's Ethan's memory to think of, you know."

"I think that's a good idea," she said, agreeing a bit too readily. "Will I see you at lunch tomorrow?"

"Wouldn't miss it for the world." Now there was no choice but to attend the lunch. I didn't trust Sunny and needed to be there to deflect any idle chatter.

The very moment we hung up my house line rang. Howard, the night doorman, informed me that Detective Malloy had arrived. I instructed him to send the evidence-gathering detective up and was waiting for him in the foyer when the elevator door opened. He took the envelope containing Ethan's letter from me and looked through the open door behind me into my residence. He whistled at the view and made a none too subtle request to see *the rest of the place*. Claiming exhaustion, I told him he would have to see it some other time. He jokingly repeated his offer to buy if I was ever in the market to sell.

The minute he left, I took a Halcion and went to bed.

I studied the St. John suit in the mirror. The way the knit hugged my curves really did compliment my shape. I regretted leaving it on the hanger for so long. Next I turned to my makeup. The day called for special care, a lighter shade of foundation than usual to create a slightly wan appearance, a subtle shade of lipstick, no mascara in the event of tears. I fluffed my hair and assessed my appearance, satisfied that I had struck the appropriate balance between sophistication and grief. Then I turned my head toward the light and caught sight of a deep volcanic fissure alongside my mouth that hadn't been there last week. Wrinkles seemed to be popping up like weeds lately. I thanked God for the paralyzing Botox injections that kept my forehead as smooth as a baby's bottom and only wished I didn't need to smile so I could use them around my mouth.

Already suitably late, I went downstairs where Jeffrey hailed me a taxi. He held the door as I dashed out into a gale-force wind, trying to get into the cab before it destroyed my hair. The weather had changed dramatically since Wednesday, and it was cold, damp, and blustery. Low-hanging clouds obscured the lake and shrouded the tops of the buildings. Like fruit just beyond reach, spring had only been tantalizing us.

It would have been a perfect day for a funeral. But I was going to lunch.

Rene greeted me at the restaurant door, referring to me as Madame Cook in his lovely French accent. Both he and Scarlet's itself were old-school, cool oases in today's desert of vulgarity. Dining at Scarlet's meant subdued elegance, white linens, and most importantly, waiters who took one's order without ever stating their names. It was light-years away from the garish dining emporiums that had become so popular, where the chairs were as comfortable as packing crates, the tables so tightly spaced one could easily eat off one's neighbor's plate, and the noise level so high one had to shout to be heard over the pandemonium. Personally, I preferred a quiet evening with my cat to dining under such stressful conditions.

Rene conducted the ritual of leading me across the room to the same table this group of women had occupied once a month, every month, for more than ten years. The sound of chatter died at my arrival and all coiffed heads turned in my direction, jaws frozen partially open and drinks frozen in mid-air. I scanned the table and noticed everyone was there, plus one extra. An unwelcome extra. Sitting at the far end of the table next to Sunny was Connie Chan, her upturned black eyes gleaming at me from her flawless oriental face. She was not one of our group, and she had no business being with us.

Then, as suddenly as they had stopped, the voices started up again, a cacophony of sentences layered one upon the other.

"Oh, Pauline, how terrible about Ethan . . ."

"It's such a tragedy."

"He was a true dear."

"He will be sorely missed."

I crossed my hands over my heart to signify my devastation and took the open seat next to Elsa Tower. Reading Elsa's column in *Pipeline,* the elitist rag of the Gold Coast and the North Shore, was a Monday morning ritual that found the better part of society holding their breaths as they scanned the highlighted names—hoping to see theirs mentioned in a good light, dreading its appearance in any other. An elfin figure with a kindly round face, Elsa had a mean streak in her that ran deeper than the Gulf Stream. She always wore a hat, and one could mark the season by her choice of chapeau. They were fur-trimmed in the winter, white and airy in the heat of summer. That day she was optimistically heralding the arrival of spring in a red straw with a flower-covered band.

"Will you tell us what happened, Pauline?" Whitney Armstrong's voice stood out among the others, the breathiness of it at odds with her sculpted face. She wore an enviable mint green suit whose designer I couldn't place. The table fell silent again, and every eye in the collection of painstakingly made-up and surgically improved faces fixed upon me.

"Well, I was waiting for Ethan to show for our Wednesday lunch at the Cape Cod. He's never late for anything you know—"

"I was at the Cape Cod and saw poor Pauline. She was at wit's end with worry," Marjorie Wilcock interrupted loudly, making no mention of who her dining partner had been. She was already running her words together, and her hand trembled ever so slightly as she raised a vast martini glass to her lips.

". . . so I started thinking, this is very unlike Ethan," I continued, ignoring Marjorie. "I tried him at home a couple of times and when I didn't get an answer, I began to suspect something might be wrong. So finally, I got in my car and drove over to check on him myself."

There was a hesitant silence. Then Suzanne Free, the young concierge from the Drake who had just recently been welcomed into our fold after her engagement to Dexter Worthington, asked sweetly, "So how did you get into his apartment?"

"It wasn't easy. I had to bribe the most horrible man. When he finally did let me in, I went directly into Ethan's bedroom and . . ." I lowered my eyes to the table. ". . . there he was."

"Oh my God, are you saying you actually saw the body?" Germaine Appleton gasped. She was stunning in wheat-colored Armani, her sable coat draped across the back of her chair. Her husband, Robert Appleton, owned the Appleton Furs chain, so Germaine nearly always sported something that once had a face, and went fur-trimmed even into the depths of summer.

"I'm afraid so."

"How gruesome that must have been for you!"

"It wasn't terribly pleasant. There was a bullet through his head, you know."

"You poor dear. What did you do then?"

"Well, called the police, naturally. And do I have to tell you how useless they were? They treated me as if I were a criminal, forcing me to wait for hours. And when they finally did allow me to leave, I went back to my car and found a hundred dollar parking ticket on it."

"The insensitive bastards." That coming from Eleanor McFardle. Her mother was an Addison from the meat packing family. Old money. It was the first time I had seen her since she had her eyes done, and the difference was remarkable.

"I heard it was a suicide, but I've also heard rumors that he was killed by a gay lover . . ." These words spoken by Jacquie Washington, the sole black member of our group. The former model had started her own agency after getting a bit old for the industry herself. Though her husband was William Brown, the fabulously wealthy owner of the eponymous publishing empire, she continued to work.

"Absolutely untrue. I received a suicide note from him in the mail yesterday."

A collective gasp was heard round the table. "I'd have never believed it," said Jacquie. "Ethan was about as unlikely a person to take his own life as anyone I know. Aside from being overly preoccupied with himself, I would think he was too squeamish."

"Ditto that," said Germaine. "Did anyone here ever pick up on a problem?"

"I sure didn't," Sunny said. "I had lunch with him on Tuesday and he seemed his normal quirky self. He told me he was working on his speech for the North Shore Writer's Guild. He even asked me to take a look at it."

There was much speculation around the table as to why Ethan might have killed himself with just about everyone agreeing that he had never given any of them the slightest indication that he had been unhappy. He had been a fixture in most of their lives, always a ready and attentive escort, quick with a compliment or juicy tidbit of gossip. No one could begin to count how many boards in town would have an empty seat.

"Not to mention, we've lost a damn good walker on top of it," Eleanor lamented. "I don't know who I'll get to go to the art openings with me now. Albert despises them."

"He was our Truman Capote, that's for sure," said Germaine, quick to add, "before Truman wrote "La Côte Basque," that is."

"Ethan had more scruples than Truman," said Jacquie.

"I wouldn't be so sure about that." All heads turned to Whitney. "I mean, well, with a writer you can never know," she added in a voice more Monroesque than Marilyn herself.

"All I know is Ethan was very good to me," said Suzanne, the soon to be former concierge. "He introduced me to everyone. He even acknowledged me in his book."

"Honey, if you bought Ethan a cup of coffee, he'd acknowledge you," Marjorie gushed sloppily.

"Who's taking care of the funeral arrangements?" The first words Connie Chan had chosen to utter caused the fine hairs on my neck to bristle. A chorus of voices echoed the same question. I shot Sunny a glance as if to say *what is this woman doing here*. Our eyes locked for a moment. She quickly looked away.

"No arrangements have been made so far. The body won't be released until the police finish searching for his next of kin," I said.

Two waiters brought our food and small satellites of conversation sprung up around the table as the fashionably slim picked away at salads with the dressing held to the side and plates of broiled fish. Sitting beside me, the usually inquisitive Elsa had been uncharacteristically quiet. Now that the others weren't paying any attention she came true to form, peering at me from under the red brim of her hat, her blue eyes ruthlessly probing above the balls of her cherubic cheeks. "Rumor has it he won't get buried until they solve the mystery of the multiple birth certificates," she whispered.

I was astonished, wondering where on earth Elsa would have gotten the information. But I didn't have to wonder long. There was only one other person at the table who knew about the birth certificates. Even though we had agreed to keep their existence under our hats, Sunny had gone back on her word and run straight to the worst hat of all. And I knew why. Always the social climber, she was trying to solidify herself with the gossip columnist. My anger was bubbling like my Perrier, and I wished at that moment that I had ordered something stronger to drink.

"So Sunny told you?"

"Of course she did," Elsa replied, slicing into a veal medallion floating in Madeira sauce. She was the only one of us who seemed to have no concern about her weight despite the extra stone she was carrying. No one would have ever dared say anything to her about it. Elsa's kindly face was deceiving and her wrath could be devastating. Her column could either deify or crucify a person, depending on her fancy. She looked at me and chewed with great satisfaction. "So why didn't you tell me?"

"I was going to, Elsa. But I wanted to wait until we knew more. I don't want to see him disparaged." I glared down the table. Sunny's traitorous dark head bobbed in animated conversation. "When did you find out?" I asked.

"Sunny called me the minute she learned about them. I asked her not to tell anyone else, to give me the exclusive," she added. Which explained why Sunny had agreed with me so readily last night. Elsa continued between bites, "It will be a delicious item in Monday's column." She lowered her voice. "Especially when Connie Chan reads it and realizes she sat through this entire meal and was still left out cold. So what do *you* make of these birth certificates?"

I acquiesced, feeling the damage was already done. "I honestly don't know. One of them was for an Ethan Campbell born in England, one for a Daniel Kehoe born in Boston. And a third for the mother of the Boston Daniel Kehoe—whoever he was."

"Strange isn't it? Ethan never said a word about coming from England. He claimed to hail from New York."

"Yes, I know. Perhaps he had a British cousin or was born overseas and his parents moved to New York when he was a baby."

"That still doesn't explain why he would have the other two birth certificates."

"Friends? Relatives?" I suggested.

"You know, Pauline, I smell fish, and when I smell fish it's usually fish. There was always something about that little man I couldn't put my finger on. He was such a name dropper it was almost as if he had studied up on them. But I never challenged him because he was one of my greatest sources. He's passed on more intelligence to me than you could ever guess. Things even I wouldn't print. So I figured why cut off your nose to spite your face."

"Well, whoever he was, he was a good friend to me." I was not surprised to learn where Elsa came up with so much of her biting material. Ethan had a way about him that encouraged people to confide in him. For a minute I wondered if he had shared any of my secrets with Elsa, but decided he hadn't. Otherwise I would have already read, *Which tall and prominent widow is dating a man nearly half her age who works in a popular eatery? Word has it that she's given him a leg up on a modeling career and he's giving her a leg over in return.* Elsa knew no loyalty when the tidbit was juicy enough. "Will you be kind to him in your article?"

"Kinder than a lot of other people would be." She forked another piece of veal into her mouth and chewed it with gusto glancing down the table at Connie Chan.

Gallons of water and pots of decaf later, with the waiters setting up the nearby tables for dinner, the party was breaking up. I wanted to speak with Sunny in private, but she was still talking to Connie Chan, so I rooted around in my purse looking for some imaginary object while I waited for them to part ways. In the meantime, Whitney, seeing that Elsa had gone and I was available, came rushing over to speak with me. As I watched her approach, moving fluidly on her heels, her hips so enviably narrow and her legs competitive to mine, I felt as green as her suit. Except for the way her man-made bosom really distracted from the designer's intent.

"I adore it," I said touching her sleeve. "Balenciaga?"

"Thierry Mugler," she replied.

"Whitney, you must forgive me for not getting back to you," I said. "I know it was terribly rude, but I simply haven't the heart to talk about Ethan. You can understand, can't you?"

"Of course I understand. Don't even think about apologizing. Our poor Ethan." Though her wispy tone was sympathetic, I thought I detected a sound of cynicism lurking beneath it. "Pauline, can I ask you a favor?"

I couldn't imagine what kind of a favor Whitney could want from me. *Fortune* magazine counted her husband among its legendary five hundred year after year, and unlike many of his wealthy brethren, Jack Armstrong clearly adored his wife. No dalliances for the lingerie baron. Not only did he beam when in her presence, he let her spend freely at her own whim without ever questioning her. What could *I* possibly do for *her*?

"I was wondering, since you and Sunny were Ethan's best friends, are the two of you going to take care of the funeral if they don't find any relatives?"

I think I grimaced. No, I know for certain I grimaced. Though Sunny and I were the obvious people for the task, I couldn't imagine Nat Livermore parting with any of his copious funds for the man he used to refer to as "that fawning little faggot." That would leave it to me. The memory of what it had cost to bury Henry resurfaced and I'm sure my expression grew even more dour.

"I'm sorry, am I'm upsetting you by talking about this?"

"No, no. I just had a sharp pain. It's gone now." I tried to look solemn. "If no family turns up, it's possible the arrangements could fall to us."

"Well, if they do, I'd like to help out monetarily," she said, taking me by surprise. "And if you need any other help, I'm available for that too. Like sorting out his things. I did that when my mother died, and I know it's a lonely job."

"That's a really lovely gesture, Whitney," I replied, thinking of the time Ethan had compared her table manners to those of a third-world refugee. I wondered if it would be fitting to accept her money. "I had no idea you and Ethan were so close."

Her expression fell as if I had told her to go to the devil. "Ethan and I had a closer relationship than most people knew." Then in the next moment she was carving out a perfect white-toothed smile. "Promise you'll call me if I can do anything. "

I was still at a loss as to why she wanted to be so helpful. Funerals were expensive and cleaning out his apartment would be an unpleasant task at best. And then it dawned on me. Perhaps she was more interested in me than in Ethan. After all, despite her lofty marriage, Whitney was still for the most part an outsider. I had true societal standing, and with Ethan gone, I was available for friendship.

"I promise to call you, Whitney," I said, looking up at that moment to see Sunny heading toward the door. I quickly excused myself and ran across the room like a madwoman to catch the traitorous wretch before she got away.

"I have some bones to pick with you," I said, standing her down in the deserted restaurant doorway, blocking her exit.

"What is it, Pauline?"

"First off, why did you invite Connie Chan to lunch?"

She turned defensive. "Connie called me this morning and asked if she could join us for a feature article she's working on. I didn't see any harm in it."

"I found it to be in incredibly bad taste, seeing how the main topic at lunch was going to be Ethan, and you knew it. You know how much he hated her. And speaking of Ethan, why didn't you tell me last night you'd already told Elsa about the birth certificates?"

"Oh, what does it matter, Pauline? After all, he is dead," she said defensively.

In my anger, I let the feline in me free. "Well, I just hope it wasn't lunch with you that put him over the edge."

Her pupils turned to mere pinpricks as her fury reached her eyes. I'd hit a nerve and I was glad. That is until she spewed her venom at me. "You know the more I think about it, Pauline, the more I think

Ethan was a fraud. And he played us all for chumps, made fools of us—especially you. Personally, I doubt we will ever know who he was, and I don't know that I care." She turned her back to me and stormed off.

I was so enraged, I did something highly undignified. I cursed aloud, referring to Sunny several times in the term applied to the ever popular female dog. When I finished with my outburst, I turned to see Whitney standing behind me, looking like a child who has interrupted her parents in the act. She smiled at me sheepishly and walked out the door.

Despite the wind blowing off the lake, I walked the six blocks home, Sunny's spiteful words echoing in my brain the entire way. I had an ardent desire to inflict mortal harm on her. The very gall of her to speak to me that way. And just as I had managed to touch a nerve with her, she had jabbed an even larger one in me. My mind was so filled with questions about Ethan I thought it might burst. Forget about the funeral. Was it now my job to defend his honor as well? Not to mention save my own face?

"Damn you, Ethan," I cursed into the wind. I resented being put into this situation. And then in an instant I decided what to do. The truth would be mine no matter what it took. I would get answers and I knew exactly where to start.

Jeffrey fought valiantly to hold the door as the wind and I blew into the lobby, my hair swirling in great spirals above my head while my skirt floated halfway up my thighs. The moment the door closed behind me, the room stilled as though the wind had been turned off by a switch. I brushed my fallen hair off my face and tugged my skirt into place.

"Jeffrey. It seems I need to go out of town for a few days. Would you be able to look after Fleur for me?"

"No problem, Mrs. Cook. The same as always?"

"Yes, a half a can of albacore tuna in the morning and a half can in the evening along with a bowl of dry cat food."

"Happy to do it. When do you leave?"

"Tomorrow."

"Going anyplace exciting?"

"London," I replied.

7
Flying Economy (No) Class

The flight to Heathrow left at seven the next evening. The price of my ticket was outrageous, especially since it was in coach, but it was the best I could do at such a late date. Naturally, the cabin was jammed. Seems *tout le monde* wanted to experience London in the spring. I wondered how much less my fellow economy travelers had paid with their advance purchases. I squeezed into my narrow window seat and avoided eye contact with the woman in jogging attire seated beside me. Though she appeared to be nervous, the last thing I wanted was to get trapped into a transatlantic conversation with the person I would be struggling over the armrest with.

I damned the misfortune that relegated me to the back of the plane, and pined for the days when all my travel was first-class. The sad truth was I could no longer afford to do so. My most closely guarded secret, and one shared only with Ethan and my accountant, was that my financial affairs were in a sorry state. Actually, I was teetering on the verge of bankruptcy. Though I still had a few assets, my portfolio had dwindled to a frightening level, one insufficient to support my lifestyle.

Financial turmoil and insecurity have been the story of my life. My father was a strikingly handsome man with a grandiose imagination and few skills. He could handle neither his liquor nor his bank account. Mother used to say that Father made Black Jack Bouvier look like a teetotaling skinflint. Due to an inheritance, he was of modest wealth when he married my mother, but by the time I turned six he had squandered every penny on can't-miss horses and business deals that went south. Soon after his money was gone, he divorced my mother for another woman, a very rich one I might add. Since he had no assets for Mother to lay claim to, this left us poor.

Grandmother disapproved of my father from the very beginning. I understand now she saw through his charms. And being a DAR Episcopalian, the worst thing she could envision was her daughter marrying an Irish Catholic. She was no great fan of the Kennedy family and used to go on ad nauseam about their uncouth manners. When Mother announced her intention to marry Father, Grandmother told her in no uncertain terms she would be disinherited if she went through with the wedding. But Mother was strong-willed and did as she wished. So did Grandmother. Mother eloped and Grandmother wrote her out of the will that very same day.

After Father left us, with no breadwinner in the picture, Mother was put in the awkward position of having to crawl to her mother for financial help. Grandmother did help us out enough to keep us fed and clothed and a roof over our heads, and to see to it that I received a proper classical education. But she begrudged Mother every penny, forcing her to endure endless *I told you so's* every time she had to go begging for money. As a result, Mother went to her as seldom as possible and luxuries were in short supply. I recall the shame of wearing last season's fashions while all my peers were dressed in the latest arrivals.

When Grandmother died, Mother remained disinherited, with the exception of a small trust set up to see that she had enough to survive. The rest of Grandmother's vast fortune went to my mother's brother and his children. A lawsuit by my mother did little to change that except cost us more money and sever all relations with my uncle forever. For the rest of her life, my mother drilled it into my head that the most important thing in life is financial independence. She didn't want to see me make the same mistake she had made. "Before you marry know his financial situation as well as his bad habits," she said. "And make sure he loves you more than you love him," she added, no doubt thinking of how my father had broken her heart on top of ruining her financially.

When I met Henry Hamilton Cook III at a party in the Hamptons, I thought I had hit the jackpot. Henry was young, well-established, and to all appearances had scads of money. We shared a love of opera, Shakespeare, Bordeaux wines, and travel. The only downside of marrying him was having to move to the Midwest, but he had a sumptuous mansion in Lake Forest and a charming summer home in Lake Geneva. When I pined for the activity of New York, he bought the East Lake Shore Drive co-op. Better yet, not only did I love him, he adored me. He lavished me with expensive gifts, Mikimoto pearls, original paintings, furs. Winters were spent skiing in St. Moritz or Aspen, and summers sailing off Palma or sunning in Cap d'Antibes.

We had been married ten years when his behavior started to change. The once adoring man suddenly became testy and sometimes verbally abusive toward me. Then one afternoon we got into the Jaguar, and Henry realized he didn't remember how to drive. X-rays revealed a brain tumor. It was an aggressive one, and over the next few months I watched the vital, handsome man turn to a shell before my very eyes. He died at the age of forty in Lake Forest Hospital with me sitting next to him holding his hand.

His death bore no resemblance to the film deaths one sees where the character slowly closes his eyes and then is gone. As he lay dying, his face grew long and his mouth formed an O, like a baby bird awaiting a worm. His eyes remained fixed on me, and I told him I loved him one last time as he slipped from this world. A nurse came in to shut his eyes, passing her hands over them like a magician over a hat.

Immediately following Henry's death, I felt relief to think he was at peace. The relief changed to misery once the funeral was over and the vacuum of free time descended upon me. Life seemed nothing more than a string of empty days. But if I thought I felt badly then, my suffering grew worse the day I learned far more was empty than my heart. Namely, our bank accounts.

Henry, as it turns out, had been living on the edge. He was leveraged to such an unbelievable degree, he made Donald Trump look conservative. This unpleasant state of affairs was brought to my attention when we got to probate. Throughout our entire married life, Henry never even hinted at any financial problems. Perhaps it was because he didn't want to see himself lessened in my eyes, but I prefer to believe that his carelessness was caused by the brain tumor.

Whatever the case, instead of finding myself a rich widow, I was faced with the harsh reality of having to sell the Lake Forest house and the Lake Geneva cottage just to pay off his debts. If they brought in enough, I could keep the East Lake Shore Drive co-op. Luckily the realtors earned their hefty commissions. Still, after all was said and done, I found myself with just slightly over a million dollars in my coffers. I cursed myself for not listening to my mother's mantra about being aware of his financial situation, but up until Henry's illness, everything seemed so secure.

I understand that to many people a million dollars may sound like a great deal of money, but it truly isn't. One must consider that even if one makes the extraordinary return of 10 percent on one's investment, one million dollars only generates a hundred thousand dollars a year, pre-tax income. This is not much to live on when one takes into consideration a lifestyle where my suits cost well over a thousand dollars each and visits to Francesco for my hair average a hundred dollars a week. Add to this travel expenses, entertaining costs, and the high price of charity balls. This does not include housing-related expenses such as property taxes, assessments, insurance, or the cost of maintaining the car. At the end of the day, I would have sailed through the interest on my million and be forced to dip into my principal, the ultimate taboo. With Mother's words about financial independence echoing in my ears, I concluded there were only two avenues I might take to remedy the situation. Remarry someone rich or make more money off of mine.

Since I wasn't feeling up to a new husband yet, I decided to invest. This is where my real trouble started. A friend told me her broker had put her in derivatives, and she said her money was doubling practically daily. This seemed like the perfect solution to my dilemma. It would certainly beat the pitiful six percent that tax-free municipals were paying.

Rule of thumb. Whenever something sounds too good to be true, one should know that it *is* too good to be true. Against my broker's advice, I insisted he buy me some derivatives. At first the returns were right in line with what I had been promised. My bottom line doubled in two years. I was delighted, drawn in by the easy money. I continued putting larger and larger chunks of my nest egg into derivatives until they finally made up the bulk of my portfolio.

Need I say what happened next? The derivative market came crashing down. One day I was worth four million dollars, the next barely several hundred thousand. Not only was the experience devastating, but humiliating. In the end, I took what was left and put it into the tax-free municipals after all. Now, after barely making ends meet for the past few years, I was on the brink. Unless some miracle occurred, I was looking at selling my beloved residence. That's why Detective Malloy's joke about giving him a call if I ever wanted to sell hit so hard. He couldn't have known how close to home he had struck. The very thought of losing my precious home broke my heart.

One might wonder why I hadn't gone for the marriage option. For one, I had loved Henry, and we had a good marriage, despite his leaving me destitute. And the market for available, attractive, rich husbands was slim to say the least. But there was another thing I had learned after being unmarried. I enjoyed the freedom of not answering to anyone. When I was growing up, I always had to do as Grandmother said because I couldn't risk angering her. When I was married, though it seemed fine at the time, we always did what Henry wanted. Since his death, I had grown accustomed to making all my own choices. I took care of my own affairs, and chose my own affairs. If not for the money, I wouldn't have traded places with any of my married friends for anything. Take Sandy St. Clair for instance. She spent her life turning her head to her husband's infidelities. I could name countless other pawns who tolerated philandering and worse, selling themselves short for financial security and status. They answered to unreasonable demands, entertained people they didn't care for, and put up with daunting criticism, merely because they feared poverty. Ethan once told me about a well-known Barrington woman who was beaten senseless by her extremely wealthy husband, and when the emergency room doctor asked her if she would like the police called in, she told him to mind his own business.

Anyhow, until now I had enjoyed the freedom of the single life. But as the plane taxied down the runway and I felt its massive bulk shudder to free itself of the earth I shuddered too: at the thought of being poor. Or might I find being destitute even more liberating than being single? *That* I sincerely doubted.

Though my seat mate was still indicating that she would welcome some conversation, I feigned ignorance to the signs. Foregoing the dismal airline meal, I took a Halcion, donned my eyeshades, and slept the entire way across the Atlantic.

I awakened to the captain informing us that we would arrive at Heathrow presently and to prepare for landing. Buckled in, with my seatback in the upright and locked position, I watched the tranquility of the English countryside pass below like an enormous green patchwork quilt. The moment the wheels of the jumbo jet made contact with the runway, the people around me began to clap. I had never heard clapping on a plane before, leaving me to wonder if my fellow passengers in coach thought there was something exceptional in the captain's performance of getting us overseas safely. Whatever the reason, it was just another sorry reminder that I was seated in the back of the plane and not in the front where I really belonged.

After clearing customs, I phoned my dear friend Lady Charmian Grace. Though it was an indecently early hour I wasn't worried about disturbing her. One of the staff would answer the phone if Lady Charmian was still sleeping. Happily, she was awake and took my call cheerfully.

"Pauline," she cooed in a clipped British accent pleasurable to the ears. "When did you arrive in London?"

"Just now actually," I said. "My trip was very last minute. I wanted to call you right away, because I'm only here for a few days and I hoped to see you."

"See me! Please come stay with me. Where are you booked? Let me call and cancel for you."

"I hadn't reserved anything. I was just now going to call over to the Connaught."

"Darling, they're full. I know it. One of Lord Grace's business associates was just turned out, a ghastly Irishman who is staying with us now because of it. But I promise to keep him out of your way. There is plenty of space for all of us. Now please do say you'll stay with us. I wouldn't hear otherwise."

"Well, how can I say no to such a gracious offer?" I replied.

"Lovely. We'll have to arrange for dinner tonight then. I must get on the telephone. I'm so glad we're in the city and not off in the country. Would have been rotten luck to have missed you. How long did you say you will be staying?"

"A few nights at the most. I have to run up to Bury St. Edmunds tomorrow and may have to spend a night up there."

"Bury St. Edmunds! Whatever for? Never mind, you can tell me all about it when you get here. Would you like me to send my driver out?"

Though I would have liked to save the quid to get into the city, I didn't want to impose on Charmian any more than I already was. Besides, there would have been quite a wait by the time the car made it through the London traffic to Heathrow. I regretted not calling ahead from the states, but my British friend could talk up a storm and I wanted to avoid a crippling international phone bill. "No, Charmian. I'll take a taxi."

"I do wish you would have let me know you were coming. I would have had Maxwell meet you. Oh, well, no matter. About an hour then?"

"About an hour."

I gave the driver the Mayfair address and sat back in the cab for the fourteen-mile drive into London. England has such a civilized feeling. For one, riding in a taxi is a pleasure. The vehicles themselves are large and immaculate, and the drivers, who are seated in a separate compartment, always know where they are going. Light-years away from the abominable service in Chicago, where not only must a passenger be prepared to direct the driver to any destination other than the airport or Lake Shore Drive, but the taxis are nearly always filthy. The one small consolation in the scheme of things is that at least Chicago cabs are superior to those of New York.

A sense of relaxation crept over me as we drove the well-maintained roads through the dewey green countryside, driving on the left, of course. Passing tidy cottages and large fields of tilled land, I was happily aware of the absence of strip malls and neon signs. As we neared the city large billboard ads started to appear and the traffic began to slow. We left the motorway and the driver worked his way through town, past the ubiquitous pubs, quaint shops, and Victorian houses of one of my favorite cities in the world. It occurred to me how I would miss the quiet elegance of the Connaught and its pampering, but oh so discreet, staff. Henry and I always stayed there on our London visits. But one pays dearly for such pleasures and the Connaught's rates are astronomical in a city known for sky-high tariffs. I had fully known the hotel would be full; it always is. My ploy of mentioning it to Charmian had brought the desired results of saving face as well as saving the expense.

After a complex series of one-way streets I would never even dare to undertake, we emerged in tony Mayfair, its elegant streets lined with proper Georgian homes. The driver pulled up in front of Charmian's townhouse as if he had been stopping there his entire life.

Lady Grace greeted me at the door. As always she looked sublime. Her peaches and cream English complexion was fresh and glowing and she was wearing her reddish hair, à la Fergie, long and onto her shoulders. It was hard for me to believe we were the same age, she looked so vital and young. I made a mental footnote to find out who had done her face, if the opportunity presented itself. One must be very cautious in broaching such subjects at risk of offending.

"Chimps," I greeted her with a laugh, using a nickname her brothers had bestowed upon her as a child when her long arms and legs had been out of proportion to her growing body.

"Pauline. You look fabulous. Oh, how I envy your height. It keeps you so slim."

We hugged and exchanged the obligatory kiss to either cheek. Maxwell, the butler, spirited my bags away, and Lady Grace led me into her salon where a tray was piled high with croissants and French pastries. Over cream tea, we caught up on old times and new. It seemed centuries ago since the party in Klosters where we first met. Her husband, Lord David Grace, and Henry had struck up as fast a friendship as Charmian and I. Though I hadn't seen her in years, it felt like only yesterday. We gossiped, or shared information rather, and I brought her up to snuff on our mutual acquaintances stateside. Likewise, she filled me in on our mutual friends overseas. Her information turned out to be far steamier than mine. As much as the English like to portray themselves as bastions of class, they are the greatest lovers of scandal of any people I know. And the largest perpetrators of it.

An hour had passed before I came around to telling her the true reason for my visit, the strange circumstances surrounding Ethan's death, and my quest to get to the bottom of who he really was. As I drew near to the end of my story, I could tell she was marking the time. Her eyes kept flicking toward the clock that ticked on the marble mantle above the gas fireplace.

"Quite curious about your friend," she said, resting her cup back in the saucer with a little flourish. "Pauline, I'm terribly sorry but I must desert you. I've got the very devil of a day. Had I known you were coming, I would have made other arrangements, but as it is I have to run off. A fitting for my Ascot wear followed by a terrifically boring luncheon engagement I'm afraid. But I've gone and planned for a splendid dinner tonight. Lord G. will be here as well as a few others. We can finish catching up then. Please make yourself at home and if you need anything at all ask Maxwell or Christina for help."

"Thank you, Charmian, I'm sure I can look after myself. I'll probably take a nap and then do a little sightseeing. I want to head up to Bury St. Edmunds first thing in the morning."

"Well, have a good lie-in then dear, and I'll see you later. Ta."

She was out the door in a flurry. I finished the last of the tea and rang for Maxwell to show me to my quarters. He led me up the stairs to a large airy room filled with Victorian antiques and decorated in flowered chintz. A vase of fresh spring flowers graced the bureau. My luggage had already found its way there and was set upon a rack.

"Will there be anything else?" he queried, standing unobtrusively in the open doorway.

"No, Maxwell, that will be fine," I said. He pointed out a buzzer for my convenience and then he closed the door ever so gently, as if I were already asleep and he didn't want to disturb me. Such service simply does not exist in the States.

After unpacking my bags, I found myself wide awake. Seems my Halcion-induced sleep on the plane had fulfilled my body's sleep requirements for the time being. I decided to put off my travel nap until the afternoon. I freshened up and headed out in search of a train ticket to Bury St. Edmunds in the morning.

8

Window Shopping

The skies were spritzing sporadically, hardly unusual for London in the spring, or any time of year for that matter. Toting the ever-indispensable umbrella, I left Chimps's townhouse and headed to Grosvenor Square, one of the oldest and largest squares in Mayfair. At the far end of the green expanse loomed the dreary but imposing American Embassy. Seeing it brought back memories of the lively reception Henry and I attended right after the Falklands War, when everyone was feeling bright and imperialistic again. For a melancholy moment I was swept up in feelings of loss, but I quickly brushed them aside. There were far more important things to do than wallow in self-pity.

Since it was a Sunday, all the travel agencies were closed, so I took a taxi to Victoria Station to buy my ticket. There, at the British Rail information window, an efficient young woman informed me that the train I wanted left the Liverpool Street station at eight thirty-five in the morning and arrived in Bury St. Edmunds just prior to eleven. I purchased a seat in first class.

My legs were still feeling somewhat cramped from the long flight in a short seat, so I decided to stretch them by taking a walk. London is truly a city to be enjoyed on foot. Each block holds its own fascination. I strolled past centuries-old pubs filled to capacity with local workers enjoying their day off and window shopped at galleries selling Turner watercolors and spiral-legged Louis XIV armchairs, feeling myself unwind with every step. Turning onto the side streets, I wandered the residential mews where flower boxes in every window spilled out riotous arrays of fuchsia and violet and peach. From there, I strolled on to Green Park where the yellow daffodils bloomed alongside the feet of Sunday joggers. The colors of spring were painted everywhere.

On a whim, I decided to pay nearby Buckingham Palace a visit. If I were to name three things I specifically admired about the British it would be their taxis, their gardens, and their appreciation for history and tradition. Having already tasted the first two, no place better represented the third than the home of every British monarch since Queen Victoria. As I drew near the gated grounds, I could see the Royal Standard flying which meant that the present queen was in residence. I stopped in front of the palace and peered between the heads of the tourists pressed against the iron gates. There stood two of the queen's guard in gold-braided scarlet jackets, their tall bearskin busbies perched high upon their heads. I watched a couple of small children make silly faces in an attempt to get the stone-faced guards to smile and remembered once doing the same thing with Henry years ago.

It was drizzling steadily now. Beneath the protection of my umbrella, I strolled back toward Mayfair, stopping on Brook Street to linger in front of the Courtenay window. The purveyors of the finest lingerie money can buy, there were times in the past I flew to London simply to shop there. Thankfully, British shopkeepers are civilized enough to shutter their stores on Sundays, or my already stressed credit cards would have suffered more damage.

As exhaustion finally began to creep in, I hailed a taxi and took it to the Connaught. The concierge recognized me immediately and addressed me by name, even after so many years' absence. For nostalgic reasons, I took a relaxing cup of tea in the understated lobby, and then walked the last few blocks to Charmian's townhouse.

By the time my tired feet climbed the stairs to my bedroom, I was more than ready to have a lie-in before dinner.

I awoke refreshed and looking forward to the evening. Since Lord and Lady Grace moved only in the best circles, there was no doubt it would be interesting. I drew a bath in the ornate marble bathroom adjoining my room and had a relaxing soak as I thought about what to wear. Though I had brought several demure suits with me, I decided the simple black cocktail dress with the deeply plunging neckline would do perfectly. Best to show off the decolletage while it's still presentable. Charmian had called for cocktails at seven-thirty, so at a quarter of eight I took a last satisfying look in the mirror and headed downstairs.

On the first floor, there were men's voices coming from the salon. I took a moment outside the door to compose myself, giving my bosom a final adjustment, before making my entrance. Two men were seated in deep leather chairs in front of the gas fire. The industrial tones of their voices told me they were conducting business. The first man was my host, Lord David Grace, his elongated face set in a deadly serious expression. Judging from his Irish brogue, the second man was the other houseguest Charmian had referred to this morning. His head of unruly copper hair topped a mildly freckled face with a square jaw. Though his skin was lined and weathered, he appeared to be somewhere in his mid-forties. They both looked up as I entered the room, the Irishman giving me the once-over in a way that made me wish I'd picked up something new at Courtenay.

Lord David's gray eyes lit up in a way that let one know one was welcome.

"Pauline," he said, standing to greet me. "How good to see you." Since I was wearing two-inch heels, I had to stoop slightly to receive his dry peck on the cheek. "You look wonderful. Let me introduce you to Terrance Sullivan."

By now, the Irishman had risen also. Even with my shoes, he was taller than I, his shoulders broad beneath the supple wool of his Saville Row suit. His eyes reflected the deep French blue of the shirt he wore, and he regarded me in an intimate, familiar manner that I found alarming yet flattering. His extended hand virtually encompassed mine in a firm but gentle grip—that lasted just a bit longer than it should have. He smiled, exposing exceptional teeth for an Irishman. I suddenly found myself feeling like a gangly ingenue at her first dance. My right kneecap began quivering involuntarily, and despite my exposed decolletage, I was flushed and overheated.

"How do you do?" I asked, trying to appear cool.

"How do *you* do?" he asked in reply. Our eyes locked for an inappropriate time before I managed to break away and turn to Lord Grace.

"Well, David," I said, fighting desperately for equilibrium. "How go things with you?"

"Exceedingly well, I must say," he replied, coming to the rescue. "Mr. Sullivan and I were just in discussion about a development he's proposing outside Dublin. We could be entering into quite an interesting venture together."

"Is that so? Where outside Dublin would the—" I started to ask, turning once again toward Terrance Sullivan. He was staring at me with such an untamed glint in his eye that my words lost themselves in midair. Thankfully, Charmian chose that moment to float into the room with two newly arrived dinner guests, an elegantly dressed elderly couple named Lord and Lady Pierce. I never got their forenames, they weren't even mentioned. Maxwell appeared on the scene with a tray of champagne glasses, and I quickly snatched one up, nearly draining it in one fell swoop to calm my palpitating heart. The next guests arrived, he related to the Rolls Royce fortune, she weighty with jewels. The last to join us were theater people. A producer and his wife.

The ensuing conversation was lively and witty, not at all stuffy as one might imagine a gathering of proper English to be. Naturally, Camilla's name came up and there was agreement all around that while she certainly wasn't Princess Diana, the princess really hadn't behaved as a princess ought to while she was alive. The Royals had practiced adultery from time immemorial, and Diana should have been a sport about it. Thankful the dalliances of the prince were no longer the primary fodder for the press, half thought Camilla received dreadful treatment in the papers while the other half felt she deserved it. Everyone hoped to be spared headlines such as those proclaiming the prince's proclivity for female hygiene products from now on.

Maxwell rang that dinner was served. On our way into the dining room, Charmian pulled me aside. "So what do you think of the Irishman. Isn't he ghastly?" she whispered. "I don't know why David puts so much stock in him. I believe they're thinking of forming some kind of a partnership. I think it's dreadful."

"I don't find him 'ghastly' at all, Chimps. I actually find him intriguing."

"You do?" She looked thoughtful.

"Yes. Is he married?"

"Confirmed bachelor according to Lord G."

Which made him all the more interesting to me. Unfortunately, Charmian had seated us at opposite ends of the table. Though he, Lord Grace, and the Rolls Royce heir were locked in a political discussion for most of the meal, every time I looked in his direction it seemed he was staring at me. Dinner was delightful, cornish hens and bread puddings followed by stilton and port, but I had little appetite and hardly touched a bite. It wasn't until we went into the drawing room for coffee that he managed to peel himself from Lord Grace and the automobile heir to have a word with me.

"We haven't really had a chance to talk," he said. "Let me reintroduce myself. My name is Terrance Sullivan."

"And I am Pauline Cook."

He was smoking a cigar and sucked upon it deeply, slowly releasing the aromatic smoke in an even stream. "Did you ever study mythology, Pauline?"

"Of course I did. In both high school and college. My favorite myth is that of Daphne and Apollo."

"Is that when Daphne turns into a tree rather than submit to Apollo's advances?"

"Exactly."

He laughed aloud, a gutsy laugh that caused a few heads in the room to turn. He quieted and asked, "So you believe in fate, then?"

I couldn't believe my ears. My heart caught in my throat making it hard to take a breath much less form words. I'm fairly certain my mouth hung open. When I didn't answer, he continued, "I only say that because when I saw you walk into the room this evening, I had this sense I knew you even though we've never met. I wonder if you felt it too?"

I was unnerved. I was feeling something, but I wasn't quite sure what. It took several seconds before I found enough voice to answer him. "Perhaps," was the best I could do.

He looked at me oddly and lowered his voice. "Maybe I'm not doing this right. Let's start over a second time. What brings you to England, Pauline?"

Which brought me back to the sad reason for my visit. "I'm hoping to find the roots of a friend who died."

"Must have been a very good friend if you've come all the way to London to do it."

"Yes, he was a very good friend. My best friend. And actually, my search is taking me farther than London. I head to Bury St. Edmunds in the morning."

"Was this friend your lover?"

I laughed. "No, I'm afraid he was more like a girlfriend."

"Ah, a puff then."

"Yes, a puff."

He furrowed his brow in thought and then said, "Tell you what. Why don't I come along? David and I have finished up our business for now. I'd welcome the opportunity to spend some time with you. Maybe we can get to know each other a little better."

"That's very kind of you, but to be perfectly honest, it might prove to be rather boring. I'm not quite sure what I'm looking for there."

At that point our conversation was interrupted by Charmian. In a gesture quite unlike her normal self she wedged in between us. "So how are my visitors doing?" she asked. It wasn't until I saw the goo-goo eyes she directed at Mr. Sullivan that it dawned on me she didn't find him nearly as ghastly as she claimed. Rather, she was coming on to him in a way that suggested there had already been some physical contact between them. Not in any sort of mood to get into a competition with my hostess, I stood to excuse myself.

"Oh, Pauline, you can't turn in yet," she said with transparent insincerity.

"I'm afraid I'm just exhausted, Chimps. And I've got an early wake-up. Thank you for a lovely evening." I said a polite good-night to Terrance Sullivan and the others and went up to my room.

I lay in bed unable to stop thinking about Terrance Sullivan. I told myself I was glad that the magic between us had been ruined. I had no need for the complication of becoming attached to someone. Things were just fine for me the way they were. I had enough escorts to fill the social end of my life, and I had Sean to fill the sexual end.

I had no illusions about Sean. There was no doubt he was using me for the money he thought I had. He assumed that I was wealthy beyond his wildest dreams, and what had I to gain by informing him otherwise? In fact, I fueled his assumption with perks like designer clothes and Gucci wallets, not to mention occasional "loans" I really couldn't afford, knowing that not a cent of the money he borrowed would ever find its way back to my brokerage account.

But I considered it fair trade, because I was using him, too. Physically. Here I was, a victim of my body's last surges of estrogen, and there he was with that which I really needed. Not only was he prodigiously attentive in the carnal way, he was tireless, unlike the rich old dinosaurs I dated from time to time. With Sean, I was enjoying sex more than I had for a long time.

In a strange way, I met Sean because of Ethan. Three months ago Ethan and I were to attend the opening of a Balthus exhibit at the Evol Gallery, and he suggested we meet beforehand at an establishment called Bertucci's, right around the corner from the gallery. For some reason that escapes me, I arrived on time for a change, and equally as unfathomable, Ethan was late. The instant I walked into the dimly lit establishment, I had a sense of having stumbled onto the set of a gangster movie. The room was full of dark-haired men in expensive suits and thick gold bracelets who greeted each other with kisses on both cheeks. They were accompanied by gum-chewing women half their age with teased blond hair and long red fingernails. Cigarettes burned in just about every ashtray next to piles of cash laid out on the bar, presumably for the drinks and not the girls. Pictures of Frank Sinatra lined the walls and his music played in the background. I seated myself on a bar stool wondering what on planet Earth possessed Ethan to select this outpost of criminality for our rendezvous. Perhaps it was his idea of a joke.

I was absorbed in the floor show, the people were actually quite interesting to watch, when I realized that someone was speaking to me. I turned my head and there behind the bar stood a most glorious specimen of youthful testosterone. With chiseled cheeks and a well-defined jaw, chestnut eyes ringed in thick black lashes and smooth olive skin, he was one of the sexiest creatures I had ever laid eyes upon. Even with his ponytail and pierced ear. He smiled at me with raw simian insolence, two dimples carving perfect parentheses into his cheeks.

"I'm sorry, did you say something?" I stammered.

"I asked if you wanted a drink, miss?"

Suddenly alive in a physical sort of way I hadn't considered for a while, I mindlessly ordered a glass of Chardonnay. Watching him reach over to get the bottle, I found myself admiring his muscular physique the same way middle-aged men drool over young female flesh. He put the wine in front of me and I took a sip. It would have caused any self-respecting Burgundian to slit his throat. Though it mattered little to me as he warmed me with another personal smile.

"I haven't seen you here before," he said.

Hardly, I thought. "No, you haven't."

"You live nearby?"

"I live along the lake."

"A Gold Coaster. I could tell the second you walked in."

I was intrigued. "Really? How is that?"

"Oh, you stand out in here." He leaned closer and I felt myself drawn into the chestnut-colored eyes. "You're way different from those bimbos over there."

"Is that any way to speak of your clientele?"

He laughed. "They know they're bimbos. They're proud of it. They make it an art form."

At that point someone named Mr. J. called him from the other end of the bar. "Aay, Sean." He quickly attended to Mr. J., pouring for him from a chilled bottle of vodka and lighting his cigarette. Mr. J. unearthed what must have been a company payroll and peeled off a bill. He gave it to Sean and waved him off with his diamond-encrusted pinky ring. "Keep da change." Sean was back with me a moment later.

"You know, I'm only doing this on the side," he said, indicating the bar and therefore his occupation. "I'm a model. Been trying to break into it for a while now. I've had a little success, you know, catalogues, Sunday paper, but I just haven't gotten the big break. I figure I'm going to give it another year and if nothing clicks, it's time to move on. I mean, I'm a college graduate and all. I don't plan on standing behind a bar forever."

For the life of me, I will never fully comprehend what I did next or why I did it, but I heard my own voice saying, "I've got a rather close acquaintance who owns an agency. Her name is Jacquie Washington. Have you heard of her?"

"Heard of her? I've been trying to get an appointment with her for months. She doesn't even take my calls."

"Well, call her tomorrow and tell her that Pauline Cook referred you. I'm certain she will take your call." The grateful look on his face warmed me to the heart, so much so that I reached into my bag and withdrew one of my personal calling cards. "And if she still won't speak with you, contact me and I will see to it personally that she does."

"I don't know how to thank you."

"It's nothing," I said.

At that point a wind-whipped and disheveled Ethan made his appearance, looking as if he had run the entire way from Rogers Park. "I'm sorry to be late, Pauline," he said, combing his hair back over the top of his head. "There was an accident on Lake Shore Drive and they were rerouting all the traffic."

"That's quite all right. I've been speaking with Mr. . . . Mr. . . . ."

"Romero. Sean Romero."

"Mr. Romero here. He has kept me well entertained," I said in all honesty. My glass was empty and we were running late for the opening, so I asked for the check. Sean would have nothing of it.

"That's on me," he insisted.

I thanked him and he gave me a very personal wink of his right eye. I coolly slid off the bar stool and walked to the door with a slightly exaggerated sway of my hips. Ethan noticed my theatrics and asked me about it the moment we were outside.

"What was going on with you and that bartender?"

"Nothing, I assure you. Though I don't know that I would rail against the possibility."

"Please, Pauline," he nearly shrieked. "Do not ever think of lowering yourself like some kind of desperate woman. It's so unbecoming."

Throughout the entire exhibit, my thoughts kept looping back to the very sexy Sean Romero. But Balthus's depictions of pubescent girls, and the strong sexual undertones his work carried, served to remind me of the great age difference between myself and the young bartender. Just the same, I phoned Jacquie the next morning and told her to expect his call. She said she would try and fit him in seeing he was such a good friend of mine. And though the flirtation had been a pleasant distraction, I figured that was that. By the end of the day, he was little more than an afterthought.

Three days later, he called to tell me he had gotten an interview with Jacquie's agency and asked if he might buy me dinner to show his gratitude. Since I had no plans for that evening, I couldn't find any harm in it. I didn't mention it to Ethan, thinking there was no sense in getting him all worked up over what would be a one-time encounter. When Sean arrived to pick me up, he was wearing a fitted Italian sport coat that only served to magnify the perfection of his body. He took me to an off-the-beaten-path restaurant in Bucktown that served a combination of Indian and Thai food. Not only was I the oldest woman in the establishment, but certainly the best-dressed. But the spicy food was sumptuous, Sean turned out to be pleasant company, and I was surprised at how quickly the evening passed.

I was even more surprised when our date ended up in my bedroom.

We had been seeing each other ever since. It was a fairly straight-forward relationship. We would dine somewhere where I was fairly certain I wouldn't see anyone I knew, and afterward spend several delirious hours in my bed. Or elsewhere in my apartment. Ethan insisted that Sean would hurt me in the end, but I assured Ethan I was old enough to look out for myself. I didn't fool myself that Sean didn't have other women in his life. Which was just as well as far as I was concerned. I certainly didn't expect any kind of commitment from this young man, and the truth be told, no matter how good he made me feel in my bedroom, there was little room for him in my world outside of it. The differences were simply too great.

Now an ocean away from Sean, he may as well have been on another planet. I tossed and turned, unable to get Terrance Sullivan off my mind. At first glance, he was everything I could ever want in a man. He was my age, had money, was single, had money, was good-looking and charming. And had money. I thought about his words to me, the ones that left me so unsettled. *Do you believe in fate?* Henry said the same thing to me at that party in the Hamptons so many years ago. And there was one other similarity between the two men. Just like me, Henry had been a redhead, too.

I thought about Terrance sleeping alone in the bedroom down the hall. My imagination carried me to his door where my gentle knock is answered by him wearing a loosely tied robe. Upon seeing me he smiles and pulls me into the dark with him. The robe slips away . . .

Then I remembered the way Charmian had looked at him, and I doubted he was either sleeping or alone.

9

Burial Grounds

After a restless night, I awoke and rang for the house servant
to bring me coffee and a pastry in my room. I needed to
shower and dress quickly in order to catch my train. Charmian knew
I had an early departure, exempting me from a copious breakfast of
eggs, bacon, potatoes, kippers, toast, and whatever other deadly foods
start the day for the British. It's a miracle they don't drop dead in waves
in the streets considering the extraordinary challenges presented to
their arteries. I put on my makeup while I drank my coffee and ate
my "biscuit." I dressed sensibly in a beige cashmere sweater and black
designer jeans for trudging about the countryside. Then I packed a
small overnight bag with a change of underwear and toiletry items in
case I missed the last train back to London and had to spend the night
in Bury St. Edmunds.

When I went downstairs, I was surprised to see Terrance Sul-
livan sitting in the salon, reading the Monday morning edition of
The London Times. Lord David had already gone to his office, and Lady
Charmian was nowhere in sight. When he saw me, Terrance folded his

newspaper and stood up immediately. He was dressed in casual slacks and a hunter green pullover, and I noticed that his blue eyes of yesterday were now a deep green.

"And here you are," he said. "I wondered if you were ever comin' down."

"Good morning," I acknowledged him nervously. "I'd love to chat, but I'm rather pressed for time. My train leaves in thirty minutes."

"No need for a train," he said. "Lord Grace has generously offered us use of his motor car. We can drive up to Bury St. Edmunds."

"We?" I hadn't forgotten his offer of the night before, but I had already filed it away under idle chatter, especially after the vibes Charmian had been emanating.

"Of course 'we.' I can't let an opportunity to know you better get past. Don't tell me you'd be preferring the services of an engineer over your own personal driver."

I might have told him he was wrong on that point. I loved the British rail system, and would have been fully content to sit back on a train indulging in a good book while the countryside glided past with a clickety-clack. But the thought of having a car at my disposal presented a great advantage. If I needed to explore outside of the town of Bury St. Edmunds itself, I wouldn't have to hire a cab. And the guidebook I had said that Bury St. Edmunds was a small town, so for all I knew, taxis could be at a premium. Also, there was one other factor to take into consideration. Despite Lady Grace's apparent interest in Terrance Sullivan, he still remained fair game. The chance to have his undivided attention had its appeal.

"Well, then," I acquiesced. "If you are serious . . ."

"Of course I'm serious," he echoed. "Then we're off. The car's just out front."

I decided not to make an issue of his presumption in having the car ready. After all he was a high-powered businessman, most likely accustomed to doing things expeditiously. Like a child being taken on holiday, I followed him blithely out the door where Lord Grace's navy blue Bentley awaited us. He opened the passenger's door for me.

"Your chariot, madame," he said.

I slipped my overnight bag into the back seat before realizing it wouldn't be needed now. With a car at our disposal, we could drive back at any hour so there was no worry about missing the last train. As we pulled away from the townhouse, I was glad that he was the one at the wheel. Though I love the taxis, I have no fondness for driving myself in England. With everything being on the opposite side, including the steering wheel, I never seem to be able to get a proper perspective for where I am on the road. Of course, this was no problem for Terrance who was from Ireland where the same rules applied. He negotiated his way through the Monday morning traffic and put us onto the carriageway to Bury St. Edmunds without ever consulting a map. I was flattered that he had gone so far as to get directions ahead of time, but I wondered how he could have been so sure I would take him up on his offer.

"Charmian tells me you're a merry widow," he said before I had a chance to think about it any further.

"I am widowed," I replied curtly. "I wouldn't say merrily."

"I'm sorry," he said. "I didn't mean offense. Charmian said it's been more than ten years since your husband's passing. I'm an insensitive clod. Please forgive me."

"You're forgiven. Actually, I'm really not sensitive to it. It *has* been a long time."

"I'm surprised you haven't remarried."

"Henry and I were the best of friends. I don't know if I could ever find anyone to fill his shoes."

"But you've dated since?"

"My husband died, not I . . . if that's what you are implying."

He laughed that low, deep-throated chuckle of his and smiled at me. The look on his face reminded me of our first meeting the night before, giving me the sense that I might just as well be sitting naked in the passenger seat. "So tell me about this friend of yours we're hunting up?" he asked.

"What would you like to know?"

"For starters, what was his name?"

"That's what I'm not quite sure about." I went on to share Ethan's entire history with him, how we met, his death and subsequent suicide note, the birth certificates found in his apartment. The only thing I omitted was Ethan's reference to some terrible deed. I didn't think it necessary. "It's so hard to believe he's gone," I said. "He was so full of life. He just loved being the center of attention. Half the women in Chicago fussed over him. Of course, a lot of them had ulterior motives. Ethan wrote an annual article for *Pipeline* about Chicago women and who he thought had class, the ones who were best dressed, whose party invitations were the most coveted. Every woman in the city wanted to see her name on those lists and being a good friend of Ethan's sure increased the odds."

Ethan had reveled in the power that occasional column brought him. I could never forget how the first time it appeared, Sunny's name hadn't even been mentioned. After that shun she made it her business to get close to him, inviting him for dinner, calling on him for advice. Her ploy worked because the next time the column ran her name was mentioned several times.

"So, where did you rank on his lists?" he asked.

"Now what would you think?" Of course Ethan always featured me prominently. I turned my head and stared at the passing countryside. "I still find it so hard to believe."

"That he's dead."

"No. That he killed himself."

The two-hour drive flew past in no time at all. I learned we had a lot in common as we talked of favorite places and found we shared a love for Capri, Auckland, and Hong Kong, not to mention Paris. We were also partial to Brahms piano concertos and Italian opera. He told me he saw *La Traviata* at La Fenice opera house in Venice the very night the Mafia burned it down. He was also a fan of James Joyce, Fitzgerald, and Yeats. We differed on Shakespeare, his favorite play being *The Taming of the Shrew*, mine *Antony and Cleopatra.*

Before I knew it we had left the motorway and were pulling into the small village of Bury St. Edmunds. With its cobblestone streets and ancient buildings, the town had the feel of a place bypassed by time. We drove into the town center where the ruins of a stone tower sat amid the dewey green of a large park. Terrance pulled the Bentley to the side and stopped.

"Would you know where Bury St. Edmunds got its name?" he queried.

"You'll have to let me plead ignorance on that one."

"King Edmund of East Anglia was buried here way back in the tenth century."

"Thank you for enlightening me."

"So I don't suppose you know what this abbey's important for?"

"I majored in English literature, not history, I'm afraid."

"One of the greatest turning points in civilization took place in there. In 1214, King John's barons put their heads together in that very building and came up with a little piece of paper outlining some liberties they forced King John to accept. They called it 'The Magna Carta.'"

"Now, *that* I have heard of."

"The tower's been sacked by the town's people a couple of times over the centuries. Once as a protest against monastic control, another in a peasants' revolt in 1327. It's lain in ruins ever since."

"You're a virtual encyclopedia, Mr. Sullivan," I said.

"See, now, aren't you glad you didn't take the train? You would've missed out on this fantastic lecture," he laughed. "So what would you like to do now, Inspector Cook?"

"Well, first I'd like to get a map."

He pointed to one of the ubiquitous blue *i*'s denoting an information center and a British Rail sign with an arrow pointing up the road. "How about the train station? I imagine you could get one there."

We pulled up to the station just as the train from London pulled in. A few people got off. If not for Terrance, I would have been one of them. We went inside the small stone building, but as luck would have it, the information booth was deserted. I asked a man sitting behind the ticket window when the booth would be reopening.

"Not until June," he replied with a ruddy-faced smile. "But maybe I can help you with something."

"Well, first off, a map of the town would be helpful."

He opened a drawer and procured a map, turning it over to me with a cheery, "Here we go now."

"Thank you." I perused the map. In a town so small, it might not be unreasonable to expect that everyone knew everyone else. I took out my copy of the British Ethan Campbell's birth certificate and handed it to the ticket agent. "Is that name familiar to you by any chance?"

He pursed his lips and looked thoughtful. "There are a few Campbells in this town, but no Ethan that I know of."

I guess one could hardly expect success on the first try. In fact, I would have been astonished if the first person I spoke to knew of this Ethan Campbell—though it would have been a nice start. I pointed out the address on the document. "Could you tell me where this is?"

"Certainly, mum," he said, obviously happy to be of help again. He circled an area on the far side of the town. "You should find it somewheres in here."

I thanked him and put the birth certificate back in my purse.

"Are you sure you don't mind being party to this adventure? It could turn out to be nothing more than a wild goose chase," I asked Terrance as we walked back to the car. He assured me that he found playing detective an amusing distraction from the demands of his usual world.

We drove two winding miles across town to the area the clerk had circled on the map and easily found the row house that corresponded to the address. It was an ancient brown brick so covered with ivy that the front window was nearly obscured. We parked directly in front of the house and went to the door where I had to push a green-leaved tendril aside in order to ring the bell. As we waited for some response, I thought about the best I could expect to find. If the parents of the Ethan Campbell on the birth certificate were still alive they would be quite elderly. If they were deceased, maybe Mr. Campbell himself lived here. Or a sibling. Nearly sixty years had passed since baby Ethan had crossed this threshold. Did it still hold any connection to him?

When a minute passed with no response, I rang again. It occurred to me that maybe it would have been better to conduct this search on a weekend. The present occupants might be at work. But then I heard a voice calling out from the other side of the door. "Coming, coming." The door opened and there stood a tiny elderly woman. Her hair was in tight curls and she wore a perfectly pressed wrapper the color of cotton candy. A pair of blue eyes paler than a winter sky looked out from a crepe paper face.

"May I 'elp you?" she asked. Her accent was a thick and rural English, heavy on the vowels.

"Good day. My name is Pauline Cook. My friend here is Mr. Sullivan. I'm terribly sorry to disturb you, but we're looking for Mr. or Mrs. Campbell. You wouldn't be Sarah Campbell by any chance?" I wondered if I had gotten lucky enough for this to be the British Ethan's mother. She certainly filled the age requirement.

"No," she replied, her tiny face showing disappointment we hadn't come to visit her. "I'm Mrs. Doney, Miriam Doney. You're American then?"

"Yes I am. "

"I'm rather fond of Americans," she said, off on her own tangent, wanting to keep us engaged. "We 'ad quite of few of your lot stationed 'ere during the war. The air bases were just outside of town, and the pilots would come into town all the time. Almost married one of them myself. Would've been living in America now."

"I see. It's a shame that we missed having you in the States, but it's quite lovely here. If you don't mind, though, about the Campbell family, Sarah and Lawrence and their son, Ethan. They lived here at one time. Would you happen to know anything about them?"

She nodded. "The woman who lived in this house before me was a Campbell. She was a widow and sold it to us some thirty odd years ago."

"Do you know where she moved when she left here?"

"I'm afraid not, love."

"Would you have a telephone directory that we might be taking a peek at, Mrs. Doney?" Terrance interjected. I looked at him questioningly, and he raised his brow back at me. "Don't you know, good sleuths always make use of the phone book."

The old woman's eyes lit up at the sound of his voice. "You're not a Yank. Irish. Dublin. I know that accent like the back of me 'and. I ended up marrying one of your lot."

"Then you've led a charmed life," he said, teasing her mischievously.

"I did—until my Warwick died. I'm afraid the whiskey did 'im in." She did not appear to be bothered by this admission, but rather accepting of it as if it were just another part of life. The pale eyes drifted off to someplace behind me. "I'm waiting to join 'im now."

"The phone book," I reminded her. "May we intrude upon you for your phone book."

"Please, come inside," she urged, delighted to have guests. We followed her through a dark and austere front room to the back of the house where a bright postage stamp–sized kitchen was located. Mrs. Doney retrieved a directory from the pantry and handed it to me. Then she asked if we would like tea. Hardly able to refuse, I looked up Campbell in the book while we waited for the kettle to boil. There were two: a James and a Robert. When I took out a pen to write down the numbers, Mrs. Doney saw what I was doing and said. "Please love, you can call from 'ere."

Using an ancient wall phone that probably dated back to just after the war, I dialed the number given for James Campbell. A woman answered after the fourth ring, her voice tense as a child cried in the background. She regretted that she was no relation to either Sarah or Ethan Campbell. I reached Robert Campbell, who had no knowledge of them either. I put the phone back in the cradle wondering why I had thought this might be easy.

"Do you suppose there's some government office that can help?" I asked Terrance.

"I have a better idea. Mrs. Doney, where is the local cemetery?" Though I found the request odd, I said nothing. The old widow told him that the village cemetery, the resting place of her dear Warwick as well as many other former friends, was located on the outskirts of the town. Terrance asked her to point it out on the map.

We drank her tea and listened patiently to her stories about England during the war. Now I understand where the expression "war stories" comes from. They stretched on endlessly. Apparently she didn't have many visitors, so she was taking advantage of the two she had. She probably would have gone on forever had I not stood after finishing my second cup. I could sense her disappointment that her visitors were leaving so soon. She walked us to the door and wished us good luck in our search.

We thanked her profusely and promised to visit again on our next trip to Bury St. Edmunds.

"Why on earth are we going to the graveyard?" We were back in the Bentley heading toward the edge of town.

"Don't you ever read spy novels?" he asked, reminding me for the briefest moment of Detective Malloy's same question about police shows on television. "Just supposing the man you knew wasn't really named Ethan Campbell at all. Suppose he was someone else and wanted a new identity. The easiest way to do it is to get the birth certificate of a dead person, someone born around your date of birth. All records revolve around birth certificates, no one ever checks them against death certificates."

"So you're suggesting my Ethan stole an identity?"

He shrugged. "Could be. At the very least, we'll have a walk around the Bury St. Edmunds cemetery. It's got to be bleeding old."

We pulled up to the cemetery. Terrance was certainly right about it being old. The stone walls around the grounds looked as if they had been built some time in the Dark Ages. There was a small caretaker's cottage just inside the gate and we parked in front of it. Inside the cottage, a balding man sat in a large worn chair that might have predated the stone walls. His nose was buried in a newspaper. He didn't move a bit when we entered. Terrance cleared his throat loudly and the man finally peered up at us over his bifocals. We explained we were looking for the grave of Ethan Campbell, and he put his paper down and went into a cabinet, unearthing a large tome that contained a map of the grounds.

"Campbell," he said finally. "Don't have an Ethan Campbell. Got a Lawrence."

"Ethan's father," I said.

"Died nineteen forty-four," he continued. "RAF pilot. He's located in the northwest sector over here." He pointed out an area on the map.

"Is there a Sarah Campbell here, too?" I asked.

He looked at the tome again and shook his head. "No Sarah. Not yet, anyway."

❋ ❋ ❋

"Don't know what help Lawrence Campbell is to us," I said once we were back outside.

"Well, we might as well visit the old boy," said Terrance, "seeing we came all the way out here."

We walked across the cemetery, stepping on top of the remains of the long dead, past headstones dating back to the thirteen hundreds and before. The sun came out and warmed our backs, a welcome contrast to the cool pull of history at our feet. I shivered as the ancient names and dates etched in the marble markers put me in a rare state of feeling insignificant.

Lawrence Campbell's grave was exactly where the caretaker said it would be. The headstone was free of grass, making it appear that it was attended to regularly. I wondered who watched this grave. Could it be Sarah? If not, might it be someone who had some information on their son? I noticed that Lawrence Campbell, the RAF pilot, had met his maker in May, a month before D-Day. His son, who would have been just a baby, must have been conceived on a furlough. I wondered if Lawrence was the victim of some training accident here in England or if he had gone down on the other side of the channel. Whatever the case, his body had made it home. I sensed he had been a brave man. I thought of the father my Ethan spoke of, the suicidal one who had squandered the family fortune. This could not be the same man.

Fifty yards from us, a matronly looking woman in a loose-fitting floral print dress was placing flowers on a grave. She eyed us curiously, her head turning our way every couple of seconds. Finally, she abandoned her basket of flowers and came over to us. She walked with surprising vigor considering her gray hair, and as she drew near I could see her pink face was dewey and unlined. The damp cloudy climate was heaven for the skin.

"Good day," she called out.

"Hello," I replied.

"Friend of his, were you?"

"Not really."

"I only ask because I'm a friend of Sarah's. My name is Lacey Blaine."
She toed the marker with a sturdy shoe. "Lawrence was Sarah's first
husband, you know. I've promised to look after his grave as well as her
second husband's whenever I come up to tend to Peter's. I don't mean
to be nosy. It's just that she's so alone and so sick now, I was hoping
you might be family."

"Sarah Campbell is alive," I stated practically numb. I was astonished at my twin stroke of good luck: to be here at the same point
in time as Lacey Blaine, and to learn that the mother of the Ethan
Campbell whose birth certificate I held in my purse was still living. I
quickly recovered and introduced Terrance and myself, adding, "No,
we're not family, but I might have known her son. Do you know if she
had a son named Ethan?"

It was Lacey Blaine's turn to look astonished. "She did, but he disappeared years and years ago. He was a queer lad, if you know what I
mean, and we always figured that was part of the reason he left. He
was just a couple of classes ahead of me in the school."

When she said queer, I knew that she meant homosexual, which
started me on a new track that maybe the British Ethan and my Ethan
were indeed one and the same. Perhaps Ethan had left England to
escape the stigma attached to his homosexuality many years back. I
explained that a man who might have been Sarah's son died recently.
She told us Sarah was in her nineties and living in a state home for the
aged, not ten miles from the cemetery, and that her last name was
Moore now, from her second marriage. She obliged us with directions
to the home, and Terrance and I headed back out to meet the woman
I hoped might hold the key to my obsession for the truth.

Although the home in which Sarah Campbell Moore lived was immaculate and the grounds manicured and well-kept, it was still depressing
simply by virtue of its inhabitants, primarily elderly and wheelchair-

bound. And my melancholy grew greater as I realized I might be delivering the message of a son's death to an aged and ailing old woman.

When we asked at the desk if it would be possible to see Sarah Moore, no one seemed in the least bit concerned with who we were. They just seemed happy that she had a visitor. We found her sitting in a wheelchair in the television room, a woman as slight and frail and lacking in color as anyone I had ever seen in my life. Her skin was almost transparent and her tiny face held a pair of tiny dark eyes, the only thing in her entire being that did not appear to be gray. Even the robe she was wrapped in was gray, the material falling in great folds of excess around her. She was extremely lucid despite her age, and seemed very curious when the attendant informed her we were there to visit her. I could tell she was racking her memory for some recollection of who we were.

"Mrs. Moore," I said, taking her outstretched hand, "you don't know me. My name is Pauline Cook, and I'm from America." Before I was able to say anything else, a loud sigh escaped her lips.

"America," she said in a hope-filled voice. She set her thin lips in a firm line and closed her eyes, raising her chin toward heaven. "It's Ethan. You have some word about Ethan."

My voice caught in my throat, and I found myself totally unequipped to do what I had to next. I wondered what in God's name had spurred me on this pilgrimage and cursed Ethan's memory for putting me in this predicament.

"I might, but I'm afraid it isn't good news," I said. "I had a friend named Ethan Campbell who recently passed away, and I am searching for his family."

The heartrending look that registered on her face made me want to cry myself. Her lips quivered, but no tears filled her eyes, giving me the unhappy sense her tears had dried up with age. She reached into the pocket of her bathrobe with a withered hand and unearthed a folded yellowed envelope. She pressed the envelope to her heart. "My Ethan, my dear Ethan. This is the last I ever heard from him."

She held out the old letter, bidding me to read it. I took it from her shaking hand. Though the ink of the return address had blurred over the years, I could make out a hotel name, The Alder Arms in Morristown, South Carolina. I removed a sheet of paper from the envelope, so thin and worn from being unfolded and refolded over the years, it felt as fragile as tissue paper. The date in the upper right hand corner was March 14, 1965.

Dearest Mum, I am finding life in the States much better for me than it was at home. I have already made dear friends, and I suspect I am going to go places in this country. People treat me as if I am royalty when they hear the British accent. I am in the South now, a charming land if you aren't a Negro, and will be heading even further south as a job opportunity has presented itself. And it's someplace very warm which you know suits me and my fragile constitution. I would tell you more about it, but I don't want to jinx it, so I will write you when I have secured the position. I love you very much and think about you daily. Look after father's grave for the both of us. I'll write again soon. Your loving son, Ethan

I refolded the letter carefully and returned it to the envelope. I was fairly certain my Ethan hadn't written the letter. The handwriting was spare and compact, a far cry from his elaborate cursive. Besides this Ethan mentioned people making a fuss over his English accent.

My Ethan never spoke with even the slightest trace of one. I didn't think the two men could be one and the same.

Still, I had to be absolutely certain.

I was carrying several photographs of Ethan in my purse for this very reason. I took them out and selected one of the more flattering ones, taken just last February at his Valentine's Day birthday bash. He was wearing a pink shirt and red tie and was smiling a satisfied yellow-toothed smile. "This is my friend. Does he look anything like your son?"

Sarah Moore unearthed a pair of thick glasses from the depths of her robe. She put them on and studied the photo. An even more desolate look crossed her face and she shook her head.

"This isn't Ethan," she said firmly. She went into the robe pocket yet again and this time pulled out a photograph. "This was taken right before he left."

I examined the fading picture. Though nearly as time-worn as the letter had been, I could tell this was not my deceased friend. The man in this picture was strikingly handsome with a full head of light-colored curls and a small cleft in his chin. I looked back at the old woman and noticed she had started to cry actual tears that ran pitifully down the creases of her gray cheeks. She had not dried up after all. "I hoped at last to know what had happened to him. I can't die in peace until I do."

As I sat helplessly by, Terrance surprised me by putting his arms around the old woman to comfort her. "Now, now mother, don't cry. When Pauline goes back to the States, she's going to ask around after your son. She'll turn him up, I promise you."

I glared at him. As badly as I felt for this poor old woman, how could he speak for me? How was I to learn what had become of her son almost thirty-five years ago? If some harm had befallen him? Or if he had gotten caught up in his life in America and forgotten about the people he had left behind? I was no detective agency, and as it was, I already had my own mission without taking on hers.

Nonetheless, feeling very much on the spot, I assured her I would do whatever was necessary to unravel the mystery of her son's disappearance all those years ago.

"Pardon me, Terrance, but don't you think you were being more than a little presumptuous in telling that poor old woman that I would find her missing son?" We were driving through the gates of the state home, leaving the pitiful and hopeless remnants of the living behind us.

"Pauline, did you see the look on the poor crone's face, the woman was brokenhearted. I wanted to give her something to live on, especially seeing how we'd just gone and churned up the waters. I feel terribly lousy about it. I believe I'll send her some money."

"I don't think money is going to make any difference to her. She wants to know about her son."

"Well, if you don't want to find the answer, maybe I'll find it for her."

I couldn't tell if he was serious, but decided there was no reason to pursue the issue any further. "My God, we've seen a lot of lonely old people today. It's frightening, isn't it?"

"Getting old? More frightening if you don't." He turned onto the main road and pressed the Bentley into action. The countryside flew past in an emerald blur. "What are you thinking about your friend now?"

I shrugged. "I don't know what to think except that I know one thing for certain. He wasn't this Ethan Campbell. Which begs the question, what was he doing with this Ethan's birth certificate?"

"Maybe they met at some time," he suggested. "Maybe there was some foul play."

"If you knew my Ethan, you would never say that," I heard myself sigh. "I was hoping to go home with some answer, but I guess I'll have to look for it in the States."

We came to a roundabout. The signs indicating the route to London or back to Bury St. Edmunds pointed in opposite directions. Terrance slowed the car and turned to me. "It's nearly half-seven, Pauline, and I'm famished. We never had lunch you know. What do you say we go into town, find the finest restaurant they have to offer, and have a leisurely dinner. We can stay here overnight and head back to London in the morning. I know that David won't mind about the car. He has plenty of them at his disposal."

I wanted to say no, not because I wasn't attracted to the man, but because I was, and it was making me squeamish. I didn't know how I felt about staying in a hotel with him. He must have sensed my indecision, because his next words were, "Separate rooms, of course."

Maybe spending the night wasn't such a bad idea after all. It would give me the opportunity to spend more time with him out from under the keen ears of David and the hungry eyes of Charmian.

"Well, I could eat," I said.

10
Two No Luggage

We checked into the Angel Hotel, a small hotel across from the abbey gate nearly as old as the abbey itself. The innkeeper handed us the keys to two rooms, regretting that he couldn't give either of us Charles Dickens's former room as it was occupied this evening. I carried my small overnight bag up to my claustrophobically small quarters and freshened up for dinner. By the time Terrance and I met in the lobby, I was truly famished, and his idea to stay in Bury St. Edmunds looked better and better.

We had booked into the restaurant recommended by the innkeeper as the finest in town. The food turned out to be atrociously bad, a poor attempt at nouvelle French, a chewy rack of lamb and vegetables cooked to a mush. Evidently the tremendous improvements the British had made in their cuisine had not made their way up to Bury St. Edmunds yet. But a bottle of '78 Chateau Palmer did much to compensate for the tasteless food, and the cellar-like room was charming and cozy, not to mention lit with soft flattering candlelight. Just the sort of lighting a middle-aged women knows shows her to her best advantage.

Over dinner, Terrance talked about the grand plans he had for some major real estate developments in Ireland. Ireland was ready for growth, he said, having the highest literacy rate in Europe as well as a high flow of returning expatriates. As he ate, I couldn't help but notice his unpolished table manners. He left his napkin on the table until the first course was served, used the wrong fork several times, and cut all his food on his plate at once instead of in bites. One's behavior at the table tells more about a person's background than anything else. His indicated a less than upper-crust background.

But these days people of pedigree are in short supply, and one must learn not to be too fussy. Any concerns I had over his lack of etiquette evaporated completely as I looked into his eyes over the glow of the candle's flame. They had turned the same transparent aquamarine as the water in the Seychelles. He rested his square chin on his marvelously crafted hands and drew his face to within inches of mine. A shiver passed through me as though a cold draft had blown into the room. Though he was only telling me the story of how he and Lord Grace had met, I found it nearly impossible to concentrate. I could only envision my body going limp in his grasp as I stared into those eyes.

"So seeing's how I was going to be in London to work on some financing, I looked up Lord David on the advice of Melton Bedford."

"Melton Bedford?" I returned to reality. Melton was an acquaintance from my college days. Scion of an old New England textile family, he had grown tired of stuffy Eastern ways and relocated to California shortly after graduation. He was an avid, no let me make that fanatic, sportsman whose passion was deep-sea fishing. In fact, in recent years it seemed he only set foot on land for weddings, funerals, and to close business deals. "I haven't seen Melton in ages. How is he, anyway?"

"Doing fine, I'm sure. He's somewhere off the coast of Mexico looking for swordfish as we speak. Where else would you be finding him in April?"

"That would be Melton."

"So anyway, I wasn't even looking for any partners, just some friendly advice, but now it looks like Lord David and I might be doing some business together. Funny how that works, isn't it?"

The mention of Lord David and partnership brought an unwelcome picture to my mind, that of Charmian and Terrance and their body language the night before. I leaned away from him and picked up my wineglass, staring through the garnet colored liquid at the candle flame. "Speaking of partners, what is the relationship between you and Lady Grace?"

He smiled an open smile. Great teeth. "It's that obvious, then?"

"It certainly was last night," I replied.

Now he laughed. "Well, it shouldn't be. There is nothing going on between me and Lady Grace, though I might say left up to her there'd be something. My God, I want the woman's husband as my partner in a venture that makes Canary Wharf look small. There's far too much money involved to jeopardize it for a minute of sweat and lather. But it's a sticky situation for me. I can't insult the woman, because I know she has her husband's ear."

"She always has," I agreed, thinking how ill-pleased she would be with Terrance and me when we failed to return to Mayfair this evening. Charmian could be very vindictive. Perhaps she would never welcome me in her home again. Oh well, I had other friends in London. Secure in knowing the Irishman wasn't doing the deed with Charmian after all, I mused on how the night might end between us and wondered if the bed in his room was as narrow as mine.

We stopped at a pub for a brandy on the way back to the hotel. There was no more talk of business or Lord and Lady Grace. We spoke of lighthearted things and I forgot all about the dreariness of Mrs. Doney and the state home and even about Ethan. When we got back to the Angel he walked me to my room, which was practically unavoidable since all the rooms in the small hotel were only doors from each other. I put my key into the lock, wondering quietly what might happen next. I opened the door and turned to say good night. He was looking at me in the same way that had put me so off balance when I first met him. Heat rose in me. So did fear.

While my affair with Sean was satisfying, I recognized it for what it was. One day Sean would tire of being with an older woman and move on. I might miss him, but the mourning period would not be long. There was no place in my future for a bartender nearly half my age. Nor had I grieved over the end of any other dalliances I had engaged in since Henry died. They were mostly with older, very wealthy men who had lavished all kinds of money and attention on me. But those affairs held no threat because, although I was genuinely fond of many of the men, with no strong emotional attachment, they were safe.

Now, standing in the ancient narrow hallway of the Angel Hotel, inches away from Terrance Sullivan with my derriere pressed against the wall, panic set in. Here was a real possibility. I was facing a man of my own age who was nearly everything I wanted: successful, good-looking, masculine. He reminded me of my deceased husband in so many ways, it was eerie. He made me feel unduly self-conscious about myself and my appearance. My attraction toward him was dangerous.

He slipped an arm behind me and clasped my buttocks, his large shoulders encompassing mine as he leaned down and brushed my lips lightly before kissing me. I sighed with internal delight. His kisses were dewey and moist, not the sloppy dog drooling of so many young men nor the sandpaper dry of the occasional senior I spent time with. The smooth taste of brandy was still in his mouth, serving to make me more drunken in my passion. My knees trembled and I kissed him back with a ferocity I didn't know existed in me. I caressed his head and felt the coarse texture of his hair in my palm. He took my hand and turned it palm up, kissing it again and again. The way he pressed himself against me made me wish I was wearing a skirt so I could hike it up about my waist and let him take me then and there in the hallway. I raised his left hand to my mouth and tasted his fingers one by one.

Then, with the abruptness of a sharp slap in the face, he pulled away. I looked up into those ever so blue eyes, my face a vast question mark.

"What's wrong?" I regretted my words the moment I spoke them, not wanting to sound needy. That was the last impression I wanted him to have, despite my extreme neediness at the moment.

"Nothing," he said, softly cupping my face in one of his strong hands. "You are a wonderful, beautiful girl, though a little too serious sometimes," he scolded. He kissed me gently on the lips and touched my nose with the tip of his finger. "I had a lovely day. Good night."

I watched him walk down the hall, my mind whirling in disbelief, wondering at what had just happened. I felt embarrassed, like I had just thrown myself at him and had been rejected. Pauline Cook threw herself at no man. I went into my room and closed the door behind me sharply. Anger began to take the place of confusion. He had made the first advances. Was he a tease? I tore off my clothes and proceeded to brush my hair with frenzied strokes for five minutes.

I climbed into bed and waited for sleep to take me. Despite my frustration, I was exhausted and soon slipped into the state where one's mind becomes a mixed-up jumble of what might have happened today and what might happen tomorrow. Just before making that soft landing in a peaceful place, the sound of steps in the creaky hall brought me back to clear consciousness. They stopped in front of my door. Lying in silent anticipation, barely breathing, I was certain that finding he couldn't sleep, he had come back to take me after all.

There was no further sound. I began to wonder if if was just the night playing tricks on me in the dark and cramped quarters of a strange hotel room. And then I heard steps again. This time they were retreating, heading back up the hall in the direction from which they had come.

More than anything else in the world I wanted to jump out of bed, tear the door open and call out his name. Of course I didn't. Now completely awake, I lay there feeling more frustrated than ever, damning him and all his male brethren to hell while at the same time thanking heaven for their very existence.

11

Don't Touch My Bag
if You Please

Terrance was already in the breakfast room when I came down, eating an artery clogging banquet of sausage, bacon, and eggs with such relish that he didn't even notice me until I pulled out the chair across from him. He looked up and quickly wiped his mouth, flashing me his beguiling smile. It was like handing a cat burglar jewels, stealing away my anger and embarrassment from his rejection the night before. He stood and waited until I was seated before taking up his chair again.

"Did you sleep well?" he asked with extraordinary nonchalance.

"I was a bit restless," I replied, wanting to add, *no thanks to you*. "And yourself?"

"Like a rock." He craned his neck and signaled to the innkeeper who was serving another table in the small room. "You'll be wanting some breakfast before we go?"

"Yes, but certainly not what you're having." I surveyed his half-eaten meal. "You might think about watching that cholesterol. That is, if you want to see old age."

"You Americans. You needn't worry about me. Good genes. My grandfather ate a hearty breakfast like this every day of his life. And when he finished you'll never believe what he would do next. He'd call for my grandmother to 'bring the sausage pan,' and he would drink down the warm grease like it was milk."

"What an unappetizing thought. Why on earth would he do that?"

"Oh, the Irish mindset I suppose. Carryover from the famine years, you know. Don't waste a bite and store as much energy as you can in the eventuality you might need it one day to survive."

"Well, all that fat certainly couldn't have done him any good. How old was he when he died?"

"Ninety-eight," he replied, putting an end to that conversation.

The innkeeper appeared and I ordered my usual breakfast of dry toast and coffee. Terrance quickly polished off the rest of his meal and waited patiently while I ate mine, making polite conversation the entire time. The moment I finished my last bite of toast, he looked at his watch and stood up.

"Sorry to be rushing you, but I've got to get back to London. I've got a meeting."

"What about the rooms?" I asked, stubbornly drinking the last drop of my coffee.

"They're taken care of," he replied. Though I wouldn't have thought he would do otherwise, I was still pleased to see at least he picked up the tab for my night of tortured sleep.

The drive back to London was a lot quieter than the drive up had been. As I tried making conversation along the way, I found myself behaving in a manner very unlike me. I was acting in an overly pleasant manner, like a lover who senses a breakup coming and is doing her best to forestall it.

"How long will you be staying in England?" I asked, trying my best to sound blasé.

"Actually, I plan on going to the airport directly from my meeting this afternoon. Hopefully, I can peel out of Lady Grace's grasp without unsettling herself. I think it's a good thing I'm not spending another night in her house, don't you know?"

I don't know if I was more jarred by the thought that he was leaving or the newfound revelation that perhaps his motivation for joining me on this trip wasn't to spend more time in my company, but rather to distance himself from Charmian so as to avoid any risk of complications with Lord Grace. If that was the case I felt used, though in reality I hadn't been used at all, at least on a physical level. Maybe that's why he didn't sleep with me. He didn't want to add insult to injury. I fought to keep the growing resentment from my voice as I asked, "So the reason you came up to Bury St. Edmunds with me was to get away from Charmian?"

He took his eyes off the road and stared at me directly. "No, it isn't."

He didn't offer any further explanation and I didn't ask. The rest of the drive was quiet.

When we arrived back at the Graceses' Mayfair townhouse, Charmian was eating a lunch of cold meats and salad alone in the dining room. Her demeanor was exceedingly cool—as I had suspected it would be. "My peripatetic guests return," she said with forced politeness, her eyes daggers plunging into my chest. "How was your adventure?"

"Well, we learned that Ethan Campbell of Bury St. Edmunds was definitely not my friend Ethan, but not without breaking the heart of an old woman I'm afraid," I babbled, pulling out a chair and sitting, even though I had not been invited to do so. Terrance remained standing in the doorway. I suspected he feared that if he drew too close to Lady Charmian, she might coil and strike him.

"I'll leave you two women to catch up. I've just got to see to my things and I'm off." He stepped from the safety of the doorway and graced us each with a peck on the cheek. I would have been crushed at receiving the same treatment as Charmian, except that as he was leaving he hesitated behind her back and caught my eye. *I'll call you,* he mouthed and he held an imaginary phone to his ear. The gesture sent me soaring.

"Would you like some lunch, Pauline?" Charmian offered in an icy tone. Her skin was decidedly white and her lips were drawn tightly across her teeth. The way she acted made me think it would be unwise to accept food from her without a taster. I decided to clear the air right away.

"Charmian, absolutely nothing happened between myself and Terrance Sullivan if that's what's concerning you."

"Me. Concerned about you and that ghastly Irishman? The thought hadn't crossed my mind for a minute." She started to butter a roll and stopped midway through, pointing at me with the butter knife. Some of the peaches were finding their way back to her cheeks, and her pale blue eyes regained their impetuous sparkle. "Nothing at all?" she queried.

"Nothing," I assured her, omitting my own disappointment over the dreary fact.

"Do you suppose the man is a homosexual?" She bit off a piece of her roll.

I thought about the scene in the hall, about the heat of his kisses. They had more steam in them than I would think a man interested in other men could generate. Then again, he *had* stopped short . . . way short.

"I couldn't say. From outside appearances he doesn't seem to be."

"Was it that obvious I was trying to make him?"

"I could tell, but that's just me. I don't think any of the others would have noticed," I lied.

"I know you must think I'm terrible, but here I am in my forties and my body is just screaming out for passion, and David, well, he's

basically done with it. It's been ages. I love him dearly, always will, but
. . . well, you know how these things are."

I knew all too well how these things were. The very reason I maintained the shallow relationship with Sean was to attend to *these things*.
I thought once again about last night and my response to Terrance's
abandoned advances. I had wanted him body and soul, not just body.
It had been a long time since I had experienced anything on that
level. But now that I had, I didn't know how I could continue my affair
with Sean.

The need for higher intimacy had been reawakened in me, an
awakening I would live to regret.

Friends again, Charmian sat on the bed while I packed to leave Wednesday morning. The thought of returning to Chicago caused the loss of
Ethan's friendship to loom larger than ever. Here I was in the throes of
unrequited love, and when I got home he wouldn't be there to shore
me up. My favorite shoulder to cry on was gone. I found myself angry
at him again, blaming him for my latest misery, for killing himself
and leaving those damned birth certificates which in turn took me to
England which in turn led to my meeting Terrance Sullivan. Then I
remembered Terrance's silent promise to call me and had that *happy
to be alive* feeling, the dreaded euphoria that can leave a worse hang-
over than the cheapest bottle of scotch in its wake.

For obvious reasons, I couldn't share these thoughts with Charmian. As it was, her endless prattling was driving me crazy and I started
to pack even faster. "I do wish you would prolong your visit, Pauline.
I have a million people I would love to introduce you to. Why you've
practically just gotten here."

"I've accomplished what I came to do," I said firmly, "and I thank
you for all your hospitality, but I've got to get back." Though she did
present some very tempting arguments for staying, including a very
first rate reception being held that evening at the Tate. But without

Terrance Sullivan in the picture, none of it held any appeal. Besides, Ethan's corpse waited for me at home.

This time I sat in the back of the Bentley as Maxwell drove me to Heathrow. Finding the thought of making another crossing in economy unbearable, I upgraded to business class for an extra three thousand dollars. The British Airways service was exemplary, and I was glad for my decision despite the expense. The magic of Terrance Sullivan had me in its grasp. Even the very attractive businessman sitting next to me, who made it clear he was open for conversation, did nothing for me. I simply wasn't interested.

I should have known better than to be rude to a customs official. One must always be cautious with bureaucrats. But the abrasive manner in which he questioned me about carrying three bags for a three-day trip and having nothing to declare merited some sort of response. I told him that there was no way in creation that I could do any real shopping in such a short period of time, which started the other agents around him laughing. Obviously needing to reestablish his manhood, he took his revenge by pulling me aside and hand-searching my luggage, piece by piece. He zeroed in right away on my unused Montana jacket and Lanvin suit, not to mention three pairs of Italian shoes I've never worn and two Italian handbags I have yet to carry.

It might have been a losing argument for me, had I not been through these hoops before. Having learned a long time ago to carry receipts for my couture clothes when traveling overseas, I strung him along, letting him think he had me. Then I produced the credit card chits proving every item in question had been purchased in the United States. It may have ruined his day, but it added to mine immeasurably.

He scribbled on my declaration form and stormed off in an impotent snit, leaving me with my trio of open and unpacked Louis Vuitton suitcases.

12
Power of the Press

Upon arriving home Wednesday afternoon, Fleur shunned me by hiding beneath one of the living room sofas well out of reach. She did this whenever I left her alone for any period of time. I tried to entice her back out with promises of a treat, but she remained obstinate. Knowing she would come out in good time, I went into the library to sort through the neat stack of mail and newspapers Jeffrey had left just inside my door.

The first letter was from the co-op board, and thinking it was the minutes from last month's board meeting, I made the mistake of opening it. Instead, it was a notice that the building needed some infrastructure repairs so there would be a seventy-five-thousand-dollar special assessment, payable next month. Considering my available resources, it may as well have been seventy-five million. This unexpected financial bomb left me with little incentive to open the rest of the mail, most of which I knew to be bills. I dropped the smoldering stack of envelopes into the top drawer of my secretary and shut them out of sight.

Telling myself the knot in my stomach was simple indigestion, I turned to my phone messages. There were the standard social invitations, a luncheon at the Women's Athletic Club followed by slides of Eunice and Amy Winston's mother-daughter trek in Burma, a private showing of collection jewelry at Bulgari with Signor Bulgari himself, a last minute wine tasting dinner at my downstairs neighbor's. Next, the sound of Sean's voice asking "How are you and where are you?" made me realize I'd never told him I was going to London. There was a tug at my heartstrings at the thought that the next time I saw Sean would be the last. If nothing else had been accomplished on my trip, my mind was made up about breaking it off with him.

Detective Velez had left a message to call him and Whitney had left three, one each day I was gone. Finally there was a message from Sunny. She made no mention of our disagreement at Scarlet's, but asked in a terse and agitated voice if I had seen today's *Tribune*.

I picked up my copy of the paper to see what had Sunny so up in arms and found it right there on the front page. In the right-hand column was a feature article written by Connie Chan entitled "A-LIST AUTHOR TURNS B-GRADE." Evidently she had learned about the existence of the phantom birth certificates without the help of either Sunny or I. It also appeared while I had been traipsing about the English countryside in search of more knowledge about Ethan, Connie had conducted her own investigation into his life, one far more thorough than my own. She had contacted the educational institutions he claimed to have attended, Boston College for his undergraduate degree and Columbia for his master's. Neither school had any record of him, either as Ethan Campbell or Daniel Kehoe. She dug even deeper, contacting society people whose names Ethan had dropped over the years, including the Eastman family, a deceased member of which he had claimed as his godfather. Not a one of them had any notion of who he was. After shamelessly repeating verbatim some anecdotes from lunch at Scarlet's, she went on to write:

But most amazing is how he deceived the very people who were his biggest supporters, who did the most to promote him. The loquacious Mrs. Nathan Livermore, known in social circles as Sunny, told me at a recent lunch that she had always thought there was something about him that didn't fit, that he was always trying too hard. But that didn't prevent her from introducing him into her circles and treating him to numerous affairs and fundraisers on her dime.

Probably best recognized as a constant sidekick was Mrs. Pauline Cook, widow of the late Henry. The two were practically inseparable, and although she was unavailable for comment, friends say she is not only devastated by Mr. Campbell's death, but by the notion that someone she had been so close to most likely had hoodwinked her.

So after being officially ruled a suicide by the County Coroner, the body sits on a cold block in the county morgue awaiting the results of an FBI fingerprint check while Chicago society asks itself, "Who was this man who called himself Ethan Campbell?"

As if that wasn't bad enough, the picture prominently accompanying the article was one of Sunny, Ethan, and myself, taken at last spring's Arts Club Gala. The camera angle made it look like Ethan's face was stuck in Sunny's breasts while I looked on in startled delight.

I laid the paper down in disgust. I understood the motive behind Connie's biting and malicious attack on Ethan. She was taking her pound of flesh, albeit dead flesh, for the times he dressed her down in public. But it didn't explain why she had chosen to include Sunny and me in the butchery.

I called Mrs. Nathan Livermore who was less than loquacious. "My God, Pauline, have you read it?"

"I've just finished."

"Skinny flat-chested Oriental bitch. You were right. I never should have invited her to that lunch. What could have prompted her to say such nasty things?"

"She and Ethan had their differences," I replied.

"Forget what she said about Ethan. What about us? She made us look like a couple of country bumpkins! And it was on the front page of *The Tribune*. Everyone is town is reading it and laughing at us. Doesn't that bother you?"

Sunny's true colors were showing, as typical as cold driving rain in March. She wasn't in the least concerned about Ethan's good name but rather her own. Of course, I too was irate over Connie's article, no fonder of being made a fool of than Sunny, but I wasn't going to admit it. Something about Sunny's anger served as a panacea to my own. With forced calm I said, "I must admit the picture of us was none too flattering."

"Don't even mention the picture." I thought she was going to cry. "I can't bear the thought that everyone in this city sees me as a dupe."

"Sunny," I said, "so what *if* Ethan was born Daniel Kehoe and used a nom de plume? It isn't as though it's a crime. Writers do it all the time. We know people who have changed a great deal more than their names."

"What about his lies about his schools and his background?"

"We don't know for certain that he lied."

"*You* don't know for certain. Connie Chan sure seems to. Oh, and by the way, Nat has announced he's not giving cent one toward the funeral."

My choke collar tightened another notch.

I hung up and picked up this week's edition of *Pipeline*, turning to Elsa's column. As promised, her treatment of Ethan was far gentler than Connie's. She sung praises of his two books and lamented his untimely death. She wrote of his irrepressible joie de vivre and his irreplaceable presence on the social scene. She commended him for always finding time in his busy schedule to give her a call just to say hello. And finally, she mentioned the mystery presented by the post-humously found birth certificates.

> So who was Ethan Campbell? We hope some family member will come forth to tell us. Or perhaps we will never know. But even if no clear answer is ever to emerge, we can remember him as a gentle man, a dear friend, a person with a great appreciation for style and class and the days of gentle restraint that have passed us by—replaced by the vulgarity and glitz so in vogue today. Quixotic as he was, he represented a way of life that is rapidly disappearing in this fast-paced computer age of ours. We will miss you greatly, Ethan Campbell, whoever you were.

I closed the paper and pushed back a tear.

After unpacking, I called Detective Velez and apologized for not getting back to him sooner, explaining that I had been out of town. I made no mention of where I'd been or that I'd learned the Ethan Campbell of Bury St. Edmunds had gone missing, telling myself it wasn't pertinent and would only add to the confusion surrounding my Ethan's death. Deep inside I knew it was to protect my friend's reputation, as well as my own, from any further savagery.

"I wanted to let you know the M.E. has officially ruled Mr. Campbell's death a suicide," the detective said, "but if you saw today's *Tribune* you already know that."

Sunny was right. Everybody was reading that article.

"So what happens to the body now?" I asked.

"The County Administrator is still waiting for the FBI's fingerprint check before releasing it. Like I told you, it could take weeks. He's not exactly a priority. If the Feds don't turn anything up, and no family has come forward by then, we can release him to you if you want him. Otherwise, the state'll take care of it.

"By the way," he continued, without taking a breath, "I nearly forgot to tell you. I contacted that Juan Cardoza in Puerto Rico you told me he used to work for. Very nice gentleman. He didn't know anything about Mr. Campbell's family background, but he did confirm Mr. Campbell was in his employ for nearly twenty-five years. He also told me, as he recalled it, Mr. Campbell was born in England but raised in the U.S."

While I digested this latest contradiction of Ethan's, my call-waiting prompt sounded. "Detective, if there's nothing else, I'm afraid I have to go. There's someone else on the line." I disconnected him and took the incoming call. It was Sean, and he sounded extremely put-out with me.

"That's it, use me and then throw me away like yesterday's trash," he said. "Don't you return phone calls?"

"I'm sorry, Sean. Something came up and I had to go to London. I didn't get a chance to call you before I left. I apologize."

"London? What were you doing in London?"

"I thought I was looking into something about Ethan. As it turns out I was just chasing my tail."

"Hey, I read all about Ethan in *The Tribune* today. What a story with the possible multiple identities and all? Did you know about that?"

"He didn't have multiple identities. He had one. We're just not sure what it was."

"Well, I guess he never hurt anybody or anything, so what's the big deal, right? If it was up to me I'd just let it go and let the guy rest in peace."

"Therein lies the problem. It seems we need to know who he was before he can rest in peace." My desire to find the truth was growing stronger than ever. Which meant another trip. This time to Boston, the birthplace of Danny Kehoe, the owner of the other birth certificate found in Ethan's apartment. If I got real lucky I might not only find out who Ethan was but find some family to bury him. Even if I ended up burying him myself, at least I would know exactly who was in the casket.

"So, how about I take you to dinner tonight, get your mind off all the craziness," Sean was saying, though I barely heard him over the static of my own brain. "Earth to Pauline, are you there? Dinner? Tonight? Eat?"

"I can't, Sean," I begged off. "I've got a terrible case of jet lag. Besides, I've got some planning to do. I'm going to Boston tomorrow."

"Boston?" he asked incredulously.

"Yes, Boston."

"Because of Ethan?"

"Because of Ethan."

"Pauline, you are possessed." There was a pause and then, "Hey, I got a great idea. I'm off for the next couple of days. How about I come with you and help?"

I imagined this proposition was based on me providing the airline ticket, and since meeting Terrance, the thought of spending a night with Sean had lost all appeal. Of course, Sean had no way of knowing this or that things between us were about to come to an end. I didn't think it fair to inform him over the phone, no matter how shallow our relationship was. The breakup would have to wait until my return. "That's a kind thought, but I think I'll be more efficient on my own."

"Yeah, but when you go back to your lonely hotel room at . . . where you gonna stay?"

"I always stay at the Four Seasons."

"Yeah, so like I was saying, when you go back to your room at the Four Seasons, don't you think it would be nice to have a little 'room service' waiting."

He was getting annoying. "Sean, really. I need to go alone."

There was a measured silence and then, "Well, we can still have dinner tonight."

Evidently, my young soon-to-be-former paramour was not getting the message. "All I can think of is getting a good night's sleep," I said firmly. "I'll call you as soon as I get back."

This time he spoke with anger in his voice, an emotion I had not yet witnessed in him. "Yeah, I'll talk to you when you get back." He hung up without a good-bye.

While I wondered if there was any logical reason for feeling badly about Sean, Fleur came into the room and mewed loudly. She had finally forgiven me for deserting her. I picked her up and stroked her, holding her ears close to her head while she purred with unabashed pleasure.

"You love me now, all right, but by tomorrow night you are going to be very upset with me again," I said to the only living breathing creature left to count on in this world.

13

Tempting Fate

The plane landed at Logan with a thump. Several of the overhead bins popped open spilling their contents onto some of my fellow passengers, causing me to wonder if taking a bargain airline had been such a good idea after all. However, we taxied to the gate without further event. While the proletariat surged to get off the plane, I remained in my seat reading from *The Collected Works of Henry James*. When the last of them had finally disembarked, along with their wheeled carts, strollers, and shopping bags, I closed my book and peacefully took leave of the aircraft myself.

Knowing a car would be indispensable, I rented one at the airport and drove into the city. Time had softened my memory of how truly atrocious Boston drivers were, undoubtedly the most brazen people I have ever encountered behind the wheel. After being cut off twice in the Ted Williams Tunnel, and several more times along the way, I managed to pull up in front of the Four Seasons unscathed. Respectably located down the street from Piano Row, where the world's finest piano makers once crafted their instruments and Steinway still does, the hotel is also near Beacon Hill, where many of my friends once resided. Though I still had several acquaintances living along its winding cobblestone streets, many of the venerable old mansions had been sold off and subdivided into that ubiquitous blight on urban living, the condominium. Still, I retained my fondness for Boston, home to poet Robert Lowell and one of the most European of all American cities.

With the sound of angry horns still ringing in my ears, I happily turned the car over to the hotel valet and went into the lobby. The cool marble expanse was adorned with carefully selected antiques. At the reception desk, I requested a room overlooking Public Garden. The young clerk looked at her computer and regretted that the only park-side rooms available were suites at a substantially higher rate than I was paying. Even though it cost several hundred dollars more than my original room would have, I ended up taking a grand suite. I simply couldn't fathom being in Boston in the spring and not having a view of the tulips in full bloom.

My suite was decorated in nineteenth-century style, brightened throughout by vases of fresh cut flowers. I went directly to the window and took in the view for which I was paying so dearly. Public Garden was a canvas of red and yellow. I watched the swan boats glide through the lagoon beneath canopies of weeping willows, my eyes tearing with nostalgia. Henry and I had stopped in Boston on our way home from our last visit to Paris, a bittersweet trip hastily arranged to beat his ever accelerating deterioration. Almost like a child, he asked to ride one of the touristy boats. Halfway across the lagoon, he was struck with fear and grabbed me, holding me so tightly I could barely breathe. My heart had nearly broken as I realized that his holding onto me was an effort to hold onto the last remnants of his life and his sanity. It wasn't long after that trip that he was gone.

Unpacking hadn't taken long, as I had brought only one suitcase on this trip, hoping to keep my visit brief. When I had finished, I put in a call to Lizbeth Parker, a Boston Brahmin who attended Radcliffe with Sandy St. Clair and me. She was delighted to hear my voice, and we made a date for lunch at Anthony's Pier 4 the next day at noon.

That done, it was time for business. After my experience in England, I decided the phone book was as good a place to start as any. Locating the Greater Metro Boston phone book in a nightstand, I turned to *K* for Kehoe. There were dozens listed. I don't know what else I might have expected in an Irish town. Looking under Patrick, the given name of Daniel's father, I found nine of them. I didn't know if I was being overly optimistic to think he might be among the living, but if the British Ethan Campbell's mother was still alive, and Terrance Sullivan's grandfather lived until ninety-eight on a diet of sausage grease, one never knew.

I began dialing. I was fortunate to get an answer at about half the numbers I called, but that was as far as my luck went. Of the five people I spoke with, no one knew anything about a Daniel Kehoe. I left messages on the answering machines of the rest. Not ruling out the possibility that Daniel's father was dead but his mother still living, I started calling the Moiras. Then the Marys. Then the initial Ms. After exhausting them I called every remaining Kehoe in the book, a daunting task as there were nearly seventy. This turned out to be another exercise in futility and by the time I finished, my efforts had brought me nothing more than an impossibly tired finger and an earache.

With hunger setting in, I made one final call. To room service. I ordered up a Caesar salad and a half bottle of wine, and soon after finishing them fell into a deep sleep.

The next morning I awoke at the highly untoward hour of five A.M. My body clock had not yet reset itself from my European jaunt. After dialing room service again for coffee and toast, I got back on the phone, calling the numbers where there had been no answer the day before. I discovered early morning is a good time to find people.

It is also a good time to learn about their temperaments as some recipients were none too pleased to be awakened at such an early hour. Naturally, I made my apologies for the intrusion, feeling in all sincerity that those who do not want to be disturbed should leave their answering machines on and turn their phones off. Regardless, not one Kehoe I spoke with was acquainted with the family of Patrick, Moira, and Daniel.

I decided to switch to plan B and try another tactic from Bury St. Edmunds. I would pay a visit to the address given on Daniel's birth certificate. Though it had been the Kehoe family residence ages ago, perhaps whoever lived there now could be of help. I naively thought it couldn't hurt to try. I dressed for my lunch with Lizbeth later on, and went down to the concierge to get directions. When I told him where I wanted to go, a peculiar look crossed his face.

"You don't want to go down there, ma'am," he stated.

"I don't?"

"Well that part of Dorchester isn't really safe."

Thinking he was being ridiculous, I ignored his warning. After all, I had braved Ethan's borderline neighborhood in my beloved Jaguar. This time I was driving a rental car that was of no concern to me. I insisted he give me directions. He reluctantly pointed out a route and advised me to stay on the main thoroughfares. I thanked him and went out front where the valet retrieved my car.

The concierge's directions were most accurate, but as I neared my destination, I began to understand the reason for his concern. His description of the area as "run-down" was charitable. Most of the buildings were boarded up and the streets were littered with glass. With the concierge's words resounding in my ears, I stopped for a traffic light and noted a large group of young black men milling in front of a burnt-out building. Their sullen faces reminded me of the youths I saw with Detective Malloy at Area Three Headquarters, their expressions alienated and angry. They stared at me in a hostile manner that made me uncomfortable, so I ran the red light—certain that any police officer would forgive such an understandable action.

As it was, I needn't have worried about the police. I never saw any. Sticking to the concierge's directions, I made a couple of turns and pulled up at 2365 Simmons St. It was a dull red-brick townhouse in an unending row of bland townhouses, structures that looked as if the architect had decided any use of imagination or vision would be wasted here. This neighborhood was quite different from Ethan's, which I was beginning to think of as merely eclectic. An underlying sense of danger in the air urged caution. I studied the garbage and empty liquor bottles in the gutter, and looked up and down the block. The street was deserted. Acting contrary to my self-preservation instincts, I figured since I had come this far I might as well go all the way.

I forced myself out of the car and up the cracked walkway to the townhouse door. A rusted barbecue grill sat on the front stoop. In the upstairs windows sheets hung in lieu of drapes. My knock was answered by a fatigued-looking black woman holding a baby. The gray at her temples and the deeply etched lines in her face told me the baby most likely wasn't her own. She stared at me as if I had just fallen from the sky.

"Who you, the Avon lady?" she asked, her eyes unabashedly taking in my lunch ensemble, a canary yellow suit and black patent leather slides. In retrospect, it probably wasn't the wisest attire for blending into the ghetto.

"Good morning. I hate to disturb you. My name is Pauline Cook, and I was hoping you might be able to help me." I willed myself to maintain my composure. "I'm trying to locate some people who lived at this address some years ago."

"How long ago?"

"A little over sixty years. I couldn't be sure of when they moved out."

The woman actually laughed out loud. "Ain't nobody here from sixty years ago. They was some run-down houses tore down 'bout thirty years back to make way for these here places. I remember, see, 'cause I was already living round here back then, not in this here building, but one further down the way."

Though I had come to realize the absurdity of my presence on this street, there was one more question still going begging. "I wonder, would you happen to know if this part of the city has always been . . . well . . . lower income?"

She made no attempt to hide the contempt on her face. "No, honey, this is where all the rich people used to live. Then it got too expensive so they up and moved to Beacon Hill."

The baby in her arms began crying, and I fancied my welcome had worn out. I thanked her for her time and hurried back to the safety of my car. Pulling away from the broken down curb, I wondered what had possessed me to come to this part of the city. What had I hoped to find? One fact was indisputable. If Daniel Kehoe and my friend Ethan were one and the same, he certainly hadn't been born into an elite family. There was a shortage of aristocracy in this neck of the woods.

I consulted the map for the best route to the harbor where Lizbeth and I were meeting for lunch. I wanted to take the Southeast expressway, but after making a series of turns I realized I had missed a street somewhere and was now lost. And if possible, the neighborhood I now found myself lost in was even more run-down than the one I had just left. The houses were beyond uninhabitable, the streets lined with windowless, abandoned wrecks. Seized by panic, I began driving aimlessly in an attempt to get out of the area, not even considering a stop sign a suggestion.

To my great relief, I finally turned onto what appeared to be a major artery. I pulled up behind a stopped car at a traffic light where yet another pack of male youths milled about on the corner. It appeared the young residents of this neighborhood had nothing so arcane as jobs to occupy their time. I looked in the rearview mirror at the car behind me. The faces inside it were as darkly intimidating as the faces on the street corner. I nervously urged the light to change, wishing I had been smart enough to leave space between myself and the car in front of me so I could maneuver out of the trapped situation if I wanted to.

And then the voices started, taunting noises coming from the group at the corner. I tried to ignore them, pretended not to hear them, but they grew more insistent, more threatening until they merged into one frightening chorus of *Lady . . . Lady . . . Lady.* Realizing my purse was sitting on the seat beside me, I hoped at the very worst this would be a smash and grab. And if that was not the worst, what would be? Gang rape? Murder? Days as a hostage in some filthy basement with rodents crawling over my legs? My heart pulsed in my ears, and I kept my eyes fixed forward, as if by refusing to acknowledge their existence, they might go away. Then, my peripheral vision picked up a movement outside the window followed by a steady persistent knock. I turned my head ever so slightly and saw a very dark young man wearing a purple knit cap framed in the window. His pupil-less eyes were level with mine, his broad lips repeating the chant. "Lady, lady. . . ."

I lifted my chin in noble defiance.

"Lady, you got a flat."

It was then I noticed the car listing to the driver's side. Something I had run over on one of the side streets must have punctured the tire. I nodded helplessly at the young man poised beside me and opened the window a crack.

"Could you tell me how bad it is?" I ventured.

"Oh, it be flat. Completely. But only on the bottom."

Choosing to ignore his ill-placed humor, I asked, "Could you direct me to the nearest service station?"

"Lady, there ain't a gas station for a good mile. You wreck the rim if you drive on it, if you can even steer. It be the front tire." As I sat there in numb disbelief, he shocked me by saying, "No worry lady, me 'n my boys, we change it for you."

The light had turned green, the car in front of me was gone, and the ones behind me were driving around the scene. By now four young men were gathered around my car. They were of various shapes and sizes, but they shared one common trait. They were all darker than a moonless midnight. I scanned the street in hopes of seeing a police car, but should have known they only made their appearances when one was parked in front of a fire hydrant, never when one's personal safety was at stake. Despite my ever-increasing terror, I had no choice in the situation. The option was to drive unfamiliar crime-ridden streets at five miles an hour in search of what might be a nonexistent gas station.

Taking my purse firmly in hand, I got out of the car. Without so much as asking, the young man in the purple cap climbed in. I wondered if that was the last I was going to see of the car, but he simply reached into the glove box and pushed the button to open the trunk. A moment later, there were dark men swarming all over the vehicle. I watched in amazement as they took the trunk apart in a symmetry of blind precision and unearthed tools and a spare tire. Within ten minutes they had jacked the car up and replaced the flat tire with a nice round one. One of them brought the bad tire to me and pointed to a six-inch nail sticking out of it. Then, in less time than it took to take it apart, they reassembled the trunk and even put the hubcap back in place.

"There you go, Paul-line, good as new," said the youth in the purple cap whose name I had learned was Jesse.

"I can't thank you enough," I said.

"My pleasure," said Jesse. "Couldn't have nobody messin' up that nice suit."

Realizing it would only be fitting to give the young men something for their efforts, I opened my purse and took out my wallet. Cash strapped as usual, all it contained was a twenty and several ones. My hand wavered back and forth above the bills before I finally settled on the twenty. "This is for you."

His smile was broad, his white teeth radiant in his dark face, as he waved off the money. "Do somebody else some time," he said, holding the car door open for me.

After climbing in I sheepishly asked for directions back to the turnpike. A moment later, I was pulling away, thinking of how a despicable creature like Desmond Keifer could hold me up for five dollars to check on a dead friend, while a hardened street character would turn down a twenty for a life-saving mission.

The world could be a strange place.

Lizbeth was fit as ever and rail thin, her ash blond hair pulled back into a neat ponytail, her skin rosy as if she had just climbed off one of her thoroughbreds. She was quite a contrast to me in my couture suit, casually dressed in slacks and a cashmere blazer. The only thing missing was her riding crop. Over a cold lobster salad and a glass of Taittinger I related the story of Ethan's death and my search for his true origins.

"Daniel Kehoe. It doesn't ring a bell. Terribly Irish isn't it? Like looking for a needle in a haystack in this town."

"Well, yes, and judging from the area in which Daniel Kehoe started out life, I don't think you would have ever come in contact with him."

"What do you mean?"

"His first home was in Dorchester. I just came from there."

"You went into Dorchester by yourself? Honestly, Pauline. What possessed you? You might have been hurt going into that area."

"Oh, Lizbeth, don't be so narrow-minded. Just because people are poor doesn't necessarily make them evil. In many ways I think the people who live there are a lot less treacherous than some of the rich people we know."

"Oh, speaking of treachery, you'll never guess who I was seated next to at the fundraiser for the Boston Pops last week—Andrew Spector of all people. It was most awkward. It was his first social function since he was acquitted of his wife's murder. I didn't have a clue what to say to him. Honestly, what would you say? 'Congratulations on getting away with it?' We all know he killed Josie, and the worst part is he got all her money. The kids are fit to be tied. Anyhow, as I said, it was a most awkward situation."

"So, did you speak with him?"

"Well, of course I did. The man was seated next to me. I couldn't be rude. But he is horrible."

Lunch stretched out for a couple of hours as we caught up on affairs, who was having them and who wasn't. Lizbeth and I seldom talk about anything really important. For all her money and education, she is poorly versed in such matters as art or politics, and is even less interested in them. Her world revolves around horses, but since I have no interest in the equines whatsoever, our conversations generally consist of vacation spots and other people. In our circles, the two are usually inextricably intertwined. Since we had already covered other people, the talk moved to travel. She had just returned from two weeks sailing in Tahiti aboard Randolph Williams's yacht and told of Randolph's young, beautiful, and overly endowed fourth wife who not only sunbathed topless but took most of her meals in the same state.

"Warren actually missed his mouth the first time she came to lunch au naturel. He dropped an entire forkful of cerviche onto his white linen shorts," she laughed.

"I just can't imagine. Were they her own?"

"I don't believe so. They defied gravity. That didn't seem to put off any of the boys though. They stared at those titties like they were the holy grail. I was ready to kill the woman. She got Warren so riled up that he pestered me the entire trip. No one was happier than I to be back on terra firma, away from his priapism and back to my horses."

The afternoon had melted away by the time we asked for the check. Though I made a gesture to grab for it, Lizbeth insisted on picking up the tab. Afterward, we walked out onto the pier, the dense smell of sea salt filling our nostrils, a mild ocean breeze tugging at our hair.

"What are you going to do next, Pauline? About your friend's mystery origins, I mean."

"I'm not sure. I'm fresh out of ideas. It doesn't appear Ethan was related to any of the Kehoes who still live in the Boston area."

"What about his mother's maiden name? Perhaps she has relations here."

I berated myself for my lack of cleverness as of late. In England, Terrance had led me around by the nose. Now it was Lizbeth, whom I hadn't given credit for having the genius to do much of anything other than look good and ride horses, coming to my aid. I told her that her idea merited thought, and we kissed cheeks and swore eternal friendship before parting ways.

Then I was back to the hotel and the telephone, and she was off to her beloved horses.

14

Getting Warmer

The Boston phone book listed even more McMahons than Kehoes. I found myself gaining appreciation for phone solicitors as I repeated my story until I thought I would take leave of my senses. But I was to learn that tenacity does indeed pay off. At my thirty-third McMahon a woman named Emily told me that she had indeed known Moira Kehoe, wife of Patrick, mother of Daniel. In an accent that combined the dropped *r*'s of Boston with soft lilt of an Irish brogue, she told me Moira had been a cousin of her husband—"may he rest in peace." When I asked the widow McMahon if I might come over and speak with her, she assured me that a visitor would be most welcome. She also suggested that some refreshment might be in order, and could I pick up some beer along the way as she hadn't been to the store recently. The price of a six-pack was a small sum to pay considering what I had spent in my quest thus far, and so I asked how to get to her house and which brand of beer she preferred.

✳   ✳   ✳

Emily McMahon lived in a bungalow in the stolidly working-class section of Brookline, a virtual garden of Eden compared to the last Boston neighborhood I visited. Each house on the immaculate block was nearly identical to its neighbor, with the exception of different shades of paint or more imaginative lawn ornaments. I headed up the walk to the tidy brick residence, where five lonely tulips sprouted in a small patch of garden beneath the picture window, carrying a six-pack of Old City beer. It had cost me all of two dollars and sixty-eight cents, increasing my fondness for Emily McMahon and lessening my suspicions that the old gal might be a hustler.

My ring of the doorbell was answered promptly, telling me that either my arrival or that of the six-pack had been eagerly anticipated. The woman who stood before me was quite unlike the one I had pictured in my mind's eye. Instead of a bloated dipsomaniac in stretch pants, she was a tiny bit of a thing with thinning silver hair, stooped at the shoulders from osteoporosis. Her print dress was faded and her blue cardigan threadbare at the elbows, but her withered cheeks glowed with a fresh dab of powdered rouge applied for the benefit of her visitor, I'm sure. Small eyes of an indistinguishable color peeked at me from behind a pair of heavy eyeglasses that gave her an owl-like appearance.

"Mrs. McMahon—" Before I could introduce myself she had the screen door open and was waving me over the threshold with surprising energy.

"It's Emily, *deah*. Come in, come in." She quickly relieved me of the six-pack. "Didn't have any trouble finding the place, did you now?"

"Your directions were excellent," I replied. I glanced around the small living room. The shopworn sofa and chairs were dressed with lace doilies and a plastic flower arrangement adorned the coffee table. At the far end of the room, an inexpensive bookshelf displayed photos and trinkets, and a crucifix hung over the light switch at the base of the stairs. Though the room was spotless, the smell of cooking lent it a slightly grimy feel. Emily invited me to take a seat on the sofa while she went into the kitchen. I did so, settling into a groove I suspected dated back to Mr. McMahon.

She returned with some saltine crackers on a china plate and two cut glass tumblers that I could only assume were reserved for special occasions. Apologizing for not having more to offer, she explained again that she hadn't been to the store lately. Despite her knobby, arthritic-looking joints, she effortlessly opened two cans of the Old City and placed one on the coffee table in front of me along with one of the tumblers. I poured some of the amber liquid into my glass. It had an offensive smell not unlike that of a cheap cigar.

Mrs. McMahon filled her own glass and drank from it with a relish that belied her size and age.

"Ah, that's good now, isn't it?" she said. "Sometimes nothing's finah in the world than a good cold *beah*."

I nodded in agreement and forced a smile. We chatted politely for a while about the spring weather and Boston politics before my hostess actually brought up the reason for my visit.

"So you're looking for Moira Kehoe, *ah* ya?"

"Yes. A man died in Chicago who may or may not have been her son. I'm hoping she can identify him, if she's still alive."

"And if you don't mind my askin', what's your *intahrest* in it, *deah*?"

"He was my friend."

"There wouldn't be any money involved, would there?" She asked the question in a manner that told me she was suspicious of me.

"I'm afraid there isn't even enough to cover his funeral expenses."

"Aw, that's a shame." She fell silent and put a knobby finger to her lip as if she was sorting things out in her mind. I remained quiet and watched her. Then, as if she had finally justified what she was about to say, she began telling me about Daniel Kehoe's mother. "Well, just like I said on the phone, Moira was my late husband's first cousin. As I recall it, she came over from Ireland after her *mothah* died, that would be my Kevin's *mothah's sistah*. She was a beautiful young thing with thick black *heyah* and black eyes and skin like . . . oh . . . like creamery *buttah*.

"Kevin and me, we were already married at the time and out on our own, I think we'd already had Margaret Mary as a matter of fact, but anyhow, Moira stayed in Kevin's family house along with Kevin's folks and his six *brothahs* and *sistahs*. They let her sleep on the couch in the living room. Then she found a job. And it was a good one. A live-in situation up at the Baincock Mansion in the fancy section of town. Everybody agreed it was a great opportunity for a young girl like her, just off the boat and all, to work for such rich people, living in their home, eating their food. She even had a private room in the servants' *quartahs*. To a *gull* like Moira that was more luxury than she'd ever seen in her life. She probably never had a bed to herself in Ireland much less a room. Her people were dirt *poah*, and everybody had to *shayah*.

"But the shame of it all, not a few months into the job she went and got herself in the family way," Emily said, still appalled at the thought after so many years. "*Poah* girl managed to hide it for a while, but when it was discovered, she was thrown off the job. So was the *fathah*, one of the *gardenahs* at the place by-the-by. Patrick Kehoe—another one straight off the boat. He did right by her though. He married her, though Lord knows why they hadn't gotten married before. Probably could have saved them both their positions."

"And did they remain in Boston?" I asked.

"I'm getting there," she said, letting me know in no uncertain terms that this was her story. She took a drink from the cut glass tumbler and followed it with a mild, closed-mouth belch. "Excuse me, *deah*. Constitution isn't what it used to be. Anyhow, Moira and Patrick were *poah* as anything, *neithah* one working and Moira going to have a baby and all. I tell you, though, that Patrick was quite a *scrappah* with a *tempah* to match his red *hayah*. He fought in neighborhood bouts to make a few cents until he could find work. Still hadn't found work when the baby came along, so Moira had to give birth at Mercy, the indigents' hospital.

"Little Daniel was a tiny sickly thing from the very first, but, oh, that Moira loved him something fierce. None of us thought he'd make it, though. He was always coming up sick and needin' *doctahs* they couldn't afford. She would sit up all night with that baby, caring for him. But he was always needing medical care, and it got so they were constantly hitting up family for money.

"Then Patrick found a job with the T and things were all right for a while. They could get medicine for Danny and all. But Patrick had that terrible *tempah* and got himself into a fight with his *supervisah* and was fired. Now just about that time Daniel got the rheumatoid. This time we thought he was really going to die. But when Moira came to Kevin's family for money again, they turned her down. They'd never gotten over the scandal of her pregnancy, after being so good to her and all, and well, there was always some whispering over *whethah* or not Patrick was really the *fathah*. And Kevin's family wasn't exactly rolling in money themselves. They had expenses of their own, and didn't want to support a man who couldn't hold down a job because of his *tempah*.

"Danny survived, but just barely, and Patrick, not taking too kindly to people second guessing his relationship with the baby, packed 'em all up and moved away. That was the last we *evah* heard of them. I haven't seen hide nor *heyah* of Moira since the day they left and that was well *ovah* fifty years ago. They were both angry at the way they had been treated, how nobody came to their help. I guess that was their way of letting everybody know it."

"Do you know where they moved to?" I asked nearly frantic, afraid I might have reached another dead end.

"Well, before they left, Moira did tell Kevin's *sistah* Maureen that Patrick had heard of work in *Rochestah*, New York, with the transit authority there. I'd imagine that's where they went though I couldn't say for *shuh*."

Emily finished her last sip of beer, savoring it fully. She looked at my still-full glass. "You don't like *beah*?" she asked incredulously.

Fearful of harming the sacred cow, I fibbed. "I do, but I'm afraid I have a bit of a sour stomach today and can't drink much. My apologies if it seems ungracious."

"You aren't going to touch that?"

"I'm afraid not."

"Do you mind?" She gestured toward my glass and I handed it to her. She gave the rim a quick swipe with the sleeve of her cardigan, and took a healthy drink.

"And no one heard from the Kehoe family after that?" I asked, hoping to put the subject back on track.

"Nope, no one. To tell the truth, I used to think about them from time to time, especially with the little boy Daniel, so sickly and all. It wouldn't have surprised me to *heah* he *nevah* made it to adulthood."

I recalled how horribly discolored Ethan's teeth were and wondered if that could have been a result of rheumatoid fever as a child. I took out my Valentine's Day photo of Ethan and showed it to Mrs. McMahon.

"If he did make it to adulthood, could this possibly be him?"

She took it in her hand and stared at it long and hard through the thick glasses before looking back at me with a furrowed brow. "I couldn't tell you for certain. You know he was just a baby and all. Maybe I see a little of Moira around the eyes. Moira had dark piecing eyes. But she was so terribly pretty, and this man . . . seems he was hiding behind the door when the good Lord was handin' out looks." She returned the photo to me. "I'm sorry I can't be of more help to you, *deah*."

My frustration mounted as I put the picture back in my purse. My visit with Emily McMahon had been another dead end after all. Yes, she had verified that Daniel Kehoe had been born to Moira McMahon

and Patrick Kehoe, but I already knew that. A copy of an old birth certificate told me that. And she had told me the story of his entry into
this world. But it still brought me no further in knowing if he was the
man who had been my friend.

With the purpose of my visit over, I thanked the elderly woman
and stood to go. She took my arm in a surprisingly firm grip and
walked me the few steps across the living room. When we reached the
door, she continued to hold on as if she were reluctant to let me go.

"This has been such a treat," she said with a full-dentured smile.
"Thank you for the *beah*. My prescriptions run me so much, there
nevah seems to be anything left over for luxuries."

"You're most welcome, Emily," I replied, mortified that a three-
dollar six-pack was outside her budget *and* that she considered it a luxury. And in another way I found myself deeply moved how sometimes
the simplest things could bring joy. "I'll let you know what I learn."

Her grip remained firm. I was trying to politely extricate myself
from her grasp without upsetting her when she said something that
stopped me in my tracks. "You know, you're not the first person to
come around asking *aftah* Danny Kehoe."

"I'm not?"

"No." Her eyes grew wider beneath the glasses as she stared into
mine. "It was a couple of years ago. There were three men who came
in the space of a month asking after Danny just like you are now.
They wanted to know if I knew where he was or leastwise, where they
might find the family. The first man who came was a real gentleman.
He had a disfigurement though, the *poah* fellow. Couldn't seem to control his right arm. I liked him right from the start. Brought me two
six-packs. Said Daniel had won a prize. Something of value, he said. I
told him what I told you, that all I knew was the family might've gone
to Rochester.

"Then two more men came about three weeks later. Young know-
it-all kinds. Real fast talkers, if you know what I mean. They said they

were from the government, but I didn't believe them. Their clothes were too nice. I didn't tell them a thing, not even about Rochester."

"Have you heard from any of them since?" I asked.

"Not a peep."

"That's curious, isn't it?" I said.

I left Emily McMahon waving at me from her doorway with four cans of beer in her refrigerator for company that night. As for me, the entire drive back was spent wondering who those men were and where they fit in the picture. If they had succeeded in their search for Daniel Kehoe maybe they'd have some answers for me.

Back at the hotel, I contemplated my next step. If I were to continue on my odyssey, the obvious thing would be to go to Rochester. But I must confess, aside from knowing that Rochester was in upstate New York, I had no idea where it was in relation to Boston. I called down to the concierge and requested a map of New York State. It arrived at my room so promptly, I tipped the young woman who brought it up a dollar.

Spreading the map out on the desk, I quickly located Rochester near Lake Ontario, hundreds of miles from Boston. That would mean a five- or six-hour drive in a rental car. Or another plane flight. And when I got to Rochester, what then? Another hotel room and another phone book? Ethan had never even mentioned Rochester in passing. I simply couldn't see it as his home.

My enthusiasm was waning. I had already invested far too much of my time and limited funds in this inane quest, and to what end? Was it to appease my ego or my curiosity? In reality, did it make a difference who Ethan really was or how he would be remembered? To hell with what others thought of him or me, I decided. Ethan had been a good friend to me and I to him and that was that. I was going home and after the body was released, I was going pay whatever it cost to bury him and be finished with it.

I was tired of traveling. I was tired of phone books. And most of all, I was tired of old people.

My mind made up to return to Chicago on the morrow, I taxied to the historical North End of Boston to have some dinner. After meandering down the tight winding streets, I found the charming restaurant where Henry and I had dined on that last trip. It was near the Old North Church where Grandmother claimed one of her ancestors had lit the crucial lantern that warned the townspeople of the approaching British. I enjoyed my solitary meal there, lobster again—what else in Boston—and washed it down with a half bottle of Puligny-Montrachet. Having come to terms with my decision to give up, I returned to the hotel and was packing my things when the phone rang. I picked it up and was irritated upon hearing the sound of Sean's voice.

"Are you sorry that I'm not there to turn down the bed?" he asked.

"Where are you?" I demanded somewhat brusquely. An eerie sense had come over me that he had followed me to Boston and was down in the lobby.

"I'm at home. Chill, Pauline. Why are you jumping down my fucking throat?"

"I'm sorry," I said, less than honestly. "I've had a devil of a trip."

"Have you learned anything about Ethan?"

"Nothing of any value," I replied. Then my own words caused me stop. I flashed back to Emily McMahon telling me about her visitors. One of them told her Daniel had won a prize. Something of value. If this were true, and Ethan was Daniel, perhaps there was something of value to be retrieved—maybe even enough to bury him. Suddenly Chicago was not my destination in the morning after all.

"So are you going to stop banging your head against the wall and come home?" he asked.

"No. I'm afraid I'm going to bang it even harder. Tomorrow, I go to Rochester."

My cat was going to hate me for this.

✳   ✳   ✳

At the check-out counter the next morning, I nearly had a heart attack upon seeing the telephone charges incurred during my stay. They far and away exceeded the cost of the room and room service combined. The first credit card I tried to pay with was declined, so I used one of my other bloated cards and drove back to Logan where I returned the rental car.

Soon after charging yet another airline ticket, I was on a commuter to Rochester.

15
The Crotch

I'll say it straight out, Rochester is an industrial and gritty city. If there are beautiful sections they are outlying, at least that's where the people with all the money live, and from what I understand there is quite a bit of it around because of local industry. But the people with the money are smart and spend as little time in Rochester proper as possible—my goal the moment I arrived there. Not only did I find it depressing, it was one of the rare cities where I didn't have a single connection.

Conscious of my mounting travel expenses, I took the complimentary airport shuttle to the downtown Hyatt. Sharing the van with me were three girls and a young man. The girls were members of a wedding party who couldn't stop talking about the single status of the groom's best man. The young man had jet black hair slicked back off his face like patent leather and wore a business suit. Our driver was a rotund, rather jovial man wearing a name tag that read ZEKE.

On the drive into downtown Rochester, Zeke enlightened us with enthralling tidbits about the city. We learned that the population was approximately a quarter of a million people, that it was New York's third-largest city, and that it had earned the nickname "The Crotch," because it straddled the Genessee River all the way to Lake Ontario.

By the time we crossed the slow-moving waters of the sulky river, I had basically tuned him out until he dropped a nugget that caused me to sit up and listen. He was talking about George Eastman and the little company he had started there, reminding us that Eastman Kodak's headquarters remained in Rochester. I recalled Ethan's claim that one of the Eastmans was his godfather, the same claim Connie Chan refuted in her article.

An indescribable otherworldly sensation crawled up my spine. Did that claim have its origins in this city?

I checked in, this time settling for a standard double, and went directly to my room, not bothering to unpack. I had no peers to visit, and besides, there was no way I intended on spending more than one night in anyplace nicknamed "The Crotch." Plopping down on the bed with the phone book, I resumed my mission by turning to *K* for Kehoe. Thankfully, from both a patience and pocketbook standpoint, there were only a few listed. In the space of a half hour I had exhausted the entire supply and none of them had ever known a Patrick, Moira, or Daniel who had fled there from Boston.

What now, Pauline, what now? I asked myself, falling back on the bed in frustration. I stretched my arms out over my head to relieve my tension. The motion must have brought a needed blood surge to my brain, because I came up with an idea. Emily McMahon suggested Patrick found work with the Rochester Transit Authority. Perhaps they might be able to tell me something about him. I called down to the concierge who told me the transit authority offices were within walking distance of the hotel.

Happy to actually walk someplace for a change even if it was in Rochester, I was soon on my way. Being tall, weight has never been an issue for me, but I've always felt walking is the best way to keep the legs toned and shapely, and I hadn't really walked since London. Reaching the transit offices a brisk ten minutes later, the unprepossessing brick structure looked exactly as a public-works building should—budget-conscious. Entering through the revolving glass doors, no doubt meant to protect against Lake Ontario's meteorological whims, I emerged into an empty lobby. A directory alongside the elevators told me the personnel office was located on the third floor.

A young blond woman sat behind the chest-high counter. She was bouncy and friendly and most of all helpful, a welcome departure from one's usual civil servant. I told her—quite honestly—that I was seeking the family of a deceased friend. I then added—somewhat less honestly—that I knew his father had worked for the transportation authority at one time. Her beaming smile never left her face the entire time.

"So I wondered if he's still collecting a pension or the like, so I might locate him," I explained.

"I'm really not supposed to give out personal information," she said with a mildly tortured look on her face. She was sizing me up, not quite sure what to make of me. It could have been my multicolored Missoni suit, something I'm sure was rarely seen in the building if not Rochester itself. Resting my Prada bag on the counter (every woman in the country had to recognize that label), I gave her a most imperious smile. I don't know if it was the smile or the designer nylon that swayed her, but a moment later she was bowing her blond curls over her computer keyboard and tapping out commands with her bright purple fingernails. I watched her wait for a response. A pause, and then more clicky-clicky of the keys. Another pause and her hands rested on the desk. With her eyes fixed on the screen, she nodded at it as if to let the machine know she understood.

"Have you found him?" My pulse accelerated in anticipation. Her next words slowed it back to a steady thump.

"Yes, here he is, but I'm afraid I don't have good news. He's listed as deceased. Died in nineteen eighty-nine. My records show his wife continued to collect his pension until she died in nineteen ninety-two. That's when the last check was sent out."

So I was in the right place, just way too late. I had found Danny Kehoe's parents, but unfortunately they were dead. Unwilling to accept defeat, I asked if she could give me the late Kehoe's former address. Once again the tortured look. She wanted so desperately to be helpful. Glancing up and down the corridor, she said in a hushed voice, "I'm not really supposed to do this, but seeing's how the party's dead, I don't see what harm it can do." She scribbled out the address on a piece of transit authority stationery and handed it to me.

"Seven fourteen Thorndale Street," I read aloud. "Could you tell me where this is?"

"Right here on the twenty-one bus route," she said, pointing to a spot on a large map mounted on the wall behind her. "It stops right outside this building."

"Is the neighborhood safe?" Though this new lead held promise, I wasn't quite ready to risk life and limb again.

"Oh, it's fine. It's a working-class area."

Of course it was.

I walked back out into the dreary Rochester day with the address still clutched in my hand. The time was two o'clock. If I caught the 21 bus as recommended, I could probably be in Daniel Kehoe's former neighborhood within a half hour. It had been years since I had ridden a bus, and that was in Paris. I wondered what the procedure was and if I had the proper change. I looked in my purse and found a dollar just as the bus was pulling up.

The fare turned out to be a dollar and a quarter, but while I explained to the bus driver that was all the change I had other than a twenty-dollar bill, a handsome young man came to the rescue and put a quarter in the till for me. I thanked him and turned to see a full bus of people staring at me, obviously in no humor to be delayed on their way home. There were no free seats, and no man rose to volunteer his, not even the one who had paid the quarter. I took hold of a hanging strap, and as the bus jerked back and forth with each stop along its route, I was grateful I didn't normally rely upon public transportation.

As to be expected, the houses in the Kehoe family neighborhood shared the same uniformity that the houses in Emily McMahon's neighborhood did. They were small and well-kept with the exception of one here and there in need of a coat of paint. Thorndale Street was a couple of blocks from the bus stop and after a couple of misses, I located the house where Moira received Patrick's last pension check. The sound of a television could be heard through the front door. I rang the bell and waited. No one answered. I rang again. The same. And again. And again.

Knowing someone was inside, and not about to be put off at this juncture, I struggled through the bushes in front of the house and peered in the picture window. A rather large man sat in front of the television smoking a cigarette. He was wearing a baseball cap and the sort of T-shirt one sees on Italian immigrants in movies. On a TV tray beside him were any number of beer cans, a couple of them over-turned. In the dimness of the room, the images on the television screen changed the light on his face.

I banged on the glass. He turned abruptly as if a whip had just been cracked in his face and peered at the window. I smiled my most becoming smile and pointed at the front door. He got out of his chair and I hurried from the bushes to meet him. A moment later the door swung open with a vengeance. Through the screen, I could see his shirt was soiled and his beard several days old.

Preparing to introduce myself and explain my purpose, he pre-empted me with a loud and foul, "What the fuck do you think you're doing?"

"Well, I'm Pauline Cook and I'm looking for Daniel Kehoe or any-one who might know where he is," I stammered, his verbal assault having taken me by surprise.

"Get the fuck out of here or I'll call the police," he shouted.

"I beg your pardon," I said, regaining my composure. Unafraid to go up against this cretin, I was about to reiterate my reason for being there, when I realized he was closing the door. "Wait, wait a minute," I called desperately. I was there. I needed an answer. "Are you Daniel Kehoe?"

He stopped and glared at me with red eyes. "Never heard of the fucker," he said and he slammed the door in my face.

The good news is I had a seat on the bus back into the city. The bad news is I had to miss the first bus that came along as the driver refused to break a twenty-dollar bill for me. After a cup of bad coffee at a local café in order to get change, I caught the next bus. During the ride, I decided that my search for Daniel Kehoe had finally come to a close. There was no place left to look. I had searched every avenue and had reached an impasse. The entire thing had been a complete waste of time, energy, and resources—unless one counted meeting Terrance Sullivan as worthwhile. That remained to be seen. Sean had been right when he said I was banging my head against the wall. It was time to stop the banging.

Completely disheartened as I disembarked the bus three blocks from my hotel, I opted to do the only thing that could cheer me up. I went shopping.

Two hours later, I walked back into the Hyatt lobby weighed down with shopping bags. They were filled with clothes I had no need for, didn't really like, and absolutely couldn't afford. Though Rochester was hardly Fifth Avenue or Rue Montaigne, I had somehow managed to make a substantial contribution to the local economy. Now, I needed a drink. Fearing if I went up to my room to unload my purchases I might not be able to summon the energy to come back down, I toted them with me into the lobby bar. I was in no mood to face four walls alone.

Taking a corner table with a clear view of the mirrored bar, I dropped the bags onto the floor and fell into a garishly upholstered chair. A plastic card in a plastic holder listed the drink specials of the day. Though a concoction called Sex on the Beach piqued my interest, I settled on a more pedestrian glass of white wine, asking the mini-skirted young waitress to make it a white Burgundy if possible. She went away looking perplexed.

The bar was half-filled, the girls from the airport shuttle sitting with a large group of young people I determined to be other members of the wedding party. Their chatter was offensively loud, fueled by Sexes on the Beach no doubt. My gaze drifted to a table at the opposite end of the room where the young man with the patent leather hair sat drinking alone. He caught my eye, and I gave him the polite smile of a fellow traveler. I immediately regretted the gesture as he picked up his drink and came over to join me.

"You look as though you could use a little company," he said.

Finding him rather bold, I was ready to say *not at all* when I stopped myself. He had a certain vulnerability about him, a je ne sais quoi that reminded me of a boy trying desperately to be a man. I stared into his narrow blue eyes and could see they were tired. He too was a stranger in a strange town. I didn't see any harm in the selfless act of permitting him to join me for a drink. That aside, having someone to talk to didn't seem such a bad idea.

"While I am perfectly content alone, I am guessing you would like some company. You are welcome to sit if you so desire."

He accepted my invitation and took the garishly upholstered chair opposite me.

"I'm Todd Matthews," he said, holding out his hand.

"Pauline Cook," I replied, clasping it briefly. The way he stared at me, I couldn't help but wonder if he was trying to determine my age.

I shifted in my chair and crossed my legs in a deliberate manner. His eyes followed my action, coming to rest on the cache of shopping bags at my feet.

"Shop 'til you drop?" he asked, raising his glossy black brows.

"Something like that," I granted him. "I've had a rather frustrating day. It helps to relieve my tension."

The waitress brought my wine and he motioned to his almost empty drink, indicating that he would like another one. "I know what you mean by needing to relieve tension," he said draining the remains of his ice-filled glass, a clear liquid I assumed to be vodka. "This relieves mine. Being on the road like this is a real drag. Lots of hotels, lots of lonely nights. Even though it may look pretty glamorous, when you get right down to it, the life of a road warrior can be a grind."

His use of the word "glamorous" caused me to wonder about his frame of reference. Glamorous was landing at Sardy Field in Aspen aboard a G5, motoring into Portofino aboard a 150-foot Hatteras, ordering the '61 Latour at Le Grand Vefour in Paris. Nowhere in that picture did I find a hotel bar in Rochester. Then again, perhaps my frame of reference was quite different from his.

"What do you do for a living, Mr. Matthews?" I inquired.

"I'm a sales rep for Tryton Athletic. Have the entire Northeast territory. It keeps me jumping."

"You're still on the road on a Friday night?"

"Trade show this weekend."

I sipped my wine. It was a dreadful domestic Chardonnay. I studied my fellow nomad. The face that most likely was clean-shaven that morning showed a distinct shadow beyond five o'clock. Aside from that everything about him was youthful. Twenty-five, maybe twenty-six. Not a minute older.

"Are you married?"

He shook his head no.

"I would venture you have a girlfriend."

"Had one. She got tired of my traveling so much and found someone closer to home. I haven't really had time to start a relationship ever since. That was about a year ago." There was a momentary silence, and then he asked, "What brings you to Rochester? The shopping?"

Hardly, I thought to myself, still trying to reconcile half of the purchases I'd made. "No, I came in search of a friend."

"And did you find him?"

"How did you know it was a he?"

"Lucky guess. So did you find him?" he repeated.

"Well, I suppose I should have phrased my statement differently. I didn't actually come in search of him, I know *where* he is. I'm just not quite sure *who* he is." And as a lonely traveler in a faraway bar, I decided to share my tale of woe. I told him of my fruitless search for Ethan's true identity, how I thought I had located Daniel Kehoe's parents but they had died, the horrid treatment I had received when I went to the family house, and how it was now left to me to bury him whoever he was. He listened raptly, and then began spewing forth suggestions on how to solve the riddle, most of them involving computers and the Internet. Though I appreciated Mr. Matthews's enthusiasm, the technological talk was causing my eyes to flutter. My long day was drawing to a close. I asked for the check. The waitress had charged me for my visitor's vodka, but I signed for it anyway and slipped it back into the faux leather folder.

"It's been quite nice speaking with you, Mr. Matthews. I wish you the best of luck in all your travels."

"Thanks. Nice talking to you too, Pauline. We road warriors have to stick together. Where you off to next?"

"This *road warrior* has had it. I return to Chicago first thing in the morning."

I was insulted when he didn't stand as I got up, and also found it presumptuous of him to call me by my first name when I had been addressing him by his surname all along. Then again, what does one expect in an era when men think nothing of dining in a fine restaurant wearing duck-billed caps and the general populace looks as if they have dressed from the community rag bag. At least he wore a suit. I forgave him his bad manners. His youthful face and guileless smile made it difficult to hold anything against him.

"I'll look you up if I ever get the Chicago territory," he said.

"Yes, do that," I replied. As I left the crowded bar, I noticed him ordering another drink. I hoped the waitress would have the presence of mind to put it on a new chit.

Once in my room I was overcome with exhaustion, both mental and physical. There was just too much weighing on my mind for any one person. The loss of Ethan, whoever he was, the disappointment of my encounter with Terrance Sullivan, the ever looming threat of financial ruin—the trilogy drained me, body and soul.

I kicked off my shoes and stretched out on the bed, too tired to undress. My eyes fluttered shut, and I felt myself slipping over the edge into a drug-like state when my ears pricked at a barely discernible sound inside my room. Coming back to consciousness, I leaned over the side of the bed and looked toward the doorway. A sheet of paper lay on the green and mauve patterned carpeting, just inside the door.

Despite my fatigue, my curiosity was piqued, so I rolled lazily out of bed to retrieve the paper. It was a piece of hotel stationery with a message scrawled on it.

Try his former neighbors

My heart pounded furiously as I tried to figure out the meaning of the message and who would have sent it. Then I remembered Mr. Todd Matthews's earnest desire to help me find out more about Ethan. He must have gotten my room number off the signed bar tab. I told myself to review my bar bill in the morning before checking out—just to make sure he hadn't enjoyed his next drink at my expense, too.

Then I thought about his suggestion and decided it wasn't such a bad idea.

Following Mr. Matthews's advice, I returned to the Kehoe family neighborhood first thing the next morning. The ride on the 21 was much quieter as it was a Saturday, so there were plenty of seats, and this time I brought correct change for both trips. I was now a pro on the Rochester bus system.

Back on Thorndale Street, I chose to ignore the residence where I had been so rudely treated the day before, and went directly to the house next door instead. A harried young woman with a frightening number of children clamoring around her legs answered the door. Unlike her neighbor, she was quite polite as she explained she had only lived in the neighborhood for a year and therefore knew nothing of a Kehoe family. But she pointed to the house across the street, one of those that needed that coat of paint.

"Try the Schmidt sisters," she said, picking up one of two crying children without breaking eye contact with me. "They've lived here since forever."

I crossed the street to the house with jagged ribbons of paint peeling from its facade and rang the bell. The living room curtain parted and a pale face peered out at me. Quicker than a memory the curtain fell back into place followed by a shrill voice from the other side of the closed door.

"Who's there?"

"Pauline Cook, Miss Schmidt," I explained through a windowless wall of oak. "Your neighbor sent me over."

"You mean Evangaline?" A second voice said something from behind the closed door to which the first voice responded even louder. "I said Evangaline sent someone over." The door opened a crack until a chain stopped it. A single cataract-covered eye stared from half a wrinkled face and half a spare chin. Another half face hovered behind it.

"What did Evangaline send you over for?" asked the Schmidt sister in front.

"She told me you might remember the Kehoe family."

"The Kehoes? You knew them? Why they've been gone for years," the front sister continued. The chain slipped away and the half faces became whole, though they held their ground on the other side of the screen door as if the thin mesh provided protection from the terrifying world outside. "What do you want to know about the Kehoes?"

"I'm trying to identify someone who has died, someone who might have been Daniel Kehoe. Did you know him?"

"Little Danny? Why sure we knew him. Small, homely thing, poor child. Terribly unhealthy. His mother was always looking after him for some ailment or another. Did I say he was homely? Never could figure out how such a beautiful looking couple like Moira and Patrick could have given birth to such an ugly child. Their daughter was pretty as could be."

"Daughter? You mean Daniel had a sister?"

"Sure he did, but she was much younger than him. Wasn't expected according to Moira. She said she thought she had a tumor. When she found out she was pregnant Danny was nearly grown up.

"We always felt so sorry for the little fellow. His father was terribly mean to him. He would cuss him out so fierce sometimes we could hear it all the way across the street. But with little Shannon he was different. He treated her like she was a little princess, always fussing over her and whatnot."

"Do you think you would be able to recognize Danny from a photograph?" I asked the elderly sisters, my adrenaline flowing thinking I might finally have some definitive answer. Their physical description of Danny was how I might have described Ethan.

"Can't," replied the sister in front. "Got the glaucoma so bad we can't even read the paper anymore. Can barely see the television."

I raised my eyebrows in appeal to the sister in back. She shook her head and her chin wobbled along with it. "Runs in the family."

"We're sure to be blind nearly anytime soon," said the first. "But we're preparing. We been practicing for years, learning all the tricks like putting your finger in your cup to find the water level."

"We've been preparing for years," the second parroted.

"Would you by any chance know where I might find Shannon Kehoe?"

"Well, she got married. Married an Italian. Magelli? Maginelli? Oh, what was it now, Esther? We went to the wedding."

"It was Maglieri, I'm sure of it. Anthony Maglieri. And I'm pretty sure they moved to Northview right afterward. At least that's where the thank-you note came from. We gave them a beautiful trivet and she wrote a lovely note. Don't know if she'd still be there now though. It was quite a few years ago."

I thanked the Schmidt sisters profusely and they closed the door against me and the demons of the outside world. A shudder passed up my spine as I thought of the cruelty life dispenses in one's declining years, especially when one was of limited means. I had seen it with Miriam Doney, Sarah Moore Campbell, Emily McMahon, and now the Schmidt sisters. Loneliness. State homes. Cheap six-packs of beer. Blithe acceptance of encroaching blindness.

I hoped I wasn't getting a glimpse of my own future.

16

The Discreet Charm of the Bourgeoisie

Shannon Maglieri did indeed live in Northview and was listed. When I contacted her and told her I might have news of her brother, there was a long silence before she said she would be happy to see me. I didn't mention that the news might be his death, since I couldn't be positive there was a relationship between my Ethan and her. If there was, then truth would out soon enough. Since no city buses serviced her suburb, I rented a car and drove to her home.

The Maglieri family lived in a subdivision called the Cotswolds on the Green, ostensibly the developer's attempt to lend an aristocratic air to imitation English manor homes built on postage stamp–sized lots. Though these houses couldn't compare to the Lake Forest house I had been forced to sell, the facades were reminiscent of it, causing me to pine for my former home and its five quiet acres. Though I loved the messy vitality and convenience of the city, there was something to be said about the peace found away from it. So many memories of Henry's and my life in Lake Forest still clung to me. Like summer breakfast on the terrace overlooking the rose gardens, listening to cardinals' mating calls, and smelling the dewey scent of damp grass. Or the cooling swims in the pool on still August nights while crickets sang their high-pitched songs. Or fireside cognacs in the winter watching snow settle gently on the massive fir trees outside the library window. These were things that had been taken from me, and I still missed them greatly.

Though the Maglieri house had a three-car garage, there were still two vehicles parked in the driveway, one a square black minivan, the other a red truck set upon such ridiculously gargantuan wheels I wondered how anyone other than a giant could possibly get into the cab. I parked behind it, my rental car so dwarfed by the monster vehicle, I seriously questioned if I was running the risk of it being run over should the owner of the truck decide to take his leave.

The walkway was lined with neatly trimmed boxwood bushes, and in front of the entry door two large terra cotta planters held fir trees I suspected would be replaced with flowers come summer. My ring was answered almost immediately by a handsome-looking woman a few years younger than I. Her thick shoulder-length hair was dyed shoe-polish black and her pale skin was enviably smooth with the exception of some character lines around the eyes and mouth. She wore a hideous blue exercise suit and smiled a wide but slightly apprehensive smile. There was something hauntingly familiar about her, though it took me some time to realize what it was. I was looking at Ethan's dark piercing eyes.

"I'm Shannon Maglieri," she said, welcoming me into her house with an extended hand.

"Pauline Cook." We shook. Her hand was cool and dry. A couple of teenage boys with shaved heads and pierced ears emerged from the back of the house and grunted quick hellos at their mother's insistence before disappearing upstairs. She led me into the living room off the entrance, a cavernous space dominated by a sectional sofa in a busy floral print and a black lacquered coffee table. Amateurish oil paintings of landscapes and still lifes ornamented the walls while crystal vases and figurines glowed from a black lacquer display case. Everything looked fresh and new and, one might say, very bourgeois. Quite very. No worn furniture or dusty heirlooms here. Across from the sectional was an enormous television that I suspected did not sit idle often.

"I don't know that I've ever seen a TV quite that large," I had to comment.

"If you think that's big, you oughta see the one in the basement. You know men and their sports. Being the only woman around here, I get out-voted all the time down there, so this is where I come for some peace and quiet. I don't know what I ever did to deserve three boys. Married my husband, I guess." She laughed a kind, sincere laugh that told me it was her joy in life to complain about her men.

I took a seat on the sectional and she sat down next to me, so close our knees nearly touched. "You said you had news about Danny?"

I felt the same twinge of guilt I had in the state home in Bury St. Edmunds, fearful of opening old wounds by digging up buried memories. But I didn't know how else to go about this. "I don't mean to upset you unnecessarily, but a man has died in Chicago who was a very good friend of mine. I knew him by the name of Ethan Campbell." I studied her face carefully to see if the name drew any reaction, but she didn't even blink. Her dark eyes remained fixed on me in anticipation of my next words. "In the aftermath of his death, several birth certificates were found in his apartment. One of them was for a Daniel Kehoe born to Moira and Patrick Kehoe. I'm here to see if my friend was the same person."

Her shoulders drooped and she shook her head sadly. "I haven't seen or heard from my brother in over thirty-five years. I was just a little girl when he left my parents' house."

"Do you think you would recognize a picture of him as an older man?" She shrugged. "I'm not sure, but I'd try."

I pulled out my well-traveled photo of Ethan at the Valentine's Day party. She took it and ran a red polished nail tenderly across his face as if she were actually touching it. She looked back at me and nodded. "This is my brother. That sad face could never change." Her eyes welled and she wiped back a tear with her finger. "How did he die?"

Having learned there was no gentle way to deliver disagreeable news, I was blunt. "I'm afraid he died of his own hand. He shot himself."

A small gasp escaped her mouth as she drew a short breath. Then she calmed herself and said, "I suppose I should be glad to know what became of him. We worried about him so much, Mama and me. He left home right after his twenty-first birthday, saying he was off to make his fortune. For the first few years, he wrote to us all the time. Sometimes, he'd even call. The last time we heard from him he was somewhere in Virginia. He said he was heading to Miami. Then we didn't hear anything else." She sighed a wistful sigh. "He always wanted to live in a warm climate."

"Well, he ended up somewhere warm for quite a while. He lived in Puerto Rico for twenty-five years."

"Puerto Rico." She sighed again and shook her head in memory. "Danny always wanted to live in exotic places, warm places. He was a real dreamer. He had what my mother called 'illusions of grandeur.' He read Fitzgerald's books about the rich like they were the bible. He read *The Great Gatsby* so many times he knew it by heart. And he spent every spare penny he had on travel magazines. He told my mom when he got rich he was going to buy a yacht and sail around the islands and he would come and get us to go with him."

"Well, you might be proud to know your brother went on to become a well-respected writer," I told her, thinking how Ethan's desire for a boat had never changed. "He published a couple of biographies and was working on a third one when he died. In fact, it really seemed that he was enjoying more success than he ever had in his life. That's why it's so baffling that he did what he did."

"He wasn't ever on a talk show or anything like that, was he?" she asked. "I always see writers on *Oprah*."

"No, I'm afraid his writing wasn't quite that popular."

Yet another sigh. "You know two years ago, someone came around looking for Danny. Said he had some very good news for him, but wouldn't tell me anything else. He was a very mysterious deformed man. I guess nowadays you'd say he had a disability. Anyhow, all I could tell him was I hadn't seen or heard from my brother in years and had no idea where he was. He left me his business card in case I ever did hear from Danny. Guess I won't need it now."

"May I see the card?" My thoughts careened back to Emily McMahon and the men who had visited her in the same time frame, also asking about Daniel Kehoe. She had said one of them had a deformity. Shannon left the room and returned a few minutes later. The speed with which she had unearthed the card told me that she kept it someplace convenient, that her brother must have been on her mind with some frequency all these years.

"You can keep it if you want. I don't have any use for it anymore," she said, handing it over to me. I read the raised type. HOLSTEIN INVESTIGATIONS—SPECIALTY—MISSING PERSONS. There was a Boston address and phone number. I zipped the card into the inside pocket of my purse.

"I know this sounds terrible, but did Danny leave money or anything?" she asked.

"Not even enough to bury himself, I'm afraid." I did not mention my prominent place in his useless will, thinking it might hurt her feelings that he made no mention of her. "In fact, I want to ask you if you'd like to see to the disposition of his remains."

"You mean, he hasn't been buried yet?" She looked shocked.

"No. The body has been under the jurisdiction of the state until we could figure out who he really was. Now that we know, it can be released—to you if you want him."

Her tone changed to a manner that I found none too encouraging. "I don't want to sound cold, but I don't feel any obligation to bury him. With three boys we're about as stretched as you can get here. Mortgage, car payments, credit card payments, tuition, you know how it is. We'll have two in college next year. Danny walked out of my and my mother's life a long time ago. In fact, sometimes I blame him for her death. She never got over the loss of him. So I can't exactly warm to him coming back into my life when he's dead. In fact, if not for you, I bet I never would have even known he died." Shannon Maglieri twisted her wedding band around her finger and looked out her picture window onto the street. "Let the state bury him."

"I see." I sensed there was something more she wanted to tell me, but she remained silent so I got up to leave. "Thank you for at least clearing up the mystery of who he really was," I said.

I walked behind the red truck and got into the rental, mired in the thought that although I finally knew who Ethan was, I was now saddled with his funeral for sure. I started pulling out of the driveway when I heard her calling out. I stopped and she came running up to the car. There were tears in her eyes.

"He was only my half-brother," she said. "I never knew it when we were young. I never knew why my father was so cruel to him until my mother was on her deathbed. That's when she told me that Danny wasn't my father's son. She wanted me to know so I could tell Danny if I ever saw him again. She wanted me to tell him she was sorry for the way my father had treated him and sorry she didn't stick up for him. She said at the time that was the only way. Those were her words."

Oh, Ethan, I thought. Do the surprises never end?

"So do you know who his real father was?" I asked.

"No, Mom never told me."

I drove away with shaking legs as it dawned on me the who part of Ethan's mystery was finally solved. My deceased friend was a bastard, born in a Boston indigent hospital and raised in working-class Rochester. There had never been a christening at St. Patrick's Cathedral, and his mother had come no closer to New York's café society than Ethel Rosenberg. At the time, I thought that was the extent of his deceit and that I would never know why he had chosen to pass himself off as an Englishman who had disappeared years before. I had to assume he was so ashamed of his humble origins that he wanted to escape them. That his father's cruelty had destroyed his psyche beyond repair.

But the bigger questions hovered untouched, the ones I had been avoiding since the start of this odyssey: the where, when and, more curiously, how he had become Ethan Campbell.

But those were questions that would have to wait and perhaps might never be answered. For now it was time to put Ethan Campbell . . . a.k.a. Daniel Kehoe . . . to rest.

17

Unrequited Lust

I caught the first flight out of Rochester Sunday morning and was back in Chicago before noon. I paid Jeffrey a very dear ten dollars for watching Fleur, and headed up to my apartment to reunite with my pet, who was angrier than ever. In fact she was so irritated with me that she fled into the recesses of my bedroom the moment I walked in the door. I knew that it was all attitude on her part, that she had been perfectly fine while I was gone. Cats are so admirably independent. Human beings would be well served to behave more like our feline friends.

It felt sublime to be chez moi again after my travels—that is until I checked my mail. Bills and late payment notices abounded, and I put them in the drawer with the others and the special assessment announcement. Then I pushed them far into the back. My answering machine told me I had twenty-two messages that I decided to ignore for the time being. There was more than enough on my mind, premier being Ethan's funeral. Doing it properly would be a burdensome expense, but I didn't see any other way. *Tout le monde* would be watching to see how it was handled. I couldn't very well let him pass to the other world without someone saying a few words in remembrance of him.

I called Detective Velez and let him know that Shannon Maglieri had positively identified Ethan as her brother, Daniel Kehoe. He said he would contact Mrs. Maglieri and send her an autopsy photo for verification. In the meantime, though, he was still waiting for the FBI fingerprint check to come through and couldn't release the body until it did. Though he felt certain it would be any day now. I sighed at the temporary reprieve and went into my room to unpack.

After putting my clothes away, I was trying to coax Fleur out from under the bed when the phone rang. I thought about letting the machine get it, but since there were already twenty-two messages waiting to be listened to, I decided not to add one more. And was glad for my decision.

"Is that you, Pauline?" My heart lurched at the sound of the Irish accent. "Finally. I was beginning to think you didn't really live there at all, just spent your time gallivanting 'round the world. I've been calling for days."

"Hello, Terrance," I said, doing my best to sound casual, hoping he couldn't detect the tremor in my voice. "Actually, I've just walked in the door after a tour of the Northeast. I haven't even gotten to my messages yet."

"Doesn't matter. I didn't leave one. Never do. Hate talking into machines. Anyways, I'm in New York and I thought we might get together, you and I, and finish that business we started in England."

The trembling in my voice migrated south to my knees, forcing me to sit on the bed. A week ago he had left me in the lurch. Now he turns up halfway around the world and wants to see me. I was flattered to the soles of my Charles Jourdan pumps.

"Unfinished business?" I purred, unconsciously tilting my head the way Fleur does when seeking a caress. An image of the heated hallway scene at the Angel Hotel popped into my head as I speculated on how that business might end.

"Yes, unfinished business. Our missing Mr. Campbell. I simply haven't been able to get his old mum out of my mind. I thought if you were game we could meet in South Carolina tomorrow and nose about a bit, see if we can solve the mystery of what happened to him."

The hissing sound in my ears was my ego deflating. "That mystery doesn't concern me anymore. I learned that my friend was born Daniel Kehoe in Rochester, New York. Now I'm waiting to bury him. So that makes this an inconvenient time to go nosing around South Carolina."

"But I've only got a couple of days before I have to be back in Ireland. Pardon my insensitivity, but hasn't your mate Ethan been on ice for a while already? What harm could it be to wait a few more days?"

"You must be kidding."

"I'm not. Come down to South Carolina and help me look for the Englishman."

"This is a folly," I said. "What could you possibly expect to find in South Carolina after all this time?"

"Oh, ye of little faith. How can you know until we get down there? He's probably bought himself a plantation and is sittin' around the day long drinking mint juleps. Probably just forgot about his old mum. We could jog his memory. Don't you want to make an old woman happy."

"And what if we learn the worst, that her son died down there?"

His voice turned serious. "Then we can at least give her some peace of mind. C'mon, Pauline. Be a sport and join me. I'm going either way, and it would be a much better adventure with your lovely self at my side."

I thought about it, not too long and not too hard. Within moments my mind was made up, and I was going to be adding yet another airfare to my credit card balances. Even if the fingerprint check came through tomorrow, the funeral could wait a few more days. After all, Terrance was living and breathing. Ethan was not.

"All right then, I'll join you," I said.

"Wonderful. Meet me tomorrow evening in Charleston. I'll be reserving two rooms at the John Rutledge House Inn. It's small and, as I understand it, quite charming. I wonder how it will compare to the Angel. I do hope the mattresses are just as lumpy."

"I know the inn and you are correct; it is quite charming, as is Charleston. I'll see you tomorrow then." I hung up and told myself not to get too excited.

I was beginning to feel as if I lived either on a plane or in the airport. After enduring two plane changes in order to get a reasonable fare, I began to seriously wonder if I was losing my sanity, still gallivanting about to some unknown end. I finally landed in Charleston at three o'clock and went directly to the hotel. As promised, a reservation had been made in my name. I went up to my room, charmingly decorated in vintage Southern with a large brass bed and a homey looking quilt. Terrance had not yet arrived, and since it was a glorious day, I decided to take a walk to ease my jittery nerves.

Charleston is one of the very most charming outposts in the country, and being there put me in a remarkably upbeat frame of mind. I strolled through the historic district, abundant with springtime flowers: tulips, daffodils, dogwood, peppermint, peach. Lavender wisteria spilled from the front porches, or piazzas as the Charlestonians prefer to call them, of Italianate brick houses dating back to the colonial days. There was a certain civility in the air, and things moved at a leisurely pace I've yet to find anywhere up north, even in the small towns of New England.

I was grateful to see the city had recovered from the devastation of Hurricane Hugo. My last visit had been shortly after the storm, and there had been so much destruction it felt like a war zone. Now, with the tarp roofs gone and the birds chirping instead of saws buzzing, it was the Charleston I knew and loved again.

I contemplated calling one of my friends in town, yet another Radcliffe schoolmate, Victoria Kendall Kovitz. Victoria was both a DAR and a daughter of the Confederacy, born and bred in Charleston. She had horrified her family and the local aristocracy twenty years ago by marrying a football player who was now the coach of a high school football team. Not only was he "from away," the term Charlestonians apply to anyone who is not of their ilk, but he had no pedigree to speak of and one of the thickest necks anyone had ever seen anyplace. Between football seasons, they lived on her parents' former plantation, where she entertained frequently in order to see the right people. But because of Gus's coarse style and lack of manners, they were seldom invited to the important doings in town—despite Victoria being a native. Charlestonians don't take kindly to people *from away* and a person *from away* with bad manners has practically no status at all.

I decided against calling Victoria, but not because I wasn't fond of Gus. I actually found him amusing in a crass sort of way. No, the reason I didn't call my friend was because I wanted to spend this time with Terrance all by myself. Had she known I was in town she would have insisted on seeing me.

When I got back to the hotel, Terrance still hadn't arrived, so I took a long cool bath to cool me down in more ways than one. I did not get dressed as I had brought a cream-colored linen dress and didn't want to be a mass of wrinkles when I saw him. I realized then I had never asked him what time he planned to arrive. When six o'clock came and I hadn't heard from him I called the desk. They informed me he still hadn't checked in. Trying not to be too anxious, I lay on the bed in my slip reading, or rather trying to read, since concentration was nearly impossible. Finally, I gave up and turned on the television. The clock ticked off seven, and I wondered if he was really going to show. It was quarter of eight when the phone finally rang.

"What," I snapped.

"Is that any way to be greeting a man who's just come from the jaws of hell?"

"I was beginning to wonder if you were coming at all." I said, having difficulty hiding my irritation.

"I'm truly sorry. Truth is, I wanted to be here earlier this afternoon, but got held up with business. As it is, I missed the last flight to Charleston and had to charter a plane to get here at all. Let me make it up to you over dinner?"

My anger cooled. After all, how can one be angry with a man who charters a plane to fulfill his obligation? "All right," I cooed.

"Meet me in the lobby in ten minutes then. I'm looking forward to seeing you, Pauline."

I hung onto the phone for a solid minute after he hung up. Then I slowly replaced it in the cradle and put on my linen dress.

We dined at the Restaurant Million, a charming establishment with exposed brick walls and Aubusson tapestries, situated above a noisy tavern. We ate crayfish and prawns and washed them down with two bottles of Corton Charlemagne. Conversation between us never lagged; it was both facile and spirited. There was no talk of Ethan being the reason we were there and, frankly, I didn't care. I learned more about Terrance, that he read mystery novels when he wasn't reading history. I told him that I had minored in art history and was therefore ingrained with a working knowledge of Greco Roman history and the Renaissance. He told me of his own love of art and admitted to owning a Renoir as well as some antiquities. I expressed to him my disdain for private collectors who take treasures out of the public domain, neglecting to mention the minor Pissarro that hung upon my own walls.

We volleyed back and forth the entire meal. He wore a light blue seersucker suit, turning the blue of his eyes pale and transparent. They still held the spark that had captured my attention the first time we met, and there was no denying that it had me under his spell once again. I found myself laughing more freely than I could remember and there was something quite liberating about it. I felt so acutely alive, my eyes must have been sparkling, too.

After dinner, we took a walk along the harbor in the sultry evening air. He guided me along, holding my arm in a loose impersonal way I found distracting. Suddenly, he let it go, stopping to lean against a railing and peer out at the Atlantic. The moon cast silver ropes upon the waves. I sidled up close to him, emboldened by the two bottles of wine we had drunk.

"Why are you really here, Terrance?" I asked. "Is this a challenge to you, like a business deal?"

"Pauline," he replied, stopping and staring ever so deeply into my eyes. "What I told you on the phone was the truth. I travel the whole world, and I see a lot of things. I find lately I've come to live mostly for business and what it gives to me. But seeing that old woman in Bury St. Edmunds really touched me heart. I've decided to make it my personal undertaking to learn what became of her son."

"I see." Disappointed, I looked into the darkness as if there was something terrifically interesting out there.

"But there's another reason I'm here," he continued. "The moment I saw you I felt something inexplicable, a kinship. I can't explain it, but I know you felt it, too, or felt something. Otherwise you wouldn't be here either."

His words were more intoxicating than the wine. I was feeling things I hadn't since I met Henry. I turned to him in the moonlight and looked up at him in a way that made it clear I was available. He bent as if to kiss me, but instead tapped his forefinger lightly on the tip of my nose.

"I think we should get an early start tomorrow," he said, taking my arm and nudging me gently back toward the hotel.

He walked me to my room and to my extreme disappointment made no effort to compromise my virtue other than a brotherly good-

night peck on the cheek. I stood in my room in the throes of unful-
filled passion trying to figure out Terrance Sullivan. He was a puzzlement. I had no idea what was going on with him, but one thing was
for certain. I was confused beyond belief.

Terrance rented a Mercedes convertible for the drive to Morristown,
the origin of British Ethan Campbell's last correspondence with his
mother. With a straw hat tied beneath my chin to protect myself from
the ravages of the Southern sun, I was glad for the wind on my face.
My head felt that it might possibly explode after all the wine the night
before. Terrance, however, seemed to be completely unaffected by
both the sun and the alcohol. He drove hatless with his wild red hair
blowing freely, humming an Irish tune as we rolled through the lush
green hills of South Carolina. Every once in a while a cluster of houses
would spring out of the countryside, a sore reminder of the unstop-
pable human encroachment upon all things beautiful.

"It's a shame to see these horrid complexes mar this exquisite countryside," I said as we passed a sign announcing Chewton Glen Estates
three miles ahead. "Who really thinks these houses are estates?"

"It's jargon," he said. "Mediocrity is in the masses."

"Well, I'd rather see the land preserved and the masses kept out.
Unfettered growth is the death of beauty."

"Watch who you're talking to here, lassie. I come from the masses.
Don't expect to keep the rest of the world out just because certain rich
people don't want to see changes that're going to make someone else
richer. Developing is how I earn my living, and proud of it I am."

"Well, don't tell anyone in Charleston," I chided him. "They won't let
you back in. Developers are on the bottom rung of their social ladder."

"Lower than the lawyers then? Impossible." He laughed heartily
at his own joke.

We drove past the Chewton Glen development, and I was reminded
of Shannon Maglieri's neighborhood, with its oversized houses push-

ing to the ends of cramped lots. Terrance honked the horn and waved and this time even I had to laugh. His frivolous and lighthearted nature was drawing me even further under his spell. So many things about him reminded me of Henry, including his love of history and his iconoclastic attitude.

After driving several more miles, we spotted the exit for Morristown and turned off the main highway. We were on a quaint country road, shaded for much of the time by a canopy of Banyon trees, the air dense with the smell of horses and dewey green grass.

"What on earth would have led young Ethan Campbell back into this neck of the woods?" he wondered aloud as the pristine countryside passed by. A few minutes later, a hand-painted sign signaled our arrival in Morristown. The road took us directly into the town's center where a white church with a tall belltower sat opposite a cooling stretch of village green. The main street was lined with early colonial and Georgian buildings, giving one the sense of going back in time. In a way, the town was an American version of Bury St. Edmunds, the type of place a homesick Englishman might be drawn to.

We found the St. Alder Arms without even looking, or rather it found us, on the main street just past the church. As if to say welcome, a parking spot was open directly in front of the wood-framed inn. Terrance pulled into it and the two of us sat looking at the reason for our journey.

"How would you feel if we walked in and a lad named Ethan Campbell greeted us?" asked Terrance, the perennial tease.

"He wouldn't be a lad anymore, he would be over sixty, and I would be in a state of shock," I replied. "Then I would insist he write to his poor old mother."

"Well, then, let's have at it," he said, getting out of the car.

* * *

The polished wood floors clicked sharply beneath our feet as we entered the old inn. The intimate lobby had a sitting room off to the right, furnished with what were now antiques, though I suspected they weren't antique when they were purchased. The registration desk directly in front of us had a coat rack and umbrella stand beside it. It was deserted, but there was a bell on the counter which Terrance picked up and rang vigorously. Almost immediately a young man emerged through a door behind the desk. He was about thirty years old with close cropped blond hair and a small yellow goatee.

"Yes, may ah help you?" he asked in a Carolina accent thicker than maple syrup.

Terrance left it to me to explain what now felt like an even more ridiculous mission than it had before.

"As unbelievable as it sounds, we are trying to track down someone who stayed here around thirty-four years ago, an Englishman. I can't begin to suppose you would know anything about him."

"'Spect I wasn't even born then, ma'am, so no, I don't suppose I would know anything about anybody who stayed here back then. Too bad my granddaddy passed last year, he probably would have remembered. I don't think he ever forgot one person who spent a night at the St. Alder Arms. This here was his hotel, and when he *dahd* he left it to Mama and me."

"You don't say." I looked at Terrance who was leafing through an old-fashioned guest register on the counter. Beside each person's signed name was a space for their hometown address.

"How many years have you been keeping this kind of guest book?" he asked.

"Since fo'ever, I suppose."

"Is there a chance you'd still be having the register from say 1965?" he asked, tapping at the guest book.

The blond man scratched at his goatee, and a small accommodating smile crept onto his face. "You know, I just maht. Granddaddy never threw a thing away, and when he passed Mama and I just left ever'thin' sitting up in the attic. Y'all are welcome to have a look around for yourself if you like."

"We'd like that very much," Terrance replied. Without asking anything more, the trusting young innkeeper led us up two flights of stairs to the third floor. The hall was lined with what I took to be guest rooms from the brass numbers mounted on each door. He pulled down a trap door in the ceiling leading into a dark attic. After unfolding some rickety steps, he disappeared into the darkness. A moment later a light came on.

"Y'all can come up now," he called.

I followed Terrance into the oppressively hot and dusty space. The young man cautioned us that there "maht be some spahders," a warning that made my blood flush cold despite the sauna-like environment of the attic. Then he pointed out some packing boxes in the corner and said, "I'm pretty sure the books is in *theyah*. Y'all just make yourselves at home and come and get me when y'all are finished."

We thanked him and climbed across nearly a century's worth of accumulated junk, furniture and tools, stacks of magazines, and even a Confederate flag. The boxes he had pointed out were carelessly stacked in a haphazard manner, but upon opening the top one we discovered that the contents were indeed old guest registers. There appeared to be one book for each year, dating all the way back to the nineteen twenties. It didn't take us long to unearth the book labeled nineteen sixty-five.

"Do you remember the exact date of Ethan's letter to his mother?" Terrance asked.

"Surely you jest," I said, thinking it a wonder that I had even held on to the address of the inn.

"Well, I recall the month anyway," he said impishly. "March, same month as my birthday."

"So, I just missed celebrating it with you?"

"You can still buy me a present if you want."

Strangely enough, my hands shook as I leafed through the yellowed pages dating back oh-so-many years. The names and addresses of the previous visitors to the St. Alder Arms were written out in a grand variety of handwriting, some flowery, some scribbled, some methodical, and some barely legible where time had eaten the color from the ink. The signers came from places all over the country and globe. There were guests from Alaska and Denmark as well as locals from Charleston and Savannah. My eye moved down the left column, looking, looking, looking for that one name, Ethan Campbell. Instead, another familiar name cropped up on the page, a name causing me to gasp aloud.

"What is it?" Terrance asked.

It was an early version of the flowery handwriting I knew so well, the same hand that had so recently written a suicide note. I turned the book toward him and pointed it out. Danny Kehoe, Rochester, New York. Wordlessly, my eyes continued down to the name of the next guest registered. And sure enough there it was, written in the same concise hand as his final letter to his mother. Ethan Campbell, Bury St. Edmunds, England.

Terrance regarded me with a raised brow. "Are you thinking what I am thinking?"

I was, but I didn't want to admit it. One Ethan Campbell disappears and another one surfaces. I suppose I had to have known in my heart that their paths crossed somewhere along the line. How else could Daniel have adopted Ethan's name? But I didn't want it to be the place where Ethan Campbell had posted his last letter to his mother. I wanted it to be some other place, not here where it implied so much wrong.

"Do you think Danny Kehoe did Ethan Campbell in and then stole his identity?"

"I don't know what to think. All this tells us is that two people stayed in the same hotel in March of nineteen sixty-five."

"C'mon, Pauline, sweet girl. Ethan Campbell from England inexplicably disappears thirty-four years ago. Ethan Campbell of Chicago dies thirty-four years later and turns out to be not Ethan Campbell after all, but rather a chap named Danny Kehoe. And the two stayed in the same hotel right around the same time the first Ethan disappeared. Seems more than a bit sinister to me."

Sinister was a mild word, I thought. Creepy was the one that kept flaring up in my mind. Very creepy, I might add. Was there to be no end to Ethan's ongoing melodrama? "I don't know what to say, Terrance."

"I suppose the next logical step would be to find out if a crime was committed."

"And how might we do that, go to the phone book?"

"No. We ask the police."

18
Another Unclaimed Body

For the second time in my life I found myself inside a police station, and for the first time, a prison. The small, brick building that housed the Morristown County Sheriff's office housed the jail as well. It appeared the building had been built some time in the early part of the twentieth century, which made it the youngest thing around. That included the staff, from the crusty bleached blonde named Lou Anne who greeted us to Sheriff Walters himself, who we were lucky enough to catch on his lunch hour.

If the sheriff wasn't retirement age then he was a few years past it. He was also enormous, his three chins and protruding belly putting him in stiff competition with Desmond Keifer, Ethan's former building superintendent. But pound for pound, he was Southern hospitality, and he welcomed Terrance and me warmly into his office. The decorating theme was fish, and the walls were covered with pictures of him and other men dangling the cold-blooded creatures from lines alongside several stuffed ones mounted on wooden blocks. A large ashtray on the desk held the remains of a half dozen cheap cigars and the overhead fan circulated the air just enough to make sure all present could smell them.

Terrance explained we were there on behalf of the mother of an Englishman who had possibly disappeared around Morristown in March of sixty-five. Did he have any recollections, Terrance asked, of any odd occurrences around that time? Perhaps a car accident, or a lightning strike. The sheriff lit up cigar number seven and leaned back in his chair, pushing his heavy hat back on his forehead while he released a thoughtful stream of putrefied smoke.

"Sixty-five. Now, that's a long time ago. A lot's happened here since. Leave me think a spell. I was a brand new deputy back then . . ." He sat in ponderous silence. "This is a white man, you say." I nodded. "No, weren't any unidentified white men around then. Now if you was talkin' about a black man, it might be different. I got plenty of nigra John Does there. But a white man in sixty-five? Don't think so."

I was strangely relieved there were no dead bodies lurking about. No body meant no crime. With nothing else to ask the sheriff, we stood, eager to beat a hasty retreat from the cheap cigar smoke. He took my hand in his and shook it so fiercely I thought it might come off at the wrist. Then he shook Terrance's hand in much the same manner except that he didn't release it.

"What's that accent you got there anyway? You from England?"

"No, just across the river from it. Little country called Ireland."

"Ireland, you don't say. My grandmother came from Ireland. County Kerry."

"Did she now? Beautiful country, Kerry."

"She was a wonderful woman," he mused. "She lived to be near a hundred years old."

"She didn't drink sausage grease by any chance?" I couldn't resist.

He released Terrance's hand and looked at me oddly. Then thinking he had misunderstood me, he said, "Nah, she drank straight whiskey. Tough old bird. Used to make me Irish soda bread and tell me bedtime stories. My favorite was about St. Patrick driving out the snakes. Ain't no snakes in Ireland, right son?"

"Sure and that's the truth, sir."

"Wish I could say the same for us here. We got lots of swamps in this here Lowcountry and they's full of snakes, all kinds of them, not to mention gators." And then the sheriff stopped talking and a look of revelation came across his face. "Now wait a minute. Sixty-five you said? Shoot fire, there was a body found round here, but it wasn't in sixty-five. Hold on."

He opened the office door and shouted for his assistant. The same woman who had greeted us scurried into the room. "Lou Anne, these nice people are looking for somebody from England who might have gone and died around here in sixty-five. What year was it that body turned up in Little Scapoose swamp?"

"Why that was 1972, Sheriff. Summer of '72, if I recall right. Only there wasn't much left of it, what I remember. Animals had cleaned it up slicker than a whistle. Wasn't much more than a skeleton."

"That's it, all comes back to me now. Them boys from Scapoose County came over here to see if we had any missing persons, but we didn't have none. Don't think they ever did find out who it was. If you got a minute, I'll call over there for you."

Of course we had a minute and more. We waited while Sheriff Walters speed-dialed a crony in Scapoose. "Yeah, Griff, Bob Walters here. You remember the stiff your daddy found in the swamp near thirty years ago, the one he tried so hard to I.D.?" There was a pause. "Yeah, that's the one. Did you ever get anything on him? Uh-huh. Well, how'd he die? Wha? Oh, yeah, I got some people here who might have been kin. You did, huh? Yeah, I'll tell 'em. Sure. Say hey to Maggie for me." He hung up and looked at us.

"Well, they did find a body but they never did I.D. it. White male about five-six. Forensics never could pinpoint a cause of death; there wasn't much left. No clear signs of violence like bullet holes or knife scrapes. They labeled the body a John Doe and cremated it."

"Sheriff, do you think that body could have been in that swamp for seven years without anyone finding it?" I asked.

"Little Scapoose? Sure thing. There're probably a few more bodies in there we ain't found yet."

"I see. I want to thank you once again for all your help, Sheriff."

"Wasn't nothin'. Let me know if I can do anything else."

"I wonder if they kept the teeth?" Terrance said as we stepped back into the now sticky South Carolina day.

"Whatever for? Certainly you wouldn't think of sending them to his mother saying, 'this is what's left of your son.'"

"Ah, so you're thinking that unlucky fellow might have been Ethan Campbell, too?"

"I didn't say that," I replied, trying to shake a feeling of gloom that was growing faster than a cancer. "I honestly don't know what I'm thinking."

"I've got an idea," he said. He put on a thick Southern accent and swayed his back so that his stomach stuck out. "What say we *drahve* over to Scapoose and have a talk with Sheriff Griff ourselves? Ma'am?" He opened the car door and held it for me, his stomach still thrust out the entire time. It was difficult not to laugh at his ridiculous posturing. My eyes darted back to the closed doors of the sheriff's office to assure myself neither the sheriff nor Lou Anne were watching his parody.

"Stop it," I insisted, unaccustomed to this sort of spontaneous behavior.

"But *ah* know how to talk to them now," he said, plucking a long blade of grass from the lawn and sticking it between his teeth.

He swaggered into the car and soon we were back on the road, the wind blowing my hair to pieces again, the ever warming sun searing down upon us. The town of Scapoose was microscopic compared to Morrisville, making its sheriff that much easier to find. The office was on the first block of town, which was also the only block. There wasn't even a second person in this station, just one uniformed man about twenty years younger than Sheriff Walters and about seventy pounds lighter.

"Can I help you folks?"

"Sheriff Griff," said Terrance, to my horror continuing to speak with his absurd accent. He sounded more like John Wayne than a Southerner. "We was just over in Morristown with Sheriff Walters and we was wonderin' if we cud ask you a few questions."

"Where you from, mister?"

"Terrance, stop it," I upbraided him, turning to the second small-town sheriff we had seen that day. "I believe Sheriff Walters spoke with you a little while ago about a body you found in 1972. We were the people making the inquiry."

"Well, I tole' Bob 'bout ever'thing I knew about the case. It was a long time ago. People don't fret over that stuff much more 'n five or ten years 'round here. After that it's ancient history."

"We just wondered if you kept anything from the body, clothes or a ring or," I grimaced as I said it, "teeth."

He shook his head. "I'm afraid not. Teeth burned with him, wasn't wearing any jewelry, and far as we can figure, he wasn't wearing any clothes. None left on him, anyhow."

"Are you saying he was naked when he went into the swamp?" I asked, digesting his words.

"Can't say for sure, but looks like it. If they was wearing clothes there's usually some rags or something left around. Clothes last longer than tissue."

The shadow of foreboding grew stronger. If the body did belong to British Ethan Campbell and he had met with foul play, why would he have been naked? I thought about my Ethan's letter to me and his reference to a bad deed. I didn't want to think about it any further.

✳   ✳   ✳

There was a small General Store at the end of the block and Terrance pulled the car over in front of it. "Be back in a minute," he said. He ran inside and reemerged a couple of minutes later carrying a brown paper bag.

"What's that?" I asked.

"A surprise," he said.

We left the little town and were soon crossing some of the most picturesque countryside we had seen so far. It was wide open and rolling green and there wasn't a house or another car anywhere in sight. Terrance pulled to the side of the road, beneath the shade of a huge willow tree on a creek. He reached into the back seat and retrieved the brown paper bag.

"Now what are you doing?"

"We're having a picnic," he said. He went into the trunk and pulled out a blanket he must have taken from the hotel in Charleston. He walked to the field and waved to me. "C'mon. What're you waiting for?"

"This has to be someone's property," I said, easing nervously out of the car.

"Well, if they catch us on it, we'll pay rent."

There was a low wooden fence which Terrance climbed easily. He stood in the open field waving me on. The breeze blew the long tufts of green field grasses, parting them before him in waves like the sea. Standing in the afternoon sunlight, his red hair looked as if it were aglow. In the distance I could see cows grazing.

"Are you coming, Pauline?"

"What about all those cows?"

"They won't bother you. I promise."

I walked to the fence and gingerly climbed the rails the same way he had, altogether too aware that my ecru Armani pants and crisp white blouse were not exactly what one would call picnic clothes. Terrance grabbed my hand and began pulling me across the field, following the creek toward a stand of trees. My low heels sunk in the soft dirt of the meadow the entire way. I was laughing and out of breath by the time we reached the trees. He was laughing, too, as he spread the blanket and both of us sank to the ground.

"Pauline, do you know when you laugh you look ten years younger?" he said.

I didn't know whether to be complimented or insulted, but his comment did serve to do one thing. It wiped the smile right off my face. But he didn't seem to notice the effect of his words, he was so busy spreading out the contents of the brown paper bag on the blanket. When he had finished I was looking at a jar of peanut butter, a loaf of presliced white bread, some Oscar Meyer bologna, a jar of mustard, two apples, a bunch of green grapes, some Hostess Twinkies, a package of napkins and some plastic silverware. Lastly, he pulled out a six-pack of beer.

"It seems that whenever we are sleuthing around together, we never take the time for lunch. Well, I'm famished."

He opened the flip-top of a can of beer and offered it to me. Reminded of the beer I had pretended to share with Emily McMahon in Boston, and with my head still aching from the night before, I started to shake my head. Then a wave of spontaneity came upon me, and I accepted the beer from his outstretched hand. I took a sip. It was cold and refreshing and delicious.

We each ate a bologna and a peanut butter sandwich, and I don't think I have ever enjoyed a meal more. I even enjoyed the beer. That day it tasted better than the liters upon liters of chateau wines I had consumed thus far in my life. If it's true that a meal tastes better in a small Roman trattoria or a casual Parisian bistro because of the ambience, I can say that the ambience of that field surpassed the best of them. Had someone put a sign and a table in the middle of that meadow, I would have become one of its greatest devotees.

When we finished eating, we lay down on the blanket and stared at the sky through the gaps in the tree branches. The beer had taken the last of my headache away and the earth beneath me was eiderdown, enveloping me in its softness. I felt ageless, like all my parts were a part of the earth beneath me. I felt important and vital. We were like children, lying there in the field. He told me about his youth in Ireland, how his father made a living as a sheep shearer and his mother took in laundry, that he had ten siblings and, though, for all intents and purposes, they had been poor, he had never even known it until he grew up and went to the city.

I told him my upbringing was the exact opposite. I had always thought we were rich. I was brought up to wear beautiful clothes, ride horses, and attend the finest schools, and I didn't learn we were poor until my father wasn't able to pay my tuition at Foxcroft anymore. I told him how stingy Grandmother had been with Mother and me after Father left because of her disapproval of him. And how Grandmother had actually gained satisfaction when my father drank himself to death during his third marriage, a secret I had never shared with anyone other than Ethan.

"I'll never forget Father's funeral. I was fifteen years old and I had to sneak out of the house to attend it because Grandmother forbade it. I sat in the back of the church all alone, and no one knew who I was. I thought I was going to be terribly sad, but when I saw how few people were there and the sort of people, well, in a way it was good for me. It woke me up to who my father had been. He had put himself first and not cared for his wife and daughter and look how he ended up. I walked out of that church and didn't even cry."

We talked of kinder things, of sports such as skiing where the Earth's gravity is the challenger, or the peace of sailing when the boat slips silently through the waves. I was so comfortable that before I knew it my eyes were closing and I fell asleep. In the cool shade of the tree, I dreamed he was lying atop me, pressing himself into me, and

I was opening myself up to him. I awakened with a start and realized I was alone. The afternoon was waning and the sun had turned into an orange bulb in the sky, its rays slanting in great gold and red streaks across the field. I looked around and saw Terrance sitting at the edge of the creek, tossing pebbles into it. He had cleaned off the blanket and packed the remains of our picnic lunch back into our brown paper picnic basket.

"Hello," I called out.

"Sleeping Beauty awakes." He dropped a handful of pebbles into the water and returned to me where I lay unmoving on the blanket.

"How long did I sleep?" I asked him.

"A couple of hours. You looked so peaceful, I didn't want to disturb you."

I stared up at him with eyes that I know communicated everything I was feeling. I would have let him take me there in the middle of that field, mosquitoes and the world be damned. He smiled his heartbreaking smile and held out his hand.

"C'mon, we best be getting back."

I left my hat off for the ride back to Charleston. The cool evening air felt damp and sensual and I wondered, yet again, whether I would be spending the night with Terrance. When we got back to the hotel, he asked me if I would like some dinner. We ate at a small Italian restaurant down the block, sharing two different pastas and a bottle of Brunello. Afterward, we took a leisurely walk. My senses were so sharpened that the smell of the spring flowers was almost overwhelming. He put his arm around me, and I rested my head on his shoulder. It felt good to disappear into the security of his body. Nestled beneath his arm, I felt insulated against the outside world.

My blood was aboil as we reached the hotel, every fiber of my body straining toward his physical presence next to me. I longed to bury my head in his chest, to discover if he was nearly as masculine as I wanted him to be. But once again I was to be disappointed. He walked me to my room and keeping his body at a distance from mine, bent to kiss my cheek.

"I had a wonderful day, Pauline," he said.

While he was still standing there, I unlocked my door and pushed it open. I wanted to grab hold of him and drag him into my room. A rose waiting to be plucked, I stared him down with heavy lidded eyes, a sorry caricature of Marlene Dietrich. "Don't you want to come in?" I invited.

There was a battle in his face. I could see his body reaching toward me, could feel his face drawing closer, could feel his warm breath on my cheek. I was willing him to come with me, wanting him like I've never wanted anything in my life. And then, just when I thought my battle may have been won, the tide turned and he pulled away. My face burned red hot with shame as he shook his head no. "I'll have to take a rain check. My flight's impossibly early in the morning. In fact I'll say good-bye here, because I'll be gone before you get up."

My ears couldn't believe what they were hearing. An early morning flight was his excuse to pass on a night of passion? Having already humiliated myself enough, I let it go. I had made my overture and it had been turned down. I had no intention of further losing face by pleading my case. "Of course," I muttered. "Good-night then, and good-bye."

"I'll call you the next time I'm in the States."

"Yes, please do that."

I shut the door behind me and threw the security lock with a firm thrust. My mind was a whirling tornado of confusion. Why had I met such a perfect man, attractive, virile, sexy and exceedingly rich, to be led down the garden path and left at the gate by the gardener himself? It was beyond my realm of comprehension. What motive could he have for chasing around the English countryside, and then the South Carolina countryside, with me if he didn't find me desirable?

There was no chance of sleep. I tossed the entire night, my torturously unrealized sexuality as disabling as a migraine. I ticked through the possible reasons that Terrance Sullivan refused to make love to me, refusing to entertain the notion that he found me unattractive. His eyes told me otherwise. Could it be he was involved with someone else? Charmian had said he was a bachelor, but that didn't rule out a long-term girlfriend. Maybe he was actually a man with principles and could not be disloyal. Or perhaps he had an embarrassing deformity. Or a social disease. He had herpes and it was active. Or he was impotent. I tried to console myself by telling myself that at least he wasn't using me.

And then, when I could think about it no longer, my mind turned to a far less tormenting but equally baffling issue. What to make of what Terrance and I had learned today about Ethan Campbell and Daniel Kehoe? Could I deny the possibility something macabre had taken place between them? Once again, I thought about my Ethan's suicide note and his mention of the guilt he could no longer live with.

Though the obvious was staring me in the face, I chose to turn my head from it. For one, I couldn't fathom Ethan performing a violent act. He was simply too small. Perhaps there had been an accident. Perhaps something had happened to the original Ethan, the English Ethan, and my Ethan had stumbled across his papers left behind in the hotel. My Ethan was a romantic. Perhaps he had just fallen in love with the name and kept it. There could probably be a million explanations for how Daniel Kehoe became Ethan Campbell.

Or there could be one.

19

Date Rape?

The next day was one of the worst in my life. I would have said it was the absolute worst, but it was superseded by what would come to pass later. After finally managing to sleep for two whole hours, I awakened to heartache and disappointment upon learning Terrance had already checked out. The entire ride to the airport and flight home he was all I could think of, my mind so preoccupied with him, I practically forgot about Ethan Campbell and Danny Kehoe.

It wasn't until I opened the door to my apartment that reality came trickling back in. My phone was ringing and I dropped my bag and ran for it. The optimist in me was hoping it was Terrance. Instead my already touchy nerves were jangled by a remotely familiar voice, one that brought to mind visions of unkempt self and the smell of unwashed bodies. I was in absolutely no frame of mind to deal with the barbarian at this specific point in time.

"What can I do for you, Mr. Keifer?" I asked, hoping to keep it brief.

"I've been leaving messages for days. I want to know when some-one is going to come over here and clean out all the junk in this apartment," he whined in his nasal voice. "I've got a renter coming in."

"I don't suppose Mr. Campbell paid his rent for the month of April?" I asked, thinking if he had it would buy some time.

"No, and it's the fourteenth. I've already lost half a month. Now if somebody don't get over here and take care of it tomorrow, everything is going into the Dumpster."

"Thank you, Mr. Keifer. I would expect no less of you."

I hung up the phone beyond aggravation with the slovenly excuse for a human. How dare he put such unnecessary pressure on me? I pictured the cluttered apartment filled with copious notes and Ethan's— he was still Ethan to me—things. Despite everything I'd learned an overwhelming sadness came over me. I recalled how excited he had been when he started research on the never-to-be-written Daisy Fellowes book. He would call me daily with anecdotes about the one-time ugly duckling who with the aid of a mountain of cash had reinvented herself as a swan. Now I wondered if he hadn't done the same, reinvented himself to escape his depressing and ugly upbringing. Maybe cleaning out his apartment wouldn't be such a bad thing after all. Maybe I might just find some more insight as to who he was. Maybe it would be therapeutic.

I played the messages I had ignored before my trip to Charleston. Sunny called twice asking what was going on with Ethan's body. Whitney called several times, asking me to please call her back. There were Mr. Keifer's messages. There was a message from Sean saying he had tried to reach me in Rochester, but I had checked out and *where was I now?*

The last message was from my accountant telling me to call him right away. It was urgent.

Ivan Epstein answered on the first ring. An intense squinty-eyed man who looked as though his nose belonged in a book, he sounded more frenzied than usual. "Pauline, do you know what day it is?"

"Tuesday, Ivan."

"Tuesday, what?"

"Tuesday, April 14."

"Which means your taxes are due tomorrow."

With all the running about I had done, I had completely forgotten about taxes. "I thought we were filing an extension."

"We are, but you still need to sign it and send in a check. You had quite a capital gain on those securities you sold."

That money was long gone. "How much do I owe?"

"In the area of fifty thousand dollars."

"Ivan, what if I don't send the check now?"

"You still have to file the extension. And you'll have penalties. The IRS starts the meter running right away." He said it in the manner of a parent chiding a child.

"Well, I'll just have to pay them later then. I'll sign the extension and get it back to you."

My next call was to Sean. I didn't want to put it off. No matter what the outcome might be, meeting Terrance had shown me the folly of this purely physical liaison. It had shown me that I wanted more, that I needed more, that after all these years of feeling dead myself after Henry's death, I wanted to care for someone again. I had forgotten what that happy-to-be-alive feeling was like, that all-consuming thrill. It frightened me to feel it again, because once one knows it, it can never be equaled.

Sean wasn't home, but I left him a message asking him if he wanted to have dinner. I had to end it while my resolve was still strong.

I called Sunny and excruciatingly told her the same story I would have to tell at least a hundred more times in the ensuing days. Ethan had been born Daniel Kehoe in Rochester, New York, his mother had been a domestic and his father had worked on the streetcar. I left out that he was a bastard and mentioned nothing of the trip to South Carolina. Connie Chan would never write a column accusing him of murder. Whatever happened at the St. Alder Arms in 1965 would remain a secret forever as far as I was concerned. The waters of time had long since run beneath Ethan's bridges. I could only judge him as I knew him.

Sunny was humiliated and angry to learn how badly she had been deceived. "You aren't still going to bury him, are you?" she asked.

"I was thinking he'd prefer cremation, but yes, whenever the body is released, I'm going to take care of it. After all he was my friend." I left it at that.

And then I called Whitney. The notion of returning to Ethan's blood-spattered apartment alone was unsettling, especially with Mr. Keifer running about at will, so I had decided to take the former lingerie model up on her offer to help me.

Her phone was answered by her housekeeper who informed me *Mrs. Armstrong was in her gym and didn't want to be disturbed.* She would pass my message on as soon as the lady of the house finished her workout. My phone rang a scant minute later. It was Whitney, huffing and puffing. If I hadn't known she was in the gym, I would have assumed she was in the middle of the act.

"Pauline," she said, "please forgive me. Miranda just gave me your message. Of course, I would have taken your call had I known it was you. I've been trying to get in touch with you for days."

"I've been traveling," I said, "and I've solved the mystery of Ethan. It isn't very glamorous, I'm afraid, but at least we know who he was now."

"Oh," said Whitney in that little girl voice of hers after I told her of Ethan's humble origins. "And to think of the way he put on airs when he was no better than anyone else." She sounded perturbed. I wondered if I should rethink my idea of asking for her help, but I was too emotionally and mentally frayed to try and come up with an alternative.

"I've got to clean out his apartment tomorrow. Are you still interested in helping?"

"Pauline, of course. When?"

I knew I would want to sleep in late. "Tomorrow afternoon. We'll have lunch at the Casino first."

After I hung up, I went into my bedroom and fished Fleur out from under the bed against her will. Forcing her to stay in my lap, I stroked her silky hair until she forgave me and broke into a contented purr. I sat there wishing a certain Irishman would stroke me like that. I would purr even stronger than my beloved cat.

I treated Sean to dinner that night at a sushi restaurant just around the corner. I'm not particularly fond of raw fish, but I knew he loved it and wanted to be extra kind to him that evening. The crowd was young and many of the young girls made no qualms about giving the eye to my date. It irritated me to no end because I'm sure they thought he was eating with his mother. I had always told him our age difference was the reason I had never taken him to any social events, but the truth of the matter was he simply wouldn't have fit in. Whereas he was a beautiful specimen to look at, our worlds were entirely different. He could never be a part of mine. He had become for me, despite all his youth and beauty, about as appealing as, well, Desmond Keifer.

As opposed to Terrance Sullivan. He had risen above his humble beginnings and carved out a place for himself in this world. I believe it was Cervantes who said, "It's not with whom you are bred, but with whom you are fed." Terrance was eating in good company. As opposed to Sean, who, at the moment, was eating with his mouth open.

"So what did you find out about Ethan?" he asked, regaling me with a brief view of rice and tuna. I wondered what had possessed me when I entered into this affair in the first place.

Picking at my food, I told him how my quest for the truth took me from England to Boston and ended in Rochester where I finally identified my old friend as Daniel Kehoe. I didn't mention Charleston. Sean didn't appear at all disturbed at Ethan's deception. He was more disturbed by the story of my flat tire in the Boston ghetto.

"Pauline, I can't friggin' believe you drove around there by your-self. Do you know what happens to white women in those neighbor-hoods? Were you crazy? You should have brought me with you."

"Well, I've lived to tell the tale," I cut him off. "And now I have my answer and I'm done."

"Unbelievable," he said. "So Ethan pulled a fast one, heh?"

"I'm afraid it looks that way."

"I wonder where he came up with the other guy's birth certificate."

"I don't suppose we'll ever know the answer to that one," I lied. "Perhaps he found the man's wallet in the street or something along those lines."

"Oh well, no harm, no foul," said Sean. "Like I said before. It's not like he hurt anybody."

I remember thinking to myself, If he only knew. Possibly there was a great deal of harm done. But I did not voice this concern. I only said, "Except perhaps some of his friends. And his own memory."

We finished our meal and I paid the check. It was only fair I pay since I was about to make the break with him. I had hoped to accom-plish the task over dinner, but hadn't been able to find the right moment. Naturally he walked me home, and since there was no rea-son for him to do otherwise, he followed me through the door Jeffrey held and into the elevator. On the ride up, I kept rehearsing the words in my mind while working up the courage to say them. The doors opened and we stepped into my foyer. I stopped short of opening the interior door. I could feel the warmth radiating off his skin as he stood next to me.

"Sean, I've done some thinking over the past week," I said, staring at the house keys in my hand. I did not want to let him in my inner sanctum where I might be tempted to compromise my resolution. "The difference in our ages is great, too great. I don't believe our friendship is a good idea anymore. I think it's best if you go home tonight."

There. I had done it.

I turned to face him. He looked stunned as though I had just slapped him with my open hand, his eyes with a hurt look I had never seen before. The thought occurred to me that perhaps I meant more to him than a "sugar mama" after all. I suffered a rare moment of self-loathing for taking his feelings so lightly, for thinking of Sean as disposable. I had always thought things would end the opposite way.

"Pauline, you aren't saying that we're through." His words were a statement, not a question. He shook his head in denial with his soft bowed lips parted slightly and his chestnut eyes penetrating me.

"Well, yes, Sean, that is exactly what I am saying." I tried to meet his gaze in a compassionate, yet firm manner.

"Don't I please you? Don't I satisfy you?"

My mind flashed back to the countless hours we had spent thrashing about under the canopy of my bed not to mention a few other select places in my apartment. There was no way of saying those times had not held some redeeming value. But the complex feelings Terrance evoked in me completely overrode the far more basic ones I had for Sean. "You have satisfied me completely. You have been . . . you are . . . a wonderful lover. But there is more to a relationship than sex. We don't make a good couple. In the long run it's not good for you and it's not good for me."

"It's up to me to decide what's good for me," he stated fiercely. His intensity overwhelmed me. "And I know I can be good for you. Pauline, don't end us like this. I need you. I need to be with you. I want to learn from you. I love the way you handle yourself, your self-confidence, the way you put yourself above other people. Even the way you talk is so different."

I didn't want to point out that the way I talked was known as proper English. This was not an appropriate time. I stared right through him, going back to last night when I stood in the open doorway of my hotel

WELL BRED AND DEAD

room begging Terrance for the same thing Sean now wanted from me: intimacy, attention, sex. Why was one willing to give it when the other was not? Sean did not appear to be getting the message, causing me to wonder if I had let my relationship with my young paramour get out of control.

"Sean, I've had a tortuous week. Maybe I just need to think a little more. Go home and I'll call you tomorrow."

My words went as unheeded as the "no" of a teenage girl in the backseat of a car. Suddenly, his supple lips were upon me, working their way down my neck until I felt them reach the point where soft tissue meets bone, an area of particular sensitivity for me. As much as I hadn't even considered sex with him a minute ago, his actions boiled up the desire that had been simmering inside me since I met Terrance Sullivan. Sean's lips never stopped as he fell to his knees, drawing me down with him. I believe I tried to resist, but he was far stronger than I was. His hands went beneath my skirt and inside my panties. What his fingers found told him I was ready. What he couldn't know was my body wasn't responding to him. It was primed by a man halfway around the world.

"And you say you don't want me, Pauline?" he growled coarsely as he pushed me back on the hardwood floor. He tore my undergarments off. My skirt was up around my hips, and he parted my legs and buried his face between them. My protestations grew weaker as my irrational body betrayed my rational mind. He rose to his knees and unzipped his pants. His erection virtually sprung from them. Climbing atop me, I could feel the hard tip of his penis begin the easy slide into my dampness.

"Sean, wait," I gasped. "Condom." But he ignored me and kept thrusting himself at me. Though my mind said to stop, my body said *what the hell* as I felt him driving rock hard inside me, finding that sweet spot that compelled me to throw the last vestiges of caution to the wind and welcome him into me even further. My thoughts were raging and it felt as if all the blood had drained from my vital organs to engorge that epicenter of pleasure. My eyes were closed and in my head the name, Terrance, Terrance, Terrance, echoed with every thrust. I clung to him, climbed him until my body released itself into a series of sublime spasms that felt they would never end.

But end they did, and as the blood began to flow back to my brain, so too did common sense. Sean was still atop me, wrangling away at the same pace that had brought me to such heights, telling me he hadn't ejaculated yet. "Sean, stop," I insisted. "You must use a condom."

"It's all right," he panted without missing a beat.

"No, it isn't." Thoughts of disease dominated my consciousness as I tried to wriggle out from beneath him. But he wouldn't let go of me and didn't let up. I was getting angry and screamed for him to stop. That only seemed to provoke him and he drove into me until he was hurting me. I pulled at his hair and tore at his shirt. Finally with a shudder and a sigh he started to release himself. I took advantage of his weakness to pull myself away, and his sperm spilled out onto my abdomen and my Chanel skirt. He raised himself onto his elbows and stared at me.

"I'm sorry, baby, I just couldn't stop." I glared into his penetrating doe-like eyes. All traces of pain were gone and I realized he had been lying. He didn't really care about me at all. He cared about having control. What I had just gone through was as close to what they call date rape as one could ever come and I cursed myself for permitting it to happen. Then I wondered if I actually could have stopped it.

I squeezed out from underneath him and stood up, pulling my damp and crumpled skirt back down over my thighs.

"Sean, I want you to go. Now," I demanded.

He turned onto his back and made a very deliberate gesture of zipping his fly. The sound reverberated through the room like a great insult. He climbed to his feet and casually pushed the call button for the elevator. Since the car was still at my floor, the doors opened immediately. He grabbed me, kissing me roughly before he stepped into the waiting elevator.

"You're a great fuck, Pauline," he said as the elevator doors closed upon his sculpted face. "For an old broad."

I was so furious I wished the elevator cable would break.

20

Spring Cleaning

"Do you know how much sperm it takes to get AIDS?"

Even as the question came out of my own mouth, I couldn't believe I had confided in Whitney Armstrong. But since losing Ethan, who had truly been my best girlfriend, there was no one to whom I felt that close. Certainly not Sunny. Not Elsa unless I wanted to read about my problems in her column. But I was finding something eminently likable about Whitney, something I couldn't quite put my finger on. Away from the lunch crowd, she was refreshing and spirited. Truth be told, had she not been married to Jack Armstrong, she wouldn't have gotten the time of day from any of the women in our group, myself included. Now I was seriously considering the possibilities of her as a good friend. And if our friendship did continue to blossom I would ask her someday who did her work. She looked outstanding.

We were dining at the Casino Club before heading up to Ethan's to sort through his possessions. The Casino was one of the few club memberships I still retained. Only the very socially elite belonged, and the board worked hard to keep the parvenus out—though even they had been forced to capitulate somewhat in recent years. There was simply too much dotcom money floating about. But at its core, the club remained an outpost of old, or at least older than last year, money. The hubris of the membership is best illustrated by the response of one-time president Mrs. John Winterbotham to the builders of the John Hancock Building next door when they wanted to buy the property in the 1960s. Their letter was found unanswered in the back of her desk drawer upon her death.

Whitney shook her head and clucked sympathetically. "I don't think you're going to get AIDS. But I can't believe he forced himself on you like that. What about pregnancy?" she asked in her wispy voice.

"That would be one for the record books," I said, giving her a poignant smile in appreciation of her womanly consideration. Though the tendency was to stretch our ages as much as Zyplast stretched our lips, we both knew my days of ovulation were drawing to a close. "Anyhow, I called my doctor first thing this morning. He said it was probably nothing to be worried about, but that I should come in for a test in a month or so if I was still worried."

"What about Sean?"

"Well, I'm never going to see him again. I've instructed all the doormen that he is not to be permitted entrance into the building." I took a bite of my salmon. It was slightly overcooked and lacking in flavor, but the single vineyard Meursault from the club's cellar more than compensated for the lackluster food.

"You know, Pauline, as much as I admire you for taking a younger lover, you have to be careful. The waters are dangerous. I had a similar experience once with an infatuation—this was way before Jack. Only he did worse than what happened to you. He beat me. Broke my nose. Tore out patches of my hair. But what hurt the most was the things he called me. He called me horrible vile names. Things so bad I can't even repeat them."

As bad as "old broad" I wanted to ask. "You poor dear. When was this?"

"Oh, years and years ago when I lived in California. It was that experience that made me decide to leave the beach and move to Chicago. I thank heaven every day that I came here and met Jack."

"And I believe Jack thanks heaven, too," I said and I meant it. The canary diamond that glimmered on her finger couldn't have been a carat shy of twelve, and a competitive sparkler hung around her neck. I had admired the Montana suit she was wearing in the couture section at Neiman's, but passed on it after seeing the price tag—and this was her chosen ensemble for cleaning out dead men's apartments. Not only did her husband give her carte blanche with his money, he actually fawned over her in front of everybody like an adolescent in heat. One would think he was about to have sex for the first time. Henry and I had been close with Jack and his first wife, an elegant and classy woman named Theresa. He had barely put his arm around her in public. With Whitney, his hands were magnets and she was the North Pole. The way she had bewitched her husband left every other woman in Chicago society wishing they had access to the spell.

"Pauline, you don't know what it means to me, getting to know you better. That's part of the reason I wanted to help you at Ethan's. I could really use a friend. I know the other women don't really like me. They've never accepted me."

"It's envy, dear, pure and simple."

"You mean my looks?"

"No, it's not looks. It's the way Jack is so dedicated to you. I think any one of them would trade that for anything."

Whitney looked down and I believe she actually blushed. I thought of Terrance and the way I felt about him, about the way he came toward me, but then turned away as if we were opposing forces. Maybe I would be better served by learning what Whitney's secret was for keeping Jack so enamored before finding out who did her cosmetic work.

*   *   *

A sullen Desmond Keifer let us into Ethan's former living quarters. The yellow crime scene tape was gone, and the apartment smelled musty and stale. "You know how much money I'm losing each day this place ain't rented?" he grumbled, pushing the door open, his eyes fixed hungrily either on the large diamond around Whitney's neck or her cleavage directly below it.

"I couldn't possibly imagine, and I don't really care," I said curtly, shutting the door in his slobbering face.

"My God," said Whitney, stepping into the cluttered living room stacked ankle deep with papers. "How did he live like this?"

"Believe me, I have no idea," I said, thinking once again it was no wonder why he'd mailed me his will.

"Where do you want me to start?" she asked.

"Why don't you check the entry closet and see if there's anything worthwhile in there, and I'll go through these materials on Daisy. Keep anything of value and the rest we'll throw out."

I began sorting through Ethan's research on the Singer heiress, reading the snippets he had collected thus far about the exceedingly flamboyant and eccentric woman who went through lovers like so much trash, throwing some away, recycling others, many of them of the darker persuasion. I wondered if the information had any monetary value. The car insurance bill for the Jaguar was on my desk at home, and it required immediate attention. Ruefully, I decided that notes without a book were probably worthless. With a broken heart, I realized that short of some miracle, my car would have to go soon. It was only a matter of time before I would be forced to place the classified ad.

I dumped the notes into a box. Whitney started going through some drawers in the dining area while I moved on to the kitchen. The cabinets held nothing but inexpensive junk, and I made the executive decision to take Mr. Keifer up on his offer of throwing it into the Dumpster himself. I had no use for any of it or the chore of packing it up. I opened the refrigerator on a whim and immediately regretted the move as my nose was assaulted by the smell of rotting produce and molding doggy bags. I quickly shut the door, deciding to leave these treasures for Mr. Keifer as well. Some of Ethan's unopened bills sat on the counter and, with a sense of liberation, I slid them from the counter into the waste bin. I only wished my own bills could be handled in the same manner.

In the meantime, Whitney was still sorting through the dining room drawers in a very studious and thorough manner. I left her and went down the hall to the bedroom, hesitating in front of the open door. The memory of a corpse missing the greater part of its head flashed into my mind. I pushed the memory aside and went in.

The dresser drawers yawned open and fingerprint dust coated much of the furniture. The bloodied sheets were still on the bed, the rust-colored stains forming abstract shapes like a Rorschach test. The matter on the wall had dried to small brown bits. Above the desk the sign saying 'Finish Chapter One' hung as an epithet. I stood like an ice sculpture in the center of the room for some time, trying to sense what had gone through his mind in his last minutes. Had his long ago contact with the original Ethan Campbell brought him to this hideous and terminal act?

"So this is where you found him." I nearly jumped out of my shoes. She had stolen up behind me so silently it was as if she herself were a ghost.

"Whitney, you just scared the living daylights out of me!"

"I'm sorry," she said timidly. "I thought you might not want to be alone in here."

I pointed to the bed. "He was laying right there. What was left of him anyhow."

"It must have been so terrible for you. It wasn't very fair of him, was it?"

I thought about it. "No, it wasn't fair."

I went through the open drawers, lifting up tired sweaters and folded undershorts while Whitney searched the closet. I could see Ethan's sport coats hanging in there as well as some starched white shirts and a selection of good ties. Whitney got down on her knees and disappeared partially into the closet. When she emerged, she was holding a stack of magazines. I was not surprised to see pictures of men in suggestive poses adorning the covers.

"I think we'll bequeath those to Mr. Keifer as well," I said to her.

I finished up with the dresser, a pair of lapis lazuli cufflinks the only thing of value, and moved on to the desk. There were some office supplies, pens, paper clips and the like, but even these were in spartan amounts. Some more notes on Daisy, a couple of newspaper clippings with reviews from his first two books, and that was about it.

Sadly there was really nothing of Ethan worth saving. When I turned, Whitney was sitting on the floor, paging through one of the magazines with an inordinate amount of interest.

"Whatever are you doing?" I had to ask.

She did not acknowledge me, but continued flicking through the pages, lost in a world of her own. She stopped at the jagged edge of a torn-out page.

"It's not here," she said to herself.

"What's not there?" I asked, standing over her shoulder, my curiosity like embers under the bellows.

"Nothing. It doesn't matter anymore." She sounded dispirited.

"What is it? What were you looking for?"

"Oh, just something Ethan and I discussed once."

I couldn't imagine what Whitney and Ethan could have discussed that had its origins in a pornographic magazine, but perhaps it had something to do with Jack's fondness for his wife. Possibly some technique no man could resist? Something else to ask Whitney when I knew her better.

And then out of the clear blue, she began to rail against Ethan. "You know he wasn't who you thought he was, Pauline. You never saw his dark side."

Astounded at her outburst, I had no idea what prompted her attack on Ethan. I assumed it had to do with what was or wasn't in those magazines. I thought about the terrible deed he mentioned in his letter and all my own unanswered questions about him in South Carolina. *Maybe I have seen the dark side of him, Whitney*, I thought. Maybe I have. But to her I said nothing.

We finished up, deciding to take only a couple of boxes of notes and some unframed photos from recent social events. The rest of the junk could find its way to the Dumpster via Mr. Keifer as far as I was concerned. I even left the manual typewriter Ethan had written his two books upon.

Whitney had left the entry closet open, and I noticed the ratty hooded parka hanging inside that Ethan sometimes wore in winter months to protect himself against the elements. For some reason, seeing it evoked an emotional response in me. I pictured his little body huddled against the cold wind, marching relentlessly up Michigan Avenue to meet his lady friends for lunch or tea or a poetry reading. He really tried his best, I thought sadly, and wondered how I could ever think ill of him. In his mind, he had lived in a world that time had given up for a hurly burly of computers and World Wide Webs. Whitney was wrong. *I did know Ethan*, I thought. *I just hadn't known his name.*

I reached into the closet and grabbed the parka off its hanger.

Just as we were leaving I remembered Ethan frequently took Halcion to get to sleep. My own supply was running low, so I thought I would avail myself of whatever he had left. While Whitney waited in the hall I ran into the bathroom to check the medicine chest. Except for some Band-Aids and mouthwash, it was empty. This really puzzled me, because Ethan was such a hypochondriac he was convinced his pills kept him alive.

I shrugged it off, assuming the police took his drugs to help with the autopsy. Damn, I thought. Halcion was expensive.

I pulled up in front of the Armstrong mansion on Astor Street, a cool concrete giant with a neoclassical facade. The gate swung open before I had come to a complete stop. Evidently, the staff recognized that Madam was home. Whitney opened the car door and started to get out, swinging perfect legs onto the drive. Then she stopped and twisted her torso back toward me. She reached out and took my hand, holding it in a loose but friendly manner.

"Pauline, let's be close. I think we both need it."

Though I found her delivery to be somewhat odd, I knew what she meant. She wanted us to be better friends. To do things together. Go to shows and openings and events Jack Armstrong would be attending too. I found it very touching because most women were generally not eager to bring a single woman along when they were with their husbands. But as I had mentioned before, the last thing in this world that Whitney Armstrong had to worry about was Jack straying. And she knew it.

I smiled my serious woman-to-woman smile. "I'll call you. We'll do lunch next week."

"Wonderful. This one's my treat," she insisted.

21
Last Rites

Whitney and I did end up doing lunch the following week, but it was along with seventy or so other close friends and hangers-on of Ethan's, and at my expense.

The FBI fingerprint search finally came through that Monday and yielded nothing, meaning that Ethan wasn't in their files for having committed a crime or for any other reason for that matter. I breathed a sigh of relief. With no dental records available from his childhood, the authorities satisfied themselves with Shannon Maglieri's identification of her brother from photos, and they released him to me.

I had the body transferred to Stapleton-Fox Funeral Home, the preferred mortuary of Gold Coasters when a loved one checks out, conveniently located only blocks from most of their homes. And on a damp April afternoon, three weeks to the day after the discovery of the body, services were finally held for Ethan Campbell (a.k.a. Daniel Kehoe), services I was paying for, services that had left me aghast when I learned their price. The cost of dying had gone up dramatically since Henry's demise. In the interest of saving some money, I decided to have the body cremated. For the time being, its final resting place would be in an urn in my apartment. Perhaps in one of the windows overlooking the lake.

The crowd that showed up for the service came as much to pay respects to Ethan as to see who else was there. Most of them were women, most without their husbands (it was after all a Wednesday afternoon and there was work to be conducted), and all were thoughtfully dressed in finest mourning couture.

Ethan would have appreciated the turnout, I thought, as I surveyed the flower-filled parlor. All of Ethan's swans were there, as well as a lot of the local creme and many who aspired to be creme. His decorator friends, Raoul and Bharrie, were in attendance, as well as his hairdresser and the many waiters and shopkeepers he had befriended who spoke in hushed tones about the people with whom they were rubbing shoulders. It seemed none of them cared a whit about having been bamboozled, either that or they didn't want to miss the circus. The only one of his friends who was missing was Sunny. She and Nat were conveniently in Paris, but she did send an ostentatious bush with a card that read, *Ethan, You will never be gone as long as you are in our minds.*

The press was in no short supply either. Ethan's friends from the society magazines, literary critics, and of course Elsa, dressed in a Genny suit with a black chapeau to match. And then there was Connie Chan who had conspicuously chosen to wear bright red. "I can't believe that bitch had the nerve to come," Elsa said to me, dabbing at her eyes in a most affected manner with her lace-edged handkerchief. "Red to a funeral. It's an affront."

"An utter lack of respect," I said, echoing her sentiment.

The volume level was high with talk of the Lincoln Park Zoo Ball and other rites of spring, lending the gathering an almost giddy feel. Mr. Fox, the funeral director, approached to tell me the minister had arrived, and suggested we get on with the services. I walked to the front of the room and took the podium beside the orchid-draped casket. The chatter slowly died with the exception of the voice of Marjorie Wilcock. I located her and silenced her with a glare.

"Good afternoon, friends of Ethan," I said. "We are here to pay our respects to a special person who touched all of our lives in one way or another. Reverend James is going to perform a service, but before he does, I've asked Elsa Tower to say a few words in remembrance of him."

Always at her best in the spotlight, Elsa walked dramatically to the podium, her head held high beneath the black rim of her hat. In her hand she held a folded sheet of paper with her notes. I stepped aside to give her center stage.

"I hope not to bore you by speaking too long," she began, "but as Pauline has asked me to speak on Ethan's behalf, I would like to convey my feelings about him to all of you.

"I first met Ethan when he was working on his book about Berthe Palmer, that icon of Chicago women who is in large part responsible for our great collection of the Impressionists at the Art Institute. She was the reason he first came to our great city, and I recall that he complained greatly about the cold here then, telling me that his years in Puerto Rico had thinned his blood and that as soon as he finished his research, he would be heading back to the south, to someplace with a more agreeable climate.

"That never happened, as we all know. The moderate success of *Berthe: A Woman Who Made an Impression*, kept him headquartered here so to speak, and he became a fixture in our circles. We embraced him, he embraced us, and in so doing, Chicago became as warm for him as any tropical destination. His second book about Gloria Guinness served to foster our appreciation of him for his great observational skills in bringing to us stories of the elite. His quick wit and repartee made him in great demand in our literary circles and at our social events.

"Now it's no secret that there has recently been some attention, too much attention in my humble opinion, paid to what his real name was and whether he was born of well-to-do parents or came from humbler origins. Some people have even concerned themselves with this so much so as to make some sort of ill-targeted vendetta to sully his name and thereby his memory."

She raised her eyes from her notes and rested them for a three count on Connie Chan, whose blazing red suit stood out like a fireplug in the Black Forest.

Elsa continued. "What I would like to say on his behalf is that who Ethan was is reflected in the faces of everyone in this room. He was our friend, he made each of us feel unique, he emulated a time where people were gentler and more polite. Surely none of this is a crime. There was a civility to him that is sorely lacking in this day and age, and I say to Ethan, most surely in heaven above us, please set every one of us a place at your table, and we promise to arrive properly dressed. Goodbye and Godspeed to you."

Handkerchiefs were emerging from Kelly bags and breast pockets like doves at a magic show. Elsa retrieved her lace hanky from her sleeve and dabbed the moisture from her eyes. She gave a meek smile and stepped down to hushed whispers of "beautiful" and "well-said." I applauded myself for asking her to speak. She was such a master of hyperbole that even my own faith in Ethan was renewed.

The minister stepped up next and, since he'd never known Ethan, said the requisite words about life and death followed by a few prayers. Finally, the funeral director resumed his post and informed the assembled grievers that "this would conclude the services" and that "Mrs. Cook would like to invite the attendees to a late lunch at the Casino."

As I scanned the crowd, I hoped not all of them planned on joining me. The liquor bill alone would be paralyzing. Raoul and Bharrie escorted me out the door to the waiting limousine. I was just getting in when Mr. Fox, the funeral director, caught up with me.

"Mrs. Cook, there's the question of the bill here." He flashed the itemized sheet in front of me. My eyes darted to the bottom line. I wasn't sure if I was paying for a wedding or a funeral.

"Of course, Mr. Fox. You have my address. Please send it to me," I said, shutting the car door.

The party afterward cost as much as the funeral. After all, I had to send Ethan out in style. I made the best of it, moving about from table to table, accepting condolences for the umpteenth time while my guests dined on tenderloin or fillet of sole. An unwelcome Connie Chan saw fit to join us, and though I begrudged her every bite, I was overly polite to her. One never knew what she might decide to write.

Three hours later, I walked through my door and laid my black pashmina on the settee in the entrance. Despite all the money I had spent, I felt relieved it was finally over. I had gone on a wild goose chase that in the end had revealed a different Ethan than I had known. Nonetheless, I had fulfilled the obligations of a friendship, and had seen to the disposal of his remains, seen to it that good words were spoken over him, and even fed all his close and not so close friends.

Ethan was now put to rest forever. Or so I thought.

22
The Unpleasant Sting
of Reality

A month passed. My cat and I were the best of friends again, she trusting that I was not going to go off and desert her again as my travel schedule had eased off to nothing. The bills poured in from my previous trips, yet another tribute to Ethan's memory, and I did my best to pretend they didn't exist. I hadn't heard a word from Terrance Sullivan, and had no way of reaching him. I was tempted to call Charmian in London under the guise of chatting and hope his name would come up. More than once I picked up the phone to initiate the probe and ended up putting the phone back in the cradle. In truth, I was afraid of what I might learn if I spoke with Charmian, that she had, after all, managed to entice him into her bed.

However, this did not stop me from pouncing upon the phone, like Fleur would on catnip, every time it rang. My obsession got so bad that I started carrying my cordless phone around the house with me, even taking it into the powder room. I couldn't risk missing a call from the elusive Irishman who refused to speak to answering machines. It even came down to me declining social invitations so I could remain home to take my calls.

My phone rang incessantly, but it was always the wrong people. Eleanor McFardle called to ask if I intended to sit on the Library Board. Whitney called to ask me to dinner. Sunny called to extend an olive branch and see how I was doing. Jacquie Washington called to tell me she was dropping Sean from her client list for his erratic behavior. She hoped I didn't mind since I was the one who referred him to her. I told her that I had absolutely no connection to him any longer, and, by all means, to do as she pleased.

Sean called, and because I was picking up my calls instead of monitoring them, I was forced to speak with him. The conversation was short and to the point. I let him know in no uncertain terms that he was no longer in the picture, that I considered what he had done tantamount to rape and that he was lucky I hadn't called the police. He apologized profusely for his actions of that evening. Then he told me that Jacquie had dropped him and asked if I could put in a good word for him. His physical violation I could almost forgive, after all I did take an active role in it, but the cruel insult he had delivered afterward— never. I pictured the calculated look on his face when he had called me an "old broad," and I knew that was one sticky wicket that could never be unstuck. After telling him I was unable to help him, I requested he remove me from his telephone book permanently.

A dear old friend, and I mean old in both senses of the word since Armand Peckles was eighty-nine, called to invite me to *La Traviata* at the Lyric. It had been Armand's car waiting to take me to *Tosca* the night Ethan called to tell me about his swollen ankles. When Armand's first wife died shortly after Henry, we had been a fixture at social events for a while. He had even hinted that our relationship could go further. Though he was flush with money, I declined his advances at the time because I was still mourning my husband and wasn't yet in dire financial circumstances, not to mention he was nearly forty years older than I.

Soon afterward, he married a woman sixty years younger than himself, and I didn't hear from him for years. But last year he divorced her in one of the more spectacular and scandalous cases to hit the papers in recent history. It seemed the new Mrs. Peckles, entrusted with overseeing the staff of their Kenilworth mansion, had hired her longtime lover as a chauffeur and to help her while away the time in anticipation of the day her much older husband preceded her in death. I imagine she figured her ten or fifteen years in purgatory would pass far more agreeably with her boyfriend nearby.

Unfortunately for her, she was naive enough to think a man who accumulates a fortune like Armand Peckles was lacking in gray matter. But he had slipped not a whit. If anything, with business on his mind less and pleasure on it more, he had grown sharper. And more demanding. There were two things expected of his young wife—to look sensational and make him feel that way.

When her absences in the house grew more protracted, and his suspicions were the only thing aroused, he hired an army of detectives to spy on her. Over the period of a year they swarmed the house under the guise of painting crews, landscapers and even window washers. The photos of Heather and her lover playing footsie just about everywhere on the estate came out during divorce proceedings, and Heather Peckles was sent packing without a sou.

Which meant the fabulously wealthy Armand Peckles was available again.

I tried my best to drum up some enthusiasm about this while I waited for his car to pick me up. I had dressed with special care, wearing an off-the-shoulder rose Valentino gown and a borrowed diamond necklace from Bulgari since I had already sold off my best pieces of jewelry. Though there wasn't a dry eye in the house by the time Violetta succumbed to death, I found myself completely unable to enjoy the opera. My only thought was I might be missing a call from Terrance. Eager to get home, I declined Armand's offer of champagne and dessert at the Chicago Club afterward. It was then I realized I had to take some kind of action or remain permanently holed-up in my apartment. After all my complaints about cell phone users, I finally joined the club, signing up for a discounted six-month trial package. From that point on I was free, forwarding all the calls from my home phone to my new cell phone.

There was a certain downside to this forwarding arrangement, however. One afternoon I was in Diabolique trying on a pair of gabardine slacks and boucle top when the phone began ringing. I frantically forced the slacks over my hips so I could get to my cell phone in my purse and ended up tearing the zipper in the process. My quite affable hello was greeted by an even more affable voice asking if I was Mrs. Pauline Cook. Upon identifying myself, the caller informed me that he was employed by an agency whose purpose was to collect on unpaid bills. Not waiting to hear on whose behalf he was calling, I snapped the phone shut.

I was shaking with vitriolic anger as I dressed. The sheer audacity of . . . whoever. I decided to buy the top, but passed on the pants, not wanting them with a broken zipper. My face must have been crimson with rage because Lucinda, the sweet salesgirl who always takes care of me, asked if I would like a glass of water. I shook my head no and handed her my credit card. She ran it through a computerized device, and then her face turned crimson also. She apologetically told me that my card had been declined.

"Impossible," I said. "Try it again." I was fairly certain I had credit left on this card.

She performed the same exercise, and the card was refused once again. The murderous expression on my face must have frightened the poor girl, because she looked as though she wanted to crawl under the counter.

"This is absurd," I declared.

"There must be something wrong with the computers, Mrs. Cook. Would you like me to just bill you directly?"

"That would be lovely, Lucinda," I said, taking my purchase and storming from the store.

The moment I got home I called my attorney.

"Ed, what I tell you is privileged, is it not?"

"Of course, Pauline. Think of me as a priest."

It was hard to think of Edward Cohen as a priest, not when it came to his transplanted hair, rolled-up cuffs, exaggerated waistline, and three ex-wives. But I was secure that what I was going to tell him was in confidence. And more importantly gratis. He had been a good friend of Henry's and usually made himself available to me without running the clock.

"It seems I have some collection agency after me. Do they have the right to call me at home?"

"It all depends, Pauline. Do you owe money to the creditor they are collecting for?"

"I wouldn't know. I hung up before the cretin got that far."

"Well, if you do owe money, and the agency is trying to collect on a legitimate debt, yes—they can use reasonable means to contact you. There are limits, however. They can't call you in the middle of the night or leave threatening messages. But they can take legal action against you."

"Oh, that's delightful." I stewed over the situation. "What should I do?"

"That's easy, Pauline. Find out who it is and pay them."

Easy for him to say.

My next call was to my broker. Thomas Slattery was both ambitious and honest as far as I knew, unlikely bedfellows, to be sure. I inherited him when Henry's original broker had retired. I must credit him with trying his best to steer me clear of the derivatives debacle, but I hadn't wanted to listen to him at the time. So I had stayed with him and his firm despite my losses. After all, my own hubris wasn't his fault. Thomas had a receded hairline which he most likely got from rubbing the top of his head when he was on the phone, as I pictured him doing right now.

"Thomas, I need to raise some cash. I'm going to have to sell some things."

"Mrs. Cook, I don't know how to tell you this, but you have nothing left to sell. Remember you had me cash in the last of your muni bonds last month?"

"That was the last of them? I thought I had a couple left."

"I'm afraid not."

"Well, how much do I have in the account, then?"

I could hear the sound of his busy fingers tapping something into his computer. "A little over three hundred dollars. In fact, if you don't make a deposit soon, you don't even qualify for an account here anymore."

"Thomas, how much did you make in commissions while I was buying all those derivatives?"

He was silent.

"My account will remain open at John Meeker and Sons."

My final call was to my accountant. Before I could say a word, he was asking me if I had sent in my income tax check.

"Not yet, Ivan. That's what I would like to speak with you about, among other things. I'm in a difficult situation—it seems I don't have any money to pay my bills. I was wondering if you might have some ingenious solution for me, a refinance on the co-op perhaps?"

"Pauline, you're already carrying two mortgages on the place and you've tapped into your equity. There's nothing for you to borrow, even if you could qualify for a loan."

It was at that moment the extreme gravity of my situation became crystal clear. Up until then it had lurked somewhere toward the back of my mind, there but unseen, like an undiscovered body in a South Carolina swamp. It was time to take some action.

"Ivan, I have bill collectors hounding me and I don't know what to do."

"Do you have anything of value you can sell? Art, jewelry, cars?"

I thought of my safety box. Its contents were down to my engagement ring and the strand of Mikimoto pearls Henry had given me after our third date. My emotional attachment was far too great to ever part with them. The other jewelry was already gone. I had the Pissarro hanging in my living room, but the world would have to be in the path of a meteor before I would part with it. Which left the car. At least if that went, I wouldn't have to pay the astronomical insurance bill that was now stuffed into my desk drawer with the other bills.

"There's the Jaguar."

"Then I suggest you sell it."

"Can't you think of anything else I could do?" I asked in desperation.

"Pauline, the way I see it, you have three other options. Borrow money from a friend—which I don't recommend—always ends in disaster, marry someone with money, or sell the co-op. No wait, there is a fourth option."

"What is that?" I was hoping for a lifeline.

"You could get a job."

I hung up on Ivan without saying good-bye, not in the least amused at his sense of humor. A job, indeed. Where? At one of the boutiques I had been patronizing for so long? Chanel? Max Mara? Ultimo? Wait on people like me? Indeed! I phoned *The Chicago Tribune* and asked for the classified ads department.

The man I spoke with was very nice and offered to help me price the car by looking it up in something called a blue book. I was astounded when he came back and told me that the price advised for sale was $12,000. The car had cost Henry far more than that when he bought it. I should have thought it would be a collector's item worth more. Certainly more than $12,000. That wasn't enough to cover the upcoming month's bills, much less make a dent in what I already owed.

I placed the ad and set the price at $25,000.

That resolved I was pushing the day's mail into my drawer when I noticed a shiny envelope that said 'Pay no interest for 6 months' on the outside. I opened it and found a pre-approved credit card inside. All I had to do was call the 800 number to activate it. Five minutes later, there was a temporary Band-Aid on my gaping wound.

23

The Circle

Elsa invited me to lunch "just to chat." She was fishing for gossip of course—Ethan's demise left a large gap in her column. While she demolished a serving of calves' liver with buttered noodles, I mentioned that Whitney had helped me clean out Ethan's apartment. Elsa's eyes actually left her plate for a moment to look into mine.

"Since when are you and Whitney Armstrong so close? She's so terribly common."

"She's refreshing," I said, picking at my sea bass.

"Lake Michigan is refreshing, but that doesn't mean I'd recommend anyone swim in it," she said from under the turned-up brim of a yellow fedora sporting a peacock feather. Using her dinner roll to sop up the remaining sauce on her plate, bringing the china to a near polish, she added, "You can dress a pig in expensive clothes and jewels, but it's still a pig."

"That's very uncharitable of you, Elsa. Besides, these days it's not where you're bred, it's where you're fed more so than ever."

"Well, there's no disputing Jack Armstrong sure is feeding her. But there's something about that woman I can't put my finger on. She's hiding something. Before he died Ethan called to tell me he had something great on Whitney, but I never got a chance to find out what it was. He said it was so volcanic that even I probably wouldn't print it."

The thought of Whitney's strange behavior in Ethan's apartment popped into my mind, but I made no mention of it to Elsa. "I find Whitney to be kind and ingenuous."

"Yes, she was ingenuous all right when she ousted Theresa Armstrong, wouldn't you say?" Elsa was a good friend of Jack Armstrong's first wife, and the initial support she gave Theresa in her columns after the breakup rivaled the support Liz Smith gave to Ivana after being jilted by the Donald. Elsa's support for Theresa faded, however, as she slipped farther off into the moonscape. "I'm saying right now they don't last another year."

Of course, everyone knows where Don and Marla's relationship went, but my money, or rather my former money, would have said that Whitney and Jack were going to stick. Jack fawned over his bride like a Japanese over his first-born son. "From what I understand, they are very happy."

"They're happy now, but just wait until he falls out of heat. Damn, I wish I knew what Ethan had on her. I'm sure it was juicy."

My cell phone rang in the taxi on the way home. I was still forwarding all calls from my home phone despite my creditor problems. But I'd gotten rather adept at avoiding the collection man, so when I heard an unfamiliar male voice I almost hung up. Then I remembered the ad for the Jaguar in *The Tribune*. Though it had been running for days, I hadn't received any calls yet.

"Are you the one with the vintage XKE for sale?" he asked.

"Yes," I replied with mixed emotions. I really didn't want to sell my car.

"Is there any wiggle in that price?"

"Pardon me, any what?"

"Any wiggle. Any room for negotiation. You're asking a lot more than the car is worth."

"That is your opinion," I said. Deciding right away I didn't care for his tone and didn't want him ever setting his pompous posterior upon my beloved car's leather seats, I ended the negotiations before they got started. "There is no wiggle, and actually the price has changed. I'm now asking $30,000."

"You're out of your nut, lady."

"And that, too, is your opinion." I ended the call and rode the rest of the way home in blessed, uninterrupted silence.

Later that evening, with my cat curled happily at my side, I looked unhappily out across the choppy waters of the lake. There had been no more calls for the car, a sign my pricing strategy was working. I knew I had to try harder to sell it. I needed the money desperately. My situation was so dire I hadn't paid the monthly maintenance on the co-op, not to mention the special assessment. When I ran into Parker Donnelly, the co-op board chairman, in the lobby the other day, I had to tell him I had forgotten and would put a check in the mail right away. Now I avoided going out at times when I might see any fellow residents.

It seemed money was everywhere except with me. I was beginning to understand how Ethan had felt being around so much wealth and having none of his own. It was so unfair. It tore me to pieces to listen to department store clerks talk about the small fortunes they were making on the stock market. E-trade. AOL. Red Hats and CMGIs. I watched the soaring Dow and Nasdaq with frustration and listened to Alan Greenspan speak out against irrational exuberance and things soared higher. I wanted to be part of the exuberance. And it was doubly tormenting to be so destitute while everyone from waiters to shopkeepers to shoe-shine boys was getting rich and richer.

A prescient chill came over me as I realized my life was making a circle. I was heading back where Mother and I had been after Father deserted us, scraping for every penny. Except the situation was graver this time. There was no Grandmother to fall back on as a last resort. Yesterday's paper ran a story about a Beverly Hills woman who had resorted to living in her car after her alimony ran out. My situation would be even more dire than hers if I sold my car.

I thought about Armand Peckles. He acted disappointed when I begged off on a drink after the opera last week. I knew he was still very fond of me. Perhaps if I acted quickly, I could seal a deal with him before the bank foreclosed on the co-op. Then I recalled something he said during the intermission, that after his last disastrous marriage he would sooner get a tattoo on his chest than ever marry again. Still, I might have given it a try, but in all truth, I was hedging. How would I feel if I secured Armand, and then Terrance Sullivan made one of his unpredictable appearances? It would be akin to Scarlet O'Hara settling for Frank Washington before she found out Rhett had all that money.

The phone rang and I answered it listlessly. The caller had a thick Southern accent, bringing back some stinging memories of Charleston. Though I was certain I had never heard this voice before, there was something hauntingly familiar about it.

"This here is Rufus James Burton, and I'm calling about the ad in the paper."

"The Jaguar?" I said trying to sound affable. Things were at the point I had to consider any serious offer.

There was a silence, and then, "No, ma'am, I don't know nothing about no Jaguar. I'm calling about the ad in *The Charlestonian*."

A mystery to me, of course. "What ad in *The Charlestonian* might I ask?"

"Why the one offering the reward, ma'am. I'm looking at it right here. 'Seeking information leading to the whereabouts of Ethan Campbell last seen in Morristown, South Carolina, March 1965. Contact Pauline Cook. 312-557-3836. Reward.'"

The phone fell out of my hand.

24

Soup to Nuts

"Are you still there?" I asked my mysterious caller, having recovered from shock enough to pick the phone up from the floor.

"Yes'm."

"I'm afraid the telephone slipped. Could we start over, please? You said there's a classified ad in *The Charlestonian* offering a *reward* for information about Ethan Campbell?"

"Yes, ma'am. 'Cept it ain't in the classifieds. It's a big ad on page three."

The word flabbergasted wouldn't even begin to describe my feelings. Someone had placed an ad in a metropolitan newspaper asking for information about Ethan Campbell and naming me as the contact. And offering a reward, no less. The ad must have cost a small fortune. If it wasn't so beyond bizarre, I might have been impressed. Then it came to me slowly, like the sun's corona peeking through the mist of a Martha's Vineyard morning. A voice was telling me who was responsible for the ad, and that voice had an Irish brogue. Terrance was really determined to make sure that old woman died in peace. Normally I would have been incensed that he had the nerve to include me in his folly without asking my permission. Instead I was elated. It meant I would hear from him after all.

"Does it state how much the reward is?"

"No, ma'am."

I thrashed about for an appropriate figure. "The reward is fifty dollars."

"Ma'am?"

I chose to ignore the disbelief in the voice. "Yes. Fifty dollars. Now do you have information or not?"

"Well, I thought for such a big ad, there might be a little more money involved."

I thought about Terrance. I thought about seeing him again, about his whimsical smile, and the possibility of someday running my fingers through his wiry red hair. I thought about how rich he was. Evidently, it was extremely important to him to find out what happened to Sarah Campbell Moore's son. "All right then. One hundred dollars. But you're going to have to prove to me that you really knew Ethan Campbell."

"Oh, I didn't know him, ma'am, but I surely remember him. I wasn't but a little boy sitting in my daddy's coffee shop. Mr. Campbell, he was at the counter eating eggs and grits, askin' my pa about what was grits anyhow. Well, you know how kids is, walls have ears and all, but damn if I couldn't barely understand him, he talked so pretty. My daddy asked him where he come from and he said England. And then he gave his name. 'I'm Ethan Campbell,' he said. I remember 'cause it reminded me of Campbell's soup, and I thought that since he talked so fancy, maybe he owned the soup company or something. You know the way a kid's mind works and all. Think the craziest things. But anyhow, that one just stuck with me all my life. Not that I ever give it any thought since then, except today when I opened the paper and saw the ad. Why, it popped right back into my brain as clear as last night's dinner."

I knew his story was true. Otherwise, how would he have known the Ethan Campbell in question was an Englishman?

"So, Mr. Burton, what makes you think that you can tell me Mr. Campbell's whereabouts when you only saw him once in a coffee shop over thirty-five years ago?"

"Well, because," he drawled, "I heard him tell my daddy where he was headed."

"And where was that?"

"Hundred bucks?"

"Yes, one hundred dollars," I acquiesced.

"He told my daddy he was going to Puerto Rico for a job."

I obtained Mr. Rufus James Burton's mailing address and promised to send out a check within the week. Then I hung up the phone and stared at it, the implications of what he had told me sinking in little by little until I grasped the entirety of it. The final piece of the puzzle was in place. In 1965 Daniel Kehoe had become Ethan Campbell so thoroughly that he had even shown up in Puerto Rico and taken his job. I knew then with certainty that the skeleton found in the South Carolina swamp was the missing Ethan Campbell. The cold calculation of what my Ethan had done became crystal clear. The knowledge frightened me and for the first time I wondered how I had lived in such close proximately to evil and never suspected it.

Suddenly, this was far too much for me to handle on my own. I needed to share the story with someone. I would certainly share it with Terrance when he called, but God only knew when that would be. I thought of Sunny and immediately ruled her out. I didn't want to hear I told-you-sos for the rest of my social life. Elsa would be even worse, because this was far too sleazy for her to leave out of her column. Then Whitney came to mind. She had said she wanted to be close. Well, we were going to be close.

The housekeeper let me into the Astor Street mansion. She led me down a long hall decorated with handpainted Chinese murals and tapestries and into a large solarium at the back of the house. The late afternoon sun was streaming in the windows and the combination of humidity and plant life, tall palms and rubber trees, leafy dieffenbachia and flowering orchids, gave one the sensation of being in the tropics. Whitney was stretched out on a wicker chair reading *Vanity Fair*, her slippered feet resting on an ottoman. She looked divinely comfortable in stretch pants and an oversized blouse. It was the first time I had seen her without makeup and I noticed her skin was just as luminous without it.

"Pauline!" She put down her magazine and leapt up upon seeing me. "I hope you're all right. You sounded so serious on the phone."

"I'm a little frazzled. I need a sounding board."

"Well, I'll be happy to listen. Can I get you something first?"

"A glass of wine would be lovely."

"Miranda," she said to the waiting housekeeper. "Could you be a love and bring us two glasses of the Jadot Puligny." Then she took another look at me. "On second thought make it the bottle."

"And I don't suppose you keep any cigarettes in the house."

She gave a pearly toothed smile. I couldn't get over how perfect her veneers were, yet another thing to ask about when the time was right. "As a matter of fact, I do. I cheat once in a while."

"That's what I hoped."

I sat down on a low-slung rattan sofa opposite her. The sound of trickling water came from a small fountain at the far corner of the room, its gentle music helping to lessen the feeling I might explode. Miranda returned with the opened bottle, an ice bucket, two white wine glasses, and a pack of Marlboro Lights. I lit a cigarette, feeling the drug-like nicotine course through my veins almost immediately. It felt good. It had been years since I had given them up—well before I married Henry.

"Can I tell you a story in complete confidence?" I asked.

She sat down next to me on the sofa, awkwardly close. Not wanting to insult her, I fought the urge to pull away from her closeness. She put a hand on my arm and said, woman to woman, "I'm your friend, Pauline. Whatever you say will stay right here."

"It's about Ethan. You were right, he wasn't as nice as I thought he was. There was a lot more to him, a lot more." My story spilled out, but this time I filled in all the blanks about everything that had happened since Ethan's death, of my trips to England, Boston, Rochester.

"Oh, Rochester. You poor thing," she said, petting my arm as she puffed from her own cigarette.

I went on to tell her about Charleston and the unidentified body found in the swamp. I told her about the phone call from Rufus James Burton and the British Ethan Campbell who was heading to Puerto Rico for a job. Then I told her the one thing I hadn't told anyone else. About Ethan's suicide note admitting to some terrible act. "I'm pretty certain now I know what that act was. He killed the first Ethan. Which is completely mind-boggling to me, because the person I thought I knew could never have done that. He could be catty at times, but overall he was a pussycat. I thought. Now I discover that he's Theodore Bundy."

Her silence made me wonder if the story had gone over her bleached-blond head. But I was proven wrong when she said, "You know, sometimes desperation drives people to take desperate measures."

"You think Ethan was desperate?"

"Yes. It sounds to me like he had a dead-end life, blue collar background, not able to find any kind of permanent job. Then he came upon Ethan Campbell. He wanted to be whoever this other Ethan was and he was desperate enough to do anything to get it."

It occurred to me that perhaps Whitney knew what lurked below Ethan's surface better than I. My mind flashed back to her odd behavior at his apartment. "Whitney, when you first offered to help me with Ethan's things, you said he had done you a favor."

She turned her blond head sideways, focused on a palm at the back of the solarium and laughed an ironic laugh. "He did in a way. He threatened to blackmail me, but then didn't go through with it."

"What?"

"Now it's my turn to tell you this goes no further. He knew something about me that wouldn't be looked upon very nicely in our social circles. It goes way back before I married Jack."

At one time I would have been stupefied by Whitney's telling me that in addition to everything else Ethan was an extortionist, but at this point nothing he had done could surprise me anymore. My only question was what did he have on Whitney? It must have been the unshared information he tantalized Elsa with. There were a lot of avenues ripe for me to take a mental stroll, among them her habit of physical closeness to women. Or maybe she had been a prostitute at one time. Certainly she wouldn't have been the first of that profession to make a lateral move. But Whitney wasn't saying anything more, and her personal life wasn't the reason behind my visit anyhow. There would be plenty of time to ruminate about Whitney after I resolved my own personal dilemma. I stubbed out my second cigarette and looked at the nearly empty bottle of wine.

"Whitney, if you were I, what would you do?"

"What do you mean?"

"About Ethan. Should I report any of it? That I believe Ethan killed someone and stole his identity?"

She mulled it over. "I don't see what it would change. Where Ethan's concerned, I think you could only stir up sewer water. Why not just forget about it and get on with your life?"

"Because it's become an obsession with me." There, I had admitted it. The thing that had been really driving me all along. I wanted, no I needed, to know the entire truth.

I took a third cigarette from the pack and readied to light it when a new avenue of pursuit popped into my head. In my excitement to get to Charleston and Terrance Sullivan, I'd completely forgotten about the odd man who visited Shannon Maglieri asking about her brother. The investigator. His card was still in the zipper lining of the purse I'd been carrying that day. I had intended to call him upon my return from Rochester, but ended up traipsing about the Low Country with Terrance instead. I tried to remember what I had been wearing that day. I'd been wearing a navy Donna Karan suit, which meant I would have been carrying my navy Kelly bag.

"Whitney," I said, putting down the unlit cigarette and draining the last drop of white Burgundy. "Thanks for the ear. And wine. And cigarettes. I've got to go."

25

The Truth Will Out

I more or less oozed out of the taxi, regretting that I had drunk so much wine on an empty stomach. I was definitely feeling tipsy. An unfamiliar young man wearing the building's uniform held the door for me. He was dark-complected with a flat nose and a sweep of thick black hair that seemed to float from his square face. He was also enormous, my head barely clearing his chest.

"Good evening, Mrs. Cook." The voice was not coming from the unknown Goliath beside me, but rather from somewhere else in the lobby. I turned to see Jeffrey's familiar blond head seated behind the desk. "Meet Tony Papanapoulous. He's replacing Edgar. I'm showing him the ropes."

"Did Edgar decide to retire?" I asked, forming my words carefully so as not to slur. I did not want to give the new help any wrong impressions. First impressions are generally the lasting ones. I hoped I didn't smell like cigarette smoke.

"Oh, Edgar didn't decide to leave. He got decided for. Sent a schwartze delivery boy up to Mrs. Cavanaugh's instead of Mrs. Stein's, and I guess her door wasn't locked, so he walked in and scared the living sh . . . daylights out of her. She nearly had a heart attack."

I learned later that Jeffrey had graciously left out the meatiest part of the story. It seems that Elizabeth Cavanaugh had been dancing naked in her living room to the strains of a Chopin Polonaise when the rather out-of-his-element young man—sporting dreadlocks, what's more—walked in on her *pas de deux*. Rumor has it her screams could be heard on the street, which sent Board Director Donnelly bounding downstairs with his passkey. He was not as close-mouthed about what he saw as Jeffrey was.

"I'm sorry to hear about Edgar. He will be missed." Holding my head regally high, I picked my way toward the elevator, but as cursed fate would have it, the edge of the area rug was curled up and caught my heel. I started to fall and the strong arm of a young man came out of nowhere to steady me. It belonged, of course, to the new doorman who I was certain struggled to maintain a straight face.

"Be careful there, Mrs. Cook," said Tony Papanapoulous. "Don't want you to go and hurt yourself."

I straightened myself up and shook my arm from his grasp. "Thank you," I said in my most dignified manner. I stepped into the waiting elevator and waited for the doors to close. As they did, I called out to Jeffrey so that everyone would know that my stumbling was not entirely of my own volition.

"We really must do something about that rug."

Fleur watched from her perch atop a shelf in my dressing room closet while I sorted through my handbags until I found my navy Kelly bag secure in its flannel sleeve, pushed to the back of the top shelf. Safe inside the zippered compartment was the card Shannon Maglieri had handed me what seemed nearly an eternity ago. I reread the engraving: HOLSTEIN INVESTIGATIONS—SPECIALTY—MISSING PERSONS.

"Ethan, let this be the end of you," I said aloud as I dialed the Boston number. It was nearly six in Chicago, making it seven on the east coast, so it was no surprise when an answering machine asked me to "leave a detailed message."

"My name is Pauline Cook and I would like to speak with Mr. Holstein regarding Daniel Kehoe," I said leaving my phone number. That was as detailed as I intended to get.

I went into the kitchen and started rooting through my barren Sub-Zero in search of something to absorb the wine. My slightly besotted brain was awhirl with thought, wondering if a professional like Mr. Holstein might help me finally come to know the real truth. Not five minutes later, as I opened a can of Fleur's tuna, the phone rang. It was the finder of missing persons himself. His speech was marked by the slow cadence of a strong Bostonian accent. He sounded like one of the Kennedys themselves.

"You left a message about Daniel Kehoe?"

"I did."

"Do you mind if I ask how you knew I was looking for him?"

"His sister passed your card on to me."

"Shannon Maglieri," he said without hesitation. "So what can you tell me about Daniel Kehoe?"

"Perhaps I might ask the same of you." I felt we were playing a game of cat and mouse, and this feline had no intention of letting him get the upper hand. "I'd like you to tell me why you were looking for him first before I tell you what I know about him."

"I am looking for him on the behalf of a *thud pahty*."

He said am. He was still looking. "And would this third party have anything to do with a man named Ethan Campbell?"

A confused hesitation. "Who?"

His tone told me I had missed the mark. This man had no idea who Ethan Campbell was. Nonetheless, I repeated the name just to make sure. "Ethan Campbell."

"*Nevah hud* of an Ethan Campbell, but I'm very interested in Daniel Kehoe."

"Well, your interest is energy wasted. Daniel Kehoe is dead."

Another hesitation only this time I could hear an exaggerated sigh before he asked, "Are you certain of this?"

"I should be. I paid for his funeral." The wine was talking. "You see, he made me his heir."

There was no hesitation on Mr. Holstein's part. I could sense his interest right through the phone lines. His voice perked up to andante as he said, "Young lady, I need to pay you a visit."

26
In the Black

Mr. Hal Holstein took the first flight out of Boston the next morning. Not comfortable inviting a total stranger into my home, we arranged to meet for lunch. I called Spiaggia and made a noon reservation, requesting my usual table in the window overlooking Oak Street Beach.

When I arrived at 12:30 for the noon reservation, Carlo informed me that my gentleman friend awaited me at the table. He escorted me across the restaurant, vibrant with expensive talk and silver service clinking on china plates and ice tinkling in crystal water glasses. Mr. Holstein did not see me approach, his angular face was turned sharply out the window. He appeared to be completely absorbed in the dark clouds rolling in off the lake, fluffy cumulus whose white tops were at odds with their dark underbellies.

I sized him up before meeting him. He looked nothing like I had pictured. He was a balding silver-haired man, dressed in a reasonable gray suit with a white shirt and red tie. Recalling that both Emily McMahon and Shannon Maglieri mentioned that he had a disability,

I saw now what it was. His right shoulder dipped forty-five degrees lower than his left, and his right arm was pressed to his chest, his fist hugging it in a ball of curled up fingers. His healthy left hand rested on the table, strumming the top of a manila envelope.

I dismissed Carlo and stood there waiting. My visitor did not notice me until I cleared my throat to get his attention. His gaze reverted from the storm broiling on the lake to me. A pair of pale blue eyes so cool they seemed nearly devoid of emotion assessed me in turn, scanning me from top to bottom, noting the tailored lines of my suit, my necklace, my watch, my handbag. He was so thorough, I wasn't shocked when I noticed him glance beneath the table to see what kind of shoes I wore.

"They're Ferragamo," I said, deciding to save him the trouble.

"Pardon my *mannahs*." He pushed his chair back to stand. I waved my hand to indicate he should remain seated, but he rose to his feet nonetheless, coming to his full height which was quite unexceptional. Maybe somewhere in the area of five foot five if he stretched. He extended his good left hand, and I took it awkwardly in my right, holding it as if we were children on a park bench.

"Mrs. Cook. I'm Hal Holstein. So good to meet you." I understood now why he spoke so slowly. His lips labored to form every word. His efforts weren't so terribly removed from the way I worked to form my words the prior evening in front of the new doorman, except there was a world's difference in the reasons.

I sat down and placed my napkin in my lap, noting that Mr. Holstein's remained on the table. I wondered if this was bad manners or an indication that he did not intend on eating. The busboy appeared and poured water. I waited until he was out of earshot to begin talking.

"So Mr. Holstein, it seems we both have some interest in Daniel Kehoe. I know what mine is, but I must confess I'm very curious as to what yours might be."

"Mrs. Cook, you said on the phone that you had *bear-rayed* Daniel Kehoe and that he had made you his *ayah*."

"That is correct," I said after deciphering his words. "I did bury him and I am his heir, his sole heir, I might add. Unfortunately, heir to nothing, I'm afraid."

"Well, Mrs. Cook, I not only search for missing persons, I am also a *trace-ah* of lost *ayahs*. I have been looking for Mr. Kehoe for some time now. I had hoped to find him alive. You see, he's inherited some money. If what you say is true, that he is deceased and left his estate to you, it stands that you are now entitled to that money. Less my *shayuh*, of course."

"Your share? Whatever for?" I asked indignantly without thinking through his words.

"*Findahs* fee."

"You didn't find me, I found you." His response was an unwavering stare that told me he was all business. His body may have been compromised, but his mind certainly was not. I could tell that despite appearances, he was an adroit thinker who knew I should be more than interested in hearing what else he had to say. And I was. "What exactly would your share be?"

"My fee is one third of the estate. Out of that sum, I will *covah* all the legal fees. But before we can go any *fathah*, you will have to sign a document agreeing to those conditions."

He slid the manila envelope he had been drumming on to my side of the table. I took a measured pause to be sure he knew I meant business too, and opened it. A one-page legal document inside basically stated what he had just told me. In very plain English I might add. There was a line for my signature at the bottom. "I would have to discuss this with my attorney, of course. One third seems a bit steep."

"It's standard, I *asshuh* you."

"Could you at least tell me the source of the inheritance?"

"I'm afraid not."

"I could most likely find out myself," I challenged him.

"Maybe you could. But I doubt it."

"I would expect you could at least give me an idea of the amount of money involved."

His eyes were so direct, it was an effort to not drop my gaze. I picked up my water glass and stared at him over the rim while I drank from it. We were not playing cat and mouse, we were playing poker. Struggling to maintain a placid demeanor, I racked my brain in search of who might have left Daniel Kehoe money. Certainly no one I had met so far. I could safely rule out any of his family members. Perhaps he had met someone on the road and done something to change their life and this was their way of showing gratitude. Or a more likely scenario was someone from his past life had simply taken pity on him. One thing was for certain. Whoever the benevolent donor was, the connection between them had its origins prior to 1965, the year Daniel stopped being Daniel and showed up for a job in Puerto Rico as Ethan Campbell.

I weighed my chances of finding this mysterious benefactor on my own. Thinking of Terrance's ad in *The Charlestonian*, I contemplated running my own ad in every major paper in the country with an announcement that I knew the whereabouts of Daniel Kehoe. Then they could contact me. But, alas, that would involve vast sums of money, something I was in short supply of. And then, how could I be certain the man sitting across from me was on the level? This could all be some kind of an elaborate hoax.

But a tempting hoax, nonetheless. My mind circled back to the alleged money. Considering my desperate situation, any sum, however paltry, would come in handy . . . a thousand . . . ten thousand. I permitted my fancy to take over and imagined that there might be a hundred thousand dollars. A hundred thousand would be minced into sixty-six and change after Mr. Holstein took his cut. Still, it was a damn good starting place, buying me time on the car, my co-op, and some of my more pressing bills.

"If I were to sign this document, how long would it take to get the money?"

"You have a valid will?"

I nodded, recalling how Detective Velez and I noticed Ethan had it notarized at the local currency exchange. "Written by Ethan Campbell."

"But he's been subsequently identified as Daniel Kehoe?"

"That's what it read on the death certificate."

He mulled it over. "I don't think it should take long. We could possibly get this cleared up in a couple of months."

I wasn't sure what kind of money was involved, but I had nothing to lose and everything to gain.

"I'd like my attorney to have a look at this document before I sign it."

"By all means. When do you want him to do it?"

"No time like the present." The sooner I got that clock ticking, the better. As they say in the south, time was a-wastin'. My cell phone proved to come in handy as I put in a call to Edward Cohen without leaving the table. Edward informed me that I was in luck, he had an entire half hour free before going into a meeting with his partners. I told him we would be right over, and tossed my napkin back on the table. Mr. Holstein and I left Spiaggia without ever ordering.

"So, what's your opinion, Edward?"

I was seated in his Michigan Avenue law office while Mr. Holstein waited in the lobby, leafing through magazines with his good hand. Edward hovered over his kingly desk, the walls behind him papered with bookshelves, his head lowered between a pair of shoulders that could have belonged to a walrus. On a lit stand beside him a roly-poly Botero sculpture held court, its contours not unlike those of its owner.

His bifocals followed his meaty finger down the single page in front of him on the desk for the third time.

When he finally leaned back, his chair made an audible groan. "It's pretty clear-cut, Pauline. If you sign this, Mr. Holstein gets one-third of whatever monies are involved, less legal expenses. In other words, if this phantom benefactor left one thousand dollars, at the end of the day you get six hundred and change."

"I've already done the math, Edward."

"So my question to you is what if this turns out to be some kind of a significant sum?"

"A problem I would love to worry about. It's highly unlikely."

He pushed the document back toward me. "Your call, Pauline."

"Frankly, Edward, at this juncture I need money, any money. If there's anything at all involved, it's a godsend. I'm going to sign it."

"Like I said, it's your choice. You want I should call him in?"

I nodded and Edward picked up his phone to summon Mr. Hal Holstein, Specialty Missing Persons, Tracer of Lost Heirs, back into his office. In no time at all, Mr. Holstein sat beside me in the chair one's husband would occupy if we were getting a divorce. Instead we were entering into a marriage, one I hoped would prove to be lucrative for both of us. His head was tilted toward me, his hand posed in the peculiar palsied manner from which it never rested.

"Let's get on with it," I said. I thought I saw the glimmer of a smile at the corner of his mouth, but the blue eyes remained emotionless. Edward called in his secretary Janice, an enviable young thing with skin unscathed by age or elements and a figure that defied gravity, to act as a second witness. In front of them, I signed and dated Mr. Holstein's contract, effectively handing over to him 33.333 percent of whatever fortune had been left to Daniel Kehoe, a.k.a Ethan Campbell, and thereby passed on to me.

I prayed the sum could keep me from the ruthless jaws of poverty for at least a few more months. Edward dismissed Janice and the moment the door closed on her youthful derriere, I could stand it no longer.

"And now that the paperwork is out of the way, might I finally learn how much money is involved here?"

For the first time Mr. Holstein showed some emotion. The corners of his dour mouth turned upward and the blue eyes conveyed a genuine spark of life. "As of this morning, the estate consists of thirty-three million, three hundred and fifty-two thousand, sixty-seven dollars and eighty one cents."

I jumped to my feet so quickly the room went black.

27

Champagne for Everyone

My eyes fluttered open to see Edward's broad face so close to mine I could count his hair plugs. He was slapping my face gently with a pillowy soft hand. Hal Holstein hovered over Edward's right shoulder wearing a look of consternation like the owner of a thoroughbred horse who had twisted its leg. The pattern of an oriental rug danced in my peripheral vision telling me I was on the floor.

"I think she stood up too fast," said my attorney.

"She probably should have eaten some lunch," said my new best friend in the world.

The door opened and Janice came running in with a glass of water. Making no effort to move from my place on the floor, I took the glass from her slim hand and smiled up at her. She might have been young and yet to suffer wrinkle one, but I had thirty-three million dollars. Make that twenty-two after Mr. Holstein's cut. I immediately wondered if there was any way that I could nullify the contract I had just signed, and then berated myself for being greedy. There was an expression that Henry had loved: Pigs get fat; hogs get slaughtered. I concluded it best to not be a hog. After all, Mr. Holstein had won his share of my fortune fair and square.

With visions of a suite at the Crillon dancing in my head, I assured everyone I was fine, and with a boost from Edward, was soon reseated in my chair. I felt happily light-headed, as if I had just been given a double dose of Valium, except I was full of rapturous energy. In fact, it was all I could do not to get up and dance. After years of penury, I was rich again. Rich! I could keep my car and pay my special assessment. I could shop to my heart's content and not have to wait for the sales. I could travel wherever I liked and eat caviar with impunity. Beluga!

It was all because I had been fortunate enough to befriend a man who turned out to be a fake and most likely a murderer, and had been obsessed enough to find out who he really was.

Mr. Holstein was sitting again too, and I watched him expectantly, squirming in my seat as I waited to hear the details. He seemed to enjoy the drama of the situation. Even Edward, who I'm sure was running the clock on me now, looked ready to burst from his ample skin. Finally, after an interminable passage of time, the tracer of lost heirs proceeded to fill us in.

"Have you ever *hud* of Joseph Baincock?"

I spun my mental rolodex. Baincock, Joseph. Wealthy Eastern scion. Boston. Beacon Hill. Wife Emily. Father founded Baincock Paper, later sold off to a large industrial concern for an amount rumored to be near a hundred million dollars. Was of my grandmother's era.

"Yes, I've heard of him. I believe I read in *Town and Country* that he died a couple of years ago."

"That is *cahrect.* Well, Joseph Baincock was Daniel Kehoe's biological father."

It took a minute for the unlikely notion to gel. Then it began to make sense. I recalled Emily McMahon pouring Old City beer into dimestore tumblers in her living room and telling me about her husband's young cousin Moira who worked in a mansion on Beacon Hill.

Moira, Danny's immigrant mother. I put myself in Moira's shoes, a beautiful naive Irish lass sleeping in her own bedroom for the first time in her life. Interrupted by a nocturnal visit from the lord of the manor, one of many such visits. Then cruelly dismissed from her job when it was learned that she was pregnant. What a wretch Joseph Baincock had been to then force her out into the street as the result of his actions. The thought honestly made me ill.

I'd already known that the family gossip had been right. Shannon Maglieri had told me that Patrick Kehoe wasn't the baby's father. But did Patrick Kehoe know who the baby's real father was? He must have really loved Moira to marry her nonetheless. How sad that Patrick's love for the mother did not extend to her son. I pictured poor little Daniel, sickly and homely, living with abuse from a man who was angered by his image every day of his life. A frail little boy who couldn't understand what he had done wrong. No wonder he had chosen to bury himself in fantasies.

And then the true irony of the situation struck me. My Ethan had been born with a silver spoon in his mouth. His love for the better things was part of his genetic makeup. Had he not taken his own life, he would have realized his greatest dream. He would have been extremely rich, richer than many of the people he kowtowed to. How tragic that he hadn't lived to enjoy his good fortune. Tragic for him, that is. Pas pour moi.

"I'm famished," I declared. "Would anyone care for some lunch?"

I believe Edward Cohen would have given any of his clients the air to join us, but it just so happened he was meeting with his partners. So Mr. Holstein and myself were a cozy twosome back at Spiaggia, reseated at the very table we had vacated earlier. The scenario was far different than before. The storm clouds had rolled past and the sky was dotted with tufts of ethereal white, so much like a Venetian sky it could have been painted by Veronese himself. The scene in the restaurant had changed too; it was subdued as the lunch crowd was mostly gone. In fact, if not for my close relationship with Carlo we probably wouldn't have been seated at all.

I buttered a slice of bread and waited to take a bite until the waiter had finished pouring from the bottle of Comtes de Champagne I had ordered. Rosé. My favorite.

"To you, Mr. Holstein." I raised my glass to my liberator. He was not drinking, but he raised his water glass and we clinked them together. I sipped the wine and felt the divine sensation of a million bubbles expanding in my mouth. "This is really marvelous. You should try some."

"I'm not much of a *drinkah*," he said. "Doesn't agree with me."

I put down my glass and felt the satisfying wash of wine work its way into my system. To say my mood was elevated would be a major understatement. "So please continue your story, Mr. Holstein."

"*Whayah* was I? Oh, *yeaher*, so in his declining *yeahs* the old man *stahted* feeling guilty. With his wife dead and no children of *theyah* own, he decided he wanted to do right by Moira and her son. He changed his will to leave half his estate to Daniel Kehoe. I can quote his actual words from the document, 'It is only just and fitting that I, having brought this life into the world, should pass onto it a goodly share of my worldly goods.' The rest of the fortune went to relatives and some charities, but he made sure the will was written in an iron-clad *mannah*, that anyone who contested the inheritance of Daniel Kehoe would be shut out. So the nieces, nephews and whatnot took *theyah* money and went off to spend it. Daniel Kehoe's *shayuh* has been sitting in limbo *evah* since."

"And may I ask how you came to learn about this money?"

"I earn my living reading the obituaries and then reading the wills. Wills are public documents, you know. Although I'm thinking of retirement after this."

"But it wasn't until yesterday that you learned what became of Daniel Kehoe?"

"That is *cahrect*. Frankly, I had given up looking for him. I believe I searched *hahdah* for Daniel Kehoe than I *evah* have for anyone. Every which way I turned all I got was a dead end. His family hadn't seen him in *yeahs*, I couldn't find any friends, he had no work record. It was as if he fell off the face of the earth in 1965. I do *wondah* why he changed his name and disappeared like he did," he ruminated.

"I think Ethan, or Daniel rather, was like a caterpillar. He wanted to shed his previous life and leave it behind, his way of shuffling off his mortal coil." I did not add that Daniel Kehoe's metamorphosis most likely had to do with the disappearance of the man whose name he assumed. I intended that knowledge remain shared by only Terrance and Whitney.

"According to his *sistah*, his *mothah* suffered greatly."

"Maybe it's the lot of mothers to suffer in this world," I said, thinking of the sad old woman in the state home in England, waiting to hear word of another missing son so that she could die in peace.

We finished eating and the champagne bottle was nearly empty before I managed to persuade Mr. Holstein to indulge in a taste. He poured himself a minuscule sip and emptied the rest into my glass. Before we could toast, the waiter appeared with the check, clearly eager to be on his way as we were the only diners left in the restaurant.

"This one is mine," I insisted, taking the check and slipping my latest credit card into the folder. The waiter whisked it away. Then Mr. Holstein and I clinked glasses together and drained the last of the champagne. He placed his glass back on the table and rearranged his malformed body so that he was leaning as close to me as he possibly could.

"There's one other thing I think you should be aware of."

It was at that precise moment the waiter returned with the check and my credit card. "Just put that down," I commanded somewhat brusquely, eager to be rid of him so I could learn what Mr. Holstein wanted to tell me. He didn't put the folder down, but looked at me with a sheepish expression on his face.

"I'm sorry, Mrs. Cook, but your card was declined."

Evidently no one had yet informed the bank card company of my good fortune.

"Why, that's impossible," I started to fib, but Mr. Holstein held up his good hand and reached into his breast pocket. Pulling out his wallet, he flicked a card onto the table.

"Let me," he insisted.

The waiter whisked the check away again, leaving the tracer of lost heirs and me alone.

"Where were we?"

"You were going to tell me something," I replied.

"Oh, yes. There was one other contingency in Joseph Baincock's will, aside from the one cutting off anyone who interfered with Daniel Kehoe's inheritance. In the event that Daniel Kehoe was not found within three years, the money was to go to Mercy Hospital, the indigent hospital where Daniel was born."

"Well, then, they're not going to be too happy to learn that I'll be getting the money they were coming so close to. Do you think they'll take legal action?"

"They don't have a leg to stand on. The will clearly states the bequest is to go to Daniel Kehoe or his heirs and assigns. I don't see it as a problem. I just wanted to make you aware of it."

I felt the ruffling of a shifting wind. "You're certain I shouldn't worry?"

"I wouldn't be *heyah* if I wasn't positive that the money will be going to you. I just wanted you to be aware of the situation, that they might be a little difficult, that's all."

The waiter returned yet again, this time with an approved voucher. Evidently, the tracer of lost heirs was in far better standing with the credit bureaus than I. Mr. Holstein picked up the pen to sign the check, and a dour look came over his face as he saw the amount for the first time. I suppose it's fair to say people in his profession are not accustomed to drinking $350 bottles of Champagne at lunch—if at all.

"Next time it's yours," he said humorlessly.

28

Does Anyone Know Anybody

Once again I entered the lobby in a slightly inebriated state. However, this time it was in a completely different mood than the last. I was soaring, an inhabitant of a sparkling new world. Tony was on duty alone for the first time, and remembered me well enough to call me Mrs. Cavanaugh. At least it started with a C. Normally, I might have taken offense at being confused with the eccentric ballerina, but instead I gave him my winningest smile and floated past him. I cared not what he or anyone thought of me anymore. I had twenty-two million dollars.

I went upstairs, drew myself a bath, and luxuriated in it for more than an hour. I was back in the chips, and life was looking up dramatically. I finished my bath and toweled off in front of the mirror, taking my usual critical look at myself. Still not bad for nearly fifty. No problems that a little cosmetic work wouldn't solve, now that I could afford the very best. And then the rebel in me thought, why bother? The reason to look one's best was to seek or keep male companionship for financial security. With my own financial security, did I really have the need for a partner?

But then, in the fading glow of the champagne, the feelings I had managed to submerge for weeks broke through the floodgates. A surge of loneliness flowed through me, choking my newfound happiness like a vine does a rose. Crazy as it may sound, I felt I would gladly trade my new-found fortune for the opportunity to see Terrance Sullivan once again.

In the grip of this insanity, I decided I had waited long enough to hear from the elusive Irishman. It was time to take some action. I needed some answers about him like a diva needs applause. Maybe he had someone else, maybe he was queer, maybe he was insufferably shy, but I was going to find out what was what.

Though it was midnight in London, I put in a call to Charmian. Considering the late hour, the crisp British voice that came over the line was chirpy, successfully conveying the impression that his sole purpose in life was waiting for the phone to ring.

"Is this Maxwell?"

"It is indeed, Madam."

"Maxwell, this is Mrs. Cook calling from Chicago. I'm sorry to disturb you at such a late hour, but something has come up and I must speak with Lady Grace."

There was a pause. I could tell that ever the faithful servant, he was gauging my level of importance, deciding if I merited disturbing his employers at such a late hour.

"Of course, I wouldn't bother Lady Grace if it wasn't urgent," I added somberly, hoping to swing his decision in my favor.

My ploy worked because a moment later he said, "I shall summon her immediately." A minute passed before I heard the click of a phone being picked up followed by Lady Charmian's sleep-encrusted voice.

"Pauline, are you all right?"

"Sorry to bother you, Chimps, it's just that . . ." It was then I realized how inappropriate it was of me to make such a frivolous call at such a late hour. In fact, it was downright nervy. I was behaving like a stalker, my obsession overruling my common sense, not to mention my manners. At one young naive time in my life, I thought life was about love. It was easy with Henry. After his death, I forgot about love and decided life was about money. Now that I had money again, I realized I wanted the love part, too. That was why I made this call. Charmian would simply have to understand. "I need to get in touch with Terrance Sullivan."

Is it possible one can feel rage through a telephone line stretching four thousand miles across a dark and turbulent ocean? I can honestly answer that question with a yes.

"Terrance Sullivan?" The name came out with venom. "Well, any number of people would like to get in touch with him. The problem is we can't find him. He's absconded with bundles of Lord G.'s money and disappeared to God only knows where." I could hear David Grace grumbling now, no doubt roused from sleep by the shrill sound of his wife's voice.

"Did I hear you say Sullivan? Is that Sullivan? Give me the phone."

"Calm yourself, it isn't him," Charmian snapped. "It's Pauline. For some reason or other, she's looking for him too."

"Hand me that phone, confound it." There was a momentary silence and then Lord G. was talking to me. "Pauline. This Sullivan man. Have you been in contact with him?"

"Not for some time. That's why I was calling you."

"Well, the man's a fucking blighter. Scam artist. If he ever shows his head around here again, I'm sure to take it off with my hunting rifle. If you have a single brain cell, you'll keep yourself, and especially your money, away from him."

He handed the phone back to Charmian. Need I say I regretted making this call. Not only was I not going to find a way to get in contact with Terrance, but my dream, my ideal, my phantasmagoric lover had in a matter of seconds been reduced to a con man.

"Pauline? Are you still there?" she asked.

"Yes," I replied, downtrodden.

"Darling, I told you from the beginning he was horrid. I told Lord G. the same thing. If only people would listen to me. He hasn't stolen money from you too, has he?"

I recalled how he hadn't seemed so horrid to Charmian during the time he spent at her house that she didn't want to bed him. However, this was not a matter for discussion at the time. Nor would it ever be. Everything had changed in a matter of a couple of minutes. "No, he hasn't stolen any money from me," I assured her. "I'll let you go now. Sorry to disturb you so late. Thanks for enlightening me."

Charmian was speaking as I hung up. I really had absolutely no interest in continuing the conversation. I was far too numb. I felt abused. Granted, what had happened with Terrance thus far didn't qualify as a relationship, but that didn't stop me from caring for him, for hoping we could be something together. I was beyond miserable. In one day I had become both rich and poor. Rich in wealth and poor in love. I wondered what law in nature dictates that life can never be perfect for more than an atomic second.

Desperately needing to talk, I called Whitney. Her housekeeper informed me that Mr. Armstrong and she had left earlier that day for New York. Of course, the Met benefit was this weekend. I had been invited to join them, but had begged off, claiming social commitments in Chicago. The truth was I couldn't afford the airfare, hotel, and the $1,000 tariff for a ticket. That was yesterday when I was only poor in money. Today, I would have given anything to be in New York with them. Instead I stood in my window watching the waves crest on the blue gray lake and break with each beat of my heart. The ethereal white clouds of the afternoon had turned dark gray in the oncoming dusk. The wind blowing off the lake bent the trees on the parkway back and forth as if they were performing a ballet.

Suddenly, the walls of my co-op started closing in on me. I had to get out of there, get some fresh air. I went into my entry closet for a warm coat and noticed Ethan's old parka hanging beside my furs. It had hung there since the day Whitney and I cleaned out his apartment. I grabbed it on a sentimental whim.

On my way down in the elevator my nose was pricked by scents that lingered in the coat. I recognized Ethan's favorite cologne, bringing back the memory of the way it radiated from him whenever we met and bussed cheeks. But beneath the sweet familiar scent lurked a musty odor, an unattractive smell of something being stored away for too long.

I walked along the lake, the wind knifing at my face while the waves pounded violently at the breakwater. An occasional huge wave would leap the barrier and crash onto the pavement, soaking my feet and splashing onto the parka wrapped tightly around me. Despite the weather I kept going. My memory pulled up a phrase from Latin class at Foxcroft. *Solvitur ambulando.* Solved by walking. I was walking off Terrance Sullivan. Like liquid oxygen freezing damaged tissue, each blast of the wind worked to exorcise a piece of him from my mind. Things were going my way now. Why torture myself thinking about him? Better to walk this through and be done with it.

It was pitch dark when I got home. Tony gave me a peculiar look as he held the elevator door and when I saw myself in my entry mirror I understood why. With my hair twisted into knots and my cheeks raw from the wind, I looked like a madwoman. But I felt one hundred percent better. My pragmatic side had overruled the romantic one. I had decided there was no reason to suffer over unrequited love when I could revel in my newfound fortune. Terrance Sullivan had been nothing more than a tempestuous dream. But there was a silver lining behind the cloud. Make that a gold lining. Solid gold.

I took off Ethan's soaking wet parka. Though the wind had blown off the cologne scent, the smell of must still clung to it, so I decided to send it out to be cleaned in the morning. As is my habit, I went through all the pockets before putting it into the dry-cleaning hamper. I've sent off far too many a pair of earrings. The outside pockets were empty except for some lint, but inside the interior breast pocket I found a tightly folded magazine page.

I unfolded it carefully. It clearly came from one of the blue magazines Ethan had kept stockpiled in his bedroom closet. The page showed a scene of partially dressed young men dancing in very close proximity beneath the garish lights of a crowded nightclub. One of the dancers was circled in red ink, his slim torso naked, his only article of clothing a silver g-string unless one counted the pair of fire engine red women's heels he wore. His reed-like arms were wrapped around the chest of another young man in homo-erotic ecstasy. As I studied his face, dominated by an overly large nose and a crooked, gap-toothed smile, there was something familiar about him I couldn't put my finger on. I wondered why Ethan had chosen to carry this particular page around with him.

Then I took another look at the young dancer's legs. They were long, slender, drop-dead gorgeous legs—legs just about any woman would give up her firstborn to possess. Legs that were even better looking than mine. I knew those legs, had seen them and envied them many times. Then I looked more closely at his face, and I don't know if I was more amused or horrified. A nose job, some dental work, cheek implants, and there she was. Whitney's cosmetic work was even better than I suspected.

I began to doubt truly knowing anyone in this world.

29
Payoff

Two months stretched into four and spring rolled right into summer while I waited for the inheritance to come to me. As it turns out, Mercy Hospital was putting up a stink after all. A huge one. It seems they weren't willing to give up their claim on Joseph Baincock's money and had started legal action to keep it. I was in daily contact with Mr. Holstein who assured me that things would be resolved to our best interest and were just taking a little longer than he had anticipated. In the meantime, I managed to stay afloat by borrowing from various sources including Whitney, Edward, and even Armand Peckles, assuring all that as soon as a certain legal matter was cleared, I would pay them back with interest.

The summer was steamy, both in temperature and events. Sunny learned that Nat was cheating on her, putting up his girlfriend at a geographically desirable (for him) luxury rental in the Rush Street area. Naturally she hadn't told me, but had confided in Elsa, a horrendous mistake on her part. Elsa, starved for gossip since Ethan's demise, and still angry at Sunny for sharing her scoop with Connie

Chan way back in April, had made a thinly veiled reference to the affair in her column.

> What wealthy and prominent man is cheating on his wife and hous-
> ing his paramour in a love nest so near to home he can slip out for
> a quick rendezvous whenever he desires? The wife is livid, but con-
> fesses she is going to play dumb. After all, with him she is Mrs. Some-
> body and without him, Mrs. Nobody. If she's lucky, his girlfriend will
> tire of the smell of his cigars and send him back home.

Sunny hadn't spoken to Elsa since.

Marjorie Wilcock and Franklin James abruptly stopped seeing each other after their divorce proceedings got serious. When Marjo-rie saw the pittance she would most likely receive, since her husband had been smart enough to hide most of his money, and Franklin, not being smart enough to hide his, saw how he was going to be hung out to dry, that put an end to their little trysts. Apparently financial dev-astation dampens even the most fiery of ardor. They were still trying to work it out with their spouses.

After swearing he would never marry again, Armand Peckles eloped with a woman the same age as his great-granddaughter and then died shortly thereafter, leaving me to wonder if his death was due to natural causes or if the new Mrs. Peckles had just been cagier than the last. The thought crossed my mind that had I succeeded in marrying him, I would be the widow. At the same time I wondered if his estate knew about his loans to me.

My friendship with Whitney actually grew stronger. I remained tight-lipped about her little secret, not even telling her what I knew and that I was in possession of a picture that could ruin her life. She had replaced Ethan as my best friend, and for once I knew exactly who I was dealing with. I shared my heartbreak over Terrance with her and told her the *whole* story of my financial situation including the money I awaited from Ethan's estate. I swore her to secrecy and then asked if I could borrow ten thousand dollars to tide me over.

Whitney couldn't write me a check fast enough. She had her own personal account that she referred to as her maintenance money, and Jack told her to do with it as she pleased. I smiled inwardly every time I saw Jack wrap himself around her at some social event. If he only knew.

As for all the women who were so jealous of her their teeth were green, yapping like Yorkshire Terriers over everything she did, the smile grew broader. After all, who would know better how to pleasure a man than someone who had once been one?

Then one sunny day in August, when the humidity was so bad I dreaded venturing out for fear my hair would curl up like Little Orphan Annie's, the phone rang with the news I had awaited for four torturous months. Mr. Holstein's words were sweet as Sauternes, lingering in my ears far longer than the honeyed wine ever could on my tongue.

"The proceedings with Mercy Hospital have been dropped. The Baincock Estate will be cutting you a check next week," he said.

The following Wednesday Mr. Holstein hand delivered the check to me, left hand of course. I thought it only fitting and proper that we conduct the transaction at the Cape Cod Room, both in remembrance of the many lunches Ethan and I shared there and in deference to my Bostonian companion. Over oysters and Comptes de Champagne (blancs de blancs this time) he handed me the rectangular sheet of paper that represented my salvation. Twenty-two million and change. Handel himself could not have sung a stronger "Alleluia" than the one sounding in my brain. My future would not be as a pauper. I wanted to kiss the check, but refrained from doing so in front of Mr. Holstein. The kiss could wait until later when it was only the two of us, check and I.

"I'm can't tell you how good it feels to have this money in my hand. Mercy Hospital was causing me many a sleepless night," I confessed.

He surprised me by saying, "I'd *ven-chah* to say I was losing more sleep than you. *Remembah* our agreement says I foot the legal bills. They threatened to fight to the *bittah* end and it was costing by the day."

"So why do you suppose they suddenly caved in?"

He pulled at a bit of fabric, a small blue nub on the right sleeve of his jacket, "I'm afraid it took a bit of creative investigating on my *paht*."

I put my oyster fork down.

"Creative investigating?"

"Yep. I was beginning to get *feahful* they might possibly win, so I started digging into the hospital's history for something that they might prefer remain buried. I found it in a former nurse whose grandson needs an operation. It's amazing what you can learn when you spread enough money around. She was all too willing to tell me about some disturbing goings-on at the institution back in the thirties, the kind of thing that would bury Mercy in lawsuits if it was *evah* unearthed—even now. Would most likely wipe out the bequest several times *ovah*."

He stopped talking, one of his peculiar games. I had learned from dealing with him that he loved to be coaxed into giving up information.

"Well, are you going to tell me or not?"

He clasped his good hand over his bad and let an elusive trace of a smile bend his narrow lips. "*Remembah*, when Daniel was born, Mercy was an indigent hospital, not the fancy institution it is now. Well, it seems back then there were some unethical *doctahs* who took advantage of the *poah* immigrant women who came to the hospital to give birth. Some of them were so destitute they simply couldn't afford to care for another baby. Others were unmarried. So when the children were born these *doctahs* would issue death certificates for the babies and then sell them for adoption on the black market."

"That's reprehensible. I can't believe how low some people will stoop for money."

"So when I pointed this out to a couple of Mercy's board members, they dropped their lawsuit. But, there's more to the story, I'm afraid. In reality, Daniel Kehoe's estate could have been half what we received."

"I don't believe I understand what you are saying," I said, looking at my beautiful check, not wanting to think of it divided by two. Then he dropped a bombshell announcement that most likely would have put me back on the floor again were it not for the numbing properties of the champagne.

"Moira *nevah* knew it, but she gave birth to twins."

"Twins! Ethan was a twin? How do you know this?"

"The nurse kept a record of all the babies that were sold off. She was afraid if they ever got caught she might be able to save herself by helping to unravel the mess they were creating. Daniel's twin was adopted by a Pennsylvania couple who are long since dead. I was able to trace him to Florida, but didn't contact him."

"Does he have any claim to the inheritance?" I asked, suddenly panicked. The check hadn't been in my possession for an hour and I was already worried about keeping it.

"Wouldn't even know it exists. He has no idea who his real father was. Even if he somehow managed to trace his roots, it would only lead him as far as Patrick Kehoe."

"Well, thank God for that," I said, greatly relieved. "But if you're so sure about this, then why are you telling me?"

"It's *peculyah*, but people have a way of coming out of the wood-work when money's involved."

True to his promise, Mr. Holstein allowed me to pick up the check this time. The very moment we parted I marched, well took a taxi actually, down to Thomas Slattery's office in the Loop. I handed him the check. Even in the raging climate of people making money hand over fist, he was impressed by the sum. So much so, he picked up his phone and told his secretary to hold his calls.

"Now, aren't you glad you didn't close my account at John Meeker and Sons," I ribbed, feeling unusually generous and forgiving.

"Pauline, we need to talk about what to do with these funds. In this hot market I can take this money and triple it for you. I've got twenty ideas right off the top of my head . . . we can put half of it into growth companies. The momentum right now is incredible."

"What's a money market paying?"

He tapped something into his computer and rubbed the top of his balding head. "Today's rate is five and a half percent."

"So quick math tells me that's roughly one million, two hundred ten thousand a year in income. Does that sound right?"

He nodded.

"Put it in the money market."

The look of disappointment on his face was measurable. "Are you sure? We're in the hottest market ever, you can do better," he taunted me.

I recalled my derivative debacle. "Cash will do fine for now, Thomas. We can talk about other options when I get back."

"Where are you going?"

"Paris."

After leaving Thomas's office, my next stop was the travel agent Henry and I had used for so many years to book all our luxury travel. She was excited to see me, her long lost prodigal customer. I booked a first-class seat on Air France and the finest suite at the Crillon. My happiness was beyond belief. Paris in September defies description. The flowers are abloom. The heat of the summer has abated, and the city takes on a relaxed feeling as the hordes of summer tourists return home. I was already thinking of the friends I was going to look up, and my mouth watered for the duck confit at Tour D'Argent. The only thing lacking was a lover to share the world's most romantic city with me, but in lieu of that, unlimited shopping funds would do rather nicely.

I stopped at Neiman's to buy some travel clothes and arrived home in a taxi filled with boxes and bags. Jeffrey was on duty and met me at the door to help transfer my bounty into the lobby.

"Jeez, did you leave anything in the stores, Mrs. Cook?" he asked. "It looks like you bought out Michigan Avenue."

"There's actually more coming, Jeffrey. Can you have this all brought up when the other packages arrive?"

"Yes, ma'am."

"Oh, and Jeffrey, I'll be going to Paris next week. Could you look after Fleur for me?"

"Of course, Mrs. Cook."

"I'll give you the details later," I said, and feeling especially generous, I handed him twenty dollars for handling my bags. He stared at it as if it was the first time he had ever seen money.

30

Never Talk to Strangers

My bedroom looked like a Bedouin marketplace, mounds of clothes, shoes and handbags strewn about as I tried to narrow down what to take with me to the City of Light. My goal was to pack lightly, since I planned on doing a lot of pent-up shopping. A trill of excitement shimmied up my spine at the thought of it. Nothing in this universe competes with French couture, and no words tickle one's ears more delightfully than the phrase uttered upon entrance to any shop along the Rue Montaigne, "*Madame desire?*"

The customs man would get his piece of flesh from me this time.

Two years having passed since my last visit to Paris, I was listening to French language tapes while packing, hoping to bring my fluency level back up to par. I had also engaged a delightful young woman from Toulouse to tutor me. Since we were scheduled for a two o'clock phone session, when the phone rang at 1:55 I went directly into my library to take the call, answering with the most flowery of *bonjours*. The responding accent was to French as chicken liver is to foie gras. Or perhaps I should say Dublin to Dunkirk.

"And a bonnie-jour to you, too."

Though one wishes it wouldn't, the heart skips several beats before coming to a suffocating stop somewhere in the middle of the throat.

"Who may I ask is calling?" I said, stirring up the frostiest tone I could find.

"Ah, you've gone and forgotten me already, have you now?"

My heart resumed beating, but with unsettling irregularity. Lowering myself shakily into my chair on legs that had turned to gelatin, I said, "No, I haven't forgotten you, Terrance, although I would like to."

"Now why would you go and say something like that?"

"Let us leave it at I don't care to associate with criminals."

"I see you've spoken to the Graces."

"I have and they informed me of what a scoundrel you are."

"Me a scoundrel? Faith and . . . his lordship's got his knickers in a knot because I caught him trying to cheat me and beat him to the punch."

"Those are my friends you're talking about," I said firmly.

"That lot? They're nobody's friend unless it involves a few quid. Lord G. and his crowd, they're the criminals. Don't kid yourself about what they're like. They'd dump you faster than ale flowing in a Dublin pub if they didn't think there was something you could do for them."

"I resent that and in fact, I resent you calling me at all. Forget about the Graces and whatever wrongs you did them, where on this planet of ours did you ever get the gall to run that ad in *The Charlestonian* and promise that I would provide reward money?" There was a shrillness in my voice I couldn't help. My emotions were getting the better of me, as vulnerable to him as Achilles' heel was to Paris's arrow.

"Well, it worked, then? You got an answer to the ad?"

"Wouldn't you like to know! You should have called sooner. I might have told you then."

"Pauline, on St. Patrick's staff, I've been meaning to call you. Time just got away from me."

"Four months?"

"Please, hear me out. I dialed you up because I've got business in Chicago in a couple of days, and I want to see you. At least give me a chance to explain."

"It's a shame, Mr. Sullivan, but in two days at this precise hour I shall be sipping Taittinger on a flight to Paris, seat reclined and footrest up."

"I'll come in tomorrow then."

"I'm afraid I'm busy all day tomorrow."

"C'mon, Pauline, be a sport. I promise . . ."

I cut him short. "Your promises are worthless. Now at risk of being rude, I really do have to go." Summoning up more resolve than any woman in this world should ever have to, I slammed down the phone. Then I stared at it mournfully, wondering if I had done the right thing. As if in answer, it began ringing again. I answered in my coolest voice. "You have a great deal of nerve."

"*Je regrette*, Pauline," came the soft French accent. "I was delayed."

"Oh, Monique." My ego deflated like a spinnaker in the doldrums. "I'm sorry. I thought you were someone else."

The tutorial was an utter and complete waste of time, for me at least. Monique would still collect her two hundred dollars. My mind was a vast wasteland, barely able to complete a coherent sentence or recall some of the most common conjugations. Even the verb for "deceive" escaped me until Monique prodded me along.

"*C'est tres simple, Pauline. Tromper comme trompe l'oeil.*"

Of course. How could I forget. To deceive the eye.

After the worthless session, I went back into my room and tried to continue packing. But my enthusiasm had waned and Paris now seemed like any other dull city. In a gesture of frustration and anger, I started tossing clothes over my shoulder onto the floor.

✻   ✻   ✻

I met Whitney and Elsa for a bon voyage lunch the next day, Elsa having cozied up to Whitney after I saw fit to befriend her. Since Elsa was always more than insufferably late, I arrived on time so as to have an opportunity to speak with Whitney in private. Sipping wine in a corner booth at R.L., I poured out my heart with my forlorn tale of unrequited love.

"You poor dear," she cooed as tears rimmed my lower lid. "What a brute! How dare he come in and out of your life as if you have nothing better to do?"

"What's worse was that for one insane moment I nearly agreed to see him! I must be crazy."

"No. Just normal. Sometimes we fall for the ones who abuse us the worst—the real bad boys, you know. That's before we get smart." She tapped at her temple and then signaled the waiter to bring two more glasses of wine. I wondered just how many bad boys she had known. And what her gender had been at the time. She continued, "Now you are to run, not walk, onto that plane tomorrow. He's no good and you've said so yourself. He is history, which means he is the past. You need to think of the future. Go and have an affair with some sexy Frenchman."

"You're right," I agreed. "I deserve that, don't I?"

"You certainly do," she said, giving me a girlish hug. Then trying to take my mind off the man who was now the future past, she asked, "Are you all ready for your trip?"

"Almost. After lunch I've got to pick up something to wear on the plane, and some time tomorrow I have to drop Fleur off at Cat-a-Lina. I was going to have one of the doormen watch her, but she got so angry with me last time I left her, I've decided a month alone is just too much for her. Jacquie Washington recommended it. She leaves her cats there when they go to Puerto Vallarta for the winter. This Natasha I spoke with assured me they'll spend quality time with her each day. It's outrageously expensive, but worth it for my peace of mind."

Our wine arrived at the same time Elsa made her entrance through the revolving doors. Her chapeau du jour was a jaunty red beret with red and blue streamers. In honor of my trip, no doubt.

"Not a word about Terrance," I whispered to Whitney.

"Do you think I was born yesterday?"

Elsa's cheeks were glowing and her eyes wide with excitement as she pushed me over in the booth. "I'm sorry I'm late," she said. "You'll never believe what's happened."

Whitney and I waited for her to release her nugget.

"It's Connie Chan. She's at Northwestern Hospital in a coma. She was mugged on her way home from work last night."

My thoughts were on Connie as I sorted through travel wear at Barney's. Though I had always found her disagreeable, it was a shame that she, or anyone for that matter, had fallen victim to such a violent act. The doctors couldn't say how severe her head injury was or even if she would come out of it the same person—if she came out of it at all. This caused me to take stock of my own life and realize how lucky I was. I was healthy, financially secure, and leaving for Paris on the morrow. How absurd it was to torment myself with thoughts of Terrance Sullivan. From that moment hence, I resolved him banished from my mind forever.

After finding the perfect travel suit as well as a few other items, and watching my credit card breeze through the system unchallenged, I took my bags and headed home. It was rush hour and the streets and sidewalks were jammed as the work force made their way home by car or on foot. I was waiting amid the throng for the light to change at Michigan and Oak when I heard someone behind me calling my name. I turned around to see a somewhat familiar young man with a briefcase work his way through the crowd toward me.

"Pauline," he called. "It's Todd Matthews. Remember me?" He came up beside me and extended his hand. The image of an icy glass of vodka in a garish hotel bar popped into my mind. It was the *roadwarrior* with patent leather hair who I shared a drink with in Rochester—the one who had slipped a sheet of paper underneath my door suggesting I check Ethan's former neighbors in my search for his identity.

"Of course I remember you, Mr. Matthews," I said. "How are you?"

"I'm doing great," he gushed, exuding the same enthusiasm he had shown on our previous encounter. "Now what are the odds of this? Running into you, I mean. I got a promotion and Chicago is my territory now."

"Congratulations," I said.

His hand was still held out, but he looked down and saw my bags made it impossible to take it. "Shopping again, huh? Here, let me get those for you."

"That's not necessary. I don't want to take you out of your way."

"It's no problem. I'm staying across the street at the Drake."

My purchases *had* become a bit cumbersome, and thinking it couldn't do any harm, I relinquished them to his sturdy young hands. The light changed and we flowed across the street with the crowd. As we walked past the Drake, he nodded at the skyscraper that towered behind it.

"I just found out that used to be the Playboy building. That's pretty cool, huh?" He sounded awestruck. "I mean Hef used to live here and all? I can't imagine what those days were like."

I could imagine. Henry and I once attended a party at the Playboy Mansion on State Street before Mr. Hefner had moved his empire west. From the very moment we entered the former turn of the century mansion, I knew we had entered a world of decadence. The outrageously modern decorating took second place only to strategically placed fireman's poles that served as an alternative to the stairs for the scads of young, scantily clad women in attendance. From the way the men's tongues practically lolled from their mouths, it was a small wonder they managed to keep the other parts of their anatomy contained. Needless to say, even though I was wearing a Peter Max print dress, I felt sorely out of place.

I made the mistake of adjourning to the ladies' room for one brief moment and returned to find a smiling young creature in a bikini top rubbing against my husband like a cat at a scratching post. When he saw me approaching, Henry raised his hands as if to say, *I have nothing to do with this.* The young woman turned and, upon realizing who I was, laid her hand squarely on my husband's crotch. Her smile faded to a pout. "You must really love your wife," she said, and she walked away.

The party was still in full swing when we left at three in the morning. The next day I told Henry I found the whole experience quite vulgar and he agreed. Although not as heartily as I would have liked. When an invitation arrived for Mr. Hefner's next party, I politely declined it.

"The building is being remodeled as condominiums," I said to Mr. Matthews, bursting his bubble.

Tony was on duty again, and he held the door for me while Mr. Matthews followed on my heels like a loyal Chihuahua. He was still holding my bags and gave no indication of putting them down. I tried to politely excuse myself. "I'm terribly sorry, Mr. Matthews, but I'll have to say goodbye here. I'm going out of town tomorrow and I still have to pack."

A look of extreme disappointment registered on his face. "I was kind of hoping to buy you some dinner or something. I don't know anyone here and it gets kind of lonely. I've got a great expense account."

I had no intention of going to dinner with Mr. Matthews. But I felt guilty not giving him some sort of attention. After all, he had done me a big favor in Rochester, one that had ultimately led to me making the connection for the inheritance. For some reason far beyond my own comprehension, my charitable side chose to make a rare appearance. "I'll tell you what. Why don't you come up for a few minutes and we can have a drink. But I really have a lot left to do, so we'll have to keep our visit brief."

He smiled widely, and I patted myself on the back for being such a giving human being.

"Just one minute," I said, and I turned back to the doorman. "Tony?"

"Yes, Mrs. Callahan?"

"It's Mrs. Cook. The Penthouse."

"Oh, sorry, Mrs. Cook," he apologized, looking sheepish at his mistake.

"I'm leaving on an extended trip tomorrow evening, and I want to make you aware I've canceled all services, so there should be no service people going up to my apartment."

"Gotcha."

"And also, this is very important, will you be sure and tell Jeffrey that I don't need him to feed Fleur. Tell him that I've made other arrangements for her."

"I'll tell him."

"Very well. Thank you, Tony."

"My pleasure, Mrs. Callahan, uh, Cook."

I gave Mr. Matthews a look that said good help is hard to find, and he followed me into the elevator, still toting my bags.

Mr. Matthews set the bags down in my interior foyer. Upon seeing him, Fleur, who had been lounging on one of the living room sofas, quickly retreated to my bedroom. Mr. Matthews walked across the room to the windows and let out a low whistle.

"Wow, what a view," he said.

"Yes, it is quite spectacular," I agreed. "What can I get you to drink?"

"Vodka on ice."

"Certainly." I went into the bar and fixed his drink. When I returned, he was standing in front of the wall where my Pissarro hung. It was one of the Impressionist's lesser works, a rural piece dominated by peasant rooftops, but it had belonged to Grandmother, and I was quite fond of it. I handed him the drink. He took a sip and then put it down on a table without so much as asking for a coaster.

"Is that a Pissarro?" he asked.

"Why, yes," I replied, astonished that he was able to identify the artist just like that. "Do you like his work?"

"I know it's worth a lot."

It was at that moment my intuition chose to make a tardy appearance. It was telling me inviting this virtual stranger into my apartment had been a horrid mistake. Suddenly, I wanted him out of my house immediately if not sooner.

"By the way, did you ever find out anything more about your writer friend?" he asked, his eyes fixed pruriently on my Pissarro.

"I found out I had never really known him at all. Now, I'm terribly sorry, Mr. Matthews, but I have just realized I have more packing to do than I had thought. I'm afraid I have to ask you to leave."

"Packing for Paris?"

My blood pressure spiked. I remembered saying I was going out of town, but I was certain I hadn't said anything about Paris. An eerie sensation crept over me, and I felt as though I was an audience watching myself from the back of the theater. Without another word I walked back into my exterior foyer and pushed the call button for the elevator. If I could get down to the lobby, I would be safe.

"I'm sorry, Pauline, but I can't let you go anywhere. I need you to stay right here."

He put his arms around me from behind, pinning my own arms to my side. It was not the grasp of a lover, but rather of a jailer. My response was to struggle against him, and I tried striking out with my fists. This was nothing like the long-ago scene in the foyer with Sean, where in my concupiscence my fight was half-hearted. This time my struggle was sincere. I twisted and turned and railed against him with every bit of strength I could summon, all the while wondering what he wanted. To rob me? Rape me? Take my life?

In a frenzy of adrenaline driven fear, I stomped on his foot and ground the heel of my pump over his instep. The tactic worked and his grip on me loosened as he choked back a howl. I broke free just as the elevator doors opened and flung myself inside, pushing the buttons for "lobby" and "close door" in rapid unison. But he was only momentarily disabled, recovering in time to join me in the elevator just as the doors shut.

We faced off from opposite ends of the car as the elevator started to descend. Though terror still held me in its grip, there was a certain victory in having escaped my apartment. While I hovered against the wall as far away from Mr. Matthews as I could get, he turned his attention to the control panel, no doubt seeking a way to turn us around. Pushing the "stop" button would sound an alarm, pushing any of the intermediary buttons would cause the doors to open into someone else's foyer, running the risk of encountering one of my neighbors. I prayed that one of them might be summoning the elevator at this very moment and join us on the ride down. If not, there was Tony the giant on duty in the lobby. He was twice the size of Mr. Matthews. To assure he would take notice of my dilemma, I formulated a plan to scream the moment the doors started opening.

Unfortunately, my adversary had anticipated this next move. As we neared the ground floor, he abandoned the control panel and came at me, grabbing me brusquely around the waist with one arm and slapping his free hand over my mouth. The force with which he held my mouth shut was so great I feared the porcelain caps of my front teeth might break off. I struggled against him with all my might, trying to put an elbow into his ribs or kick his knee with my dangling foot, but it was all to no avail. His youth and strength were simply too overwhelming.

The elevator reached the ground floor and as the doors slid open and the paneled lobby came into view, my terror-filled eyes couldn't believe what they were seeing. The hulking back of Tony bent over a newspaper. Unlike Jeffrey, or even Edgar, whose eyes were always glued on the elevator doors in order to greet whoever was coming down, the oblivious Neanderthal didn't even look up. My attempt at a scream was nothing more than a muffled whimper in my captor's hand.

Mr. Matthews pushed the penthouse button and the elevator doors closed on my hope. I was isolated with this stranger and on the way back up to my apartment. When the doors reopened in my entry, he dragged me forcibly from the car. As I listened downheartedly, the elevator doors shut behind me. My attacker's grip loosened for a moment, and I twisted my body in an effort to squirm free. Instead I ended up facing him, staring up into the eyes of a beast of prey. He tightened his grip, his left arm clenched so tightly about me I could barely breathe. Then, he pulled something out of his pocket with his free hand, and a moment later a horrid-smelling piece of cloth was pressed to my nose.

"Take the painting," I gasped, trying not to inhale. Whether my offer was heard or not, I was retreating, my legs turning to putty beneath me, my body going limp like a Belon oyster sliding off its shell. I tried to rise above the danger, to some safe place far away.

The last I remember is trying to bite his hand. Then everything faded to gray.

31

Unwelcome Guests

I awoke seated at my dining room table, my hands and feet bound to one of my Queen Anne chairs. A piece of thick tape over my mouth kept me mute. My head pounded as though I had consumed several bottles of cheap domestic champagne, and my mouth felt as though it had been filled with dirt before the tape was applied. I could hear Mr. Matthews in my library on the house line, speaking to the doorman.

"Yes, this is Todd Matthews calling from Mrs. Cook's apartment," he said most affably. "She asked me to let you know she's expecting a couple of visitors this evening, a Mr. Prince and Mr. Fantome. She said no need to announce them, just send them up." There was a pause and then, "Right. Prince and Fantome. F-A-N-T-O-M-E. Yes, that's right. Thank you."

Of course I had no idea who these two people might be, though my French studies had brought me far enough to recognize that Fantome is French for ghost. I howled in fury from behind the tape at the stupidity of the new doorman. Jeffrey would never have accepted such instructions without speaking to me directly, nor would Edgar, no matter how old and senile he had gotten. Guests were simply not "just sent up." I was outraged that the co-op board had hired such an imbecile, and I made a mental note to let the board president know my opinion at the first opportunity. But while I was formulating exactly what I was going to say to Parker Donnelly, I heard the unmistakable beeping of a cell phone being dialed. I calmed myself and listened intently. "Hi, it's me," I heard him say after making his connection. "The package is wrapped and the door is open."

He clicked the phone shut as he entered the room.

"Oh, you're awake." I noticed his ring finger was wrapped with a strip of material that looked suspiciously like it had come from one of the tea towels in my kitchen. A wave of satisfaction coursed through me to know my bite had found its mark, hoping he didn't have AIDS. He knelt down in front of me and patted me on the leg. His skin was flushed and his eyes dilated and gleaming, but his ebullience did not appear to be sexual. It was more that of a man who has just won the lottery. "Sorry about this, Pauline, knocking you out and all, but don't worry. No one is going to hurt you."

Unable to respond, I communicated my disdain by jerking my head away from him. The resulting pain resounded in my eyeballs. He slapped me on the leg with undue familiarity and stood up, going into the kitchen where I could hear him opening the refrigerator and cabinets. If he was searching for something to eat, he had best look elsewhere. My refrigerator had already been cleaned out in anticipation of my trip. The only food in the house was a jar of capers, some nicoise olives, and several boxes of Carr's Table Water crackers for cheese. And the Albacore tuna I bought by the case for Fleur.

After a while he came back into the dining room eating from an open can of the tuna with a fork. I glared at him.

"You sure don't keep much food around here, do you?" he said. He walked past me and went into the living room, settling noisily onto one of my couches. I shuddered to think of him violating my Scalamandre upholstery, most probably still wearing his street shoes.

Half an hour ticked by. Fleur ventured into the dining room and stared at me questioningly. She leapt into my lap and tried to nuzzle, but since my hands were tied behind my back I was unable to respond to her overtures. Giving up, she jumped down and meandered into the living room where, upon seeing our uninvited guest was still in residence, she turned tail and scurried past me, back down the hall and into my bedroom.

Though I was situated facing the wall, if I turned my head far enough, I could see out the window. The long shadows the high rises cast onto the water told me the sun had fallen low in the western sky. Twenty stories below, the taillights of evening commuters blinked on and off as they jockeyed for position in the four gray lanes of Lake Shore Drive. How I envied those people their freedom at that moment, crawling along in traffic on their way home to their pedestrian lives.

I didn't speculate about my own situation and what Mr. Matthews and his soon-to-arrive accomplices wanted from me. There were simply too many options to consider, the majority of them unpleasant. I chose to take myself overseas, to Paris and a morning visit to view the Fragonards at the Musée Jacquemart-André followed by lunch at Brasserie Lipp in Saint Germaine. This is all a dream I told myself. Soon I would awaken, nestled between my velvety soft Egyptian cotton sheets with their four hundred thread count. My eyelids grew heavy and my head slumped forward and I once again succumbed to unconsciousness.

The sky was dusty gray and the buildings' shadows no longer visible on the water when my eyes fluttered open again. It took me a minute to realize that the pounding in my temples was in synchronization to the sound of someone rapping at my front door. I looked up and caught a glimpse of Mr. Matthews crossing the living room. Then

I heard the low rumble of voices. Finally, Mr. Matthews reappeared followed by two pairs of feet.

My eyes traveled from the first pair of feet the entire length of the body to the head. I blinked hard and told myself this couldn't possibly be happening. Now I was certain this had to be a dream. Or rather a nightmare. There could be no other possible explanation.

"Hello, Pauline," said Terrance Sullivan, gracing me with the same smile that had caused me to melt in previous times. He carried a large box which he dropped thoughtlessly onto my newly purchased Chippendale table as if it was a picnic table. Oddly enough, I felt embarrassed that he see me in this subordinate position, even though I fully realized he had something to do with it. I tried speaking but as my mouth was still sealed shut, the best I could do was indignant squeaks.

"Don't you think we can take that tape off, Todd?" The manner in which he said Mr. Matthews's forename sounded so unnatural I knew immediately that it was an alias. I also recognized that sometime between his last call to me and the present, Terrance had lost his brogue, not to mention his red hair was now dishwater brown. My eyes darted between the two men as my brain tried to make the connection between them, the first a man I had thought I was in love with, the other a lonely traveler I once shared a drink with in a faraway bar.

"I don't know. She got wild before," said Mr. Matthews, brandishing the bandaged finger.

"Doesn't surprise me," he chuckled. "I knew she was feisty. But you'll be good now, won't you, Pauline? No shouting?"

I nodded obediently. At this point I wanted more than anything in the world to be able to communicate. Terrance, or the man who called himself Terrance, leaned over and pulled the tape from my mouth with a quick ripping motion. It stung, but not much more than a lip wax. What really stung was his presence. I didn't know whether to give him a piece of my mind or venture one of the dozens of questions burning a hole in my brain.

It was then I happened to look at the third man for the first time, and the scene soared to Felliniesque proportions. Up to this point, Terrance Sullivan's presence had me so rattled that I hadn't even glanced in this other person's direction. Now my attention was riveted to him. He had died his hair blond and sported a rather poor excuse for a mustache, but there was no mistaking who he was.

"I hope you'll accept my apology for standing you up last March," said his lyrical voice.

"Ethan!" I gasped. "How can you be here? You're dead."

"Do I look dead to you?"

"Then whose ashes are in my entry closet?"

He shrugged his narrow shoulders.

I was beyond astonished, beyond bewildered, beyond confused. My senses were so overloaded I felt like I was sailing in high seas, the deck dropping out from beneath me as the boat breached the waves. Had I not been tied to my chair, I most likely would have fallen from it.

"Why are you here?" I managed to eke out.

"I've come for my money," he said.

32

Restitution

I thought I knew fear when Mr. Todd Matthews grabbed me outside my apartment. I thought I knew fear when he struggled with me in the elevator and then used his ether or whatever it was to knock me out. I thought I knew fear when I awakened to find myself bound hand and foot in my own dining room. But it came nowhere near the panic that seized me as the meaning of Ethan's words sank in. *He had come for his money.* For a minute, I forgot how to breathe. My circulation staggered to a halt and the pooled blood hummed in my ears. Pinpricks of light flashed before my eyes and within seconds consciousness and I separated yet again.

This time when I came to my situation was far more comfortable. I lay on one of my sofas with my head tenderly propped upon a pillow. My hands and feet remained bound, but my hands were now tied in front of my body instead of behind my back. Ethan sat beside me, fanning me with the September issue of *Town and Country*. When he saw my eyes were open, he took a glass of water off the cocktail table and held it to my lips.

"Here, dear," he said sympathetically. "Drink something. It will help."

I crooked my head up and took a sip, gagging as the water went down my windpipe. He waited until I stopped coughing and then put the glass to my mouth again, this time holding my head in his free hand. The water went down much more easily. I drank nearly the entire glass before resting my head back on the pillow.

Coming from the kitchen, I could hear the raised voices of Terrance and Mr. Matthews. Terrance's very American accent was spiked with anger. "I told you to not to overdo it. What'd you want to do, kill her?"

"I swear I only used what you told me to. I don't know why she passed out again."

"If anything's happened to her, it's over, you know that?"

"You really think I'm an idiot don't you? Don't forget, if not for me, we wouldn't even be here. Who was it that found his brother in the first place?"

"Pauline is back with us, gentlemen," Ethan called out loudly. The argument stopped abruptly and the two *gentlemen* presented themselves in the doorway, staring at me as if I were a kitten just rescued from a bucket of water. It might have made a touching scene, Ethan at my side like a loyal lap dog while two dear friends looked on with concern, had not my restraints added another dimension to the picture.

"Glad to see you're all right, Pauline, you scared the hell out of us," said Terrance, his white teeth flashing in his strong face. The best I could do was a withering glare. He turned to Ethan. "Have you explained things to her yet?"

"No, she just woke up this very instant."

"Well, no time like the present, wouldn't you say?"

"All right," said Ethan, turning his head back toward me on the couch. "But I think it would be better if you left us alone."

Terrance deigned me yet another calculated smile, and I mentally flagellated myself for having been so taken in by him. I knew his teeth were far too good for an Irishman. I cursed myself for not paying heed to Lord and Lady Grace's warning about him, wondering why I chose to flutter so close to the fire. Had I slammed down the phone yesterday the very moment I heard his voice, he wouldn't have known about my trip to Paris. Maybe this rogue's gallery wouldn't have made their appearance until later in the week, and by then I would have been eating madeleines at Fouguet's.

Terrance and Mr. Matthews went into my library and turned on my only television set. The roar of a crowd told me they were watching some sporting event. Ethan cleared his throat in a serious manner, and I turned my gaze toward him. Everything about him, his pockmarked face, his nostrils flaring over the pitiable trace of hair lining his upper lip, his black beady eyes staring down at me, was so tragically pathetic that even though I was the one in the compromised position, I felt infinitely superior.

"If we are to speak, I should like to sit up," I demanded, some of my bravado coming back to me.

"Of course," he replied, the obsequious Ethan I had known in another life. "Here. Let me help you." Placing his small hands upon my shoulders, he pivoted me from my supine position to an upright one.

"What do I call you? Ethan or Daniel?" I asked before he had a chance to say anything else.

His response was static as he calmly looked down at his hands. They were folded neatly in his lap, as they often were when he was thinking. His narrow shoulders were rounded making his chest concave, and he held his arms close to his sides as if he was only allowed to occupy so much space. I noticed the trace of a smile lift the wispy mustache as he said with complete indifference, "Call me what you like."

"Well, since I've always known you as Ethan, I'd prefer to continue addressing you that way." There was an awkward silence. At a stretch, could one call this old friends getting reacquainted? Then why not put forth a question or two? Where have you been and what have you been doing? Do you have plans for New Year's? Or maybe something a little more profound, such as, "So tell me, Ethan, did you kill the original Ethan Campbell for his name or his job or both?"

His hands flew from his lap and stirred the air like hummingbirds in search of a feeder. "I did not kill him," he said unequivocally. "His death was an accident. A terrible, tragic accident."

"Then why did you hide it? Why didn't you contact the authorities?"

"A homosexual in the deep South in the sixties? Are you serious, Pauline? They would have hanged me first and asked questions later." His eyes drifted toward the ceiling and stayed there, focused vaguely on the eggs and darts of my crown molding. It didn't appear he was going to volunteer more.

"Did you know his mother is still alive and wondering what happened to her son?"

"I feel badly about that. He carried all her letters with him. They were so loving. But no matter how you look at it, Pauline, he's dead. What difference would knowing that make to her?"

"The difference that she could die in peace."

Clearly he did not want to be challenged. A physical change came over him as if he suddenly remembered he was the one in charge. Our question and answer period had drawn to a close. It wasn't until later that night, when I lay handcuffed to my headboard, that I would have the opportunity to fill in the blanks. He squared his shoulders and turned his gaze from the ceiling back to me. Leaning in so close I could smell the sour milk scent of his breath, he said, "Pauline, I knew you would find out who I was. I knew you couldn't rest until you did. That's why I left you the money. But it's mine and I want it back."

Now, I must agree that Ethan was right when he said he knew I would find out who he was. He had known me well enough to know

I would do it in order to satisfy both my curiosity and my pride. He had assumed I would fly to England in my quest and also assumed that I would stay with Charmian and David Grace, friends I had talked about for years. And he knew from my descriptions of Henry that my head would be easily turned by a red-haired Terrance Sullivan. Yes, he had hit the mark on all those things.

But he didn't know me nearly as well as he thought if he believed for one psychotic instant that I was simply going to get out my checkbook and write him a check for twenty-two million dollars.

"Over my dead body, Ethan. And, might I add, there's no mention of *you* in *my* will."

The eyes I had once found shining and lively took on an evil dimension, shrinking back in their sockets like a vampire avoiding a crucifix. "Pauline, I feared you might be difficult. And I know you worked hard trying to find out who I was, so I'm going to give you something for your troubles. In appreciation of all the effort you've put in, I'm going to permit you to keep a million dollars for yourself."

This caused me to laugh aloud. "Hah! Clearly you've lost your mind. I'm not going to give you a sou, you fraud. Now get out of my house before I expose you and see you in jail."

This time it was Ethan's turn to laugh. "Would you really expose me, Pauline? Think about it. If I'm exposed as alive, then the inheritance you are now enjoying belongs to me and not you. It makes no difference if I'm incarcerated or not, by rights it belongs to Daniel Kehoe."

He had a good point. The thought had not occurred to me that his very existence was a threat to my windfall, that Ethan's being alive meant the money legally belonged to him. Having always been pragmatic, I began to consider his offer. I came to the conclusion that other than murdering him, highly unlikely in light of my situation, my only recourse was negotiation.

"Ethan, I liked you so much better dead," I said. "Make it ten million and you have a deal."

"Two million. I have partners to be paid."

"Five million."

"Two is my best offer."

"Interest on two million might bring me one hundred twenty thousand dollars a year. I can't survive on that."

"I've survived on a lot less. Maybe you should learn to budget." His callousness was such an affront that I wanted to reach up and slap his sallow, wormy face with my bound hands. But I managed to keep my demeanor, calling to mind my broker Thomas Slattery's argument that in this growth economy I was losing vast sums of money by not being in the equity market. If I could get Ethan to pony up just a bit more, I could put the money into stock and parlay it into something substantial. Certainly with stock there could be no repeat of my previous derivatives debacle.

"I won't go lower than three million."

He considered. "Done." He clasped my tied hands and shook them to seal our agreement. "This is what you are going to do. First thing tomorrow morning you will transfer nineteen million dollars to my offshore bank account, and then we will take our leave. In the meantime, Mr. Sullivan, Mr. Matthews and I will stay and keep you company until the transaction has been completed."

33

A Quiet Evening at Home

And so, Mr. Matthews, Terrance, Ethan, and I spent an intimate evening together. I remained in the living room trying to read Jane Austen with tied hands while they rotated between watching me and some abomination on the television set. The only time they untied me was when I needed to make a trip to the rest room whereupon Terrance or Mr. Matthews would follow me and station himself at the door, threatening to break it down if I took any longer than a few minutes to attend to my personal needs. It was humiliating and degrading, but I'm sure it was in their minds that if I was somehow able to get free, I would disappear and they might never find me again. And they were right. The thought never left my mind that if I could somehow escape my apartment, I would run to Whitney's and hide until my flight tomorrow. Were it not for my apartment being on the twentieth floor, I would have climbed out the window.

At seven-thirty, we supped on tuna and crackers, washed down with a couple of bottles of chilled Puligny from my cellar. Mr. Matthews complained about the food selection as if I were a poor hostess for not having laid out better provisions for my uninvited guests. Need I say his moaning failed to arouse any sympathy in me.

Some time after eleven it was deigned time for all to sleep. Ethan and Mr. Matthews disappeared into my guest rooms while Terrance marched me to the master bedroom and ordered me onto the bed where he handcuffed my right hand to the post on the headboard. For a dubious moment, I wondered if he planned to take advantage of me. But instead of ravaging me, he settled into the chaise lounge across from the bed. With a sense of revulsion it dawned on me that he intended to sleep there. This was not exactly how I had envisioned our first night together back when he was someone else.

"There's no need for you to stay in here. I'm not going anywhere," I assured him, tugging at my handcuffed arm as proof. "And it's not as if I would benefit by calling any authorities. You know as well as I if Ethan is discovered alive I lose everything. I am cooperating so I can retain my paltry three millions dollars."

"Ethan was pretty damn generous to give you that much—far more generous than I would have been," he said.

"Ah, and another nail in the coffin of the philanthropic, sensitive man I met in England. I can get how you deceived me, but for the life of me, I'll never understand how you slipped through Lord Grace's radar."

"I didn't need to slip through Lord Grace's radar. It was jammed by greed. Would you like to hear the deal I proposed to him? A low-income housing development in Dublin to be underwritten by public funds and then turned into private investment for big profit in the end. I *invented* some loophole in the law that would permit us to do it. I never expected him to go for it, it was only an excuse to meet him so I could meet you."

"But I can't believe he took you seriously without even knowing you."

"He took me seriously because I introduced myself to him backed up by a list of gold-plated names Ethan gave me, names of people who couldn't be located, like your college friend Melton Bedford who was fishing off the coast of California. And your buddy, the Lord, he couldn't put up money fast enough at the thought of fleecing someone else. He started calling in his friends."

"Well, you're quite an actor. Is this what you've been doing your entire life? Deceiving people in order to take their money?"

This time he answered me in a backwater accent that made my skin crawl. "Me, well I'm just a good ole' boy from down south, trying to get by, same as you. Fact is, that reminds me, I b'lieve you still owe me one hundred American dollars."

His words were yet another shot across the bow, and I found myself wondering when in my life I had become so thick-witted. No wonder the check I mailed out to Mr. James Rufus Burton had been returned by the U.S. Postal service marked "No such address." At the time I had given it little thought, figuring that Mr. Burton would find me if he wanted his money. But there had never been a Mr. James Rufus Burton, just as there most certainly had never been an ad in *The Charlestonian.*

"That was you with the cockamamie story about Campbell's Soup?"

"None other than."

"You are despicable," I hissed.

"And you're so much better?"

"What is that supposed to mean?"

"Take it any way you want. For instance, let's talk about that old woman in England you cared so much about. Have you contacted her to tell her what you've learned about her son or sent her a penny since you got the money? Have you shared any of the inheritance with anyone who might be more deserving of it than you, like maybe Daniel's sister or aunt? No, it's a safe bet you never contacted any of them.

Danny said it was a slam dunk you'd keep it all for yourself and we didn't have to worry about you giving any of it away." He leaned forward in the chaise, his eyes nearly purple reflecting the shirt he was wearing. "You were attracted to me because you thought I was rolling in dough. How good do I look to you now?"

I glared back at him, a man I had once craved so carnally that I would have done almost anything to get into his bed. The emotional roller coaster ride he had taken me on in the past months was unlike any I had experienced for years prior. My mind drifted back to the heated scene in the hallway of the Angel Hotel, and the desire I had for him in that field outside Charleston. My face flamed with heat the same way it had on those two occasions, only this time the heat was vitriolic anger. "I am so glad I never slept with you."

"As if you had a choice in the matter," he taunted. "Though I really did want to fuck you, Pauline. But I never sleep where I shit."

This time he had gone too far. With my free hand, I plucked a Lalique cat figurine from the nightstand and hurled it at him with all my might. He ducked in time to avoid the missile and it smashed into the wall behind him, shattering into thousands of crystal shards. The noise brought Ethan running, his face puffy with sleep, his overcombed strands of hair hanging down about his ear. As he blinked himself to wakefulness, his eyes flicked from Terrance to me to the blanket of crystal on the floor.

"What in hell happened here?"

"Ethan, I want this cretin removed from my presence this very instant," I demanded. "If you refuse there will be no transactions in the morning, do with me what you will, the money be damned."

Ethan knew better than to cross me when my temper was like this. "Maybe it's better if I keep an eye on her the rest of the night," he said.

"Suit yourself. It's your own life you're taking into your hands." Coolly unaffected by my rage, Terrance got up and picked up a few of the larger pieces of crystal from the floor. He started out the door before stopping to deliver a final crushing blow. "Pauline, I gotta tell ya, you are one of the most shallow broads I've ever met in my life. Which makes it so easy to screw you like this."

Ethan took up Terrance's post on my chaise while I fumed over Terrance's last words, so angry my vision blurred. Who was *he* to call *me* shallow? I tried to minimize the insult by bringing to mind one of my mother's pet expressions, "consider the source," but it did little to soften the blow. No matter how much I told myself that the slur had been issued from the two-sided mouth of a con man, somehow his epithet still had teeth.

"Don't look so unhappy," Ethan chirped in an effort to placate me. "He's far too common to recognize class when he sees it." I looked at him and Mother's words came back to mind. *Consider the source.* Was he validating or invalidating my mother's expression?

"Don't look so unhappy!" I snapped. "Surely you jest. It's nearly midnight and I am handcuffed to my bed wearing the same clothes I've had on all day. I am scheduled to leave for Paris tomorrow afternoon and I haven't finished packing. I haven't had a proper meal, I haven't been permitted to do so much as apply my face cream, and my net worth is going to go down by ninety percent tomorrow. As if that isn't enough, now I am forced to take insults in my own house from a common vulgarian who I once fantasized as my ideal mate. How dare you have the gall to say 'don't look so unhappy!'"

Having finished my speech, unable to contain myself any longer, my fury gave way to tears, scalding rivers of them spewing forth from my exhausted eyes. Being handcuffed made it impossible to flip over and bury my face in my pillow, so I buried it instead in the crook of my arm, crying great heaving sobs of frustration and anger. A moment later I could feel Ethan's weight settling beside on the bed. I looked up to see him holding out a box of tissues. I took several and blew my nose messily into them.

"Dear lady, dear friend, I know this wasn't exactly the best way to go about this, but it was the only way. After tomorrow we will be out of your hair and you can get on with your life."

"Don't call me your friend. I'm not your friend," I sobbed.

He sounded genuinely hurt. "Please don't say that."

"It's the truth. I despise you and I shall never forgive you for this, Ethan. Never."

"Oh, Pauline, I can't bear for you to hate me this way. Is there something I can say to change your mind?" he whined. Some of the Ethan I used to know, the one who desperately sought acceptance, was coming to the surface.

My tears slowed to a mere spring, and for a capricious moment I toyed with the idea of asking for more money. There could be no better salve for my wounds. But I knew the request would be futile. So instead I took the opportunity to seek satisfaction of another kind, non-monetary, but desirable nonetheless.

"Well, you could give me some answers."

A wry smile passed across his thin lips, reminding me of a teenager whose mother has just caught him self-pleasuring with his father's men's magazine sprawled across his knees. Nodding a series of short quirky jerks, he got up from the bed and resumed his place opposite me on the chaise, pulling my cashmere throw over his narrow shoulders as if preparing to settle in for a while. The open look on his face reminded me of my lost friend, the one whose shoulder I could always cry upon, the one whose engaging voice had so intrigued me years ago.

"What would you like to know, Pauline?"

"For starters who are they and how did they find you?" I gestured down the hall in the direction of the other two chameleons.

"They didn't find me. They found my twin. He found me."

In a burst of clarity, I realized whose ashes were in my entry closet, the son Joseph Baincock never knew he had sired and Moira McMahon Kehoe never knew she had delivered into this world. When Mr. Holstein told me about the twin's existence, he suggested that people had a way of coming out of the woodwork where money was involved. He hadn't known known how on target he was. And just as he had in Morristown, South Carolina, in 1965, Ethan had recreated himself again, this time metamorphosing into his twin. But according to Hal Holstein the twin lived in Miami. How did he and Ethan come together?

"Ethan," I begged him. "In consideration of what I've been through, you do owe me one thing."

He looked at me glassy-eyed. "What's that, Pauline?"

"You owe me your story."

"My story? What do you mean?"

"I mean your story. The true one. From the moment you left your family home until this very minute."

I gave him my most obstinate look. He smiled his first smile since invading my home. Still the same yellow teeth. "All right, Pauline. I suppose you do deserve it."

And he started telling me everything. I became so absorbed in his story, I forgot about being held captive in my own house and the specter of poverty once again looming large before me. All that existed was Ethan and his tale, and he enraptured his audience of one much the same way I am sure that storytellers in ancient days enthralled battle weary warriors around the fire.

It was a story that would have made him the bestselling author he so longed to be—had he only been able to bring it to print.

34
A Tale of Two Ethans

"You know, Pauline, I always knew I was different. It was an overwhelming feeling. The environment I lived in was contrary to my nature, surrounded by blue collar people with lack of aspirations. Though my mother was loving, my father was a pig, and my sister . . . well, she was young. Anyhow, I don't think there was a day in my life I didn't tell myself, 'I don't belong here with these people.'

"My so-called father was terribly abusive, though I don't think we called it that when I was young. He had a pugilist's fists and never hesitated to use them on me. By the time I turned twelve, I don't think there was an inch on my body that hadn't been bruised at one time or another. But worse than the physical cruelty was the mental cruelty he dished out. He rode me night and day about my worthlessness, and for a long time I fulfilled his prophesy. I felt I was incapable of doing anything, which kept me from leaving home. For survival, I'd hide in my room and read about exotic places and fancy people and think 'I belong there, not here.'

"Finally, or I should say, fortuitously, one day shortly after my twenty-first birthday, he came after me with a garden hoe. If I hadn't had quick reflexes I'm sure he would have killed me. My mother was afraid for my life and told me now that I was a grown man, it was time for me to go off on my own. She gave me some money and an envelope with my birth certificate, and oddly enough, hers too. She said, 'I just want you to remember who you came from.'

"So I left home and went to New York City. I only lasted there a couple of weeks. It ate me up alive. Things were too fast for a naive young man like me. I meandered for a few years after that, moving from town to town, working odd jobs, until I somehow ended up in Charleston. I fell in love with that city almost immediately, even though I realized it was yet another place I wouldn't be accepted. Then one afternoon while I was watching the shrimp boats pull into the harbor on Sullivan's Island, I struck up a conversation with an Englishman named Ethan Campbell. He told me he was going to Morristown for a few days' holiday before heading down to Puerto Rico to start a writing job he'd just secured. He invited me to come to Morristown with him. I figured, why not? I tagged along and we checked into the St. Alder Arms, separate rooms, of course, so that no one would suspect our sexual orientation."

He fell silent, and I could tell he was contemplating what to say next. Then suddenly he began speaking rapid fire, the words churning to his lips and bubbling over as if he had been waiting forever to share them. "It was an accident. We were two consenting adults. He told me what to do, showed me how to do it. I never could have thought up anything like that myself. One minute he was in the throes of ecstasy, the next he was dead at my feet—with me standing over him holding a nylon stocking. "

So that was how the British Ethan Campbell had died—of erotic strangulation. I only knew of it because it had been in the paper recently, explaining away a rash of suicides among young men that most probably hadn't been suicides at all. The deadly dangerous sexual act involved cutting off oxygen at the point of orgasm to increase its intensity. That explained how one so small as Ethan had been able to cause the Englishman's death, and why the skeleton found in the swamp had shown no indication of how he died or of any clothes.

"Pauline, I was terrified beyond belief. I didn't know what to do. I stayed in the room with Ethan's body until the middle of the night when everyone in the inn was asleep. Then I wrapped it in a blanket and dragged it down the stairs, praying that no one would wake up. Every creak of the steps echoed like a scream, it was so quiet in there. Luckily, he was a small man like me, but it still pushed me to my limits to move him. Somehow, though, when it means your survival you find superhuman strength.

"Ethan's rental car was parked on the street, so I dragged the body to it and loaded it into the trunk. Then I got into the car and started driving. I had no idea where I was going or what I was doing, I just got on the interstate and drove. That's when I spotted an exit sign for Little Scapoose Swamp.

"It was as if Providence was looking out for me," he said, his eyes turned inwardly as he relived that night. "I turned off the highway and drove into the swamp until the road ended. Then I pulled the body out of the car and dragged it through the marsh until I thought my arms were going to pull out of their sockets. Mosquitoes were eating me alive, and I didn't dare think about the snakes and reptiles I knew lived in swamps. I just kept dragging him and dragging him, thinking that if I could get that body far enough away they wouldn't find it until I was long gone."

Finally, so exhausted he couldn't drag the dead man another inch, Ethan left him in the water and returned to the car to decide his next course of action. He could go back to the St. Alder Arms, check out in the morning and catch the first bus out of town, or he could keep the dead man's rented car and just continue driving. If he didn't go back to the inn, he worried about what would happen when the innkeeper went into their rooms the next day and found all their belongings but neither of them. He would most likely call the police, and there would be an investigation that might lead to the swamp. And they would most certainly connect Daniel Kehoe to the body since the two men had been inseparable since their arrival.

Then a solution came to him. If Ethan Campbell continued to exist, there would be no reason for the authorities to search for him.

Daniel sped back to the inn, arriving just before dawn. He went into the dead man's room and packed up his belongings, taking his wallet with all his documentation as well as a substantial amount of cash. Then he went back to his own room, cleaned himself up and packed his things. An hour later, while the innkeeper and his wife were busy setting up for breakfast, he asked to check out for both of them. He settled their bills in cash from Ethan's wallet, climbed into the rented car and headed south.

"It may sound strange, Pauline, but for the first time in my life I felt liberated. I had all of Ethan's papers, his birth certificate, his driver's license, his passport, his work visas and, most important, a writing job in Puerto Rico. Our physical descriptions were nearly identical, height, weight, hair color, eyes, and so on and since this was before pictures on driver's licenses, it was perfect. I kept all his identification except his passport which did have a picture on it, so I burned it. When I got to Miami, I turned in the rental car and caught the boat to Puerto Rico."

"But didn't Juan Cardoza know you weren't Ethan Campbell?"

"Juan had never met Ethan, they had only corresponded by mail. He did know that Ethan was a British citizen, so I told him I was born in England but grew up in New York to explain why I didn't have an accent. He never questioned it. So Ethan Campbell flourished and Daniel Kehoe ceased to exist. Which was good. No one would miss Danny Kehoe."

"Except your mother and sister."

For the first time a look of regret came over his face, but it lifted quickly. "I felt slight remorse over that, but I knew my sister would be okay. As for my mother, I did love her and I know she loved me, but when I think back on the way she let that son of a bitch treat me . . ." His voice trailed off as he relived a part of his life ugly enough to turn him into the creature who now sat beside me.

So Daniel Kehoe as Ethan Campbell spent twenty-five years in Puerto Rico, writing for Juan Cardoza's paper and living his life with ever increasing self-confidence. It was as if becoming Ethan Campbell negated his sad history. He would read the loving letters Ethan's mother had written him and pretend that his own mother had been so adoring. And after the years he spent hiding in his bedroom and reading of exotic things, he found out he was engaging. Though his writing job didn't pay a great deal, he built a fairly happy life for himself in Puerto Rico.

"But then I started getting wanderlust. I really wanted to be in a metropolitan area where there was more culture to draw from. I figured enough time had passed since the death of the original Ethan that it would be safe for me to move somewhere else, but I worried about New York City since I might see someone from Rochester there. So I looked at all the cities in the United States, and I settled on Chicago. I wanted to write, and was fascinated with Berthe Palmer, so I thought what better place than the city where she had lived? Of course, no one had ever clued me in about the weather in this godforsaken place. It was worse than Rochester, with one exception. When my book was published I received a warm reception. That's when I decided Chicago would be home for me. And it was a good choice. I made so many friends. I've never seen so many women starved for companionship, so happy to be on the coattails of an author no matter how small.

"I'm sure I don't have to fill in the blanks for you in the intervening years, Pauline, except that I always had this feeling of being more—that I was deserving of more. But I pushed it back and contented myself with my life here.

"Then one day last March my whole world started to implode. I received a phone call from a man named Norbert claiming to be my brother. I knew the original Ethan Campbell had no siblings, so I told the caller he'd made a mistake. Then he said something that sent shock waves through me. He said he was Daniel Kehoe's brother.

"Can you imagine, Pauline, what was going through my mind? No one had seen or heard from Daniel Kehoe since 1965 and here was a complete stranger on the phone, not only claiming to know I was Daniel Kehoe, but claiming to be my brother as well. I kept my cool and asked him what made him think he was my brother. He said I would know when I saw him. I tried putting him off and then he said something that caught my attention. He said that Daniel Kehoe had inherited a lot of money. He wouldn't tell me anything more unless I agreed to meet with him.

"He came to my apartment that Tuesday night, the day before you found the body. Can you imagine my shock when I opened the door and saw myself standing in the hall? I invited him in and in the course of our conversation I learned that his parents had died many years before and he was on his own. They had left him a modest sum which was almost gone. He told me he dabbled in writing himself, had started his own autobiography but hadn't gotten very far. He worked in a bookstore because, like me, he loved the written word.

"Then Norbert told me that the week before, two men had come into the bookstore and told him that he had a twin named Daniel Kehoe who had come into a lot of money. In their search for Daniel they had learned of his existence, and they hoped by some fluke of fate he might have connected with his brother. At the very least they would know what Daniel looked like."

The two men, of course, turned out to be none other than Terrance and Mr. Matthews. So they were "estate" bounty hunters just like Mr. Holstein. Which meant in their quest to find the rightful heir of Joseph Baincock, they too had visited the hospital where Daniel was born, and had dug deep enough to find the nurse who kept track of the black market babies. Only they had found her well before Mr. Holstein had, and unlike Mr. Holstein, they had looked Ethan's twin up. It must have been a lucrative year for the former baby trader. I hoped her grandson had gotten his operation.

"But how would Norbert know where to find you?" I asked, lost in the labyrinth of Ethan's tale.

"He had read my book on Gloria. He was fascinated with her too. He said when he saw the picture of the author inside the book's dust jacket it was like looking in a mirror. So when Terrance and Matt told him he had a twin, he knew right away who his twin was. He assumed that Ethan Campbell was just a pen name."

Of course his twin would have read his book. What is it that sociologists say? That identical twins separated at birth tend to have the same interests in life, from their favorite colors to the work they do to the type of people they choose to marry. And so it was only natural Norbert would have taken an interest in books about society women. Since Ethan's bio stated that he lived in Chicago, he was easy to find from there. His phone number was even listed. He claimed he listed it so that people could find him during his research, but I personally thought it was because he didn't want to risk missing out on any invitations.

Ethan continued. "So Norbert made me an offer, that in exchange for putting me and the inheritance together, he'd get half. Which would have been perfectly fine with me except for one problem. In order for me to claim the money I would have to prove I was Daniel Kehoe. How could I possibly explain who I had become instead? A naturalized citizen named Ethan Campbell? I believe I was more terrified that night than the night the real Ethan died. And what made matters worse was that I had been right all along! I was extraordinary. Now I was to be denied my birthright because of an accident in the past.

"I decided to play it safe, and insisted I had no idea who Daniel Kehoe was. Norbert shrugged and acted like he accepted my denial. The next thing I knew he was holding a gun on me. He forced me into the bedroom and made me sit on the bed.

"'What could you possibly get by killing me?' I asked him.

"And his answer was, 'I'll say I'm you, that's what, and I'll get the money.'

"'You don't understand, you can't get away with it,' I told him, but he refused to listen. I jumped up and grabbed for the gun. We struggled and it went off. Norbert fell onto the bed. I stepped back in horror. He was dead and I was right back in Morristown, South Carolina, standing over a dead body that I would take the blame for."

Wondering if anyone had heard the shot, Ethan went to his front door and put an ear to it, listening for any changes in the rhythm of the building. Thankfully there was rap music blasting in the hall and he hoped it was loud enough to cover the sound of the gunshot. He waited a long time, and when thirty minutes passed with no knock at his door, he decided the shot had gone unnoticed. Feeling he had bought some time, he paced back and forth around the piles of paper in his living room, thinking over his options.

"Number one, I could call the police and explain his death was an accident. But even if they believed me, they would most likely do some investigating into me. That could be a real problem. Or number two, I could do what I had done thirty-four years ago in Morristown, grab a new identity and run. This was the more appealing of the two. Only this time I would bury Daniel Kehoe and Ethan Campbell for good. I would leave the birth certificates my mother had given me along with Ethan's identification.

"Since my twin was wearing a tropical weight suit, I had to undress him. No one would believe I would wear a light suit like that in March. I put the bloody clothes into a grocery bag and called you. I had to make sure you'd come to check on me. I needed someone to identify that body as me before it decomposed. That's why I made up the story about the bad reaction to my new medication. You were just heading out to the opera as I recall."

"Have you any idea how much guilt I suffered thinking I cut you short when you were suicidal?"

"I apologize for that, Pauline. But I'm sure you can understand that I had to do it." He paused to gather his thoughts and continued. "I grabbed my prescriptions and left the apartment. I had found my brother's wallet and hotel key in his pockets, so I figured I'd be safe in his hotel room. When I got there I changed into his clothes. They were a perfect fit. Except it was obvious he never visited Chicago in March. On top of the bloody tropical suit I had to throw out, everything in his suitcase was summer wear. He must have thought we actually have spring here."

He laughed a merry lighthearted chortle at his joke and continued. "So there I was, standing in front of a mirror in a Hawaiian shirt and yellow slacks wondering if I could really walk outside in them, when someone knocked at the door. I didn't even draw a breath hoping whoever it was would go away. But the knocking didn't stop. It got louder until I was ready to crawl under the bed to hide. Then someone shouted, 'C'mon Norbert, we know you're in there. Open this door before we fucking kick it in.'

"At that point I resigned myself to fate and opened the door. There were two men standing in the hall. One seemed quite agitated, the other calm. They pushed me back into the room. The agitated one swore 'You cheating bastard. Did you think we wouldn't find you here? If you think you're going to claim jump on us, you've got another thing coming. Now where's that brother of yours?'

And that was Ethan's first introduction to Todd Matthews and Terrance Sullivan, or whatever their real names were. As he stood silently trembling in front of them, they continued haranguing him about finding his brother. He began to realize they were no great friends of the dead man, merely interested in something involving a great deal of money.

"'Aren't you going to fucking say anything?' Terrance asked me.

"Having no idea what to do outside pleading amnesia, I finally said, 'I'm sorry, gentlemen, I seem to be having a memory problem.' The moment the words crossed my lips, I knew I had made a mistake. In my nervousness, I had completely forgotten that my brother had a Southern accent. They both stared at me dumbfounded.

"Then Terrance said, 'Who are you?'

"Suddenly, Pauline, I was just too tired to fake it anymore. I'd been faking it for too many years. I had reached the end of the road. Resigning myself to the fact that I would most likely go to jail, I told them about the accidental shooting in my apartment.

"At first I was sure they were going to pick up the phone and call the police, but instead Todd started ranting about how much they had put into finding me, that I had inherited a fortune and I was damn well going to collect it. They wanted their finder's fee. Then I heard the sum involved for the first time. Thirty-three million dollars? Could it be possible?"

It was more than possible they assured him. It was then Ethan set his mind to work, thinking of how he could get his hands on his birthright without going to prison. And an idea came to him in a flash of brilliance. He would bequeath the money to someone else and come back to get it at a later date.

"Why me?" I asked, remembering my jubilance the day I learned of the inheritance.

"Pauline, you were the ideal candidate. Don't you see it? It's because of you and what you did that I'm standing here today."

He was right. I was the ideal candidate, and I played right into their hands. After the three of them worked out their plan, Ethan wrote out a will and went back to his local currency exchange to have it notarized. Thinking it too dangerous to go back to his apartment, he dropped the will into the neighborhood mailbox and it found its way to me two days later. Ethan couldn't very well remain in Chicago, so he flew to Miami under his new name to wait things out. It wasn't difficult to pass himself off as his twin since he not only had Norbert's identification, but his brother had conveniently left his unfinished autobiography laying on the kitchen table. Terrance went on to London to meet up with me. And Mr. Matthews in turn followed me to Boston and Rochester. Each time, they moved me in the direction they needed like a lowly pawn in a chess game.

"Ethan," I asked. "Don't you have the slightest remorse over what you've done to me? How manipulative it was to let Terrance play with my feelings like that?"

"Another apology to offer you, Pauline. We needed Sean out of the way. You having a boyfriend could only cause complications. Besides, Terrance had to keep prodding you. We needed you to draw the attention of Holstein so you could collect the money." Ethan yawned widely as he finished his confession. "Now you know it all. I've got to get some sleep. Tomorrow's a big day."

"Wait, just one more question, Ethan. What makes you think after the money's been transferred they won't kill you and cheat you out of it?"

"Oh, I've already thought that one out, Pauline. The money is going to a joint account in my name and Mr. Sullivan's name. It's set up that both parties need to be present to make any withdrawals."

His eyes began to flutter, and he turned on his side in the chaise. In what seemed like a matter of seconds, he was asleep. I, however, lay there wide awake, a victim of my own curiosity and stupid luck. Ethan slept an untroubled sleep, each exhale marked by a slight whistle, while I thought about how my dreams had once again been shattered.

How simple and foolproof Ethan had made things for himself. He and his partners would appear at the bank, withdraw their certified checks and disperse to the ends of the earth. I wondered where Ethan would go. Somewhere warm most certainly. He never cared much for the cold. He would moan and complain during Chicago's winter, saying the years in Puerto Rico had thinned his blood. One time his whining got so bad I asked him why he didn't just move someplace warmer. "For the life of me, Pauline, I have no idea," he answered and then added, "I guess I had to come someplace miserable to write."

But what was to happen if he were to see someone from his former life, Marjorie Wilcock on vacation in Belize, Sunny in Cabo, Sandy St. Clair just about anywhere within range of the Hatteras? The odds of such an encounter were high based on all the connections he had made in his life as Ethan Campbell, and the high profile places he would undoubtedly visit. But if he encountered anyone on some far away island who knew him as Ethan Campbell, he would simply say, "Oh, no, fair lady. My name is Norbert *whatever his new last name was* and I'm from Miami. My entire life. You must be mistaken."

"But I used to know someone who looked exactly like you," the other party would say to which Ethan would reply, "Yes, I've heard that before. I was adopted so I don't know my biological family. Perhaps I have an unknown sibling out there—maybe even a twin." And then he most likely would buy whomever a bottle of chilled Taittinger in exchange for tidbits of gossip about the world he had left.

There would be no reason to doubt his story, after all everyone knew that Ethan Campbell had committed suicide. No one in the world would know the truth except for his partners in crime . . . and me.

For the first time since our domain had been invaded, Fleur emerged from her hiding place beneath the bed. She gave the sleeping Ethan a wary look and then wandered off, to the kitchen no doubt. She returned and mewed, a demand for her already tardy dinner. Ethan's eyes remained shut.

"Ethan, wake up. Wake up."

He grumbled in his sleep. "What?"

"It's Fleur. She needs to be fed. She hasn't had her dinner yet."

He opened a sly eye and glared at me. "She'll be fine until morning." He settled himself back into sleep.

"Heartless," I said to him, a mother suffering the pain of her hungry child. My cat meant more to me than any person. I patted the bed, and she hopped up and curled up next to me protectively. In the tumultuous years since Henry's death, this little creature had been the only consistent thing in my life. As I lay there stroking her, the true cruelty of these men dawned on me. Despite his small stature, Ethan had grand desires. Nothing stood in the way of him getting what he wanted.

My insomniac eyes went back to him snoring softly on the chaise, the cashmere throw tucked under his neck, his knees drawn up toward his chin. He looked so comically small compared to Terrance who had dwarfed the piece of furniture, his large feet hanging over the edge, his broad shoulders filling it from armrest to armrest. But though there was a great difference in their physical statures, there was a sameness to them that couldn't be denied, their single-mindedness in their pursuit of my money.

I called to mind an expression Sean sometimes used when imitating one of his more colorful customers. 'If I tell you, I'll have to kill you,' he'd say gruffly. Ethan had told me. For the first time, it occurred to me how dire my straits were, that in the morning after making the transfer, I could be a dead woman.

35

On the Morrow

Dawn came all too quickly, the gradations of color visible through the crack of my bedroom drapes as the sky changed from murky gray to dusty rose. In no time at all, I would be transferring my fortune into an abyss, and then . . . who knew. I scanned my room in the dim glow of the floor lamp that had been left on all night, the scattered piles of clothing on the rug reminders of the extended trip I was never to take, the shards of glass from my Lalique cat sharp reminders of love that never existed. I turned my eyes back to the crack in the drapes and kept them there as the dusty rose turned to the color of a robin's egg. It appeared it was going to be a lovely day.

Lying there, trying to squeeze the last minutes from the night, I contemplated my life which I was beginning to see as worthless. Aside from my cat, I was leaving nothing behind, no offspring, no legacy, no accomplishment people might remember me by. My life could be summed up as a string of fine meals, travels, society functions, biting talk, and a closet overflowing with clothes and shoes.

Somehow, I should have come to more than this. Perhaps Terrance had been right. Maybe I was shallow.

"Good morning, my dear. I hope you slept well."

Ethan's melodious voice was startling. I looked over to see him watching me, as he probably had been for some time. The very sight of him sickened me now, the vulgarity of his skin, the miserly wisp of mustache above his rail of a lip, his yellow teeth and black beady eyes. I felt the sting of true hatred, without doubt the largest emotion I had ever experienced in my life.

"You're going to kill me, aren't you?"

"Don't be absurd, Pauline. I'm not going to do you any harm. As soon as I get the money, we will be out of your hair and you're free to live your life as you please. You must believe me."

"I would like to believe you, Ethan, but by your own admission, your track record hasn't exactly been sterling."

At that moment Terrance chose to enter the room, his curls damp and coiled in upon themselves from his shower. He was wearing a terry cloth bathrobe from one of the guest bathrooms. It was too small for him, the sleeves barely clearing his elbows. Fleur climbed to all fours and hissed, the hair on the back of her neck rising. She leapt from the bed and bolted past him down the hall.

"I see my cat has good taste," I said.

"And a good morning to you too, Mrs. Cook," he said. "I hope you don't mind that I used your shower."

"Would it make a difference if I did?" I hissed just like my cat. I turned toward Ethan. "I don't suppose I might be able to use my own facilities."

"Of course." He reddened with embarrassment. "Terrance, would you take her to the bathroom?"

Terrance unlocked the handcuff, and my hand fell free. It was so swollen and numb it felt as though it was no longer connected to me. I rubbed at the mean red mark encircling my wrist, at the same time opening and closing my fingers to get the circulation going. I swung myself out of bed and stood in front of him defiantly.

"You're not thinking of coming in with me."

"I'm going to stand outside the door and you have exactly sixty seconds," he said.

"I beg your pardon, but what can any woman accomplish in sixty seconds? The equipment is not the same as yours in case you didn't know."

"Just do it or I will be in there with you. And don't even think about locking the door."

I went into the bathroom and slowly closed the door. The moment it clicked shut I flew to the vanity and opened the top drawer, counting backward from sixty as I perused its contents for anything I might be able to use in self-defense. Unfortunately, I owned no discreet derringer or pearl-handled switchblade. I settled upon my nail scissors and a pair of tweezers and quickly secreted them into my trouser pocket. I opened the next drawer down, searching for anything else that might come in useful, and my eyes settled on a plastic bottle of nail polish remover.

"Thirty seconds," Terrance called from outside the door. I picked up the nail polish remover and stuffed it into my bra. The shape was cumbersome and it stuck out like a third breast. I could hear the heathen bastard calling out "fifteen seconds," and with no better solution coming to mind, I turned the bottle sideways and pressed it under my left bosom. It was awkward and the plastic was cold, but the bottle was camouflaged beneath the drape of my pullover.

"Five seconds."

I unzipped my pants and was seated upon the throne when he burst through the door.

"I beg your pardon," I hissed, holding my hands in front of my private area. "I believe I warned you this would take longer than sixty seconds."

"You have thirty more seconds to wipe your ass and get outside or I'm coming back in to do it for you. Got it?"

He disappeared once again behind the closed door. I did as I was instructed and reassembled my clothes. The moment I pushed the flush, he reappeared and took me roughly by the arm.

"Let's go."

"May I at least wash my hands?"

"No. You can wash them all you want when we are finished here."

"You are an ill-mannered pig. I don't know what I ever saw in you."

Ethan was waiting in my office, and now I saw what had been in the brown box Terrance had carried in the day before. There was a fax machine set up on my desk.

"It's showtime," he said, smiling.

I shook my head. "No it's not. I've changed my mind. Ethan, you can expose yourself as alive and I don't really care. I'm not transferring the money."

Then Mr. Matthews walked in carrying a struggling Fleur in his arms. He handed her over to Terrance who held her by the scruff of her neck and took her small head in one of his powerful hands.

"What a beautiful cat," he said. As I watched him warily, he wrapped his thumb and middle finger around her throat. "I could snap her neck like that, you know."

"You wouldn't!"

"I would."

Looking at my beloved pet held so vulnerably in his cruel hand, I realized I was beat.

"All right, all right. Don't hurt her. Now tell me what to do."

After being given explicit instructions, I phoned James Slattery's office. My young broker took my call immediately, answering in the jocund manner of one who is making more money than he ever truly expected to in his life. I am quite certain I put a rather large clink in his bonhomie when I announced what I wanted.

"Did I hear you right? You want to transfer nineteen million dollars to another account?" he asked in astonishment.

"That is correct."

"Mrs. Cook, may I ask you why? I've told you I can take excellent care of your money for you. In this market we can easily grow it to twice, three times what it is, in practically no time at all. Let me put you into some Intel options."

"James, I am not interested in stock at this time. I plan on buying some foreign real estate and the transaction will go much smoother if I have the money in place there," I said, repeating the scenario I had been instructed to give. "I'm expecting a bidding war."

"It's your money, of course, but—"

"No, buts, James. I want the money transferred and I want it done right away."

"No can do right away, Mrs. Cook. When you're transferring a sum like this out of the country the government demands some paperwork. Even if we get it all approved today, the earliest I can effect the transfer would be tomorrow morning."

I looked at Terrance Sullivan holding a purring Fleur in his lap. The fraud had won her over as easily as he had won me. Ethan was standing behind me, listening in on my conversation as best he could. I wanted them gone, out of my house. The government was buying me another day of my money and perhaps my life, but it was another day to be shared with these sociopaths.

"Fax the papers over to me right away. It is imperative that I get this done as soon as possible."

I hung up the phone. "I'm afraid the transfer can't be made today," I announced.

"I heard," said Ethan and then to Terrance he added, "It's going to take until tomorrow."

"Crap," said Terrance as he dropped my cat onto the floor.

36

Such Sweet Sorrow

James Slattery faxed over some documents requesting the source of the money to be transferred and the reason for its transfer, the government's way of tracing the flow of money out of the country, done to check drug trafficking and other illegal activity, he explained. I filled the forms out with a weary heart and sent them back. James assured me he would get back to me as soon as the transfer of funds was approved.

Time passed insufferably slowly. Breakfast was tea and tuna and the last of the crackers. Afterward, I was taken back into my living room where I tried to read more Jane Austen, but gave up after reading the same paragraph for the third time. The phone rang incessantly throughout the morning while my answering machine fielded calls from friends and acquaintances wishing me bon voyage, people who were free to capriciously go about their lives while mine was limited to my present surroundings. I listened without response as Elsa, Jacquie, and Whitney left me fond adieus, Whitney's girlish voice especially warm in its well wishes. "You must be out running last-minute errands. Have a great trip. I can't tell you how envious I am!" Had she seen me, I doubt she would have felt so strongly.

My captors monitored the incoming messages, including one that came in at eleven o'clock from Natasha at Cat-a-Lina. "Mrs. Cook, we thought you were going to bring Fleur in this morning. Maybe there's a mistake. In any event, we're just going to assume you've made other arrangements for her unless we hear from you."

One tedious hour segued into the next without any word from James Slattery. Even my captors were growing fatigued with the situation, especially Terrance, who was getting jumpier by the moment. I hadn't been allowed to bathe or even cleanse my face, and the necessary forays to the bathroom were both stressful and brief as I was no longer even permitted the dignity of closing the door completely anymore.

The tweezers and scissors were still secreted in my pocket and the plastic bottle of nail polish remover was still beneath my left breast, digging into the flesh of my ribs. It was causing me such a disagreeable amount of pain, I contemplated taking it out and tossing it in the trash my next trip to the loo. But reminding myself it might serve as my only line of self-defense, I willed myself to rise above the discomfort. The bottle remained painfully secured under my left breast.

Lunch was tuna again. Mr. Matthews, growing increasingly frustrated with the menu, added some capers to the mix, making a dissatisfied face as he chewed. "I don't suppose we could order in a pizza?" he suggested to Terrance.

"Are you crazy?" Terrance replied more than sharply. "We don't want anyone getting anywhere near this apartment until we're long gone. After tomorrow, you can buy a chain of pizza parlors."

The afternoon crawled past even more slowly than the morning, if that was at all possible. Ethan entertained himself by pulling all the travel books out of my library and spreading them across the living room floor. The other two were glued to the television, hitting the mute button every time the phone rang in order to monitor the incoming call. I settled on staring vacuously out the window. A bank of low clouds had rolled in, turning the day beyond dreary, and the lake reflected them in a colorless gray that only served to compound the hopelessness that welled inside me.

Finally at four-thirty the phone rang again. It was the call everyone had been waiting for, the sound of James Slattery's voice leaving a message on my answering machine. I was plucked from my perch on the couch and hustled into the library before he was able to finish.

"Mrs. Cook, this is James. I've gotten all the paperwork back and—"

Ethan hit the stop button and lifted the phone from the hook.

"James," I said, fighting hard to keep my voice from trembling. "I'm here."

"Oh, there you are. Let's see, where was I? Oh, yeah. I guess all the documentation is okay and I just need you to sign one last piece and if it's all in order we can do this transfer first thing in the A.M. I'll fax the paper over."

"Thank you, James."

And then out of the blue, "Hey, weren't you going to Paris or something?"

"I've had a change in plans," I replied listlessly.

The last document signed and delivered, I returned to my perch in the living room. My ankles hurt from my restraints, my wrists were practically raw, and the plastic bottle of nail polish remover had begun to dig a hole in my flesh. The phone had stopped ringing with personal calls, my peers assuming incorrectly that I was in the first-class lounge at O'Hare sipping champagne and awaiting my boarding call. At six-fifty, a deep sigh escaped me as I thought of my plane taxiing down the runway with a vacancy in seat 2A. It was small consolation that my full-fare ticket was refundable. One had to be alive to obtain it. In fact, at this point my mental state had so deteriorated that all I longed for, aside from a proper bath, was one last walk in the park.

The evening hours were a blur. I declined the tuna dinner, having completely lost my appetite, and was escorted to my bedroom sometime afterward. Sleep eluded me as I spent yet another night wondering if it was my last. Ethan shared my room again and fell almost immediately into what appeared to be sound untroubled sleep. As for the other two, I could hear the dull tone of the television until late into the night.

Through the crack in my drapes I watched the sky turn from black to a troubled gray day with rain pelting the windows. Ethan was down the hall in the bathroom when Terrance came in to rouse me from my bed. He looked clean and fresh, having undoubtedly availed himself of my shower again. I felt greasier and dirtier than ever.

After unlocking the handcuff, he walked me to the library where Mr. Matthews was situated in front of the television holding Fleur and watching some inane program with a man named Regis and some vapid blond woman whose name I didn't catch. Ethan traipsed in behind us and the television was turned off. Terrance picked up the phone, dialed, and handed the receiver over to me one final time. A moment later I heard the chipper voice of my broker.

"Good morning, James. It's Pauline Cook. About that wire transfer."

The chipper tone vanished. "Right, Mrs. Cook. It's all arranged. Just waiting for your final O.K. You know it's not too late to put you into some Cisco, some CMGI—"

I cut him short. My heart was breaking, but I had no choice. "James, I would like you to effect the transfer now."

I could feel the ship of his last hopes sinking over the phone line, as was mine. "All right, I've pulled up your account and one, two, three. Done." The words came out as if he had just pushed a button for a nuclear device.

"Very good," I said with true irony. Ethan, who was listening in on my cordless phone, started mouthing something at me. "What now?" I asked testily.

"Did you say something, Mrs. Cook?"

"Oh, fax me a confirmation as soon as you have one."

"Will do, Mrs. Cook."

The deed done, I said goodbye to my broker and my money, and contemplated what was to come next. After the thieves had gotten what they wanted, would they do as they promised and leave me alone? The television was turned back on as we sat awaiting the fax that would bring this travail to a close. Their presence was almost more offensive than what they had done to me. During a commercial for Sara Lee, Mr. Matthews began to wax eloquently about what he was going to eat as soon as he was out of my apartment. He covered nearly every fast food chain in the known universe.

"One thing's for sure," he said, "I'll never look at a fucking can of tuna again."

While the clock ticked off the minutes, I began to feel myself reaching the breaking point. For the past couple of days, my emotions had run the gamut from fear to heartbreak to disappointment to acceptance of loss. But now the apex of all emotions, anger, was making a tardy appearance. It raged inside me, churning and fueling, growing larger until I felt I might explode. Like oxygen feeding a fire, it flared with life. I was no longer afraid, I was incensed. How dare they do to me what they had done?

That was when the fax machine rang.

Huddling around it like so many stooges, they waited for the proof that the money they had so meticulously, diligently, and underhandedly plotted for was now theirs. As the machine rhythmically spit out the sheet advising them their fortune had been delivered, they started dancing about and slapping each other on the back in congratulations. So caught up in their reverie were they, that they had forgotten me for the moment, sitting in quiet fury with my hands and feet untied. A prolonged beep sounded the end of the fax, and Ethan held the sheet up victoriously.

"This is it," he announced. "Our money is home. Now I suggest we depart posthaste to go greet it."

No one noticed me backing to the door. While they had been celebrating I had prepared my weaponry to be brought into play. Held behind my back in my left hand was an open bottle of nail polish remover. In my right, the nail scissors.

"Todd, get Pauline," Terrance commanded while he and Ethan examined the sheet of paper as if they had just discovered a new gospel. "Tie her and take her back to her room."

Mr. Matthews came to me and grabbed my arm brusquely. Using my anger as fuel, I drove the nail scissors deep into the flesh of his upper arm, sinking the small blades in as far as they would go. His howl told me I had hit bone. Terrance jerked about and saw the scissors sticking out of Mr. Matthews's arm. He darted to grab me, and I let loose with the nail polish, hurling it into his face. His eyes went wide in momentarily disbelief before shutting tight against the searing of the chemical. Amazingly he did not cry out, but groped past me in a bizarre dance of shock and pain, feeling his way urgently down the hall toward one of my bathrooms.

Taking advantage of the confusion, I started to run, down the hall past the living room toward the entry. I could feel Mr. Matthews in pursuit though I did not turn to look. I just kept running. If I could make it into my private foyer before he caught me, I just might have a chance. There would be no time to summon the elevator, but next to the elevator was the entrance to the fire stairs. That was how I planned to escape.

I reached the entry ahead of him. The other side of the foyer door was freedom. I put my hand upon the knob to open it, and felt the warm dry touch of another hand clamp down on mine. Mr. Matthews was standing behind me, his hot breath on my neck. Reaching into my pocket with my free hand I grabbed hold of my last weapon, the pair of tweezers. With the power of a woman possessed, I began jabbing at his hand like a chef chipping ice. His grip was abruptly released and without a second's hesitation, I opened the door and slipped into the foyer, slamming it shut behind me.

My adrenaline was flowing like that of a sailor in the final lengths of a regatta. I raced to the fire door and slammed on the bar to release the catch. It didn't budge. Panic gurgled like a volcano as I pushed it again and again with the same non-result. Certainly this wasn't possible. The fire code read that the exit stairs must be available at all times.

I looked down and was filled with the hopelessness of a stray cat cornered by a pack of dogs. My captors had already anticipated I might use the stairs to flee. The bar was wired shut. In desperation, I began banging on the door with my fist. Then came the inevitable footsteps behind me. I stopped banging and slumped to the floor, still grasping the bloody tweezers in my hand. Through strands of greasy red hair, I could see Mr. Matthews glaring at me with uncontained anger. His hand was spouting blood, drops of which splashed onto my face.

"I'm going to beat the crap out of you," he said raising his foot parallel to my head. "That face is going to need a lot of work when I'm finished."

"Todd, stop!" Ethan was behind him, tugging at the younger man's arm to hold him back. Mr. Matthews lowered his foot while I cowered on the hardwood floor. Ethan bent over me. "I don't know why you've chosen to be so difficult, Pauline. I promised you we were going to leave you alone after we got our money. Now come with me. We've got to tie you up again before we leave, just until we reach our safe haven without any complications. After that, you're free. Don't forget, you've still got three million dollars, Pauline. Now be a sport."

Terrance appeared in the doorway, his eyes swollen like lemons, peering at me through cherry red slits. "You bitch," he said in a voice raspy with pain.

Mr. Matthews wrenched the tweezers from my hand and yanked me to my feet. Then he and Terrance literally dragged me down the hall to my bedroom. Terrance threw me on the bed and the handcuff went back onto my right wrist. My left was tied to the headboard with a mercilessly tight piece of rope. They forced my legs apart and tied one to each post of the footboard, so that I was bound to the corners of my bed like one to be drawn and quartered. I tried to squirm and found myself unable to move more than an inch or two. Mr. Matthews rummaged through my drawers and found a pair of panties which he stuffed into my mouth. Terrance finished the procedure by wrapping duct tape around my head several times.

"All right, that's that. Let's blow out of this dump," said Terrance.

Ethan stood at the foot of my bed wearing a look of true sympathy on his face. "Don't worry, Pauline. As soon as we have our money, we'll make a call and let someone know you are here. But just in case you forgot, if anything happens in the meantime and I'm detained, the entire fortune reverts to me, even the three million dollars you still have in your possession."

And then they were out of my sight. I could hear Terrance's voice in the hall, ugly with anger and pain. "The fuck we'll make a call. The cunt can starve to death. And I hope she suffers."

Shortly thereafter there was the sound of the foyer doors closing. Despite my circumstances, it was a relief just to know they were no longer in my apartment. In a minute, the elevator doors would open into the lobby, and they would walk out the door to freedom and my money. But as I lay there, mentally making the trip down the elevator with them, I called to mind words that Detective Velez had uttered to me in the precinct one day, at the very beginning of this escapade. *Thank God they're stupid. If they had brains we'd be in trouble.*

I took comfort in those words.

37

Nemo Me Impune Lacessit

And there I lay through the long morning, hungry and thirsty, frightened and in pain. I finally gave up on retaining my dignity and relieved myself in my bed. The immediate gratification of emptying my bladder gave way to cold damp discomfort a couple of minutes later. My humiliation was complete.

With nothing else to occupy me, I actually dozed on and off, waking from dreams of ordinary life to the nightmare that had become my actual life. I tried to think of some way to free myself and tugged at the restraints relentlessly, but the work they had done was too thorough, and all I did was exhaust myself. Not that it mattered. Fleur stayed beside me most of the time, leaving once to go and drink from the toilet, and mewing occasionally that she was hungry. It really disturbed me that they hadn't thought to feed her before they left. Did she have to suffer as well as I?

Then in the early afternoon I heard my entry doors opening and the sound of a heavy foot in the hall. My heart caught as I thought they had returned to finish the job. The steps receded in the opposite direction toward the kitchen and there was silence for some time. Then my heart started pounding uncontrollably again as the sound of the heavy footfall came down the hall toward my bedroom.

A deep male voice called out, "Fleur?"

She started mewing at the sound of her name. The footsteps followed the sound and a moment later the body building hulk of Jeffrey was framed in the doorway. His eyes grew wide, his expression incredulous at the sight of me spread eagle like a porno star awaiting the cameras. Thank God, that idiot Tony had forgotten to deliver the message about not feeding my cat.

"Mrs. Cook?" he whispered. He sprang into action, trying to remove the duct tape first, but stopped at my muffled scream as it tore out a chunk of my hair. He untied my left hand instead, and I worked the duct tape myself while he untied my feet.

"Mrs. Cook, are you all right?" he asked when I was finally able to speak.

"I'm better," I said as I smoothed my greasy hair, certain I resembled Joan Crawford in *Baby Jane*. My right hand remained handcuffed to the headboard and would have to stay that way until we could obtain some bolt cutters. "Quickly, Jeffrey. Bring my cordless phone."

"Yes, ma'am. To call the police?"

"Lord, no. First I've got to call my broker."

As if it happened every day, James Slattery knew exactly what to do. Within a short time foreign authorities had been notified that a crime had been committed and the account in Grand Cayman to which I had transferred nineteen million dollars was frozen. The police arrested all three of the cretins hours later when they tried to withdraw the money.

I traded in my Air France ticket for one on Cayman Air. But not before putting in a call to Hal Holstein. After exchanging the customary pleasantries with the tracer of lost heirs, I got down to business.

"Mr. Holstein," I said, "tell me everything you know about Ethan's twin, from his last name to his favorite designer."

Then I flew down to Grand Cayman to identify the scoundrels in person. I had not forgotten Ethan's admonition that if he were to get caught, he would make certain that I was left penniless. I would never know if he meant for me to die in my apartment, but I can assume he felt secure that if I didn't, I would remain quiet about him in order to retain my three million dollars. But he was wrong, and he was about to see how wrong he was.

I was escorted into the local jail, my third since my discovery of the body back in March. The three of them were detained in the same cell awaiting extradition. They were lying on narrow cots, and one must say, they looked exceptionally good behind bars. Upon seeing me, Mr. Matthews turned his face to the wall while Terrance stared at me languidly with sore-looking red eyes.

Only Ethan rose to greet me. He came to the edge of the cell and pressed his narrow face between the bars. Prison garb made him look more pitiable than ever, but I had no sympathy for him. Aside from what he had done to me, I strongly suspected that his brother's shooting was no accident, that Connie Chan had not been mugged by a stranger, and that even the original Ethan's death had been intentional. He was evil, even more so than the two grifters who had accompanied him in this latest of evil acts.

"Pauline, you've really screwed yourself," he hissed, his once melodious voice now venomous and acrid.

"I'm sure I don't know what you are talking about," I said.

"Dis man here, he acting crazy sometimes," said the local gendarme standing beside me at the cell. "He keep saying he somebody else."

"Somebody else?"

"He keep saying he Daniel Kehoe, or supthin like that."

"He says he's Daniel Kehoe? He must be delusional. Daniel Kehoe is dead. I paid for his funeral. This man is Norbert Blakely of Miami

Beach. He works at La Fenestra Bookstore and drinks piña coladas at Sharkey's."

Hal Holstein had delivered.

Ethan's obscenity-laced screams echoed down the hall as I walked away.

When all is said and done, I must say I did benefit from the experience. After all, I walked away with my twenty-two million dollars intact. Ethan hung himself in prison before even coming to trial. He knew me well enough to know I would never back down on my story that he was Norbert Blakely, his dead twin. Poor Ethan or should I say Daniel. He would have done so much better had he led an honest life.

While waiting in Grand Cayman for the other two to be charged, I met a sexy Swedish sailor who invited me to accompany him to Saint Martin on his boat. It wasn't quite Paris, but the natives do speak French. And my Swede was all too happy to fill the present-day needs that Terrance had so neglected. We plan on getting together again some time in the near future, after his divorce goes through.

I had lunch with Whitney shortly after returning home. Over smoked salmon and toast points, I told her the entire story from beginning to end. It always feels good to share the truth with someone. Her response to my handling of things was just as any good friend's should be. "Pauline, you did the right thing," she said in her wispy voice. "Ethan was a bad man. Remember I told you he tried to extort money from me one time. I told him to go to hell."

Which brought me to the magazine page I carried in my new Lana Marks handbag. Ever since my discovery of it in Ethan's parka, I had wanted to give it to her. I thought this was as appropriate a moment as any, so I took it out and slid the folded sheet across the table.

"I imagine you might have been hoping to find this in Ethan's apartment."

She unfolded the picture of the dancers and stared at the young man circled in red. Then she folded it back up and looked at me with dark wide pupils. "So you know."

I nodded. "I wanted you to know your secret is safe with me, that you don't have to worry about that picture turning up and Jack finding out."

She giggled girlishly and her full lips broke into a cheek to cheek smile. "Pauline, you're so sweet. But, honey, Jack knows. You don't think I would have married him without telling him, do you?"

There were a few other things to be taken care of, things I had sworn I would do if I survived the ordeal in my apartment. I went back to England to visit the real Ethan Campbell's mother. I told her I'd learned her son died in a car accident shortly after his last letter, that it had been swift and painless and he never saw it coming. I saw no reason to torment her with the truth. She seemed greatly consoled, and I suspect it's just a short matter of time before she takes her final rest now.

I did not give Lord and Lady Grace a call.

Emily McMahon received a check large enough to keep her both in Old City beer and prescriptions until her dying day. And I contacted Shannon Maglieri to set up a fund paying for all her boys' college educations.

As for myself, the only special man in my life right now is James Slattery and our relationship is purely business. In light of all he has done for me, I have decided to take his investment advice. He has been highly recommending an energy stock that everyone seems to be getting rich on, so I've decided to put a substantial portion of my portfolio into his recommendation. It's called Enron, and I have great faith in it. After all, everyone needs energy.

So as I head toward the close of my fiftieth year, for the first time in my life, my financial future is secure.

ACKNOWLEDGMENTS

I would like to express my gratitude to some of the special people who helped bring *Well Bred and Dead* to fruition.

My agent, Helen Breitwieser, who called after reading the manuscript and said those four words so dear to a writer's ears: "I love your book."

My first editors, Erin Brown and Jill Schwartzman, who helped polish my words to their final shine, and my current editor, Sarah Durand, who brought those words to print.

Amy Singh, who has always been there throughout my writing career, offering her expert legal and literary advice.

Here's to Donna Curry for attending a certain luncheon years ago that provided the inspiration for Ethan, and to Roseann Moranetz for being such a thorough reader.

Big thanks to everyone at the Aspen Writers' Foundation for what they do to bring readers and writers together, and to my fellow writers in the weekly writers' group for their valuable input and critiques.

And to all my family and friends for their love and support. I am truly blessed.